MOTHERS AND DAUGHTERS

Crete, present day. A woman anxiously awaits the arrival of someone who could change her life for ever...
Lancashire, the 1950s. Three young girls make their way in a post-war world. Bookworm Connie dreams of university, but her world is turned upside down when she learns the truth about her father. Joy wins over local heart-throb Denny Gregson when she wins the 'Miss Mercury' contest, but he's not all he seems. Convent-educated Rosa is a born rebel, desperate for a life on the stage. As all three girls face tragedy, can they learn from their mothers' mistakes – or will history repeat itself?

Mothers And Daughters

by

Leah Fleming

Magna Large Print Books
Long Preston, North Yorkshire,
BD23 4ND, England.

1439684

British Library Cataloguing in Publication Data.

Fleming, Leah
Mothers and daughters.

A catalogue record of this book is
available from the British Library

ISBN   978-0-7505-3185-6

First published in Great Britain by Avon
A division of HarperCollins Publishers 2009

Published in Large Print 2010 by arrangement with
HarperCollins Publishers

Magna Large Print is an imprint of Library Magna Books Ltd.

Printed and bound in Great Britain by
T.J. (International) Ltd., Cornwall, PL28 8RW

For Elf and Lyz who found each other.

Somewhere out between ideas of right doing
and wrong doing, there is a field.
I'll meet you there.

Jalalud'din Rumi

Crete

2007

She sits under the crisscross shade of the apricot trees, hidden from view by an arch of fuchsia bougain-villaea, beside a pool rippling like blue silk, glancing at her watch. Is it time yet?

She's not one for too much sun even though she's half Cretan. There are enough life-lines etched on her face without adding more. She is content to soak in the colours around her, the brown earth, the white villa walls, the olive trees in blossom, the white jasmine under an ink-blue sky. She can hear the chink of sheep bells in the distance where the mountains rise up above the hilltop village. The fish van calls out on its Tuesday round. The cicadas are screeching.

She never tires of the colours of Crete: blues and whites, and the sandy ochre of the monasteries nearby. When she thinks of her English life, she sees millstone grit and slate grey, the shrub green of bay and yew, burning autumn shades in the garden and a paler sun.

She's not ready to go home yet. There is one more thing she must do.

She is miles too early for the plane's arrival, pausing to watch the charter flights from Britain sink down from the gap in Soudha Bay onto the Akrotiri landing strip in a cloud of red dust. For once, she's dressed up: a bright turquoise sundress and gold sandals, what's left of her hair hennaed, clipped up with combs, her

11

shades holding back the straggles, her legs waxed and nails polished.

The new arrivals stagger off the plane and into the heat of the afternoon, and pile into a bus to the entrance and the long wait for baggage. She knows the routine by heart, watching the departing lobster skins in skimpy tops queuing patiently. Wait till they return to the chill of Manchester in the night, she smiles, bags full of olive oil, raki and leather shoes.

How many times has she stood here waiting for friends? Will she come? Will she recognise her?

She smiles at the holiday reps with their clipboards at the ready and the car-hire locals, with their mis-spelled surnames written on cardboard. It is a place for expectant first-timers, blown away by the heat and the dust, for old hands, ex-pats home from the old country with their cases full of cheeses, Marmite, smoked salmon, curry spices, DVDs and home-made marmalade.

Did their emails cross?

Sit down, relax, she tells herself. She'll be ages yet, so get a paper, a coffee, anything to take your mind off what is to come.

How can I relax when I've been waiting for this day all my life...?

She sits on a bench trying not to shake. Will they recognise each other from the snapshots; a middle-aged woman, an ageing hippy, with sun-bleached hair, freckles, a necklace of turquoise stones clunking over her flat chest?

Breathe in deep. Remember your yoga, focus on the present, not what might yet be. How long it has taken to come to this meeting point. How do I even start to explain?

She sinks back with a sigh. To answer she must go back to the beginning, right back, back to the 1950s. She will want to know it all.

PART I

SCHOLARSHIP GIRLS

1

Grimbleton, Lancashire,

June 1953

'Be careful with that box, Levi,' yelled Susan Win-stanley as he guided the precious cargo through the tiled entrance of the Waverley Guesthouse. 'To the left into the residents' lounge...' the petite woman ordered as her brother-in-law squeezed his way through the door.

'No,' shouted Ana, his other sister-in-law. 'To the right ... into the dining room. It will be safer in there.'

Joy and Connie, their respective daughters, looked on with excitement as their uncle Levi lifted the box that was to be the talk of Division Street.

'Take no notice of her. We can get more people in the lounge,' countered Su.

'Will you two make your minds up? I'm standing here like your black servant. Do us a favour, one way or t'other, but my arms are aching. Which way is it to be?'

Ana shrugged. 'Poof! Suit yourself, don't blame me if half the street trample over your new carpets. Better close the curtains or they'll see it through the window.'

Connie wanted everyone in the street to know

this good fortune. They would be the first in Division Street to own a proper television set in time for the Coronation in three days' time.

'Put it down there ... no ... over there.' Susan was pointing. For such a little woman she could be bossy. 'We need a table to raise it to eye level.'

'If you put it there, the sun will shine on the screen,' Ana argued. She may only be a nurse but even she could see it was in the wrong place. 'Then no one see nothing,' she added in a Lancashire accent broken by guttural Greek vowels. How different the two of them were, thought seven-year-old Connie: Mama so tall and wide, with red hair scraped back into a thick bun, her fierce green eyes missing nothing. Susan, dark with flashing brown eyes and a tiny body.

'But there's no socket to plug it in there,' Su argued back.

Levi was up and down like a yo-yo at their command, a big barrel on two legs, who huffed and puffed a lot but was always there to do jobs for them in his old home.

'Just shut up and let the dog see the rabbit. If we pull out the sofa from the wall, there's a spare socket behind there, as I recall, and it's out of the window light.' He pushed the sofa forward and Connie scrambled into the space to retrieve a crumpled hanky, two mouldy sweets and a broken pipe.

The carpet square didn't reach that far back and the wooden floor was full of fluff on the skirting board where no one had bothered to dust.

That set Su in a panic. 'When did these corners last get a fright? We shall have to bottom this all out right now. Joy! Go and fetch the mop and brush. I don't want the neighbours to think we keep a dirty house.'

The furniture was shunted one way and another and then back. How could one small box create such havoc? They all set to with a vengeance to spruce up the room.

Levi tried to slope off to his van but Su collared him at the front door.

'Not so fast, my good man... There's a bit more shifting yet.'

'Hurry up or Ivy will send out a search party and there'll be all hell to pay.'

Everyone knew Ivy didn't like him helping out in the family home. She never called 'round because of the 'B.F.O.', the Big Fall-Out, that, to Connie's dismay, nobody ever talked about. She and Levi had lived in Waverley House themselves before the bust-up. Connie didn't know why she never invited them round now to play with Neville to watch *Muffin the Mule*.

Eventually the object of future worship was placed with great reverence on the pie-crust table: a twelve-inch screen Pye set with walnut-effect cabinet and cathode ray tube, the workings of which Mr Pickles had tried to explain to a bewildered Connie and Joy in Junior Science Club. The piano was demoted to the cold dining room.

Connie and Joy had done loads of stuff on the Coronation itself in school: the history of the Crown Jewels, the ceremony and the royal family. Connie's class had made crowns, orbs and sceptres out of cardboard and gold cigarette papers, sweet wrappers and milk-bottle tops. Joy, who was in the class above, was making scrap-books about the royal family, cutting out every picture she could find about the Queen.

Then there was the pageant in King's Park on Sunday afternoon and the Lemody Liptrot Little Lovelies, to which Connie and Joy belonged, were appearing in the finale as flag bearers. Their best friend, Rosa Santini, was doing a solo. She was coming to watch TV with them on Coronation Day, along with her mum, Maria, and Sylvio, her new husband, and little Salvi and Serafina.

There were flags and bunting right down Division Street, pictures of the Queen in every window, and posters showing the Golden Coach. Best of all they were having their very own street party. If only it would stay fine, Connie sighed. Everything depended on the weather and, being near the hills, they got more than their fair share of the wet stuff.

Still, nothing could spoil the fun and the thrill of seeing it all on telly. Sometimes their house felt like Grimbleton Station at the start of Wakes Week holiday, always comings and goings, suitcases in the hall, visitors up and down stairs. They had per-manent guests like Dr Friedmann, who worked in the General Hospital, as did Mama. There was Miss Pinkerton, who visited her nieces for weeks on end, and then regular travellers and salesmen, who popped in on their rounds. The washing machine in the scullery out back was always on the go and Auntie Su had to have help with the iron-ing. Then there were the state visits from Grandma Esme, who'd retired to a bungalow up Sutter's Fold. She liked to descend without warning just to check everything was shipshape – the Waverley would always really be her house.

They were going to pack in as many visitors as they could to watch events unfold from palace to cathedral and procession. It was going to be just as good as going there and, Granny Esme said, even better 'cos they'd get to go inside.

'But you've got to behave. The Queen may not see you, but she's watching, just the same. Remember our motto: "Family First and Foremost"... No slacking in the back row.'

Connie loved her granny Esme. She never called round without bringing them something in her brown crocodile handbag: coloured pencils, foreign stamps for their album, Spangles in a tube. She sometimes helped in the kitchen when she could and was kind to Susan and Ana.

Connie wasn't quite sure how they were all related and no one ever explained why they all lived together. Auntie Su came from Burma with little Joy, and Mama came from Athens with her. There were loads of aunties who weren't proper aunties but her mama's special friends. Again it was something to do with the B.F.O. and the fact their daddies had died in the war. Whatever the case, the Winstanleys were an important family.

They were the first to have a proper washing machine and two cars, a business in town – Winstanley Health and Herbs, the family herbal stall in the Market Hall – and now a guesthouse with a television.

Connie had to share a room with Mama, and Joy with Auntie Susan, but when they were older they were promised two of the attic bedrooms for themselves. For the moment every room had to be let out. Dr Friedmann had a bedsitting room upstairs with a dressing room he used as a study. Miss Pinkerton had to have the room nearest to the bathroom on a account of her 'delicate condition', which no one would explain whenever Connie asked.

Breakfast and evening meals were eaten in the dining room and the lounge was a smoky fug where guests could sit and read the papers. The family lived in the back living room and kitchen. Connie would have loved the TV in there but it was much too important to get chip fat and grease all over it, Mama said.

Now it sat with a crocheted lace tablecloth over it to keep the dust off. Then the man from the shop came to fix the aerial and half the street stood outside to watch him attach it to the chimney as he pointed it towards Winter Hill near Bolton to get the best signal. Connie couldn't imagine how invisible waves could make a picture.

Uncle Levi had got one ages ago so he could watch Bolton Wanderers and Blackpool slog it out in the Cup Final. He was cheering for Stanley Matthews to get his medal as Bolton were rivals of the local team, the Grasshoppers, where her Auntie Lee's husband was coach.

Connie kept watching the sky anxiously in case the rain might spoil their day. It was going to be so exciting. Auntie Su had made them both special seersucker cotton dresses to wear in red, white and blue stripes. Mama had bought them striped ribbons for their bunches. There were special serviettes and paper hats, balloons and the crowns they'd made at school for their parties.

Then it rained and Joy cried as the pageant in the park was cancelled, and Rosa wouldn't speak to anyone, her big brown eyes filled with tears of frustration. Why did it rain so much round here? The television kept juddering so the aerial man was called back to fix it, but nothing could stop the thrill of hearing that Mount Everest had been conquered by Hillary and Tensing on the BBC News on Coronation morning, and it was raining in London too, which was only fair.

Soon their visitors started piling in: old Mrs Pickvance, and Mr Beddows from next door, who was a bit deaf; Granny Esme, who arrived in a taxi; Auntie Lee and her husband, who ran Longsight Travel in town, the Bertorellis crammed in with all the kids, sitting on the floor, staring in awe at all the soldiers and carriages and people waving flags. Kings and queens in robes from all over the world parading their finery.

'Mark my words,' said Granny. 'Such splendour ... the sun may have set on our empire but no one does it better than us.'

They had to stand up every time the National Anthem was played, but after three times everyone agreed they'd done it enough respect.

The screen was so small but the sound was clear; the fanfares rang out, the bells, the cheering crowds. Connie sat transfixed, but Joy kept pinching her for more space so she pulled her bunches and Joy squealed. Connie got a clip from her mama. 'We are in church now, so behave...'

They passed round a red, white and blue plate

with red, white and blue sandwiches on it, well nearly: red tomatoes and tongue, white bread, and pickled cabbage, which was about as blue as they could get.

They'd made Coronation biscuits shaped like crowns with silver balls for jewels and cake. There were potato crisps, and port and lemons for the ladies, Mackeson's Stout for the men, and Vimto for the kids. They sat glued to the box, feeding their food to their mouths, afraid to miss a second of the spectacle. Auntie Su cried when the Queen made her vows. 'She's always been fiercely patriotic,' Mama smiled, then whispered, 'Look at her, she thinks she's more British than the Queen herself.' They saw little Prince Charles in his silk outfit, with his granny. He was so well behaved.

No one saw Neville creep through the door and plonk himself down beside them. Cousin Neville was Levi's son. He lived round the corner, off Green Lane, and was an 'only one' so liked to boss them around. They all went to the same primary school but he was in Joy's class.

'Budge up,' he whispered, sitting on Connie's skirt.

'What's up?' she asked. 'Your telly gone wonky?'

'Nah ... they're at it again, Mum and Dad, argy-bargy all morning long. Dad's gone to the British Legion for a pint. It's not much fun being an only one.'

Connie didn't consider that Cousin Neville had it hard. She never got a minute to be on her own. There was always someone in the room or in the kitchen. Oh, to have a room to herself, like Neville, and time to read her Enid Blytons in peace without someone shouting, 'Connie, love, can you just...?' She had to share everything with Joy as if they were sisters, not second cousins.

'Sit still and shut up,' she ordered him, and for once Neville did as he was told.

After the service and the procession were over, and it was still raining in London but drying off in Grimbleton, they began to set the tables up with white cloths and more paper plates and balloons, while Jackie Dodd's father organised a game of French cricket in the street, odds against the evens. The Winstanleys were number twenty-two so they tagged along on the even team, trying to make the ball hit the legs of the person holding the bat.

Then they sat down to more sandwiches, sausage rolls, buns with coloured icing and rubber jelly with hundreds and thousands on top. The boys were flicking it on their spoons, shouting, 'Ice cream and jelly ... a punch on the belly! A whole lot of fun and punch up yer bum!'

Granny was not amused.

Then Sylvio and Uncle Pete pushed the piano out to the open dining-room window and they had a singsong and knees-up, dancing and laughing until it was nearly dark.

Someone from the *Mercury* took a street photograph. There were Rosa, Neville, Joy and Connie all grinning in their home-made paper crowns; Ana, Su and Maria, and Gran in her straw hat, staring at their offspring proudly.

'Golden Kids for a Golden Age' said the headline, but it didn't go down well in Division Street as most of the people on the shot were visitors, muttered Noreen Broadhurst's mum from number fifteen. 'They're all furriners,' she sniffed.

Then thunder clapped overhead at the same time as Ivy stormed round the corner from Green Lane. 'So there you are! Trust you to sneak off here. If I've told you once ... Division Street is no place for you. I've been searching everywhere. Come on home!' she ordered Neville, wagging her finger. Everything about Auntie Ivy bounced, Connie thought: her curls, her frilly blouse, her busts, the pleats on her skirt, just like a pink blancmange on a plate. Connie giggled as Neville backed away from his mother's outstretched hand.

Ivy looked daggers at her. 'And you can cut that smirk off your face, cheeky madam! Do as you're told, young man. I'll not have you show me up before this lot.' Now she stared at Mama and Auntie Su. 'I might have known you lot would be making this racket,' ignoring the fact that half the street was dancing and enjoying themselves.

'Let the lad be, Ivy,' ordered Granny. 'He's been no trouble. Let him play a bit longer. I'll see he gets home before dark. Is Levi not with you?'

'No, he wandered off down the pub as usual. Come on, Neville, or you'll see the palm of my hand!'

'There's no need for that ... come and join the party,' Auntie Su invited her with a sweep of her arm. Big mistake.

'No thank you. I know when I'm not welcome,' Ivy huffed, looking pointedly at Maria and Sylvio. 'Didn't take you long to get yer feet under the table, did it?' she said to Sylvio.

'None of that. Remember where you are ... in a

public place. I think you've had a few too many sherries. I'll come and keep you company, if you like,' Gran offered.

'I prefer my own company, thank you,' Ivy replied. 'Neville, are you coming or do I have to drag you back?'

'I want to play with my sisters,' he shouted, shaking his black curls and folding his arms across his chest in defiance.

'Don't you go calling them girls sisters! You're a *proper* Winstanley. Them's just chancers, interlopers and their mothers ... war widows! My aunt Fanny!'

'Ivy!' Granny Esme's voice rose. 'That's *enough.*'

'I don't know why you take their side over me every time. They stole our inheritance. Mark my words, you'll rue the day!' And off Ivy wobbled, her high heels clickety-clacking on the pavement as she made her way back to their semi in Richman Crescent.

'What was all that about?' whispered Joy to Neville. Then they all smiled. The B.F.O. had reared up again.

It was an eternal mystery to the three children.

'Inside,' Granny ordered, scooping her family up like a flock of unruly sheep. 'Floor show is over, ladies and gentlemen. I think we'll go and watch a bit more TV.' When Grandma barked, everyone jumped. This time no one else was invited inside.

Connie winked at Neville. He'd called them his sisters and that was good.

Connie wakes from her reverie. Perhaps she will show those snapshots from the family album back at the

27

villa. Everyone who mattered then is in there, she muses, checking the Arrivals screen for what must be the hundredth time.

Looking back, to her the colours of her childhood blend with the patterned Axminster rug where they lay absorbed in comics, watching firelight and shoes, the grey ballet blankets where Rosa, Joy and she stretched out growing limbs and caught splinters from the dancing studio's wooden floor. School was somewhere you sat cross-legged with scabby knees, absorbing knowledge like a sponge, she smiled.

The real-life dramas, past and present, unfolding in the Waverley wafted over their heads but they felt the draughts of them now and then. She can never recall a time when Joy and Neville weren't always by her side. They bartered allegiances like the swapping of stamps and picture cards, argued over Monopoly on wet Sunday afternoons when the TV was forbidden, aware that in the kitchen their mothers were hatching plans, golden schemes to give them the best education and the chance to fulfil their own dreams. What mother doesn't want her child to have more than she ever had?

2

The Big Day

The two girls clung together as they walked up the long stone driveway to the Girls' Division of Grimbleton School, looking towards the red brick castle with turrets and crenellated rooftops set high on the hill overlooking the town. The building was surrounded by parkland and tennis courts with grassy sports pitches and a hedge separating them from the Boys' Division next door.

Connie thought it was just like the thorny hedge in *The Sleeping Beauty*, separating one world from the other. She felt very small besides the big prefects in smart grey skirts and red jumpers covered in badges, who ushered them towards the quadrangle and the examination rooms ahead.

Every ten and eleven-year-old was gathered on either side of the hedge to sit 'The Scholarship', the big one. This was to be the most important day of her life so far.

Auntie Su had insisted they came in school gymslips and shirt and tie, with hair tied in pigtails. 'It is important to make a good impression. It will help you concentrate,' she had argued.

Rosa had been allowed to wear her tartan trews and a sweater, with her hair done up in a ponytail. She was going for a place at Our Lady of Sorrows Convent. Connie and Joy were separated from Rosa by their surname initials, and Neville was going for the Boys' Division next door.

There were clusters of anxious mothers waiting at the gateway, hoping that their darlings would past muster on the day, but the three girls had come on the bus with a gaggle of entrants from St Saviour's Primary School.

Mama was on duty in the hospital but had left her a little sacred picture of St John of Patmos for luck. She had gone into Manchester to buy a special tama to pin to the icon of the saint in the church. Dr Friedmann had given Connie a new pen to write with. Auntie Susan was doing break-fasts and insisted they had porridge and eggs to help them concentrate. Now Connie felt sick and kept swallowing with nerves.

For nearly a year they had all been sent to Miss Scorah's at the end of the road for extra coaching in arithmetic and spatial intelligence tests. She was a retired teacher who liked to shout mental arithmetic and tables at them and gave lessons in her front room for half a crown each. They had to leave the half-crown under the bell on the mantel-piece because Miss Scorah didn't like taking money from children.

Neville called her a witch – he had twice as many lessons. Miss Scorah was kind if you tried, but threw the books across the room if you were careless.

'Connie Winstanley! You can do better than this drivel. I think you were watching television while you did this work,' she screamed, her grey eyes hard as playground ice, and she was right. 'I am not going to waste your mother's precious money on such rubbish! Go home and come next week with a clean page and no scribblings. I expect only the best from my best pupils.'

She'd run home crying with shame. That was when she realised that much was expected of her, not only by her mother and Auntie Lee and Grandma, but by the School, which liked to get as many of the top class past the scholarship and brag about it in the papers.

Her teacher, Mr Pedley, didn't hold with extra coaching. He said it was unfair but with fifty-five children to teach, the clever ones were put to the front and caned more often if they didn't come up to scratch. That was his way of making them work. Connie was taking her scholarship a year early as a try-out.

Auntie Su said it was everyone for themselves these days and they must take their chance. Granny Esme had said she would buy their uniforms if they passed. They all went to visit her on the bus. Her bungalow was almost in the country and looked down on the town with its forest of smoking chimneys. Sometimes she made them a picnic and took them for a walk into the woods, showing them bluebells and mushrooms and trees. They ate ginger parkin and Lucozade, and raced back down to the house for sugary tea in china cups with flowers on them.

Connie loved Granny Esme's sitting room, with its rows of china plates in the cabinet and pictures of all the relatives on the piano, especially the one of her daddy, Freddie, in his army uniform. He looked so handsome.

'I'm expecting great things of you two,' Granny would say. 'It'll give me great satisfaction to take you down to Grundy's outfitters and kit you out in those red-trimmed felt hats and striped blazers. You must keep up the tradition even though you are girls. It is no excuse – the Winstanleys expect,' she smiled.

Joy bowed her head. She was not confident of passing anything. Then she looked at the photo of Freddie on the mantelpiece with envy. 'Did my daddy, Cedric, go to the grammar school like Connie's?' she asked.

'I'm sure he did, dear, and so did Uncle Levi.

Not that you'd notice it now,' Gran sighed, and looked at him as a young soldier in a cap.

Why would no one tell them more about Cedric, the cousin from London who died before Joy was born? There were no pictures. All his family were killed in the Blitz.

Connie knew all about the Blitz because she could see the broken houses from the bus when they went shopping to Manchester and visited the Greek church. Mama wasn't much better. She said nothing about Crete and Greece and how she had met Connie's daddy. It was if their history was all wrapped in a parcel with a label: 'Do not open or else...' It wasn't fair. She had no medals or souvenirs like some of the children in her class whose daddies were killed in the war.

Then there was the business of her name. Why was she called Connie when her mother called her Dina? When she asked, all she got was a shrug. 'It is my special name for you. You were named for your grandma, Constance Esme. It is an honour to carry her name. It is tradition.'

All she knew was she looked just like Daddy Freddie. She could see that by the photograph. She had the sandy curls and fair looks.

She often wondered about how her mama and daddy had come to have her. It was something to do with Daddy putting seeds in Mummy's tummy so they grew like tomatoes in the glass shed. Joy said they grew into fat bulbs but Rosa said her mummy grew her brother, Salvatore, and sister, Serafina in her tummy until it was a balloon which burst one night while she was asleep.

The Santinis had lived at the Waverley for a while

and it had been fun. Then they went to live over Uncle Sylvio's new hairdressing salon and there was a big fight with the Santinis, which no one was allowed to talk about. That was another B.F.O.

When Auntie Ria and Mama and Auntie Su got together there was always noise and bottles of wine and laughing. Sometimes Dr Friedmann joined them and Auntie Diana who worked in London, and her friend Pam from the hospital: Connie acknowledged she may not have many relatives but she had plenty of aunties and uncles now.

Every week the girls met at the dancing class and went for ices afterwards, and Rosa gave them a blow-by-blow account of which stars came into the salon for a shampoo and set. She was going to appear in the next pantomime at the King's Theatre, but Mama said they were not allowed to audition for the kiddy chorus because they needed all their sleep for the scholarship. Connie was sick of the scholarship.

Now it was Saturday morning, and instead of being in the studio doing tap-dancing she had to put on her gymslip and go and sit three tests. The thought of sitting at a desk all morning was a bore. Saturday mornings were for tap-dancing and sitting on the upstairs of the bus, spending her pocket money in the market stalls on gob-stoppers and kayli and Spanish liquorish and a copy of *Schoolfriend* to swap with Joy when it was finished. She liked browsing through the button stall and the rows of shiny sequins, choosing a packet of stamps from the stamp shop for her collection. Sixpence didn't go very far. It burned a hole in her pocket and she never managed to save it up.

She looked up at the tall windows and the arched doorways. It was all very grand and scary but did she really want to take a bus every day across town and be stared at in her stripy uniform? What if she got lost and missed her lessons?

'You will sit next to me?' whispered Joy. 'I'm scared.'

Joy was always worrying about lessons and about being clever enough to pass. She never missed her homework or her music practice, and Auntie Su fussed over her in a way Connie's own mother never did. Auntie Su was always in the kitchen at home while Mama was on shift or out at night school to improve her English.

Since Mama worked full time there was not a lot of time for them to be alone together except when they went to church in Manchester. Then she used to chatter in Greek. They sat together on the bus and Connie felt close to her mother and longed to ask about her homeland. She understood a little of the language but her mother always talked to her in English now as if she were ashamed of her own country.

One thing was certain: they were all expecting her to do well, but when she saw the hundreds of girls all walking so confidently into the school, all competing for a few places, it seemed hopeless. She and Joy didn't stand a chance of being among the chosen few, Connie reckoned.

'Come on, Joy, let's just enjoy ourselves and walk around as if we own the place. It doesn't matter if we don't get in. There are plenty of other good schools to go at,' she laughed.

'But Mummy says this is the best in the district. Everyone wants to come here. The girls go to university and become famous,' Joy replied, clutching her arm.

'I don't care. Miss Scorah said you can only do your best,' Connie offered, trying to be brave. 'We must leave the rest to Providence.'

'What does that mean?'

'Don't ask me, something to do with church, I suppose. You go to church more than me,' she replied, already bored with all the fuss. 'Let's get this over with and then we can look forward to the Christmas charity dancing display.'

Dr Friedmann suggested it might help to read all the books on the reading list. She had cried at the first bit of *Jane Eyre*, and loved *Susannah of the Mounties* and *Wind in the Willows*, but she could not make head nor tail of *Through the Looking-Glass*. It had given her nightmares.

She liked Dr Friedmann, though. He was kind and explained things. He had a sad crumpled face and since he had stopped smoking he was always eating sweets, which he kept unwrapped in his pocket. Whenever he dished her one, it was covered in fluff. She had to rinse it under the tap. Now he went round telling Maria and Sylvio and Uncle Levi not to smoke, but no one listened to him.

Connie knew he was very clever. The books in his room were piled high everywhere and he helped her with her homework whenever she asked. It was Dr Friedmann who explained about the ballet music being called classical, and he knew all the tunes that she practised her exercises to at the home-made barre in the hallway while he played on the piano. Sometimes he would play Chopin on his gramophone and cry into his hanky when he thought she wasn't looking. Classical seemed to make him sad but he played it just the same.

Joy preferred to knit blankets for her dollies and embroider tea cloths for Christmas presents. She liked watching television, saying the doctor in their house didn't look like any of the doctors in *Doctor in the House.*

Mama nursed old ladies in the hospital, and sometimes they had to go and dance and sing for them on the ward. The old ladies cried out and dribbled a lot and slept in cots with bars on the side, which frightened her. The hospital itself scared her with its silent squeaky corridors and horrible smells. She would never want to be a nurse, or do breakfasts and sewing like Auntie Su, so she must crack on and sit the tests.

She wanted to be more like Auntie Lee. Sometimes on Saturday afternoon, Auntie Lee shut up the travel shop and took them to the football match at Brogden Park to watch the Grass-hoppers, standing under the sheltered end in the wind, shouting and cheering them on. They had fish and chips on the way home and that was the best bit, sniffing the salt and vinegar, the hot fat and warm bodies. They walked uphill with hot chips held on the edge of their teeth and the journey always went quicker.

Auntie Lee passed for the grammar school but

left at sixteen to work for the Tax Office and the market stall, and then she went travelling abroad, which Connie thought was incredibly glamorous.

Now she and Joy were sitting side by side as rivals, Connie supposed. Both of them knew this was the moment when their whole future would be decided. She knew what it meant to fail the eleven-plus.

She would have to go to Broad Lane secondary Modern where the rough boys from the council estate, with shaven heads, went. Rosa would have to go to St Vincent's RC and leave at fifteen to work in Woolies or the Co-Op.

Mr Pedley kept drumming into them the importance of passing; this was the one chance to show your metal. But she didn't have any iron or silver or gold in her to show. Now they were sitting waiting to turn over the page and a stern lady in a black gown was pacing up and down making sure they couldn't copy from each other.

'CONSTANCE ESME WINSTANLEY' was typed on the paper in front of her and suddenly it was all very real and very frightening.

She put her Timex wristwatch on the desk to keep an eye on the time as they had practised with Miss Scorah. She had them all in for practice runs. 'Read the questions three times and answer only the question,' she had instructed.

'Turn your papers over and begin,' ordered the teacher now. This was the composition paper and she had to fill the pages with her own story.

CHOOSE ONE OF THESE TOPICS
1) My favourite day out.

2) Where I will be in ten years time...
3) A day in the life of...

That last was the one she fancied doing and she knew just what she was going to say.

'Wasn't that hard?' sighed Joy, who was chewing on her pencil after the final arithmetic exam was over, while her mother was fussing over them in Santini's, where they'd gone with Rosa.

'Well? How did it go, Rosa?' Auntie Su asked.

She shrugged nonchalantly. 'I can kiss Our Lady of Sorrows goodbye,' she sighed, tucking into a huge triple Neapolitan ice. They rarely came to Santini's since Auntie Ria had the B.F.O. with her family, but Rosa was allowed to come in on her own with them. Old Nonna Valentina still wanted to treat her grandchild and her friends.

Auntie Su was giving them a grilling and wanted to know about every question and how they answered. 'What essay did you do, Joy?' she whispered.

'The one about being a ballerina when I grow up, like we practised,' she replied. Joy had no intention of being a ballet dancer. She had barely scraped through her last Royal Academy exam.

'What did you do?' Joy smiled turning to Connie.

'A day in the life of a bag of chips,' Connie said, watching their faces gape with surprise.

'That's not one we practised with Miss Scorah,' Joy replied, and Mama's face dropped with disappointment.

'I know, I know, but it just came into my head

38

and it was a good story about a fish landed from the sea and a potato pulled out of the earth who didn't feel very special but when they got together with the newspaper they were turned into magic food and made us warm and happy. The newspaper was thrown in the bin but jumped out and began another adventure.'

Suddenly her idea seemed silly and she knew she had blown her chance, but she didn't want to be a ballerina, not like Rosa, who was the best dancer in the school.

'You've all done your best, I'm sure,' said Mama, patting her arm and giving her a two-bob bit to spend as a treat. All she could think of was that the exam was over and now she could forget it and get on with Christmas.

On the spring morning that the letters allocating scholarship places arrived, Connie had to go to school not knowing her fate.

There were tears and tantrums and mums squeezing letters through the playground railings. 'You've got a place at the technical school.' 'You've passed for Moor Bank.' It was an agony to wait until dinnertime to rush home to see what fate was waiting for them on the kitchen table.

Auntie Su was sitting smiling at Joy. 'You've passed, you passed for Moor Bank.' This was the council grammar school in the centre of town and strictly second division, but everyone knew it was better than Broad Lane Secondary.

Connie's own result lay unopened on the table. Mama was on duty but she couldn't wait until teatime to know her fate. The envelope was torn open and the letter read.

'Crikey Moses! I don't believe it!' she cried, shoving the letter across the table to Auntie Su, who went pink when she read it.

'Congratulations, Connie, Grimbleton School, Girls' Division for you! They must have liked that fish and chip story after all.'

Connie wakes from her dreaming, looking at her watch with dismay. How time crawls when you watch it. Turning the pages of that family album is like stepping into another world for her children; a world where girls wore frocks and sandals – patent leather with ankle straps – and boys wore shorts until they were thirteen or more. How they laugh when it comes out. Kids played in the street until it was dark, walking unmolested through parks, sat in cinemas, mooched around for miles, playing out all day. Not like now.

With hindsight Connie realises that there must have been other kids who were not so lucky as the Winstanley tribe. Judging by the books in the shops, they have a different story to tell of blighted childhoods and abuse. Whatever half-truths she was fobbed off with were accepted as gospel. In this fifties world, grownups knew best. Parents often had their reasons to lie.

Just three girls and Neville, living in a bubble, protected by aunties, friends, neighbours who made up for there being no fathers around. So many of their school friends had none either, because of the war.

What you don't have, you don't miss, they say... That's a lie! Together, war babies like Rosa, Joy and me might be children of peace, but each of our own private battles was devastating none the less.

40

We had no fathers to guide us through those difficult years. Is that why we made so many mistakes?

3

Rosa

Rosa stood in the dining queue daydreaming. She was rehearsing her audition routine in her head: *dégagé derrière ... jeté ... pas de bourrée* and *plié*. There would only be minutes to impress the judges for a place in the Royal Academy, Manchester classes. There would be lines of competition from other twelve-year-olds in their white leotards and sashes. Miss Liptrot was giving Rosa extra lessons to make every movement perfect.

Every morning she went into the chapel early to beg Our Lady for a place. Sweets were sacrificed in favour of buying a strip of photos of little black babies for Jesus, saved by the missionaries in Africa from starvation. Sometimes she would practise her *port de bras* as she pleaded to the Holy Mother for this special favour. Then Sister Gilberte caught her prancing and there'd been trouble ever since.

Her arms were extended and fingers outstretched. They were her best feature, for her legs were a little on the short side and her arches were not fully rounded to make her pointed foot look as good as it should. She did all her barre exer-

41

cises faithfully hanging onto the banister rail at the top of the stairs, but there wasn't enough space to extend out and stretch properly because of the pram in the hall.

She stretched out her brown brogues to see if her ankles had shrunk. They looked awful in her grey wool socks with the gold and brown stripes at the knee. If only she could wear stockings like the sixth-form girls. Her brown serge pinafore was shaped and fitted, and a size too big, having once belonged to her cousin Marcella. Everything was handed down, shiny with wear and had hems and tucks. She felt like a cross between a wasp and a bumblebee.

Our Lady of Sorrows liked their girls in shapeless drab uniforms the colour of a ploughed field or a 'number-two job', as her friend Maureen Brady had whispered to her. She lifted her skirt to examine her knees. As usual they were scuffed and pitted with ash marks from chasing her brother, Salvi, round the park.

'Put that skirt down, Rosaria,' shouted Sister Gilberte, who had eyes like radar for any fidgeting and infringement of the rules. 'How many times do I have to drum into this numbskull that Sorrows girls do not display bodily parts except on the playing field? Sorrows girls are ladies first and foremost, even if we do have to suffer the *scruffier* elements of our community from time to time. We will have no common boldness in this school, do you hear, Santini? What can you expect from Italian peasant stock!' the nun sniffed, pulling Rosa roughly back into line.

'Virtue and decorum at all times, girls. You are

the Holy Mother's little flagships sailing on a sea of wickedness and heresy.'

Rosa hated Sister Gilberte, in her long black habit, swishing along the corridor like a black swan gliding over a polished sea of oak. She was Odile to her Odette in *Swan Lake*, the sorcerer's evil daughter, all sweetness and light on the outside but a black heart at the core. How she had cried when poor Odette was denied her prince. It wasn't fair.

Sister Gilberte knew her every move, caught her running when she should be walking, skipping when she should be walking crocodile, told her off for singing too loud, sneezing in chapel, for having dirty hands and knees, and her hair ribbon missing.

Mamma would sigh and find sixpence for another hair ribbon, for they could only be bought from the school. It was not fair. There must be hundreds of ribbons hidden in Sister Gilberte's desk.

It was a good job lessons were easy and she could do her prep on the bus home or tucked under a spare hair dryer in the salon when it was quiet. If only her exercise books didn't end up smelling of ammonia and bleach. Once she got hair tint splashed on her work and got the cane again. She needed all the gold stars she could get so that she might ask for the afternoon off to attend the ballet audition. A place at the Academy morning school was another rung on the ladder to becoming the next Fonteyn, Beryl Grey or Markova. She was not fussy which. She already had a good stage name.

'Rosa Santini, rising star of the Royal Ballet School dances at the King's Theatre, Grimbleton as a gesture to her home town and alma mater, the Lemody Liptrot School of Dance,' the paper would read. The whole convent would come to see her perform and Sister Gilberte would not have a ticket but would sit alone eating her words about the Santinis being common and bold.

For the moment she must suffer for her art; a little drone at the court of the big fat queen bee in the wimple, fussing over her favourites with their sashes and big busts. She would like a Sabrina bust one day, but not until she was famous. Busts got in the way of *jetés* and *entrechats;* they bounced and wobbled and hung over flimsy tunics. Sister Gilberte said they were bodily parts that gave occasions for sin and lust, and must be bound over at all times.

Hers were like two half lemons but they still had to be encased in a tiny cotton dancing bra so that nothing showed under the white leotard. Her body was changing and she hated the hair sprouting at the top of her legs; it was coarse and dark, and showed through her leotard without a lining sewn into it.

Nuns didn't have busts but wore long white spatulas over their habit like penguins waddling down the shore in squeaky brogues that looked like coal barges.

Sister Gilberte had spies everywhere feeding her morsels of information. How else did she know that Rosaria cavorted in ice-cream parlours with Protestants and danced to juke box music, which everyone knew was of the very devil himself? If only she could fit in with the rest of her class.

When she giggled with Maureen, who was clever and wanted to be a teacher, they were separated and Rosa was told she was a bad influence so she was sat next to poor Celia White-house, who had red hair and spots and was working hard to be a saint, and whose parents had a sweet shop and tobacconist's and gave the school lots of prizes for the Christmas parties.

Somehow Sister Gilberte knew all about the Santini scandal and the Big Fall-Out after Dada went to heaven. How her mother had left the café and had a baby and lived with Protestants before Sylvio Bertorelli made an honest woman of her. The Santini stock was not rated highly after cousin Marcella left at fifteen before her exams to work in the café. Enzo went to St Vincent's so no one was expecting much from this humble offcut. Rosa's scholarship had been a surprise even to herself. It was a burden she had to bear.

'I hope you last longer than your cousin,' sniffed the nun. 'Girls from your background should not be entered for scholarships. They take up valuable places. You will do cookery and extra religious studies to nip any contrariness in the bud. The Sorrows girls are the future home-makers of Catholic Grimbleton, shining beacons of motherhood within the sanctity of holy matri-mony fortified by Papal Blessing and Nuptial Mass. I can't see you qualifying for anything much. Good Catholic girls do not go on the stage and we don't want show-offs in our midst. I shall be watching you, Santini.'

It was hard enough kitting her out for the

grammar school now that baby Serafina had followed Salvi and they were bursting at the seams living above the salon. Mamma was so busy downstairs seeing to customers that Rosa was lumbered with watching the babies whilst trying to practise her barre work on the banister rail in the hallway.

A place at the Royal Academy would change all that. School was just something to do between ballet lessons and listening to the juke box, but she still needed a letter to get her off classes so she could catch the bus to Manchester.

Mamma was not good at spelling, and Sylvio was even worse. In the end it was Queenie Quigley, one of the Olive Oil Supper Club, who came to the rescue and wrote the letter on peach-coloured scented notepaper, which was all they had to hand, and Mamma signed it. Rosa handed it in to the school office and thought nothing of it until she was summoned by her form teacher at the end of registration.

'We don't give days off to go cavorting with theatricals, Rosaria. There aren't enough days in the week to drum the basics into a schoolgirl's head if she is to avoid all the temptations of the flesh and the devil in this day and age,' said Sister Gilberte drawing herself up into a puffball of indignation. 'Dancing and prancing half naked on a stage for men to lust after – is that what any good mother wants for her daughter? Permission is withheld for your own good and let's hear no more about it. Do you understand?'

Rosa nodded, feeling sick in the pit of her stomach. A nun's word was second only to the priest's but she just *had* to go. There was nothing for it but to ignore the order and lie, for Mamma would never argue with a nun. She was on sticky ground already, being in mortal sin. Disobedience was unthinkable for someone who was in disgrace with her own Church. It was only one measly afternoon's leave. But how could she lie to her own mother?

She was glad that Joy and Connie were waiting in Santini's after school. They always met up there on Fridays. Connie was sitting in her red uniform looking like a stick of striped rock, and poor Joy, in her heavy navy-blue coat and felt hat, was sipping an ice-cream soda. They were already comparing their homework.

'When's the audition?' they asked, for the whole dancing school was thrilled that someone had got through to the last selection day. It was a good job they were her oldest friends and she could trust them with the truth.

'That cow Gilberte won't let me off school,' Rosa whispered 'But I have to go. What shall I do?' she asked as she tucked into a huge bowl of vanilla, raspberry sauce staining her tongue.

'Say nothing and just go,' said Connie, trying to be helpful. But she was so clever Rosa knew she would never miss school. She was destined for certificates and prizes, and her pockets were always stuffed with library books.

'Pretend to be sick,' whispered Joy, who often stayed off school. She said it was to help Auntie Susan with the lodgers at Waverley House. She hardly ever came to dancing class now, but preferred to meet them in the café afterwards.

Joy didn't seem to have her own gang of friends

47

at Moor Bank and was always hanging around the girls from the Girls' Division with Connie. None of them bothered with her much, which was a shame, for Joy was kind and good at window-shopping and choosing materials on the market stalls. She was pretty even if she was plump. Rosa felt sorry for Joy.

On the morning before the audition, she double-checked everything in her ballet box, a round case with a handle that was her pride and joy. She decided to skip school altogether. If she brought a sick note no one could say anything the next day.

She deliberately missed the bus and walked into town as if she was going to the dentist, dawdling back home slowly and checking her bag once more.

Sylvio offered to take them all in his van so he could call in at the warehouse for his salon supplies. It was half-day, and Mamma wanted a trip into Manchester herself. It would have been better if just the two of them had gone on the bus but Sylvio couldn't be expected to look after babies.

Rosa's selection class was at two thirty: barre work, dance, interview and medical examination. She was so excited she was shaking. It was hard to hurry everyone along into the van for the fifteen-mile journey into the city centre.

They were almost at Salford when they got a puncture and everyone had to get out. That was when Sylvio discovered he had forgotten to put the spare tyre back and Rosa felt a wave of panic as she looked at her wristwatch. None of them knew the right bus route but Mamma was not going to let a little matter of a lift get in the way of her daughter's future so she flagged down the first car that passed as if it was a national emergency, checking to see if there was a woman in the passenger seat.

It was a couple on their way to Cheetham Hill and, hearing her story, offered to drop Rosa off at the foot of Deansgate so she could walk up to the studio halfway along the street. Mamma promised to join her there as soon as she could organise Sylvio with a new tyre. She kissed her and shoved a little crucifix into her palm.

'Put it in your bra for good luck,' she smiled. 'I will be praying for you.'

By the time she got to Deansgate it was ten past two and there was a long way to run to the top-floor studio. The street was much bigger than she'd thought and she was not so sure just which doorway staircase to take. Panic was turning her limbs to lead and she was in tears as she kept stopping shoppers and asking the way. Nobody knew where it was.

It was half-past two when she recognised the doorway and found the right staircase, flying up two at a time. In the foyer she stripped off her uniform and flung herself into her leotard and ballet skirt. In her rush she knotted her ballet ribbons up wrong, her hair was flying out of her bun and she was pink with anxiety as she crept into the dancing studio, late, breathless and dishevelled. She took herself to the end of the barre, trying to catch up and keep in time.

'*Plié* ... *battement tendu*...' came the orders from the dancing master, who marched up and down

49

with a tall stick, watching them carefully. There was no time to cry that this was not how it was meant to be. Rosa tried to concentrate and gather her trembling limbs into shape. Then her ballet shoe fell off and spun across the wooden floor. She crumpled and forgot everything she had ever learned. Mamma's lucky crucifix was still in her coat pocket.

The letter of rejection when it came was no surprise. From the moment she entered the class late, there was never any hope of retrieving her poise. After all, had she not sold her soul and lied to gain this precious opportunity and now she was being punished?

'I'm sorry,' said Sylvio. 'I should carry spare. You should have gone on the bus.'

'Never mind,' said Mamma, looking sad for her. 'Next time, perhaps.' But there would be no next time. She would be too old and too developed to get a place.

'Never mind, you did your best,' smiled Miss Liptrot, patting her on the shoulder. 'It was always a long shot, Rosa.'

'Hard cheese, Rosie,' whispered Connie, and gave her a gobstopper that changed colour. 'It's their loss not to choose you.'

'Poor you,' said Joy, looking at her with tears in her eyes. 'It's not fair.'

No, it wasn't a bit fair. How could she tell them that she had done her absolute worst and had not shown off Miss Liptrot's good teaching one iota? Given the right start she would have danced the competition out of the door but nerves had got to her and the real Fonteyns of this world *never* showed nerves.

Perhaps she was not good enough for the classical ballet schools? Perhaps her legs were too short and her turn-out was too poor. It was time to lay it all at the foot of Our Lady in supplication and contrition.

'I have let everyone down,' Rosa wept, 'especially myself.'

Comfort came from an unexpected source when she went to spend the night with Nonna Valentina, who slept in the back bedroom of Angelo's house. The old lady was sitting at her dressing table pulling the jet-black hairs out of her brush and winding them very carefully over her bun pad, which was pinned onto her long thin hair, while Rosa was telling her an edited version of this sad disappointment.

Nonna looked up and smiled as she secured the pad tighter to the nape of her neck with long grips. 'Old age is not for the faint-hearted, little one. Once I could scarce grasp my plait in one fist. Now it is a pitiable little scrap. Do not fret. There are lots of ways to skin a rabbit. Lots of dancing to try, I think. I see you tap-dancing and making beautiful movements across the stage. There must be operas and musicals that need good dancers and singers. I once had the voice and looks of an angel but good looks are only lent for a season. Your talent is your gift for ever. It will never fade. It runs in the family. You are a beautiful Santini and we are proud people. We do not fail when we set our hearts on something. How else would Pepe and I have made such a great business? Never forget your dada in heaven is looking over you,' she jabbered in rapid Italian.

Rosa was struggling to keep up. They spoke only English at home. Mamma had never spoken a word of Italian since the Big Fall-out.

'You are English now... no more peasant talk,' Mamma had said when they went to live with the Winstanleys in Division Street all those years ago. Rosa now depended on her *nonna* to hear the old tongue.

Perhaps Nonna was right and she could try another way. She was going to learn rock and roll and jive for the next charity show. There was the silver medal tap exam coming up soon. Perhaps there was another way to get on a stage.

They were practising her jive routine in the playground, Maureen, Celia and a group of older girls who were trying to copy the moves, when Sister Gilberte and Sister Monica caught her doing the split jump and throwing her legs around Bernadette Dumphy with her brown knickers bared for all to see.

'Santini, put your legs down this minute and get back into the form room! The devil is in your drawers already and you're not above twelve years old. We shall have to knock some sense into you before you shame the good name of the Sorrows.'

She took the full force of the beating without a sound. It was only what she deserved for all her devilment, lies and deceit. Sin would always be punished, they were told often enough, so she would offer this pain for the starving orphans of Hungary. She winced at each stroke but bit back her pain, swallowed her tears. No one was going to thrash out her determination. Do your worst, she thought, you can't touch me. I'm a Santini.

Now she could start over with a clean slate to make her dreams come true. This time she would not fail.

4

Neville

It was Neville's big idea to start a skiffle band. Everyone wanted to be Lonnie Donegan in the youth clubs and coffee bars around the town in 1957. There were enough lads around the Green Lane Club to form a group, and once Neville got an idea in his head there was no stopping him. Connie's Youth Club at Zion Chapel was getting a bit tame, with its ping pong table and weekly Brains Trusts. All the best boys were chucked out for smoking, swearing and wearing drainpipes. She and Joy just hung around to see the talent that was getting thinner by the week and so they soon drifted over in Neville's direction.

He'd got a tea chest with strings to make a bass, a real washboard that they could thrash with thimbles and a biscuit-tin drum, banging away for all they were worth, even though their rendition of 'Rock Island Line' was so awful that the rest of the club backed off to make tea in the kitchen of the tennis clubhouse, away from the racket.

Neville had a guitar for Christmas and was still learning chords from his Bert Weedon tutor book but he could only manage a decent E chord. All the band had bought trousers that Auntie Su had taken in at the sides.

However loyal the girls were to their cousin, Connie thought his group tuneless and wooden.

'You need someone up front to sing in tune,' she suggested, but Nev took the hump.

'Well, none of you are up for it,' he snapped.

This snub was just the call to arms Connie needed and she was round to Rosa's in a flash, along with Joy.

Sometimes she didn't know what to make of Neville. He mooned around Division Street with them, chatting and gossiping with Su and the lodgers. He was very up to date with the hit parade but when he was crossed he sulked like a schoolgirl.

His parents gave him everything he wanted, even when he failed his eleven-plus twice, and he got his bike and a posh new uniform for the Lawns School for Boys in the west end of town.

Going to Rosa's was always fun. It was generally chaos in the Bertorelli flat above the salon, smelling of rotten eggs and ammonia and nappy buckets – Maria had produced another son, Luca – but Rosa was fed up of baby-minding and glad to get out of the house.

'We're going to form our own skiffle band,' Connie announced. 'If Nev's lot are all that's going then we three can do better. You can sing up front, Rosa, you can do percussion, Joy, and I'll do tambourine.'

'That's not a proper skiffle,' Rosa said. 'We need instruments and a guitar.'

'Have you seen the prices of kit? Even a Junior Skiffle set is twenty-three and six. Where will we get a hooter, cowbells or a tap box?'

'Auntie Lee has cowbells from Austria. I've seen them,' Joy suggested. 'But who will play guitar?'

'Don't need one yet. We can all sing in tune; we're in school choirs.' Connie was not going to let a little thing like string instruments get in the way of her big idea.

'Not me. I got chucked out months ago,' quipped Rosa.

'I know, but you can sing when you want to, and in tune. We'll practise in Mama's allotment shed so we won't disturb the guests. We can show Neville he's not the cock of the midden.'

'We'll have to have a name,' Joy added. 'Something pretty to go with our outfits.'

'That's just a detail. What we need is to sing in tune, play a few percussion bits and look "with it", like beatniks.' Connie was full of ideas now, not outfits.

'Mummy will want us to look smart on stage,' Joy argued. She was so plump, thought Connie, she'd look like a sack of potatoes in the full skirts and petticoats that were all the rage.

'We'll wear black, with scarves round our necks and cut-off trews like Audrey Hepburn,' added Rosa who was heavily into the beat scene. 'And ponytails, lots of black eye make-up and mascara.'

'Mummy says we're too young for eye make-up,' Joy persisted, and they each gave her one of their stares.

'Mummy says, Mummy says…We're practically teenagers now, not babies. We do what we like.'

Rosa wouldn't budge. 'I'm not dressing like Shirley Temple.'

'Oh, shut up, both of you. Let's find a good song and learn it and see how we can dance and jig a bit. But don't tell Nev. He'll have a hissy fit if he's not the boss of the show.'

'But he is very good-looking,' Joy offered.

'Mamma says he's a big soft quilt,' Rosa replied.

'What's that supposed to mean?' the Winstanley girls asked as one.

'You know, a mummy's boy... She never lets him do anything.'

'Nev's all right,' Joy defended.

'In small doses,' Rosa replied.

'Stop bitching, you two. Let's get our act together. This is going to be fun.'

Soon they were all dashing from school to do their prep before changing into their trews and carrying the Dansette up the field to the shed for rehearsals. Connie was listening under the bedclothes to Radio Luxembourg into the small hours to find a good skiffle hit number, something a bit folksy that suited girls' voices.

'What about "Last Train to San Fernando"? We can do that with comb and paper, hooter and a tambourine. It has a swing to it, don't you think?'

They practised for weeks, and Neville noticed their absence at the club.

'What's up?'

'We're doing something with Rosa, and she can't come to our club 'cos she's Catholic.'

'They've plenty of clubs of their own without gatecrashing ours. So what's so important that keeps you from listening to the Railroaders?'

'Nothing,' Connie smiled, seeing his lips purse just like his mother's when she was thwarted.

'You can tell me,' he grinned, waiting for the gossip to unfold. 'You've got a boyfriend at long last?'

'Buzz off, I'm busy.'

'Suit yourself,' he snapped 'But don't forget the Youth Club Skiffle comp next week. We're doing "Freight Train".'

'Better you than me; it's fast,' Connie replied.

'So? Since when has your cousin ever been afraid of a challenge?'

'Good luck,' she waved, smiling sweetly. Now they had something to aim for too. May the best one win.

On the night of the competition, the girls tucked themselves in a corner of the Drill Hall out of sight. They'd painted their faces as if for the stage, with lashings of black mascara, eyeliner, and lips with 'Gone Lilac' lipstick from Woolworths. Their hair was scraped back into ponytails wrapped with gold and black scarves made from one of Auntie Su's silk offcuts. They'd borrowed long droopy sweaters, worn over their black ballet tights and pumps. This was their Juliette Greco look.

They'd begged and borrowed enough instruments to qualify as a skiffle band but there was no guitar, only Rosa up front and Joy on the beat at the back.

'Which one are you lot?' shouted an official with his list. 'I've got two Winstanleys. Are you the Railroaders?'

'No,' Connie blushed. In all their rehearsing they'd never agreed on a name.

57

'Hurry up, I've not got all day.'

'We're the Silkies,' Joy said, looking to them both and pointing to their scarves.

'So we are,' smiled Connie. She liked the name. It rolled off the tongue.

'You're number twenty... God help the poor judges. We've got a right load of rubbish here tonight. The rules is on the sheet: no swearing, no smoking on stage, nothing smutty or you're off. Miss your turn and you're out, so no sneaking off for a pint.'

Neville spotted them and came rushing across, his quiff lacquered into a Tony Curtis do, his black shirt neatly pressed. 'What's all this? Come to lend your support? Dig the get-up!' he exclaimed, taking in the girls' outfits.

'You've got competition. You're not the only Winstanley who can sing!' Connie replied with more bravado than she was feeling.

'You dark horses! And behind my back too ... lambs to the slaughter,' he laughed. 'Skiffle's for guys, not girls. What are you going to attempt then?'

'Wait and see.' Rosa batted her thick black lashes at him.

'Still, the outfit should cause a sensation, all that black leg on show. Gives our Joy a bit of shape too, very sensible.' He eyed them up and down with a sly smile. 'Break a leg then!'

'And you too ... both of them,' muttered Rosa.

Neville paused. 'I heard that. Any road, the trophy's as good as ours from the lot I've seen so far. I don't think you Winstanley Warblers are going to rattle my maracas.'

'Just you wait and see...' they all replied.

Sitting on the floor of the back room, waiting their turn, Connie felt stupid, trying to stay calm. After all, this was her idea. What if they died on stage and made fools of themselves? Neville would tease the life out of them. Her face was ashen under the panstick. 'Oh heck, if I go to the lav one more time...'

It was Rosa who steadied them. 'This is no different from going on stage with the Liptrot Lovelies. Look how many godforsaken outfits we've had to dance in – prefabs, cold church halls, rickety platforms on top of pews – but we smiled and did the routines. Stare to the back and look up, don't search out faces. We'll be great.'

Then they stood on the side of the stage shaking as the compere announced them.

'Give a hand to the Silkies, brave lasses come to challenge the lads. Rosa, Connie and Joy Winstans...'

They had a minute to set the microphones to their heights, to rearrange the stage, and all Connie could think about was how much leg they must be showing. Rosa was right: this was no different from any other performance. Turn, smile, take a deep breath and look as if you were born to it.

Connie shook the tambourine, Joy kept them to the beat with her makeshift drum and hooter, and Rosa sang her heart out. To her surprise they got more than a polite clap at the end. Bowing, scuttling off stage in a daze, all she could think of was that it was over. They twittered like starlings, unaware that the clapping continued.

'Go back and do an encore ... back on,' yelled Neville from the wings.

'But we haven't rehearsed anything else to sing,' Connie shouted.

'Just go and do a reprise.'

'What's that?'

'Do the last bit and chorus all over again, and enjoy your moment!'

Back they went, smiling, tripping over the wires in shock. Was 'Last Train to San Fernando' going to be the first train on the Silkies' route to fame?

Sadly not. The Silkies got a special commendation but they didn't make the last six. Neither did the Railroaders. Neville was looking at his cousins' act with fresh eyes.

'You need to polish this act – more instruments, more songs, a little more pizzazz – but you were good on stage.' Then he whispered to Connie, 'If only Joy wasn't so dumpy; she spoils the look of you.'

'She can't help her puppy fat,' Connie replied.

'It's Auntie Su who stuffs her with chips and puddings. She could be a real looker.'

'Don't you dare say anything. She's very sensitive about her size,' Connie warned, making sure Joy was out of earshot.

'I think you could do with a mixed group – boys on drums and bass. I like the name though: smooth as silk... Let me think about it.'

And somehow after that Neville took them over as if they were his idea; introduced them to his own group, Barry, Stan and Roger, all spotty herberts in flannel shirts, who were not that keen on mixing with them either. After a few dismal rehearsals when everyone sat round listening to Neville sounding forth, his gang walked away to found yet another skiffle group, leaving him in the lurch.

'You're much better than them. I'll try to get you some gigs,' he smiled. And soon the Silkies were entertaining round the district for little more than a round of Vimto and crisps. Neville somehow pushed his way up front. He appointed himself as their manager on the strength of the fact that he had more access to a private telephone than they did. They even returned to Zion Youth Club to do a gig, but the minister was not keen on devil's music so they had to tone it down to Negro spirituals, 'Michael, Row the Boat Ashore', and Rosa belting out a rendition of 'I Believe', the big hit that was almost a hymn.

They'd packed the schoolroom with friends and family. Even Auntie Ivy turned up, with Uncle Levi on her arm for once, looking like Shirley Bassey in her big fur stole. Nev was so embarrassed.

'Mother, this is only a youth club gig, not the London Palladium.'

'Darling, it's the beginning of big things for you, but I'd get rid of the little dumpling on the back row. She spoils the act,' said Ivy, in a voice loud enough for everyone to hear, including Joy.

Connie saw Joy's face crumple. 'Take no notice, she's only jealous. We're young and she's lost her figure and her face.'

'But it's true. Look at me – I'm fat and horrible,' Joy cried, and tears rolled down her cheeks.

'You'll grow out of it... Any road, who cares? You keep the beat better than anyone else. You're one of us, one of the team.' It was the best Connie could say to comfort her cousin. Why did Ivy always spoil their fun? Why did she hate them so?

5

Joy

There was a window in the form room on the top storey of Moor Bank County Grammar School that looked out over the centre of the town, over the roof tiles and chimneys and the steeple of the Our Lady of Sorrows and the railway sidings, across to the great chimney of Standard's Cotton Mill and Magellan's Foundry. In a gap Joy could see the turrets of Connie's school as it nestled in the foot of the hillside before the moors stretched far into the distance. She knew they would be finishing the last two periods of art. She knew Connie's timetable better than her own.

She sometimes sneaked back up into this form just to catch a glimpse of Connie's world because it seemed better than her scruffy building sandwiched in the middle of town; its red brick blackened with soot. She was supposed to be finishing off her chemistry, wrapped in her blue cotton overall that barely stretched across her tummy. They were doing experiments mixing chemicals over a Bunsen burner while Mr Kopek droned on about safety and not larking about. Joy hated her figure. She was the plumpest girl in her class when they undressed to do PE. They had to wear these bright blue romper suits for gym with knickers attached to a bodice that showed every curve.

Most of the girls were flat-chested and neat, but Joy had busts that wobbled. It was bad enough having skin a shade darker than anyone else and blacker hair, and, worst of all, having the curse once a month.

'Do your bosoms hurt when you run down stairs?' she'd asked Connie, who looked blank and then burst out laughing.

'If only... My bosoms aren't worth a second glance. I have to stuff my bra with socks,' she confessed. 'Be grateful you've got a figure.'

Joy was not impressed.

She had not forgiven Ivy for those cruel words, lashing herself with them inside her head over and over again. She was a big fat dumpling, anyone could see that. Thanks goodness it was Friday afternoon and they'd meet up in Santini's with Rosa to plan their outfits for the next Silkie gig.

Every time she looked in the mirror all Joy could see was her bulging tummy and fat chest. Connie was so thin and tall, and Rosa so wiry. Joy felt like a big lump of lard beside them. Mummy liked to cook for the guests and she was expected to eat the leftovers even when she wasn't hungry. 'Eat up, you are a growing girl. A clean plate, please. Think of all those starving orphans in China!'

There was no escaping food. Every month they all trouped to Auntie Ria's flat for spaghetti and ice cream after a concert, and Mr Milburn, who was a new permanent and rented the front bedroom while Dr Friedmann was abroad studying, was kind and brought her sweets in boxes from his trips during the week: boxes of fudge that said, 'A Present from Filey' or 'Southport' or 'Whitehaven'. He had a small Morris car and gave Joy lifts into town. The back seat was crammed with cases of medical supplies and surgical appliances that were like strange corsets with tubes and straps and funny bulbous ends, harnesses coiled in his case like snakes. The front was a squash and their knees were jammed together when he drove. 'He gives me the creeps,' she'd once sniggered to Connie. 'I'm not his "dusky princess".'

She wished it was hometime. There were five floors from the gym and the physics lab in the basement, to the chemistry lab and forms at the top. There was cookery in an outbuilding and separate yards for boys and girls. It was not a bit like Connie's school and there were boys: spotty and swotty with armpits smelling from their Bri-Nylon shirts.

Rosa was full of the Catholic College boys, heartthrobs called Julian, Chris, Howard, and especially Paul Jerviss, who swaggered around thinking he was James Dean at the bus stop.

Moor Bank didn't seem to sport anyone handsome, just a load of lads making jokes about girls' figures, lads called Eric, Brian and Tom, who treated the girls as if they were simpletons.

Only last week she'd accidentally bumped into Graham Best, one of the boys in her class on the bus, and he had called her a 'fat, slit-eyed wog'.

If only she was as slender as Mummy, who was tiny-boned, with small feet, but Joy was made like the Winstanleys, curvy and awkward. Everyone called her bonny. She hated that word.

'Bonny means I'm fat, not pretty. Why can't I be like the others?' she sighed. 'Tall, skinny and clever.' If only she was into sports like Connie. Moor Bank had playing fields miles out of town, so their teams were hopeless at cricket and tennis and football. Joy managed to skive off hockey by missing the bus and arriving too late to be picked. She hated exercise, although Latin dancing and jive was fun, but no one ever asked her to practise in the playground with them.

Only last week she'd made the mistake of complaining to Mr Milburn as he sat at the breakfast table eating Force Flakes and toast. He was a vegetarian and so one of her jobs on a Saturday was to buy tins of nut cutlets from Uncle Levi's herbal store on the market, where Neville sometimes helped out.

Mr Milburn had offered to teach her to waltz and quickstep once. They practised on the wind-up gramophone in the front room. That was not much fun either, for he'd held her so tight she could hardly breathe, close enough to smell his tobacco breath, and he stepped on her toes. He had no sense of rhythm.

'If only I was good at something,' Joy moaned. 'It's no fun being C plus in homework, in dancing class, in the school choir. I didn't make the semi chorus. They sing all the best bits in the Speech Day concert.'

Rosa was appearing in the King's Theatre again, as the leader of the Mini Maids dancing chorus in the pantomime. Rosa didn't have to try hard at anything; even her curls bounced naturally and

65

needed no rags in them. Her eyes were dark and bright and she was tiny and full of energy. She talked for hours about her rehearsals and how the chorus girls went to the digs of Jonnie and the Giraffes, the rock band who were heading up the star cast. She got autographs to sell and time off school to head up the children's ballet when Miss Liptrot, who was once a pupil at the Sorrows, persuaded the head teacher, Sister Assumpta, to let her dance and guide the youngsters.

Rosa always got what she wanted and now she was into boys big time, which was boring, chasing them at the bus stop and hanging around just to catch the right ones. She was shameless.

Connie didn't like Joy clinging on to her school gang either. Only at weekends did they all get together for rehearsals, when Nev bossed them around. Sometimes she just wished the week away, waiting for the weekend to come along.

'I love Thursday,' she said. 'It's the turning point of the week after sports afternoon, on the homeward run to the Friday gathering in Santini's.'

Connie stared at her as if she was talking Spanish when they met at the bus stop later.

It was no wonder she stuffed herself with Mars Bars and Fry's Five Boys dark chocolate, she thought miserably. She would sit on the bus looking out of the window, stuffing toffees in her mouth, dreaming she was in Hollywood, chosen as a child star like Mandy Miller or Diana Day.

'I wish I was France Nuyen, the tragic Liat in *South Pacific*, mysterious and beautiful,' she murmured.

They'd been to see the film five times and Joy

cried every time, trying to imagine herself in the arms of John Kerr, the handsome Yank who had to choose between duty and love.

Joy found romance in the pages of the red-covered Mills & Boons in the library. Enid Blytons were boring now that there was something more grown up to interest her. These books were in the adult section so they were sneaked out on her mother's tickets and read with a torch in her room. They gave her wonderful dreams of handsome men ready to carry her away to happiness and marriage, but who would lift her onto their horse when she weighed in at a massive ten stone?

Connie always laughed at her reading romances and said they were sloppy.

'It's all right for you, Connie,' Joy sighed to herself, staring into mirror. 'Look at me. Who'll want to marry me? I'm a freak,' she said, and hung a silk *longyi* over the mirror in disgust.

'See you tomorrow, for rehearsal,' she said now, slurping her ice cream through a straw in Santini's after school.

'Sorry, I've been meaning to tell you, I've got a place in the second lacrosse team,' Connie mumbled, sipping her frothy cappuccino. 'It's an away match and some of my gang are going to the flicks afterwards.'

'That's OK, I'll join you later,' Joy smiled, trying not to look too disappointed.

'Sorry, but we're not too sure of our plans yet. We may go into Bolton, it depends,' Connie replied quickly. 'Another time, perhaps?'

She was being mean and wanted to be with her own crowd. They didn't want a Moor Banker around, thought Joy, bowing her head into her soda before turning to Rosa.

'What are you doing tomorrow?'

'What?' said Rosa, as if she were miles away. 'Extra practices for my Intermediate exam. If I pass this I can become an assistant teacher at the studio. I'll be too tired then to do anything but sleep.'

'I could come and join you,' Joy offered. Her weekend was fast melting into nothing, like her ice cream.

'Thanks, but it's a bit of a crush in the flat with the babies, and I've a pile of homework to catch up on. Yes, even *I* do prep. It's part of the deal with the Head,' said Rosa, trying to let her down gently.

She would just have to make her own amusement. Saturday would drone on for ever. Mummy expected help with the bed-changing and linen. Shopping was Joy's job, to earn her pocket money. She would buy a pile of sweets to make up for all the boredom. There was only a second division home match and Auntie Lee was resting now – having another go for a baby, Mummy whispered – so she mustn't bother her either. Perhaps a trip to see Granny Esme would while away a few hours. None of it would be any fun on her own but it was better than staying in.

There she was, standing at the bus stop in her navy-blue gabardine mac and felt hat on a Friday night, knowing she was going home to fish pie, and feeling like a lump of lard.

She had resigned herself to a lonely ride home when who should come and sit beside her but Neville, looking like a Belisha beacon in his black and white striped blazer and cap. He was fast losing his Lancashire accent, being at the Lawns School, and talking like one of the Battle of Britain pilots in *The Way to the Stars.*

'I say, what luck. How's things?' He plonked himself down beside her. His voice was high-pitched and unbroken but his legs were sprouting like rhubarb stalks. He didn't give her a chance to answer, going on about getting the Silkies a turn in some talent competition near Bury, and about his part in the school play.

They were doing Shakespeare – an all-boys production of *As You Like It* – and he was playing Rosalind. 'I'm the only boy in my year whose voice hasn't broken,' he laughed. 'But I get all the best costumes. What are you up to this grey wet weekend? Hope it's better than mine.'

For all his gossip and banter, there was something about his confidences that made Joy think that he too was a bit out of place with the toffs from the Lawns. Boys could be just as cruel as girls, she knew.

'What are you up to tomorrow?' Joy asked.

'I have to do my stint on the stall and then nothing but prep. I *hate* prep.'

'So you're not in the football team?'

'What me, with my two left feet? And it's rugby, not football, at the Lawns. I'm hopeless.' No surprises there, she thought.

'Me too,' Joy said, smiling at his blue eyes and mass of freckles. 'I'm too slow and too fat.'

Neville looked her up and down. 'You are a bit on the podgy side for an oriental, but you could always change that,' he said, looking out of the steaming window.

'How?' Joy said.

'Go on a diet. Cut down your meals, eat only certain things and you'll lose weight. I read about it in *Woman's Own*. The Banana Diet, it's called. It works miracles but you have to stick to it for two weeks.'

'I hate bananas, won't apples do?' Joy asked, curious now.

'I don't think so. It's bananas or nothing,' Neville replied. 'Fancy going round the shops tomorrow? We can buy some bananas off the market, if you like.'

'Go on then, seeing as you've twisted my arm. We can have fish and chips and go to the Gaumont, if you like,' continued Joy, all smiles now.

'I thought you wanted to go on a diet?' he said, pinching the flab on her arm. 'You can weigh yourself on the scales in the market hall. Those won't break!' he laughed.

'Don't be so rude. If I go on this diet you'll have to keep it a secret. I'm not very good at doing new things,' Joy added, feeling now as if a whole new opportunity was slowly presenting itself. Going round town with Neville was better than nothing, and he liked window shopping as much as she did. He knew all the latest fashions and the latest hits. Starving yourself on bananas didn't sound so thrilling, though.

'Have you heard of the Banana Diet?' she asked Connie later on Friday night.

'No. Diets are for invalids. I expect it's some craze from America. Why?'

'Neville was asking about it,' Joy lied, sensing it

wouldn't do to spill the beans.

'Bananas are the perfect food,' said Mr Milburn, listening into their conversations, as usual. 'Troops in the jungle lived off them. I hope you're not thinking of dieting. You are just right as you are.'

'What's Neville bothering about diets for?' said Mummy.

'Nothing. We're just going shopping and then to see *Seven Brides for Seven Brothers*. Connie's got a match and plans, haven't you?'

'Don't be late back. Ivy won't like you going out with her precious son. She has him wrapped around her little finger. They spoil him rotten, sending him to that private school and giving him airs.' It was not like Mummy to be snappy.

'Neville's OK on his own,' Joy said.

Mr Milburn snapped two half-crowns on the table. 'You go and enjoy yourself, dusky maiden from the Far East, lovely lotus. You're only young once,' he winked, and Mummy whipped his plate away with a sniff.

'That's enough of that, Mr Milburn. Your grandmother, Ma Nu, was Burmese, and her father an English man, but you are a British girl, not an oriental,' she explained.

'British men have a thing about oriental girls with bright smiles and flowers in their hair. They gave them such a welcome in Rangoon after the war.'

Milburn was at it again, teasing Mummy, and for a second Joy thought she was going to swipe him one with his plate.

But I'm not like Mummy, she sighed. I am fat and dumpy and slow.

71

Perhaps if she went on this Banana Diet, things might change. How exciting to think she might change her shape, merge in with the rest of the girls and not be different or picked on. She would get to like bananas even if it killed her.

To Joy's surprise the Banana Diet was much easier than she thought it would be if she shut her eyes and swallowed quickly before she felt the gagging in her throat. She started getting up late and had no time to sit down for the usual cooked breakfast, producing some Energen rolls and breaking them into bits and nibbling them when she felt hungry, or took some fruit instead. At break she ate another banana and instead of school dinner she walked around the town to make the time pass. She felt a bit queasy by home time, deciding to walk all the way home uphill for the fresh air. She ate her evening meal without a pudding and no one bothered her when she went to bed early with a hot-water bottle, to read in bed and take her mind off the hunger pangs.

The first few days were the worst, but she found to her amazement that she was good at something at last. She felt such a sense of achievement and power when she said no to tempting foods and treats. Joy was on a mission to succeed and once she got over the emptiness in her stomach, and her stale breath, she felt fine.

When she turned up at jazz class the next weekend, and they all gathered round the juke box in Santini's, to everyone's amazement she said she felt sick and didn't want ice cream but drank only a plain soda.

No one guessed her ploy but it got increasingly harder to skip meals around the table without a lot of planning. If she ate slowly and talked, chasing her dinner around the plate, no one noticed how little she ate, but it had to be put in the bin before Mummy caught sight of the waste. She hated waste. On Friday afternoons all Joy could think about was weigh-in day tomorrow so she tried not to eat at all before then.

On Saturday morning she walked into town and got herself weighed on the machine tucked behind the herbal stall.

At nine stone the results of her efforts were obvious. Her bust was shrinking before her eyes and her tartan trews felt slack.

After two hours of dance and a long walk home, she allowed herself a banana milkshake. Sometimes in school she felt a bit wobbly but she could tell by her gym suit that her shape was changing. Everyone was beginning to admire her determination. Girls kept asking her about the Banana Diet after lessons. She had to prove she could see it through to the end.

Once or twice Connie stared at her oddly. 'Have you been sick or something? You look different,' she said, sipping her frothy coffee while Joy sipped her black coffee, making it last.

'Still a long way to go,' she said, mentally adding, *until I look like you.*

If she'd lost enough weight, the treat of the week was a milky coffee with no sugar in Santini's, but it made her head spin. She was in control now and she was finding the art of eating very little easier. If she felt ravenous she walked faster until it passed. The weight loss was getting slower now she was under eight stone, and so she had to step up the dancing and uphill walking. It all took so much time.

By the time she was down to seven stone it was almost impossible to disguise her skinny shape, so Joy knitted herself thick sloppy joes in the evenings with wool bought from the money saved from school dinners and bus fares. The best bit of all was her periods had stopped. When she told Connie the glad tidings she was so envious she began the Banana Diet, but she lasted only two days. Joy was euphoric. Here was something she could do better than her cousin.

Mr Milburn kept looking at her closely. Joy had no breasts now to make his eyes goggle. She was disappearing into her sweaters and she had fine hair growing on her face, which was a bore. She felt tired all the time, and when they were in dancing class she was pushed to keep up with the music.

Mummy started to hover over her at mealtimes now, watching and spying on her, so she had to slip bits of food into her lap when no one was looking, or fill her cheeks and then go to the lav and spit them into the bowl.

Connie noticed one lunchtime. 'Why are you doing that?'

'It's none of your business,' Joy snapped, surprised how angry she felt being spied on. She was so hungry but she was terrified that each mouthful might make her put on weight and grow fat again.

By the time she hit the six-stone mark everyone

kept looking at her but no one dared say anything. Auntie Ana and Mummy were worried, and Connie was furious with her for being so devious.

'You are making yourself ill not eating your dinner,' Mummy accused. 'People will think we can't afford decent meals. Put a potato on your plate to please me. Please, darling, just the one.'

Joy sighed and plonked the smallest one on her plate to oblige, but when Mummy went to the phone she whisked it into her gymslip pocket.

'There,' she said smiling, pretending to swallow on her return. 'I've eaten it all and now I'm full.'

Rosa kept shoving sweets in her hand but it was as if every mouthful was a battle and she was not going to fail. For the first time in her life she was the strongest and the toughest of the Silkies. Even if she was hungry every waking moment, Joy was determined to win this battle, come what may. But she sensed the frightened looks around her. They were ganging up to make her eat and that scared her so much she wanted to run away.

When she looked in the mirror now she saw only podgy thighs and belly as well as the bones of her ribs sticking out. Connie said she looked like one of the starving children of China in the posters, and pleaded with her not to be so daft.

She might have kept it up for ever, slowly shrinking away, but one morning she fell over on the studio floor, flat on her back, the room spinning.

'This has gone far enough, Joy Winstanley,' said Miss Liptrot, the dancing teacher, standing over her. 'I don't have skeletons in my class with bones clanking every time they move. Get up – I am taking you home this minute. Whatever is your mother thinking of, letting you out in this state? It's about time someone took you to the doctor before it's too late!'

By now even Joy hadn't the energy to put up a protest.

6

Esme

'I don't know what Susan was thinking of, letting Joy get into that state,' said Esme from the saddle of her very high horse.

They were on their third pot of tea, putting the world to rights as Joy lay asleep in the spare bedroom of the bungalow at Sutter's Fold. Everyone was in a flap, and the peace and quiet of Esme's orderly retirement was suddenly interrupted by this unexpected development.

'Don't be hard on her,' said Ana, 'and we don't want her to hear us. Girls of that age are a law unto themselves.' She was giving Connie the eye as if it was her fault that Joy had got herself in such a pickle.

'I don't care if she hears me or not. It's only what any sensible grandmother should say to such a silly child. Fancy, starving herself into a bag of bones! Why was I not told until the damage was done?'

Esme continued, sipping the strong brew and biting into her second Eccles cake, the flaky pastry sticking to her lips. 'How long has it been going on?'

Everyone was looking at Connie again as if she knew something they didn't. Who was to blame for the pitiful sight of that young girl hardly able to stagger up the bungalow steps, holding on to her mother, looking like something out of Belsen death camp, her cheeks sunken and her eyes dull and lifeless? For a moment Connie had seriously thought she was at death's door.

'Long enough to weaken her system,' Ana sighed. 'Dr Friedmann says anorexia is a cry for help. I think she must be a very unhappy girl to do this to herself. You are kind to take her in. A good rest and fresh air will do her good.'

Esme was not convinced. 'A good talking-to is what she needs right now, worrying her mother half to death, and us besides. You don't feed up your bairns just to watch them turn their nose up at everything you offer them; finding bits of dinner stuffed in coat pockets and behind the wardrobe. What a carry-on! She's living off broth and lemon barley water now. How's that going to build up her constitution again?'

Would she have a skeleton on her hands? Everyone was expecting her to sort it all out as some sort of expert, and what with poor Lily – Lee, she liked to be called now – on bed rest for the umpteenth time. She hoped this baby would stick. No one must worry her with such awful news.

It was all right for Dr Friedmann to say his piece. He was a nice enough chap, for a foreigner, bit of a garden gnome in looks, but he meant well. Anorexia. What kind of disease was that?

'It's a good job one of you has brought up a sensible girl.' She nodded towards Connie, who looked as if she wanted to sink into the carpet. 'I hear you've been getting good grades in Latin and Ancient Greek. Still, it's only to be expected with your background.'

'It's not that easy, Granny. There're girls so clever who never do a stroke of prep but still come out above me, no matter how hard I try. Can I go in and see Joy now?' she added.

'The doctor says no visitors for the moment. How could you not tell us she was in this state? All this dieting nonsense: did you ever hear the like at your age!'

There was Susan beside herself with worry, hovering over her daughter, trying to force-feed her but getting nowhere. 'I have tried everything, Daw Esme, but still she defies me. What have I done to make her want to starve herself? Now the doctor says she must go into hospital to build up her strength... I am so afraid.' And that was how she was landed with the task of coaxing the silly girl to eat, but how? If that didn't work she'd have to go into a mental hospital. No Winstanley ever went in one of those places!

'That Milburn's brought Susan to visit in his Morris Traveller every day. I hope she's more sense than to be taken in by a commercial traveller,' Esme sniffed. 'They're all the same: old goats with moustaches, side partings slicked with Brylcreem, flashy suits and a woman tucked away in every town to give comfort after a long day on the road.' It helped thinking about something else rather than the problem next door.

'Don't be a snob, Mother,' Ana replied, not taking the bait. 'It's kind of him to go out of his way. I'm glad Jacob Friedmann is coming back. He will know what to do.'

Susan came every day, more for sympathy and support than to see Joy lying in bed. Only yesterday she'd been a bag of nerves.

'What is wrong with me, Daw Esme? I can't reach my own child. I told her to think about the starving children in China and Africa,' she'd moaned. 'I've seen true starvation on the trek out of Burma. The people were trying to save themselves. I know they teach the girls about Belsen... I don't understand her doing this to us. Now she cannot go to school and do lessons. How will she pass examinations with no lessons?'

'It'll be only a few weeks,' Esme had lied. Even she knew this was going to take months to sort itself out.

'If I get my hands on that Neville...' Susan had added. 'I hear he's been stuffing her head full of bananas. Joy hates bananas. This's all his fault!'

'That's not fair,' Connie had interrupted. 'He was only trying to help. None of us thought she'd be so daft as to starve herself. He'd tried to talk sense to her but she won't listen to us or anyone.'

'How can she do this to us?' Susan had been crying by then.

'Children are good at getting to us. I can remember Travis not taking to the breast and spitting out his food. I was that worried. It became personal and I always reckon it was his faddy eating that did for him in the end,' said Esme.

'You think this will kill her? What will people

79

think of me that I did not notice until she collapsed?' Su cried.

'Stop this, Su,' Ana ordered. 'Don't be so dramatic. Something turned the girl's head. She's done this to herself. No one *made* her do it. We just have to get to the bottom of it.'

'But she will miss her lessons. I want her to go to college like Connie will, and not end up like Rosa, skipping school,' Su replied.

'What you want for her may not be what *she* wants at the moment,' Ana had argued.

Those two would still argue black was white to each other, Esme mused. This was a time for pulling together, not pulling apart. Susan was ambitious and hardworking, and keen to make the business work. Perhaps she thought Joy would be just like herself one day, but Joy was now a jigsaw puzzle in pieces all over the floor.

Esme sighed! 'Your children are not your own, they're only borrowed. They come and go their own gait, as they say. Look how different Levi and Freddie turned out, not a bit like Redvers or me. Then there's our Lily and all that travelling malarkey. Now she's trying to hold a bairn inside her at thirty-odd. I don't understand any of it, but they are family, flesh and blood, so we go along with what makes them happy.'

Connie was sitting biting her nails, looking sheepish. 'I'm sorry, perhaps if I had been nicer to Joy she might not have gone on this dieting lark. Only it wasn't a lark, it was deadly serious. She won't die, will she?'

'We must take it one day at a time,' Ana said in her calm, nursey voice. 'Just let's get her taking a bit of nourishment into herself. Time enough to make plans when she's well. Together the family'll sort her out somehow and give her a reason to start eating again.'

Esme wanted to say that the girl had to learn the world didn't run around her, but felt mean. 'I'll not be spoiling her. We'll just have to find something to distract her from all this nonsense. She will stay in bed with books and a hot-water bottle until she gets bored. Then when we've talked a bit and sat a while, happen she'll get up and doing, but only if she takes nourishment. I'll not let her run rings round me. I'll give you a tinkle if I need you, but rest is what she needs right now and time to think what she's done to herself. You just have to think of her as convalescing. That's what we must all tell anyone who asks,' she said signalling it was time for them to go.

'Thank you, Daw Esme. You are good woman. Your seat is reserved at the heavenly table,' Susan had whispered as she rose.

'Not just yet, I hope,' Esme laughed. 'There's a few more miles on the engine clock yet, I reckon.'

When Connie and Rosa turned up after school the following week, Esme made them hot Vimto and told them they could have half an hour with the patient and no more.

'We're rationing visitors. She has to earn them by eating a little more. When she is stronger then you can stay longer,' she continued, primping up the pillows. 'I'm glad your friends are making the effort, so you must try too. You can't get strong on nothing, Joy.'

Neville popped in too, carrying his plug-in record player and soon music was blaring out, Tommy Steele banging rock and roll hits. Joy sat up and took an interest on what was in the hit parade but she did look dreadful, with sunken cheeks, not like herself at all. All Connie's mean thoughts seemed to evaporate and she just wanted her to be back to normal.

They had told Moor Bank and Division Street that she had influenza with complications and that she was suffering from nervous exhaustion, which just about covered everything. The Winstanleys were used to covering their tracks, 'keeping things in the family' and away from nosy parkers. No one seemed any the wiser.

Anorexia Nervosa was what Dr Gilchrist called her symptoms, and the three children looked it up in the medical dictionary in the reference library. They could see why it was not something Granny wanted bandying about outside the immediate family.

Joy slept a lot and read old children's annuals and picture books, and received a constant supply of other reading matter from Gran and Auntie Lee, who was still on bed rest.

Joy sipped Horlicks and Ovaltine, Bengers Food and milky cocoa as if they were poison.

'I told my mam, if Joy dies it will be all her fault, calling her names in public. I hate her sometimes. If only I hadn't told Joy about that stupid diet. I never thought she'd got it in her to be so tough. It was such a shock to see her looking so ill, and for what? She looks like a wounded animal in that bed, not a million dollars,' said Neville.

'She'll live,' said Ana. 'The will to keep breathing is strong but what damage she's done to her
organs only time will tell.'

'What can we do?' Connie asked, feeling out of
her depth.

'Give her something to look forward to,' her
mama suggested. 'Your singing group, what
happened to that?'

'It's sort of fizzled out,' Connie replied, looking
at Neville, 'what with exams and then Joy being
ill. She gave us a good beat. She's got a good
sense of rhythm. We'd be rubbish without her.'

'Then tell her! Give her a rope to hold on to,
get some concerts booked and make her sing
again.'

Sometimes Mama surprised her daughter with
good ideas. Perhaps old people did know a few
useful things after all.

Joy was making slow progress but a week later she
managed mashed potato enriched with butter and
the top of the milk. As a reward she was allowed
up into the sitting room to look out on the early
spring sunshine on the crocus border.

Soup was Esme's next goal, and what went into
them was an art in itself: ham bones, marrow, len-
tils and pearl barley, pot herbs and root vegetables.
You could stand a spoon in the broth, it was that
thick. The smell alone would tempt a fasting
monk, although Joy pretended not to notice.

She was sure she was hungry but some force
within her needed to reject more than a few
spoonfuls. It was hard for Esme not to show her
disappointment and fury but nagging didn't

seem to do any good. There was a stubbornness in Joy that defied all reasoning.

'Just a little is all I'm asking you. Perhaps then we can go out into the fresh air and see the first flowers in Sutter's Wood,' Esme bribed, knowing Joy loved exploring. She didn't know if she was doing the right thing or not, but was past caring. A walk in the fresh air would do them both good. Everyone was trying to be patient but she had forced Susan to stay away to give her a chance to get to the bottom of this funny business. The young ones brought news of school and dancing but it was as if Joy was living in her own little world. Perhaps a walk in the fresh air might build her strength.

It mustn't be easy bringing up a lass single-handed. Her own husband, Redvers, had been such good support to her with the children, and a godsend when she had lost little Travis. Susan had a good friend in Ana but there were still flare-ups now and then, and jealousy over their girls. It was only natural, given their history. If only they'd got a husband between them. But not one like Horace Milburn. Esme didn't trust him. The creases on his slacks were too crisp and he smelled of fancy Cologne.

Years of widowhood had taught her it was lonely when she closed the door of a night with no one to chew over the day with. Having Joy here gave her company, at least. She winged up a swift prayer to the Almighty. 'Find me the right words, Lord. I'm out of my depth here.'

Later, Joy was dressed in her usual baggy sweater and tartan trews that hung from her bony hips, making her look like a refugee. They took the path down the side of the little housing estate and walked up into an avenue of oaks and birch trees arching overhead. The birds twittered and flapped out of their way.

'Did I ever tell you about my friend Alice Chadwick?' Esme paused. Joy shook her head. They were walking at snail's pace, all Joy could manage. Esme never thought to see a youngster walking more slowly than she.

'It was seeing you as reminded me about that time when we went to prison,' she continued, seeing Joy pause to catch her breath and look at her wide-eyed with astonishment.

'You went to prison? When?' she asked.

Esme nodded with satisfaction. That had got the girl interested. 'When I were a lass not much older than you, just for a night or two.'

'Why?' Joy asked all ears.

'We got caught up in a riot in Bolton when Winston Churchill came to the election hustings. Some of us jumped on his car and got arrested. I was a right tearaway then. We women wanted the Vote, and the local groups all ganged together for a bit of a lark. There was me and Alice from Grimbleton, and the vicar's young wife, Mabel Ollenshaw, as was, which caused a stir, I can tell you. We wore sashes in white, green and purple to show we were followers of the Pankhursts. There were thousands in that riot from all over. We were taken to court and then to Preston Gaol. That were a right eye-opener, I can tell you, being stripped and made to wear sackcloth and caps. To tell the truth I was glad when my dad paid the bail to get me released, but Alice stayed on and went on hunger strike with the other suffragettes. Alice was very fervent about her rights.'

'Did you get into trouble?' Joy asked.

'Just an ear-wigging from Dad. He said no daughter of his would go on hunger strike and come out looking like a consumptive. It was bad for business and if I wanted the Vote I had to show I was as good as any man and go about it the proper way. Alice didn't have any parents, just an aunt who was as committed as she was, so they went on hunger strike and when she came out of prison she looked like you do, all skin and bone, with a terrible cough. I were that shocked I cried at the sight of her – she was so weak she couldn't swallow. They stuck tubes down her throat and pumped gruel into her stomach whether she wanted it or not.'

'That's cruel,' declared Joy.

'Not half as cruel as watching your own kith and kin starving herself for no good reason! Alice had her principles and I admired her for that, but I don't understand why *you* won't eat. It made her ill, and when the Spanish flu came after the Great War she was one of the first to pass away. She never lived to see us get the full Vote in 1928.'

'What else did you do for the cause?' Joy asked, changing the subject neatly, her face crumpling as if she were struggling with something inside.

'This and that: fundraising mostly, going on marches to London with our banners. We'd set off at dawn on a special train and march all day and sing all the way home. Alice could never march with us unless we had a basket chair. She was too sick, and that's not going to happen to you, do you hear me? I want to see you wed with kiddies, and being happy. How are you going to do that in this state? Your insides won't stand it.'

Joy said nothing more, but after the walk managed tea and a digestive biscuit.

Then Lily turned up out of the blue carrying a half-finished peg rug. She'd decided that lying in bed all day was not for her. If this baby wanted to stay inside it would have to take its chance.

They all sat by the fire, cutting up the cloth pieces to prod into the hessian, a mindless task. Joy handed the pieces over and watched the two of them at work.

'Would you like to try it?' asked Lily. 'I could do with a hand, then it'll get done quicker. It's a present for my friend Cynthia at work. She's getting married soon.' She then gave them the run-down about all the goings-on at the travel agency.

'Cynthia lost her mam and dad in the war. She's been looking after her little brothers and sisters. She thought Cupid had passed her by until one morning a policeman brought home young Terry from the recreation ground; the scallywag was bunking off school. He was kind and kept calling to see how the lad was shaping up. He came off duty and offered to take them all to see Bolton Wanderers play Manchester United. After that it was wedding bells ringing in the air,' she laughed.

'Is he handsome?' asked Joy, prodding the wool into the sacking.

'Not especially ... but Arthur's got a kind way with him and he's made Cynthia very happy. Neither of them is an oil painting but looks are only skin deep. What matters is a golden heart. Why do you ask that, love?' said Lily, who had once considered herself plain, but with love and friends had blossomed into a handsome woman, Esme thought. Esme prayed that Baby would stay put for another few months and give those two lovebirds the joy they deserved.

'I'll never marry,' answered Joy with a sigh.

'Why ever not?' Esme jumped in.

'I'm ugly and fat. You heard what that boy at school said ... a slit-eyed wog. He called me a Sherman tank, as well,' she replied in a matter-of-fact voice. 'And Auntie Ivy said I was a dumpling.'

Esme was horrified. 'Whoever said that wants his backside tanning with a leather strap! I bet he's a boss-eyed pea brain with spots.'

Joy's eyes flickered with amusement. 'Neville said I was podgy too, and that you have to be good-looking to marry someone nice,' she added.

Esme was so incensed she grabbed her by the arm. 'You've been reading too many silly romances, lass. It's rubbish, the lot of it. Look at me and Auntie Lily; we're not film stars but Redvers Winstanley liked what he saw and had no complaints. It doesn't work like that, love. Just get those silly ideas out of your head once and for all.'

She smiled and pointed to the mirror. 'Have a look in there if you don't believe me. Some would say you have a special beauty. Exotic is the word that comes to mind. Your father certainly found Susan attractive. Never be ashamed of who you are. We all care for you, and your mother is beside herself with worry and you've given us all a fright just because some pimple-head calls you names?

There's more to life than looks, young lady,' she added. 'There's kind hearts and brains and good works and a bit of a sense of humour. I think we've all had enough of this caper.'

'Mother!' whispered Lily. 'Don't go on about it. It's hard to be that age, all betwixt and between. I'm not so old that I don't recall how I felt about being flat-chested and plain when I went to dances.'

Turning to Joy, she said gently, 'If you help me finish this rug then I'll take you to Whiteleys for some material and I'll make you up some pretty summer dresses. We'll celebrate you being on the mend. Is that a deal?'

Joy gave a weak smile and blushed.

'Thank you, Lord.' Esme kneeled by her bed in gratitude later that night. A light had switched on in Joy's head. Somehow she would turn the corner by the summer. One way or another they would help her pick up the reins on her life.

In the weeks that followed, Rosa, Connie and Neville were never far away and brought the precious Dansette with a selection of EPs for them to rehearse to. Neville was being his usual bossy self again and told Joy they were resurrecting the Silkies.

'There's one I like by the Big Bopper. Listen, it'll suit you. It's called "Chantilly Lace".'

They sat in the garden, out of Gran's earshot, tapping their feet to the beat. It was hard to stand still and they formed a line and started making moves like in the old days.

'But it's not skiffle.' Joy looked up.

'Skiffle's old hat now. Rock 'n' roll is the thing, and you'll look the part. I can see you all in pink lace and bobby sox. You can dance and make an act. What do you think, Joy?' Nev asked anxiously. He was trying so hard to make up for his gaff in suggesting the diet. 'I'll get the sheet music, you learn the words and moves, and we'll get the Silkies back on the road.'

They all went into town window shopping like old times. Auntie Lee coughed up for the gingham for their outfits and Auntie Su made them up.

Joy returned to Division Street again. No doubt Granny Esme was glad to see the back of all her visitors but Joy would miss spending so much time with her. Under her tutelage she'd learned how to make tray bakes and a good sponge cake.

'The way to any man's heart is through his stomach,' Gran kept saying. Joy went to watch Cynthia go down the aisle with her policeman, wearing a new pale blue and white fitted dress with lace edging, and her first pair of Cuban heels, her black hair up in a long ponytail. Connie wore her usual blue jeans.

There were girls from Moor Bank Grammar School watching the goings-on on the pavement, who greeted Joy shyly.

'By heck, Joy Winstanley, is that you? You've shifted some lard! We heard you've been sick. I like your dress. Is it a Mary Quant? You look like a model. Where did you get the pattern?'

Connie took a step back and let them get on with their gossip. There would be other hurdles for Joy to jump, she thought, but being fat or ugly was no longer going to be one of them. She was going to have to take a back seat when this new Joy went out into the world. If being ill paid off, there was something about going into a decline, but Connie was always starving and loved food. Joy didn't need tanning lotion. Her skin was olive and shiny and she looked so confident. Looking in the mirror was agony these days. There were spots and freckles and thin legs. It was a good job clothes didn't interest her that much. To listen to Rosa and Joy rabbiting on, you would think the whole world revolved around what the pop stars were wearing, Connie sniffed.

She'd begged for blue jeans with a zip up the front and Neville found her a pair in a shop that fitted her long legs. With a sloppy joe on top, that became her uniform out of school. She hated her skinny legs.

Connie was glad Joy had come back home, though. Now she could concentrate on her exams. Starving was a mug's game, except that it got Joy lots of attention and new clothes, but it had been a close thing. Connie prayed she'd never do it again.

There are kids rampaging down the airport foyer with all that pent-up energy only the young have. Connie watches them with envy. It is hard to contain herself watching the Arrivals board and still no information.

If only youth knew and age could, went the saying...

The innocence of her childhood turned to the arrogance of teenage years when only she knew best. The Silkies went from strength to strength once Joy returned, so fragile but a show-stopper in her cancan underskirts, which were always fluffier and starched better than Connie's own. Those paper nylon dreams of stardom with Rosa at the front, belting out songs, didn't last long but they served their purpose in bringing Joy back to life.

Connie had been the musician though, mastering chords on the guitar with an ease that surprised her. It was Mama who had told her that her grandfather, Kostas, was one of the great lute players of the Apokoronas region of Crete.

How little she knew of that side of her family, and Mama was reticent to the point of being downright unhelpful when she fished for more information. But there were ways and she was curious.

I was devious then and that was my undoing.

Sometimes it is better not to know until someone is ready to talk. Better not to stir the dregs at the bottom of the pot, just in case...

7

Secrets in the Sideboard

Everyone in Connie's form was talking about the school trip to Austria. There would be a whistle-stop tour of France and Switzerland, Lake Geneva, Lake Constance, finishing off in the little town of Bregenz. They would visit châteaux on the Loire, glaciers in Switzerland, the cathedrals of Rouen, Chartres, Tours, Brussels; so many unfamiliar names on the map of Europe that she was poring over every night with excitement.

'I just have to go, Mama. I want to go abroad and see what Europe is like. I can go, can't I?' she pleaded, but her mother was vague and dismissive.

'We'll see,' was all that was forthcoming.

'The list has gone up. I'll die if I don't get a place. Everyone's going – Jane, Polly, Tonia; all the gang,' Connie added, just to make sure that Mama got the urgency.

'I'm not made of money, Connie,' said Mama, turning to the mound of ironing in the wicker basket.

Why was she so snappy these days with a distracted look in her green eyes? Connie sighed. It was not a good time to pester but time was short.

'I can get a part-time job in the Market Hall. Uncle Levi will find me something. I'll save all my pocket money for spends, I promise...' she continued.

'You have GCE exams coming up next year, nine subjects to pass. You need weekends for revision work, not standing behind a counter,' Mama snapped.

'I know, I know, but I've given up dancing class to study. I can work on Sundays. I've done my mocks. It's a doddle. Please say I can put my name down! I've never asked for anything like this before.'

For weeks Mama had been busy revising for her own nursing exams. There were books everywhere and Susan complained she was not doing her fair share of housework. They weren't speaking now, even when they all went to see Auntie Lee's new baby in his pram. They'd called him Arthur Redvers. Connie thought it must be embarrassing to wheel a pram about at her age.

Auntie Lee looked as tired as Mama. Art sat in his high chair, borrowed from Auntie Ria, who was always producing babies, much to Rosa's disgust.

At least they knew now where they came from, with this constant biology lesson in their midst. Rosa said childbirth was disgusting, like pushing a football out of your back passage. Mama said Auntie Lee had had a rough time and the baby was very small, but it went to show that miracles did happen. Now all the Winstanleys worshipped at his throne and Granny Esme was never away. Surely it was Connie's turn to have something to make up for the disruption in the household now that they'd be usurped?

'Not another word on the subject. I'll chew things over. There'll be plenty of chances to go abroad when you go to university. I see no need to disrupt your studies,' Mama added, but Connie was not for changing this subject.

'If it's money you are worried about, Miss Kent says we can pay on the drip.'

'What is this "on the drip"?' Mama asked, busy folding sheets. 'They teach you slang now, do they?'

'You can pay by instalments, a bit each week. Oh, please, can I put my name down?' she begged.

'I'm not promising anything. I must talk it over with Dr Friedmann and Susan. There are complications. He will know what to do,' muttered Mama.

'What complications?' Connie asked.

'Nothing for you to worry about but I really could do without you pestering me right now.

There's other stuff on my mind,' said Mama, turning away. 'Please finish off this ironing so I can study. I have such backache.'

'It won't cost you much, I promise. I can make my own clothes. I have my Post Office savings and birthday money. You will talk to them?'

There was a glint of steel in Mama's green eyes and her cheeks were flushed. Why did she not want to commit to such a wonderful holiday? Connie's sandy brows puckered into a frown of anxiety. Was there something she didn't know about? Dr Friedmann would be her ally. He was always trying to broaden her horizons.

Was it because the school was going to Germany? But the war was over yonks ago. Surely it didn't matter that they were ending up there? The war was nothing to do with her generation. It was history.

But maybe not to Mama. She had never gone back to Crete or talked about her relatives. It was as if that part of her life didn't exist. She had stopped going to the Orthodox church in Manchester. She never spoke the language and her English accent was broad Lancashire now. Somehow this holiday proposal was reminding her of something.

How mean of her to refuse to consider what it might mean for her daughter to have a treat. Connie was feeling fobbed off like a child whining for some expensive toy.

She would be fifteen next year and the horizon was full of exciting possibilities: travel, boyfriends, college and getting away from the sooty drabness of Grimbleton. Why was Mama such a spoilsport? Auntie Susan would have let Joy go on such a trip.

They were all glad Joy was back at school. The illness had changed her so much. Now she wore bright colours and got herself noticed at the bus stop. She went dancing with friends from her form at the Queen's Hall and went to the pictures with boys in a group. Auntie Susan was always making her new clothes.

It took some getting used to seeing Joy so glamorous and grown up. They were drifting apart, each with different friends and interested in different things. Joy was going to leave school next summer. Auntie Lee was hoping to give her a job in the travel agency.

Sometimes they all still met up at Santini's like in the old days but it wasn't the same.

They didn't share 'confessions' any more as they stirred the cappuccinos in glass cups, pouring on brown sugar. It was all very polite and a bit boring, talking about the boys at the bus stop from the grammar school, and who was going out with who amongst Rosa's friends.

Was there something wrong with Connie's development that she didn't fancy a single boy? She preferred to stay in and read and study and watch documentaries on TV. She wrote poems in a special notebook that was hidden under the bed and sometimes set them to music. Her bedroom was a sanctum sanctorum in the attic of the Waverley.

From her window there was a sky full of stars and the outline of the purple moors. She loved the old desk and bookshelves, and chintzy curtains made from offcuts from a market stall. There was a record player and a small radio set to catch the top twenty hits.

Here she could be Jane Eyre, Elizabeth Bennet, Natasha in *War and Peace*, living their lives over and over again in dreams. Sometimes she had company – Jane Shilling and Tonia Carter came home for coffee and they talked school all evening.

Why couldn't she go on the school trip with them? There had to be a way. Maybe she could convince Mama if she offered to pay for most of it herself? Rosa had promised to give her the secret recipe for suntanning lotion. They were going to make up a batch to sell in their schools before the long holidays.

This recipe was famous for giving the Mediterranean tan that was all the rage now, to set off the skinny white tops and shorts. Olive oil, iodine and vinegar mixed together in small bottles and smeared over the body. Only Rosa had the right measurements. Get it wrong and limbs would fry in the sun. Rosa wanted a cut of the profits and they'd spent whole Saturday afternoons gathering the ingredients from pantries and begging small bottles from the Winstanley stall.

Rosa was planning to leave school next year too, to train as a dancing assistant at the Lemody Liptrot School of Dance, while waiting to be discovered. She wanted to make it in a West End show and she'd written off to an agent in Manchester called Dilly Sherman. She was doing no study for her GCEs, and helped out in Sylvio's salon as a shampoo girl. She earned enough to buy fashion, not sew it, and always looked that bit ahead of the gang. She had blonde streaks in her fringe, which she had to paint over with mascara each morning when she went to school or she would be expelled on the spot.

How could Connie not go on the trip? She'd miss out on all the friendship and fun. If all else failed there was always Granny Esme to ask for a loan.

Granny had been kind to Joy and bought her new clothes. Everyone had made such a fuss of her when she was ill. It wasn't fair. Nobody was bothering with Connie.

Deep down she was jealous of this new Joy, so trim and neat, with not a hair out of place. It was hard to think they'd once all played together as little girls. Now their future plans were so different. Where would they all be in ten years' time?

By the end of half-term the list for the trip abroad was almost full when Connie sneaked her name on the bottom. There was an official meeting to hear the details of the itinerary. It started with an overnight ferry crossing from Dover to Calais, first night in Tours, via Rouen, and then the Loire Valley, across to Dijon. It sounded fantastic. The first hurdle to cross was getting a signed form of parental consent.

'I shall also need your birth certificate and two Polyfotos for the passport application,' said Miss Kent, who was co-organiser of the trip with Miss Spencer, the deputy head. 'Those who want payment cards see me after the meeting.'

Connie was first in the queue for the payment card and consent form. It would be easy to forge

Mama's signature, and once she had the birth certificate, which she knew was in the document box on top of the wardrobe, she'd be on her way, paying the deposit from her savings. When Mama saw she was serious, the rest would be forthcoming.

The rosewood box was always kept locked but the key was on Mama's dressing table in the casket that contained jewellery, a silver cross and chain, earrings and some foreign coins. She used to root about when she was little, lifting up the old papers in foreign writing, unable to translate their meaning.

The box was easy to find and she opened it eagerly, but besides nursing certificates, an old identity card and medical card there was no sign of Connie's own papers, just a cutting of her name in the paper for winning the scholarship.

Her birth certificate wasn't there and with a sinking heart Connie realised that she would have to ask Mama.

Perhaps if this was left to the last minute and she kept up the payments no one would be any the wiser for a few weeks? Evenings rolled by with Connie tracing this foreign journey on the map and planning a list of all her outfits and toiletries.

They all compared notes together, Connie, Tonia and Jane, whose parents had paid up in one lump sum.

Then it was the dreaded exam revision and heads down until all the papers were finished in June. By then Connie's funds had run out and she was three weeks behind on her dues.

Selling the olive oil lotion had not brought in as

much as they'd hoped. It was a wet summer and nobody was in the mood for suntanning. Jane complained that when she put it on that it had stained her best top. 'I smelled like a fish-and-chip shop.' Connie had had to give her the money back as they were going to share a room.

'I'm going to take Nivea Crème,' Jane said, 'not this rubbish. Tell Rosa Santini to check her recipe next time.'

Two weeks before the trip Miss Kent asked to see Connie, demanding all the proper documents. 'You're holding up the passport, Connie. I need them by tomorrow and your final payment too. You still owe forty pounds. Shall I contact your mother?'

'No, no. I'll bring it tomorrow,' she croaked, heart thumping, knowing her plan was unravelling fast. Surely Mama would see sense, but every time she had badgered Mama, there was always the same reply: 'Not now, Connie. Can't you see I'm busy?'

Tonight, though, she was going to have to face them with the truth, but she was sure Mama would not let her down.

She waited until Dr Friedmann left the dining room and went to his study and Auntie Su and Joy were in the kitchen. Mama was glancing through the *Guardian* and listening to the wireless while she was putting away the spare cutlery, clearing the table for her swotting-up.

'Mama, I have to tell you something and it won't wait,' Connie said, turning the knob of the radio to off.

Mama looked up curious.

'I need forty pounds and my birth certificate,' Connie said all in one breath.

'You need what?' Mama replied, putting down the paper and looking up at her with amazement.

'It's for the school trip. I've got to have all the money in by tomorrow,' she confessed quickly, hoping to disguise her rising panic.

'But we've not decided,' said Mama.

'I know, so I've been paying bits up until now. I've no savings left. Please, you promised,' she begged.

'I did no such thing. I said we would talk about it with the others. It slipped my mind.' Mama shook her head. 'I thought you'd forgotten about it, and just as well.'

'I didn't pester you. You want me to go, don't you, or did you deliberately forget? It's all arranged now. I can't let them down, it'll spoil it for everyone. It's all been carefully costed out and they need my balance.'

Mama was shaking her head. 'We never saw any forms, any details...'

'I filled them in for you. I know how you hate forms,' she lied. 'I've been searching everywhere for my birth certificate but it's not in the box. Where is it? I need it for tomorrow.'

'Never mind where it is... You are too young to have it,' shouted Mama, standing up.

'I'll soon be old enough to leave school and get married and get into trouble. You've no right to hide it from me!' The words were spitting themselves out of her mouth. 'School just need to check my identity for the group passport, that's all.'

Mama was pacing around the room like a

trapped tiger in a cage muttering to herself in Greek. 'You've no right to be going behind my back. You've brought all this on yourself, you silly girl. I never said you could go. I promised nothing and now you demand forty pounds out of the blue as if I can just take it out of my purse. You are a wicked girl. No! I don't give my consent,' she said, banging the table, so Connie picked up a willow-pattern dinner plate and hurled it at the wall in frustration.

'I hate you! I hate you! You spoil everything. You are so mean,' she screamed, throwing another plate on the floor.

'You can pay for those, young madam!' shouted Mama as Dr Friedmann flew down the stairs to see what the racket was.

'What is this?' he asked, as they both screamed at him and he held his hands up. 'One at a time!'

'Why did she not bring this to you sooner?' he was whispering to Mama after she told him the tale and had buried her face in her striped cotton apron.

Looking up, he smiled at Connie. 'Your mother only wants to protect you. She has always looked out for you. It is not easy for her to talk about past things,' he replied.

How dare he take her side in this? Connie fumed. He was no relation, or was there something going on she didn't know about?

'What has this got to do with Mama? It is my holiday, my school trip. I have saved and saved, and put down all my money as a deposit. She wouldn't even let me get a Saturday job. I shall ask Granny Esme, if you won't help me,' she yelled, storming to the door.

'Wait, Connie. Your mama has something to tell you, something which explains everything. You will understand then,' said Dr Friedmann, beckoning her back from the vestibule to sit down.

'Go on then,' she said, trying to play the grown-up. 'If my father was alive he would pay for me to go on this trip.' It was a mean jibe but she couldn't help herself. They were holding her fate in the palm of their hands.

'Ana, go and get the papers. Better it is settled. The child has a right to see them now,' he ordered.

'No!' Mama was shaking her head but she scuttled into the hall and ferreted in the back of the sideboard, which stood by the hatstand. Why hadn't she thought to look there, Connie wondered.

'Your mother is doing what is best for everyone, Connie. Don't be angry with her,' said Jacob Friedmann, as she returned and threw a pile of tattered papers contained in a shabby wallet onto the table.

'There, are you satisfied now? Take your papers, for all the good they'll do you! You won't get onto the Continent with them as they are,' she snapped, and Connie could see she was shaking. She'd never seen Mama like this before, even when she and Susan had set-tos in the kitchen.

The battered documents were well thumbed and handwritten in Greek, hard to decipher. There were official stamps and military papers. Even with Connie's knowledge of Classical Greek, they made no sense to her at all.

'What does it say?' Connie asked with hands

103

trembling, trying to pretend she was not scared.

Mama lifted them up. 'I met your father in Athens at the end of the war. Then you were born and there was nothing official,' she replied with a shaking voice.

'Did Freddie marry you after I was born then?' Connie said with relief knowing that when girls got into trouble this sometimes happened. They 'had' to get married. Was that what all this was about? A question of timing?

'There was no marriage. He was killed. There were complications. It was better to say nothing. Everyone assumed I was a war widow.' Mama was looking at her with graveyard eyes while Dr Friedmann put his arms around both their shoulders as if to soften this news.

'So I'm not a real Winstanley. I'm illegitimate. Who was my father then? Somebody from Crete? A Yank, like Melanie Allport in the Lower Sixth?' Connie was trying to pretend she didn't care but her legs were trembling under the table.

'You know who your father is. I met Freddie Winstanley in Athens on shore leave. We were very friendly. I didn't know then about Auntie Susan in Burma. It was a wartime romance. It was not meant to happen like this.' Mama's voice faltered.

'Like what? You tell me I was not meant to happen? That I am a bastard, an accident? And what has Auntie Susan got to do with this?'

Nobody spoke for a second and then the awful knowledge flashed like a bulb before her eyes. 'Oh, no! Not Joy as well... Was she some accident too? You both ... with my father. It's disgusting! All these years, you've lied to us. Joy and I are

104

half-sisters and nobody said anything to us? Granny wouldn't lie about all that stuff about Cedric,' she sneered.

'It was Esme who thought up the whole story to protect you both. She took us in when she could have turned her back on us,' Mama said. 'She didn't want you to be pointed at in the street.'

Connie could hardly breathe for shock and anger. To be fobbed off with a pack of lies when all the time the Winstanleys kept their grubby little secret, making up fictitious characters like out of Charles Dickens.

'I don't believe you. She lied to protect the good name of Winstanley, more like. What is my real name then?'

'Konstandina Papadaki... See, you are registered here but you will need a special visa to visit another country. It's too late for all that now. I didn't want the school to know our business.' Mama was not looking her in the face. 'I'm sorry but you brought this on yourself.'

'I don't really exist, do I?' Connie shouted. 'Does Joy know she's a bastard?'

'No, and don't you go blabbing your mouth off to her. She has been through a bad time. It is not our business to tell her, and Susan may never want to. She has a British passport, as does her mother,' said Mama.

'But it's not fair. She got all that fuss when she was ill. Please let me go!'

'Connie, I'm tired, my back aches, change the record. It is too late. You are half-Greek, be proud of that.'

'You're not or you'd not be so quick to let them

105

change my name to Constance Winstanley!'

'You are named after your grandmother, Constance Esme, your father's mother. It is tradition. Joy must wait until Auntie Susan chooses to reveal her story. If she ever does.'

'On her wedding day most likely... Oh, by the way, did you know your bridesmaid is your sister? It *is* my business if she is my half-sister. How dare you not tell me? Why have you waited so long?' Connie cried out, wanting to run away to her room and hide.

'That's enough! Let your mother rest. This is hard for her too. She is only trying to shield you. She means for the best,' said Dr Friedmann, and Connie turned on him.

'I don't need your opinion. *You're* not my father. All this baloney about doing well at school... What, so you can show me off to pay back the Winstanleys for taking you in? "Look, we have made a clever daughter for you?"' She was pointing her fingers at them both like daggers.

'Your mother has had a bad day without all this, Connie. She'll do what she can.' But ears were closed to his plea.

'I suppose Auntie Lee knows, and Uncle Levi, and no wonder Ivy never liked us. Does Neville know? It will be all round Grimbleton if he finds out my mother and auntie are sluts, camp followers to the British Army!'

'God in heaven! Stop that at once! Don't dare talk to your mother like that!' Dr Friedmann yelled.

'I speak as I find. She goes with soldiers and gets pregnant.' Connie was weeping with frustration.

'You have no idea how it was then, and I hope to God you never will. I was young and hungry, and the soldiers were kind and gave us food. They were lonely and we were exhausted. Freddie was handsome and charming and we went dancing and we did all the things you take for granted now. Those freedoms were bought with the blood of young men and women like him. We were fighting in the mountains at an age when you were sitting in your room playing music. The war was over, the Germans were defeated and everyone wanted to go home. Don't you tell me what I should or shouldn't've done then. Don't judge when you have no idea what we went through for victory. I have fought dogs for crusts of bread...' She shivered. 'I can say no more. I will never talk of that time.' Mama was sobbing now and Dr Friedmann held her hand.

'She's right. She brought you here to be safe and to have a future. She has done well for you and now you have good family, yes?' he said.

'They are not my family. It is all lies,' Connie said, running out into the hallway. Where should she go? To Rosa in town? To Sutter's Fold and Granny Esme ... who was really Joy's gran as much as hers? They were all Winstanleys but she didn't feel like one of them any more.

Suddenly the school trip crumbled before her eyes, all that scrimping and saving for nothing. Someone on the waiting list would jump into the place and share a room with Jane, and they would become best friends and come back into the new school year all pally.

Connie had no legs to run away, but sat on the

107

bottom step of the stairs and cried until she thought her heart would burst with anger. Then the door opened and Dr Friedmann came to sit down beside her.

'I know you are disappointed but I promise you there will be other trips,' he whispered.

She turned her back on him. 'How do you know?' she sniffed, snot running down her lips. 'I hate her. I hate you all!'

'I know you do now but your mama loves you. Give her a chance to make amends. One day when you are a mother you will understand what it is to do the best for your child. One day perhaps you will go to Greece and see it for yourself through her eyes. You will see the world we grown-ups have made a mess of. We will sort out your documents. We will make it right for you somehow. You have my word,' he said, leaning over to put his arm on her shoulder.

Of course she knew he would honour the promise but she was too angry to give him any quarter.

'She has ruined my life,' she snapped at him.

'She is your mother and she gave you life,' he retorted. 'It is not the end of the world. You have life and a family that love you. I have no family of my own. The Nazis saw to that in the death camps. They never got a chance of life. I have been blessed with good friends here. Don't be angry with your mother or Esme. They thought they were doing the best by hiding the truth, but the truth has a way of coming out all on its own at the wrong time.'

'But I wanted to go on the school trip, that's all.

I didn't want all this. Why didn't she tell me?' Connie said, standing up and running up the stairs.

Dr Friedmann stood in the stairwell patiently, his voice echoing into her room. 'Perhaps just for this very reason – that when you knew, you would be ashamed of her. Have you never done something like that? Forged a signature ... made promises you can't keep? Your mama is human and run down. We all make mistakes. Think about it.'

She burrowed under the eiderdown, not wanting to hear him. Tomorrow she was going to have to tell the world that she didn't exist. Tomorrow she would have to let her teachers down and there was only one person to blame. How could she ever trust Mama again?

Yet, if she were honest, somewhere hidden in the secret drawer of her mind the news had come as no surprise. She'd sensed the mystery surrounding their coming to Grimbleton, but to be taken in under such circumstances... How many times had Granny Esme patted her curls and sighed?

Joy was in for a big shock, that was for sure.

Next morning on the bus she whispered the news to Nev and swore him to secrecy. He hardly raised his eyebrow.

'Honestly, Connie, you're such a simpleton. Did you never wonder why my mother hasn't a good word for the Olive Oil Club?' He paused and then whispered, 'My theory is she once fancied Uncle Freddie herself.'

'Never! Has she spilled the beans to anyone?'

'What do you think? My mother has a mouth as big as the Mersey Tunnel but she's too frightened what others will think to let slip a family secret. We might not get the Winstanley millions,' he hooted.

'You knew about Joy too?'

'Of course,' Nev winked.

'So who was Uncle Cedric?'

Neville pursed his lips. 'That was Auntie Su's nice touch, don't you think, to explain away her presence: just another war widow in the district.'

'But for us to be sisters like this?' Connie shook her head. 'I just can't take it in.'

'Don't worry my lips are sealed. I won't breathe a word. I'm in enough trouble as it is. Mother thinks I'll fail my exams and she's threatening coaching again. She has such big ideas for my small brain.'

'You'll get the shop when Uncle Levi retires. You're made up.'

'But I don't want to spend my life dishing out powders and corn plasters, growing fat like him. They sleep in separate rooms, Mum and Dad, you know. Have done for years. I think my dad has a girlfriend on the sly... "The flighty piece from the stocking bar," Mum calls her.'

'I'm sorry,' Connie offered.

'Don't be. She's no angel either, if truth be told. There's rumours that the Betterware sales-man lingers ere long over her dusters of a morn-ing. I just let them get on with it. Anyhow, enough of all that. I've got another idea for the Silkies. I saw the Kaye sisters on TV, the ones who had a hit with "Paper Roses". Let's get a proper act together like them again. I've got some good contacts in Manchester who'll help us.'

'How did you manage that?' Connie was all

ears despite her misery.

'Never you mind. Let's just say, your cousin is getting himself well connected, if you catch my drift.' Neville winked again.

She didn't, but was too polite to say. She was glad he was distracting her from all the doom and gloom ahead. Poor Joy was living in joyful ignorance but it would be cruel to blurt the truth out now.

Connie smiled at her cousin. There was more to him than a mop of curls and flash clothes. It was something to do with taking himself off to Manchester on Saturdays with another dressy lad from the Lawns called Basil Philpot, poor sod. Where they went to he'd never say, just that he'd made some mates at a jazz club who were very theatrical. She'd asked if she might come along but he'd given her a funny look. 'I don't think so, Connie, not your scene at all.'

8

Connie

There was nothing for it but to head upstairs to the staff-room door to break the news to Miss Kent. Connie spun a sad tale about her mother being ill and off work that was partly true, because she had been having a lot of doctor's appointments lately about her bad back. 'We can't make the final payments and I must stay close to home,' she lied, holding her breath.

'I'm sure we could raise some special funding to tip the balance,' answered Miss Kent. 'It's a pity for you to lose your place, Constance. We know how keen you are.'

For one second she was tempted to defy everyone but then she remembered the family secret. 'Thank you, but no. Mama is very independent. I wouldn't shame her by taking charity.' She almost convinced herself with all these fibs. 'It's just not meant to be this time.'

'Well, I am so sorry and I hope your mother gets well soon. We will refund what we can, of course. There is a waiting list.'

'Thank you, Miss Kent.' Connie bowed her head, shamed. How easy it was to deceive when you were trusted. Now she'd have to make do with reviving the Silkies over the summer hols. They might make some dosh if they learned a few more numbers from the hit parade, or she put some of her own songs to music. Maybe they could get a record made... Girl groups were still popular: the Beverley Sisters, the Kayes and the Vernons Girls...

The startling revelations about her parentage buzzed round in her head like a demented bee. She and Joy had lived like sisters all their lives, sharing a house, trying to smooth over the rows between their mothers. Now she knew why there was always tension in the air over silly things, like which girl was doing better at school.

What a to-do there must have been the day they first turned up.

Now she must keep all this from Joy until Su

decided to come clean. Did Rosa know? Had the whole street put two and two together?

Joy had once told her there was a photo of Uncle Cedric in Su's dressing-table drawer that puzzled her, for when she pulled it from the frame to see if there was writing on the back, the picture was cut out from a magazine. It had puzzled them both at the time. But now she knew they were half-sisters, and that there was no real Cedric.

Suddenly Connie felt ashamed to have called Mama such awful names when she'd done her best, as a refugee, to bring them to safety, finding them a safe home and making a new life in a foreign country after such a sad time. Now she'd used her in a big lie to her teacher. She'd let everyone down.

She couldn't wait for school to end to rush home and apologise, to make things right between them, but she had lacrosse team practice first.

It was like the first day of her new life as Konstandina Eleni Papadaki. She rolled the names over her tongue. Yesterday she was plain Connie. Today she was someone quite different. Somewhere in the back of her memory she recalled Mama calling her Dina. Then one day when she went to school she'd become Connie.

As she stared out of the bus window, she marvelled that nothing outside had changed though she felt so different: grey skies, smoking chimneys, silent mills with broken windows. King Cotton had crashed in the town making many out of work.

The Winstanleys were the fortunate ones in their tall red brick house standing proud at the

113

top of Division Street on three floors, comfortably off by the standards of most of her school pals. They had a family to protect them and what Mama, Su and Granny had done, she could now see, was done out of love and concern, not spite. How stupid she'd been to be so cruel.

She leaped off the bus and sped home but there was no one around. Then she saw Auntie Su, standing in the kitchen, ringing her hands.

'Connie, you're so late!'

'Where's Mama?'

'She's had to go into hospital ... for some tests. She had another of her bleeds this lunchtime after her shift so they took her straight onto a ward.'

'A bleed? Did she fall?' asked Connie but Su was shaking her head.

'Not that sort of bleed ... a monthly bleed ... too many bleeds. You've seen how pale and tired she gets.'

Connie had been so wrapped up in this holiday business, living in her own world, she hardly noticed anyone else, especially her own mother. 'When can I go and see her?'

'Not tonight, she may go into theatre. Dr Friedmann will bring us news.'

'But I have to see her now... I said some awful things last night...' Connie broke down and suddenly Joy was with her.

'Uncle Levi will take you in as soon as he can. It's just an investigation, isn't it, Mummy?'

Connie didn't like the sound of that word. Investigation meant prodding and prying into organs, X-rays, blood samples. Mama was a nurse; she would make a rotten patient. She knew too

114

much. 'She will be all right, won't she?' Her eyes pleaded to Su for some crumbs of comfort. She felt like a three-year-old lost in the street, unsafe, frightened, searching for Mama in the crowd.

'She's in the best place. I've made you some tea ... sit down. It's been a shock, I know.' Auntie Su fussed but her dark eyes looked worried.

Connie sat limp, feeling sick, thinking of the lies she'd made up only that morning, never suspecting for a moment that there might be truth waiting to explode over her head. Had her lie caused this funny bleeding? Had she betrayed her mama for the sake of a two-week coach trip to the Continent?

Oh, please, God, I hope not, she prayed, crossing herself many times. She must buy a candle to light, pray for a quick recovery. Only then would she be forgiven, only then would she feel safe. There was only one thing she wanted to do and that was to sit by Mama's bedside and tell her what a silly, selfish, stupid daughter she'd been, and how she loved her with all her heart.

In the nightmare weeks that followed, Connie got to know the inside of Ward 9, gynaecological ward, as if it were her own home. Mama had an emergency hysterectomy and lay prostrate, white-faced, trying to smile at Connie.

'She's had it all taken away,' whispered Granny trying to explain the operation, not looking at her while she spoke. 'There were growths in it ... she'll be better now.'

Connie wasn't fooled for a minute. There was more to this than just the operation. She could sense the way the nurses fussed and smiled and fobbed off her own questions. The next day she searched out the medical section of the civic reference library, reading every textbook she could find on the reasons for such an operation. There were the usual words like 'ovaries' and 'fibroids'; biology lessons came in handy but one word kept coming up, over and over again: *carcinoma*. Any Greek scholar could tell the root of that: *Kackinoma* ... the word no one ever mentioned when a neighbour fell sick, got thin and died.

The same evening Connie cornered Dr Friedmann in his study. 'What's really wrong with Mama?' she demanded.

'She had a growth and it's been removed.'

'Was it benign?' she said, using the only word she dared speak.

He hesitated but she stared him out. 'I have to know the truth. Will she get better?'

'Sit down, child,' motioning her to the little armchair squeezed into the corner. 'We hope so. There are special treatments in Manchester.'

'Radium treatments, you mean? I know about Marie Curie. How long will it take?' So it *was* cancer, but still she daren't speak the word.

'There'll be a course of treatment at the Christie. It's the best in the North of England,' he replied, taking her hand. But she pulled it away.

'Has the disease spread?' She'd read up enough to know about metastasis, but she wasn't sure how to pronounce it.

'A little ... but it's not too late to give her treatments.'

'It's all my fault,' Connie cried. 'I pretended she was ill so I wouldn't get into trouble at school. I told lies and I brought this on her...' Her body was racked with sobs.

'No, you didn't.' He shoved a handkerchief in her hand. 'Your mama has been unwell for some time but kept it to herself. Now we've a chance to fight it. Ana must have hope and see smiling faces. She is a tough lady, strong in mind, but her body suffered in the war. It will be a battle but the Olive Oils will battle with her and you will give her strength too. You're her bright star, her golden girl. It is enough that she's you in her life to live for, so no dark thoughts now. Dry your eyes. We must all be strong together.' There was something in those sad grey eyes that worried her. He was breaking bad news gently. He was doing the best he could, but underneath she sensed his own fears.

The autumn term began, the holiday girls rolled back from their trip, but Connie had no ears to listen to their tales: who had palled up with who, who had stayed out all night with some American soldiers... What did she care when her whole week was focused on those trips to the hospital to be with Mama?

There was always a lift: Diana came up from London, Queenie Quigley and Maria brought their van, Levi and Neville chauffered Gran. Nev had passed his driving test and Auntie Su had bought a little Morris Minor that she shared with Dr Friedmann.

Connie watched all Mama's beautiful red hair fall out, just a few fuzzy tufts left, her skin tissuey and yellowy silver. She grew thin but everyone tried to keep cheerful and strong.

Only Dr Friedmann would tell her the truth.

'It's not going to be as easy as we'd hoped but no one will give up, Connie.'

How could she study Ancient Greek and history with this burden on her back, however understanding the teachers were? None of it mattered. All she wanted to do was be with Mama and make her better, clinging on to any sign of hope. Sometimes when she went, Mama was sitting in the chair by the bed but the beautiful silk dressing gown that Su had given her with peacock feathers printed on it, hung off her bony frame. They talked in Greek to be private from the other patients, wrapping the curtains round the bed. Then Mama was tired and needed to rest, and it took many attempts to get her back into bed. Connie cried all the way down the corridor. Why? Why her mama? Why now?

Rosa and Joy dropped their own plans to include her. They took her dancing, practised their singing routines, but her mind was in only one place: beside Mama's bed.

She took herself back to the Greek church to ask Father Nikos to visit, but he was already a regular at Mama's side. She bought a silver tama with a whole body on it to pin to the icon and pray to the saints for her recovery.

'Find me music, Dina,' Mama whispered one day. 'Cretan music.'

Father Nikos found an old wind-up record player and a scratchy 78 of ancient mantinades. Ana's face changed when she heard the music and her eyes looked far away.

'You must go back for me, see the island for yourself, say a prayer by my mother's grave … for

118

my sister, Eleni, light a candle for me ... find my cousins near Canea. There'll be Papadakis who'll remember me. Make it your own. Promise me...'

'We will go together, Mama,' Connie whispered back. 'When you are better. Auntie Lee will fix it for us ... by train to Italy, by boat. I will take you there.' There was a faint smile on Mama's lips.

'You will go... I will be already there... Promise.'

'No, Mama, *mazi* ... together, you and me. My Greek is almost forgotten.'

'You learned it at my breast. It is still there in your heart but you'll go one day. It is waiting for you.' It took all her strength to utter that command.

Connie couldn't bear such words and ran out of the cubicle. Auntie Su caught her.

'Don't worry, she has little pain now. She is going to sleep and not wake up.'

'But I don't want her to sleep. She is my mama ... who will look after me now? How will I live without her?' Connie sobbed. 'And I know about you and my dad.'

'Shush! Now is not the time for all that,' whispered Susan. 'None of that matters now. You are a Winstanley; we are all family. We look after our own. It is your mama's wish. Don't let her see you upset. Go back and say goodbye. It is time for her to rest.'

But when they tiptoed back through the curtain to say good night, Ana Papadaki was no longer there. She'd slipped away quietly. In her place was a cooling shell, a stranger with vacant eyes staring out towards the window.

They sat each holding a hand, silent, lost in

their own thoughts and memories. Connie couldn't breathe for panic. *She's gone to Crete and left me behind.*

'She was a very good woman,' Su said, picking some of the bedside flowers and arranging them round her head. 'Rest in peace, my sister.'

Connie blinks back the tears, blinks herself back to the blue bench in Chania airport. When will that plane ever land?

Mothers always get the blame, she sighs. When you lose your mother young, it changes everything. Fifteen was no age to be orphaned, everything taken for granted is suddenly not there. There was so much she didn't know then about her mama's early life, her life with Freddie, short though it was. So many unanswered questions that only a mother could give. Life could never be the same and she was different from Joy and Rosa, kind though they all were to her then.

No prayers, lavish wreaths and anthems at the funeral could make up for that huge loss. It had been like some never-ending dream she sleepwalked through.

I have felt the loss of you all my life. I wasn't ready to say goodbye and when I was, you'd gone and I was bereft.

She thinks about the string shopping bag with leather handles that they took to the market each week to buy vegetables, carrying it between them when it was heavy.

She lost herself in her studies as Mama would've wished, not wanting to finish school to come home to the empty chair. Doing prep in the reference library delayed the moment when she must return to face the hubbub in the Waverley.

I was told to be brave and cope, and I did, she thinks. There was no grief counselling in those days. You just got on with loss like they did in the war, buried it deep, as if Mama had gone on some long journey and would send a postcard telling of her return.

The Olive Oils still met for their suppers. Perhaps they drew comfort from each other but she found she resented their gatherings. Neville encouraged her into singing again. Miss Kent pushed her hard to take GCEs and go into the sixth form early. Happy to oblige, it was easier to be lost in a book than face Mama's absence. Dr Friedmann's door was always open but she shrank from any intimate discussion. This grief was not for sharing.

No point in going back to church either. It had let her down big time.

Music was the solace – any music, the louder the better. Pop, jazz, they drowned out all worries with their raucous beat. It was an escape. It was then she wrote the first draft of Colours of My Love *and shoved it in a drawer. There was no music in her head to put the words to back then.*

If she had lived would things have been any different, I wonder?

Of course they would. I would not be sitting in this airport waiting for someone who may never come.

9

Rosa

Rosa knew the part was hers, the minute that Grimbleton Little Theatre announced in the *Mercury* that they were doing an updated open-air *Romeo and Juliet* in the Town Hall Square. *West Side Story* was all the rage and she'd seen a touring company perform it in Manchester. This one was going to be Teddy Boys versus Rockers.

'I have to be Juliet, Connie.' Who else but a fresh-faced Italian could carry the passion of the role? Besides, she needed the experience, the exposure and the chance to take a leading role. No one was going to get in her way. She'd been too busy at the dancing school to join the Youth Theatre, but the *Mercury* had stated it was an open audition.

Connie nodded half-heartedly, tagging along with her, knowing she herself would be lucky to get in the chorus. Since her mother's death she'd grown a shell round herself. It was hard to interest her in anything but Rosa thought that being in this production might help.

Their acting experience was limited to school plays, but Mamma and Rosa both adored Shakespeare and Rosa was word-perfect since it was one of the set texts for GCE English Literature she'd actually managed to swot.

It was important to look the part for the audition, so that meant catching her long hair up in an Alice band to make her seem young and innocent. She wore her Sunday church summer dress, which was a princess line and not too short. It showed off her lithe little figure.

Connie and Joy had spent hours getting her 'in role' for the big day. When her name was called she sprang onto the stage, forgot her nerves and danced through the lines as if she already was in the ballroom scene.

'I am Rosa Santini,' she announced into the darkness, and lived out the script, scarcely glancing at the text. Besides, she was madly in love, smitten with lust, and that only added to the intensity of her performance.

Paul Jerviss had just left the Boys' Grammar School to go to medical school. They met at one of the end-of-term all-night parties held while someone's parents were on holiday, parties to which Connie and Joy were invited but never wanted to go. Now he was waiting on tables at Uncle Angelo's diner bar, while she was washing up.

He was everything a Paul Newman hero should be: tall, fair with sultry eyes and a slight sneer on his lips; he'd been Head of School and cricket and rugby; his blue denim jeans fitted snugly on his bum like James Dean's. He smouldered in the direction of any decent-looking girl. Geraldine Keane said he left a tramline of lovebites from the tip to the toe of her torso and in between. But for some reason he was playing hard to get, which infuriated Rosa. Perhaps he didn't want to tangle with his boss's niece in case there was some Mafia revenge.

He'd have been the perfect candidate to practise on to get that knowing passion that came to Juliet once she and Romeo were lovers. If she had to pretend to smoulder with lust then it was time to find out what it was all about. His friend Miles Black was giving her the glad eye, though... Any port in a storm, strictly for the sake of her art.

Looking smart and sassy in her washing-up gear at the diner wasn't easy, but it was the bust, the hair and the eyes that counted. She pretended she couldn't care less when the boys were on shift hoping Paul would be narked; he was used to girls falling at his feet. He was the love 'em and leave 'em type once he got to home base, but two could play at that game. Rosa was showing just enough interest to get noticed and then ignoring him and pretending he didn't exist. It was Miles who kept taking the bait.

To be a theatrical star she needed to practice 'allure' so she spent hours pinning up her heavy hair into a wild Bardot style, piled carelessly on top of her head with strands falling down the sides. She wore the tightest of boy's jeans and skimpy tops cut low, lots of cleavage by padding her bra so it made the best of her meagre assets. Too much dancing reduced your bust to nothing, but there were ways and means to create an illusion and she knew them all.

All this had to be done without Mamma noticing so she came to the Waverley in a sloppy joe sweater and promptly removed it upstairs saying it was too hot to keep it on.

Eye make-up was the next key to allure. She and

Joy practised using lots of mascara and smudgy eyeliner, smoky shadow and pale lipstick, and most of all that knowing look, which Rosa knew you didn't get by keeping your legs crossed.

Susan kept staring at them. 'I hope you're not going out like that!'

'Don't worry, we're just getting in role,' Rosa replied, and that usually stopped any further criticism.

Connie looked on with a shrug. She'd be happy to go out in a sack. Poor lamb didn't smile much either. Every time Mamma and Rosa had a blazing row, not speaking just barking orders at each other, mumbling under their breath and generally keeping out of each other's way, Rosa would recall what happened to Connie and rush home and give her Mamma a big hug, and all was forgiven.

She practised a whole repertoire of characters to act: demure schoolgirls, innocent ingénues, Audrey Hepburn-style; waspish Left Bank students à la Juliette Greco, all in black, and vamps. Rosa could do them all, but extra lessons courtesy of Paul Jerviss might put the seal of truth on her seductive powers.

'One must suffer for one's art.' She sat back on the last day of school with her Panama hat crushed into a ball and her school blazer screwed under her seat.

Connie was slumped on the café seat, weighed down by a satchel full of exercise books.

'You're such a swot! School's out! No more brown knickers for me, no more Sister Gilberte breathing down my neck. Today Grimbleton, tomorrow the world!'

Rosa leaned back on her chair to admire all the trendy alterations to Santini's. It was now the 'Casablanca', covered with posters of Humphrey Bogart's film. It was dark with netting on the walls and posters of gendarmes, and wine bottles with candles in them for lights. They served cappuccinos with brown sugar. You could smoke and no one would see you. Best of all was the bulbous new juke box, with its glass front and handwritten song titles to choose from.

'Did you get the part?' Connie asked, looking up.

'Do ducks swim?' Rosa replied. 'I knocked the opposition out of the water and I heard the producer say, "And who is *that?*" Rehearsals start on Monday. Don't look so interested,' she snapped. 'You're on the list too. I put your name down as a helper.'

'Thanks a bundle,' came Connie's flat reply.

'Come on, what's up with you? Another bad night again?' Rosa was trying to be sympathetic but Connie was not easy to reach.

'I'm fine. Joy's late again. I expect she's snogging John Seddon down the ginnel. Honestly, have you seen him? I could do better than that with my eyes shut.'

'I thought you two were friends, not rivals. What's up?' Rosa was fishing. Since Ana's death, Connie was funny about Joy; critical, snappy. It wasn't like her.

'Nothing. Oh, here she comes, the late Joy Winstanley, as usual. Just look at her. You'd think it was a fashion parade,' Connie sneered.

Rosa had to admit since Joy's illness she looked

so different, neat and petite, with immaculate skirt and nylons showing such tiny feet. Her hair hung down in a huge ponytail, thick and glossy like a mane. Someone wolf-whistled as she went past and she pretended not to notice.

'Sorry I'm late. I popped into the travel agency to see Auntie Lee. I start work on Monday.' She looked so excited that it was hard to be cross.

'Connie's being a misery guts – she must have the curse,' Rosa laughed.

'No, I've not. It's all right for you two. I'm stuck with a huge pile of prep for next term,' she snapped.

'You're such a swot! We're not good enough for her now, are we?' Rosa laughed. Nothing was going to spoil her excitement. The summer was going to be so thrilling for her. Who knew where she might be by September? A bit part in *Coronation Street*, assistant stage manager at a Manchester theatre or even the West End? A film extra would do until she got on a decent drama course.

'How much has Auntie Su told you about Cedric Winstanley?' Connie suddenly whispered to Joy.

'You mean my daddy? He was a soldier in the war and he died a hero. They met in Burma after the occupation in a concert party in Rangoon, I think,' said Joy.

'When did he marry her?' Connie continued.

'I'm not sure, not right away. Why do you want to know?' Joy replied. Trust Connie to be so serious on the last day of term.

'Have you seen your birth certificate?'

'No. Why should I? Mummy has it somewhere

127

safe.' Joy looked puzzled.

'Well, ask to see it, that's all I'm saying,' Connie snapped. 'The Winstanleys have a lot of explaining to do.'

'Don't talk about them like that!' Joy spat.

'I speak as I find.' Connie glared at her.

Why was she spoiling the fun and being unkind? Rosa leaned forward, almost knocking the candle onto the floor and smashing the bottle.

'Come on, Con, we understand how you're feeling at the moment, but–'

'You don't understand anything at all, either of you. Ask your precious mummy, Joy. Ask Gran about Freddie Winstanley, that's all I'm saying.' Connie rose to gather her stray bits of uniform, making for the door in tears.

'Don't go, Connie, please stay,' whispered Rosa. 'I've got something to confess, something exciting to tell you. I want you to be the first to know.'

Connie paused and sat down, trying not to look interested.

'I've "gone all the way",' Rosa blurted.

'When?' Con whispered, her blue eyes wide and curious.

'*Who?*' Joy added. They were in a huddle now, all animosity forgotten.

'Last Saturday afternoon in Queen's Park ... with Paul Jerviss's–' she said. Their faces were a picture of fascinated horror.

'Not *the* Paul Jerviss, the spin-the-bottle champion, the love-bite king? Rosaria Santini, you devil.' They were all ears and smiling, wanting to know every embellished detail.

'Well, his mate, actually. More's the pity,' she

sighed to herself. Try as she might, Paul didn't show any interest in her at all.

'Paul and Miles're working for my uncle now. We went to an all-nighter up Albert Drive, with loads of bedrooms for snogging. Miles and I got to number seven and then I left him wanting more, but we went for a walk before work. I thought, let's do it, let's find out what all the fuss is about, so we did,' she revealed.

'So ... what's it like?' whispered Joy, looking shocked.

'Having an ice cream cone that melts inside you after a lot of jumping about,' Rosa sniggered. It wasn't like that at all, just a lot of fumbling and messing about, but she wasn't going to spoil the moment.

'Is that all? What if you get yourself pregnant?' Connie said, ever the practical one.

'We did it standing up so it doesn't count,' Rosa countered.

'Are you going to marry him now?' Joy asked. She was romantic, and keen on sex and marriage going hand in hand.

'Not likely. I just wanted to know how it feels. I'm getting in the part for Juliet's love scenes,' she replied.

'Did it hurt?' Joy grimaced. 'They say you bleed and tear.'

'Not a drop. Doing all those splits sort of stretches you out, and Tampax, of course,' she lied. They hadn't got that far at all but Miles had blurted it out in excitement.

'I think it's wrong to do it just out of curiosity. Look where it got Mama and Auntie Su, dumped with babies. You're daft not to take precautions,' Connie sniffed – being a po-faced pain-in-the-bum again, Rosa thought sulkily.

'Why are you being so mean? They were married ladies,' snapped Joy.

'Were they now? I'd check on that, if I were you,' Connie said.

'There you go again! If a *bambina* comes along, Mamma will look after it for me. No big deal.' Rosa was lying again. It would be a disgrace in the family if she shamed them. She would have to be sent away and there would be no West End, only penitence and lots of Church. 'I'll say one thing, it's better to journey than to arrive,' she winked.

'What do you mean?' Joy said.

'You'll find out for yourself one day.' She sipped her coffee, leaving a frothy moustache on her lips. 'So, no more school. What shall we do to celebrate?' she asked, changing tack.

'Are you going to do it again?' asked Joy, still eager for information.

'I suppose so, when I've got a spare minute, what with teaching baby class for Lemody Liptrot and I've got rehearsals. You must come and see us. Romeo is a professional from Manchester, a friend of Simon Marks, the producer. Isn't it exciting? You can have my autograph now, if you like,' she sniggered. 'And the coffees are on me, I'm feeling flushed with success.'

'Lucky you,' Connie sighed.

Her confession had fallen flat as a pancake, a bit like Miles Black's efforts, but one must suffer for one's art, she sighed.

Soon the rehearsals were well underway and the leading man, Alex Macauley, made it quite clear he was doing a friend a favour while he was 'resting'. Rosa thought he was a bit old for Romeo but she was sure her fresh interpretation of Juliet, would meet with his approval. She was going to show him she was no mere amateur.

Neville was playing one of the Capulet gang, full of energy and presence on the stage, much better than his skiffling efforts. He looked good in Teddy Boy drapes, Rosa thought. Alex seemed to take to him and his friend Basil. No hope then of him sweeping her off her feet and off to London as his protégée, she sighed, sensing his interest lay elsewhere.

Romeo was professional enough in his delivery but there was something missing, some zest, some conviction. His performance lacked Rosa's passion. He drank too much before rehearsals and his breath smelled of yesterday's Guinness. It was hard trying to show your grand passion when his armpits smelled of old socks.

Troupers must soldier on, she sighed. This is my big chance to be noticed.

They used the classical stone frontispiece of the town hall, with its gradations of steps as the stage, and floodlit the ornate carving. For a few days it would become Verona, not sooty Grimbleton. The seating was raised up in tiers to create a pit in which the company were acting to three sides The balcony scene would use the stone balustrade round the window where the mayor and corporation came out to read the election results on polling night.

131

Imagine stepping out before a huge audience and being queen of all she surveyed. It made her heart flutter, but Rosa was full of confidence.

The others tried to appear unimpressed by her sudden fame. They were all so different now. Connie was going into the sixth form and on to university. Joy was working nine until five and going steady with one of her friends from church. All she could talk about was saving up for her 'Big Day'.

Rosa was already bored with Miles Black and his rugby team antics so she bragged about her leading man and his brilliant career. She wanted to tell him he was dumped but there was Joy standing next to him, talking about Longsight Travel. All Rosa could think of was about getting away from Grimbleton, with its narrow minds and narrow streets, to head for brighter lights, but it wasn't easy. She felt sorry for Miles, hanging around the rehearsals waiting for this Madame Bernhardt to grant him an audience.

Watching the scaffolding going up in the Town Hall Square brought the performance dates into reality. Connie was happy in the end to stay in the background and do props with a friend from school. The whole place was transformed. There was an interview with the reporter from the rival papers, the *Gazette* and the *Mercury*, but Alex Macauley got most of the reportage with his name-dropping stunts. But nothing could stop Rosa from acting like a star.

The Santinis had booked front seats but not on the same night as the Bertorellis; some things never changed. Rosa was caught as usual in the middle of their feud. They were just like the

Montagues and Capulets themselves.

She was lucky to be free at last; no more Sisters of the Sorrows breathing down her neck about the evils of the stage or sex. She pitied their poor frozen little lives, wrapped in petty sins and wickednesses. She was now free to explore the whole gamut of emotions, to be open to life and lust.

By the week of the performance Rosa's feet were six inches off the floor, expecting the whole town would stop to watch the production. She felt stunning in the silver and apricot brocade dress, with puffed-out skirt, and so tight across the chest she could hardly breathe. Her ponytail was dressed in a coronet of fresh flowers and leaves. For the balcony scene she wore a chiffony négligée dyed with cold tea, and when the light was in a certain direction, it left little to the imagination.

Neville told her that she'd better wear a leotard and ballet tights underneath if she was not to give Granny Esme a heart attack.

Everyone was so wrapped up in preparations that no one noticed the storm clouds gathering from the west. The torrential deluge, when it came, threw buckets of water over the set and the seats, and fused the lights.

The first night was cancelled and the second was a half-cock performance in the Little Theatre. By the third night there was talk of taking all the scenery down and people wanted their money back. It wasn't fair!

All that expense and drama, ruined by typical Grimbleton summer downpours. Why did she have to live in the wettest climate? It wasn't the same atmosphere inside the theatre, and the sets were rushed together and kept falling over.

Mr Stale Armpits had a tantrum and said he was not going to perform with a bunch of amateurs again. On the last night, as if to make amends for the week's rain, the sun blazed out and they decided it was a shit or bust performance in the Town Hall Square as a gesture of defiance to a packed audience, who sat where they could to watch them perform.

Only then did the play come alive. The gangs raced up and down the steps fighting and shouting, the crowd danced in the pit by the setting sun and it was all magical. The cast gave it everything, and for once Romeo came to life, swashing and buckling his way into the audience's hearts.

Mamma was out there weeping with pride at her *bambina*. Dr Friedmann and Auntie Su were sitting together, and Granny Esme was with all the other Winstanleys cheering Neville on to glory. Even the dreaded Ivy seemed to be enjoying her son's debut.

For those magical hours Rosa gave her best performance, centre stage, alive, exalted, feeling the admiration of the town at her plucky attempt to portray one of the world's tragic heroines. Her death scene had the audience gasping with sadness. Why did such passion have to end in the tomb?

When they took their bows there was a roar of applause. She knew she was born to perform. This is my life now, she smiled.

Even Alex relaxed and took her in his arms, kissing her. 'Well done! You were wonderful... We were brilliant, darling!'

She hoped Paul Jerviss was out there some-where to see what he was missing. Now Alex would take her in hand and make her dreams come true.

Connie watched the performance with a keen eye. She didn't think much of Alex's turn. It was wooden and lacklustre. He showed no passion towards his Juliet, who upstaged him at every turn. She was fed up with Shakespeare's tragedies, any-way. All the girls ever got were poison, death and oblivion.

She was clearing up after the show when she saw Auntie Su hovering by the platform, beckoning.

'I'm glad I've caught you,' she whispered. 'Joy's been asking such awkward questions. You mustn't say anything to Joy yet.'

'Why not?' Connie blushed.

'It will only upset her. We don't want her to get upset, not when she is doing so well at work,' Auntie Su replied.

'We are half-sisters. What's wrong about her knowing that?'

'She thinks I was married to Cedric. It will upset her to know the truth. It is better you say nothing. I will deal with it in my time, Connie.'

'Suit yourself,' Connie said, walking away from her. Why had she got to remind her of all that? Why was everyone trying to interfere? Why couldn't they just leave her alone? Her grief was stuck like a shadow hovering over her from which there was no escape.

Rosa had her career mapped out, Joy had her

work. All she had was a pile of books and sad memories. Why should she have to carry the family secret as well? It was time Joy knew the truth too. What harm could it do now?

'Come on, Con, time to party!' yelled Rosa, racing out of the dressing room.

'Count me out,' Connie replied.

'No way! Your mama wouldn't want you to live like a nun. Everyone's going, it'll be fun. Don't shut yourself away ... please?' Rosa wasn't going to take no for an answer.

Connie shrugged her shoulders and sighed. It was going to be a long night.

The after-show party was held in the producer's house, high on a hill overlooking the town. It was an old stone farmhouse, with low ceilings and lots of atmosphere, reeking of soot from the inglenook fireplace, and wet dogs. Everyone was chatting about their performances and Connie felt like a spare part. There were lots of hangers-on, and she saw Miles Black trying to entice Rosa into a dark corner. She was busy playing Queen for the night and had no intentions of being seduced from the limelight.

Connie observed his clumsy attempts to get her attention and felt sorry for him. Then who should sashay into her path but Mr Love-Bite King himself, waving a drink and a grin in her direction.

'Hi there, aren't you one of Rosa's Silkies?' was his chat-up line. She wanted to say, 'Piss off', but it didn't seem fair. She turned away ignoring him.

'She's Little Miss Frigid,' snapped Miles, who was peeved at Rosa and already drunk.

'Little Miss Sensible, actually, so you can forget

all your chat-up lines. I'm not the sort of girl who snogs any old creep who preys on girls for their favours.'

'Ouch! Who trod on your corns?' Paul said, still grinning. 'What have we here?' He started humming the tune 'Whole Lotta Woman'.

Connie saw red. 'I'll be a whole lotta woman when I find a whole lotta man, but not yet ... and not you!'

He stepped back at her rebuff and had the decency to blush. 'Pardon me for breathing in your space. Who's your friend, Rosa ... Miss Chilly Knickers?'

'Oh, go and suck your dummy,' Connie shouted, but found herself laughing.

He turned, paused, puzzled, half squinting at her with blue eyes to take her in. Was that a flicker of admiration and respect she saw in them or was he just trying to think up a riposte?

'Paul! Over here.' A siren voice lured him into a shady alcove, out of harm's way. Rosa was at her back. 'Why did you say all that? He's the mostest guy in the room and I've been after him for weeks, and he comes and chats you up. You're such a prude.'

'No, I'm not, I'm just picky and I don't flirt.'

'You just scare them off with remarks like that.'

'So? All this snogging in dark rooms is silly. This isn't a party, it's just an excuse for ... sex.'

'Oh, grow up. That's what this play was about – sex, sex, sex. Now everyone's drunk and frisky. You're only young once.'

'And look where it gets a girl: a kitchen sink and prams in the hall. I'd rather read a good book.'

'Well, go and find one then. You're spoiling my fun.'

Connie picked up her cardigan and bag and made for the door. She'd catch the next bus home on her own.

'No buses after ten, love,' someone yelled.

'Shit!' she thought. Now she'd have to wait until she could cadge a lift with the others.

It was a rambling house with a study, and she clambered over some prostrate bodies to search the bookshelves, not easy in the dark, but she eventually found a lightswitch.

'Shut it off!' yelled a voice.

'Sorry,' she said, but not before she grabbed something off the shelf. It was *Brighton Rock* by Graham Greene. All about Pinkie and his violent gang. She was hooked from the first page and found a stool in the kitchen to read on.

There was a shadow over her shoulder and she turned to see Paul Jerviss peering at her paperback. *'Brighton Rock*. It's a bit tough for a girl.'

She turned away, ignoring him again. He didn't leave.

'Sorry about next door but you cut a bit deep.'

'Hmm.' She continued to ignore him. 'I'm reading.'

'Do you do anything other than read and sing?' He was not going to go away, she realised.

'I might. Ask Rosa. She'll tell you all.'

'You related then?'

'Our mothers are ... were friends.'

'Did they fall out?' He was so persistent.

'My mother died in March.'

'I'm sorry.' He hesitated then added, 'My

138

brother died of polio when he was nine. It's a bummer.' She recognised the sadness in his voice and looked up. He really was a dish, with his blond hair and blue eyes, all legs, and teeth like a shark when he grinned.

'That must have been hard for your parents...'

'They split up ... three years ago. That's why I'm doing medicine. There's got to be cures for things like that.' He was leaning on a bar stool, looking out of the window into the darkness.

'But there is a cure for polio now... We all had to have the Salk vaccine on a lump of sugar.'

'Daniel didn't... He was only nine before they started immunising, but there's loads of other diseases that need curing.'

'Like cancer,' she replied, hardly believing she'd spoken the word out loud to a stranger. 'Mama went to the Christie, but ... you know it was too late–' Connie broke off before she got upset. 'You'd better go back to the party.'

'Come and have a dance.' Paul held out his hand.

'No, I'm reading.' She turned away, trying to ignore him.

'Am I really so awful that you prefer Graham Greene?'

'He's such a good writer ... and you're just fooling around.'

'Are you always so serious?'

'No, but I know what I want and when I want it, so shove off and let me finish the chapter in peace.'

'Sorry about your mother... It's Connie, isn't it? You're one of the Winstanley girls?'

'What if I am?'

139

'Nothing ... sorry for interrupting you.' He backed off.

'That's OK.'

'Friends?'

Connie looked up. 'Only if you and your friend treat my friend Rosa like a lady.'

'Rosa Santini, a lady? That'll be the day!' he sniggered.

'Oh, go away and come back when you're a grown-up,' she barked back.

'I might well do that.' He saluted her with a grin. 'But you'd better grow up too.'

Damn, he'd got the last word over hers. She saw his backside retreating, those long arrogant legs striding into the mêlée.

He'd be a great dancer but she was not going to be one of his one-night conquests. Oh, no! Paul Jerviss was just another shark on the prowl for young fish. She'd not given him the satisfaction of letting him see for a second she'd been sorely tempted.

10

Miss *Mercury*

Joy blamed Connie for the chilly atmosphere in Division Street of late. Over the months she'd become increasingly curious, but try as she might she couldn't get a straight answer from her mother about Cedric. Mummy went quietly about her chores, not looking her in the face, hiding behind a wall of silence that worried her.

'You have to tell me what you meant, Connie,' Joy snapped, picking at her hints like a scab. 'What don't I know that I should?'

Connie shrugged and went to her room as usual. Joy would have to go to the fount of all Winstanley knowledge and get this sorted once and for all.

'What's going on, Granny? Connie knows something I don't about my daddy.' She threw her question across the kitchen on that fateful afternoon when the two of them arrived at Sutter's Fold within minutes of each other.

Granny was knitting, and put down her needles, took off her glasses and sighed. Her voice was soft and deliberate. 'We will talk about this later, Joy. This is not the time,' she whispered, fingering the wool in slow motion and looking pointedly at Connie.

'I don't care. I have to know now! Connie says Mummy and Ana never married. Is this true? Are we bastards?' she screamed.

'Show respect for your grandmother! Don't use such words in this house. You'd better sit down, both of you. I suppose you'll have to know now, seeing as Miss Curiosity here is determined to spill the beans.' She looked at Connie, shaking her head. 'Where do I start? You have to understand that it was one of those strange coincidences of life, such a queer do.'

The old woman sipped her tea, looking out of the window. Granny Esme was shrinking these days, looking older, and breathless, and it

141

frightened Connie.

'I think Freddie thought Susan was not going to get permission to leave Burma. His ship stopped off in the Mediterranean on the way home – mechanical failure, I expect – and they docked in Athens. Greece was in a terrible state after the war. He met poor Ana there. These things happen in wartime...' Her blue eyes filled up with tears. 'He died shortly after. I never saw him again,' she whispered.

'Did Cedric marry my mummy then?' Joy asked, hoping at last for a proper answer.

'Not exactly. They do things differently in Burma. It was a difficult time for soldiers. You have to make allowances for wartime romances. They're like storms coming out of nowhere, drenching and soaking, and then whoosh, the storm is over and the sky is clear,' Gran smiled with a faraway look on her face. 'The first we knew about you nippers was when you all turned up together. Quite a to-do there was about that, but it was just another of those strange God-incidences, come to test our Christian forbearance,' she added as if Joy understood a word of what she was saying.

'What's all this got to do with Uncle Freddie?' Joy was looking at them both, puzzled. 'Or Auntie Ana?'

'Weren't you listening to a word she said? Me and you are half-sisters,' Connie explained, seeing the look of unbelief on her face.

'What is she on about?' There was a pause. Joy was slow to make the connection. To drink in this strange notion.

'Why do you think we all turned up at the same

address, at the same time, looking for Mr Winstanley?' Connie was spelling it out slowly. 'I don't think Freddie meant to have two wives. They made up a pack of lies about Cedric for us. At least we got part of the truth. But the dead can't defend themselves, can they?' she added, seeing Esme wiping a tear from her eye.

'Are we not Winstanleys then? Why wouldn't Mummy tell me the truth?' she said.

'Of course you are a Winstanley. All that's missing is a piece of paper. Who is to know any different? Don't blame your poor mothers. It was wartime. Everything was upside down. They were frightened that you'd be ashamed of them. Sometimes a lie is better than the sting of the truth.' Granny sighed and turned her face away from their fierce gazes.

Joy was struggling to contain the shock of it all. Where was she going to put this knowledge? She liked everything in compartments like the savings box she kept in her bedroom, with its slot for clothes, bus fares, church collection and holiday fund. There was her new job five days a week, shopping and laundry on Saturday, cleaning chores for Mummy, church and Sunday school class to prepare. On Saturday she went to the pictures or dancing at the Astoria Palais in Bootle Street. Joy was so predictable but now she was lost for words.

'Isn't it weird? We're sisters, not cousins,' Connie offered, but Joy ignored her. If only she'd not opened her big gob, none of this would matter, but Connie had and it did. No stuffing this back out of sight, and why was she the last to know?

'Your mother stole my daddy then,' Joy snapped.

'We don't know that,' said Gran. 'It was all a misunderstanding.'

Joy was having none of it. She made to leave without saying goodbye.

'Now look what you've done, opened up Pandora's box,' said Gran with a sigh.

'Why is it my fault?' Connie snapped. 'Don't blame me ... blame them!'

Joy ran down the road to the bus stop, her head ringing with this terrible news, Connie chasing after her.

'Don't blame me ... please!'

Since Joy had been ill they'd grown apart a bit and now this, but Connie was hurting too after her mum's death.

'Let's go and see Auntie Lee. She'll explain. You can't go and shout at your mother. Come on, please. I didn't mean to hurt you but it wasn't fair you didn't know. I'll treat you to a cappuccino in Santini's, if you like.'

'No I don't like. I'm walking home to clear my head. You shouldn't've have told me. I'd rather not know. It spoils everything.'

'How come? We're half-sisters. Now that funny photograph of Cedric, cut out of a mag, makes sense, doesn't it? How Mama and Su always clammed up when Freddie was mentioned? I didn't mean to spoil things, honest.'

'But you have, Connie. You have broken my dreams of my daddy. He's not who I thought he was in my heart.' She walked on, head in the air.

'None of us is who we think we are. Look at me

– Konstandina Papadaki, for God's sake, what a mouthful!'

'Oh, shut it. Me, me, me. It's all you think about. I'm tired of hearing about you.' Joy pushed ahead, leaving Connie stunned and winded. 'Go away.'

'Don't worry, I won't go where I'm not wanted but it doesn't change anything, Joy. You're still my sister,' she yelled, but Joy was beyond hearing.

It was miles back through the suburbs and town, but Joy was on fire. She'd been cruel to Connie. She was on her own now but why had she spoiled her romantic dreams of Mummy and poor Cedric? It must be just jealousy. It would be good to talk it all over with Auntie Lee, but she was so busy with little Art now. Dr Friedmann was kind, but he was Connie's confidant, she sensed, and she would never trust Horace Milburn an inch.

There was something creepy about the way he hovered round the bathroom when she was nipping in and out in her undies. He still called her his 'dusky princess'. She didn't like being alone in the Waverley if Mummy was out and he was in. He tried to tell her rude jokes and made her blush. His octopus hands were everywhere, brushing her thighs and bottom. He was always staring at her bust as if it was something special.

To her surprise, since she was ill they had grown back full and heavy, just like Gran Esme's bolstered bosoms. 'Top heavy' was what Cynthia's fashion magazines would call them, and everyone envied her sweater shape, but Joy was always squashing them down with the dark jumpers that she wore in the office. They said she was glamorous but still she saw the fat little girl staring at her from the mirror.

Perhaps it was time to go on a diet again. On she walked, feeling sapped of strength, but she'd not give in. She was stubborn like old Gran.

She felt calmer just putting one foot in front of the other. Perhaps Connie was right, it was better to know the truth than a lie. It didn't alter anything except her birth certificate. She still had her mummy, the family and her home, and Connie as a sister.

Connie might have a point but she was not going to give her satisfaction of seeing her give in and agree. She was dead meat for the foreseeable future.

As if to make her point Joy refused to go to anything with Connie and went to the football match with Enid Greenhalgh and Auntie Lee instead. The Grasshoppers were doing well in the First Division and were hoping for a good cup run. Their two best forwards, Denny Gregson and Vinnie Gratton, were local heroes when they beat some hot shots in Arsenal, Pompey, Blackpool and Bolton Wanderers.

Vinnie Gratton was a cousin of Cynthia Howarden at work. Cynthia had got some tickets for the annual Press Ball in the Town Hall. Joan Regan was doing the cabaret turn and there was to be a beauty contest to find Miss Grimbleton *Mercury*, 1962.

'Vinnie's one of the judges. Shall I put your name down as a contestant?' asked Cynthia in front of all the girls in the office.

'Not a chance,' Joy snapped. There was no way she was going to parade around.

'Don't be a spoilsport. Anyway, it's the best dance of the year. Tickets are like gold dust. The prize is a night out with a star and a ball gown from Diana Costa's boutique, worth fifty pounds,' sighed Cynthia.

Soon their talk was of nothing else and Joy gave in: a Helen Shapiro bob or a beehive chignon? Ballerina pumps or stilettos? Mascara and eye-liner, short dress or three-quarter length? So many decisions to make.

It was not the sort of do to take a regular boy-friend to. Her latest beau had fizzled out in any case because he had the usual desert sickness, wandering palms. He was another who wanted to rummage up her jumper and feel her bra cups.

'Why do they always want to get their hands on my bits?' she said to Rosa.

'Because they're the best bits in town,' she laughed. 'You should be so lucky.'

The dancing crowd always went hunting in a pack. The ball enthusiasts grew from a handful to a gaggle of Connie's grammar school pals, including her friend Tonia, who sniffed at the beauty contest.

'Parading in front of old men like that is very demeaning,' she said as they sipped their frothy coffees in Santini's.

Rosa laughed and whispered, 'She's no oil painting. No wonder she daren't put herself in the line-up.'

'So why are you two coming then?' Joy snapped,

surprised that Connie was keen to come with them. They were still barely speaking since the afternoon of their own B.F.O., and Rosa was desperately trying to bridge the gap between them. Nothing Connie could say to make amends had any effect. Now there was a standoff.

'We all want to have a decent bop and twist and see what Denny Gregson's like up close. There's nothing else to do in this godforsaken hole,' Tonia sneered. Connie looked embarrassed. Joy gave them each a haughty look. I hate you, she thought. Your mother stole my daddy and broke my mother's heart. But then she felt mean. How do you stay cross with someone who's lost their own mother? It was all so confusing.

'I hope you're going to enter that contest.' Connie was trying to make amends. 'It would be great if you won.'

Joy shrugged and linked arms with Rosa, leaving Connie with her own friends to trail behind them.

'What have I said?' sniffed Tonia, seeing the look on Connie's face.

'Nothing,' she sighed.

'Why didn't you tell me Freddie was my father too?' Joy had kept the discovery bottled up all week but now she stormed into the kitchen at the Waverley, all guns blazing, to blast her mother with the discovery. 'Why am I the last to know?'

'Because I was waiting for the right time... You were ill and Ana died. It didn't seem right.' Her mother was spluttering, her cheeks flushed.

'How can you say that?' Joy argued. 'I feel such

a twerp, and all this time Connie was sniggering behind my back. Why did I have to hear it from her and not you?' She was trying to swallow back tears of anger and frustration. 'How can you bear to live with the Winstanleys after all this?'

'We are family too, and we owe them for a roof over our heads. Be grateful!'

'You owe them nothing, slaving away at their beck and call. Connie's mum stole my father from you. It's disgusting!'

'Stop it, you know nothing! It wasn't like that at all. I have good business now. What has Ana got but flowers on her grave? Show some respect!'

'Huh!' Joy slammed the kitchen door, making the plates rattle on the dresser. She was not in the mood for listening to any lame excuses. All those lies and half-truths. How could her own mummy deceive her so?

As the date for the ball grew closer there was panic over what to wear, and Auntie Lee and Mummy promised to help the girls cut out dress patterns if they could find some suitable fabric on the market stalls. They would have to find a pattern from the rows of books in Whiteleys. Cocktail, bouffant skirt, sheath, strapless, bow neck, scooped, deep back with a bow – Joy's head was spinning with the choice.

The fabrics on the stalls were mostly delicate brocades in sugared almond colours, pale blue and turquoise, apricot, lemon and tangerine. She would look like a bridesmaid. There was nothing that took her eye.

Then Mummy produced a length of gorgeous silk brocade from the bottom of her carved trunk. It was a deep purple with gold flowers woven in, the sort of fabric no one in Grimbleton would ever get to buy.

'Here, take this. It will suit you and make you stand out,' she smiled. 'It is the last of my hoard. I was saving it to make a dress for your wedding.'

Joy was thrilled and knew it was a peace offering, a gift in recognition of all the tensions of the past few weeks.

'Thanks, but are you sure?' she said.

'Of course. It's better for it to be used and admired on a beautiful young blossom than on some faded old bloom.'

'You're not old, Mummy,' she smiled.

'When I stand next to you, child, I feel my age. Enjoy your youth. May the silk bring you luck and happiness.'

They hugged each other, both with tears in their eyes, the tension between them over until the next time.

'It's really beautiful, Joy,' Rosa said when they took their own choices to Auntie Lee for some help.

She was holding the silk to the light with reverence. 'I daren't put my scissors into this in case I slip up. There's just enough to make a shift, straight up and down with a kick pleat down the back seam.'

In the end they settled for a deep V-necked back with a bow to emphasise the line, sleeveless, with a thin golden stole, elbow gloves and shoes to finish off the regal effect.

Rosa practised backcombing Joy's thick hair into high beehive cones folded into French pleats draped over her ears like curtains. The effect was dramatic on Joy and turned a seventeen-year-old into a sleek sophisticate of twenty-seven.

'You look like a film star,' Connie whispered.

Joy said nothing.

'Our dad would be proud.'

How dare she say that? Joy had no intention of being friendly now. She didn't need Connie. She was one of the girls in the travel agency now, dreaming of weddings and *Brides* magazine, saving up for G Plan furniture and honeymoons on the Continent. What they were looking for was a steady romance, an engagement ring and wedding band and children, in the right order. She wanted a kind husband to protect her and cherish her, her own home far away from Horace Milburn's prying eyes. To be mistress of all she surveyed would be wonderful: a new house on a new estate with integral garage, central heating and a washing machine, a patio and garden to the rear where the baby would sit in an Osnath pram like Prince Andrew. She wanted a proper family of her own to cherish, a proper wedding and respectability that everyone could see. That would be the way to make sure that her sordid heritage no longer mattered.

Once she was engaged she would be on the road from Division Street towards fulfilment. What did she care for Connie's degree, or a career with intellectual satisfaction?

It was Rosa's idea for them all to arrive by taxi, squashed together, an overwhelming mêlée of perfumes mingling like the cosmetics counter at

Kendal Milne's. Hours of agonising preparations and grooming, make-up, spare nylons in the handbag, powder puffs, hair lacquer and Kirbi-grips in case the weight of their hairdos tumbled down and ruined the style; all the armoury for a modern girl. Auntie Lee had sewn underarm pads into the dresses to protect them from telltale signs of nerves, a back seat crammed with Cinderellas going to the ball.

The town hall was transformed from the churchy assembly room where Connie sometimes sat for hours listening to the Hallé Orchestra, into a candlelit ballroom with a glittery dome spinning like a diamond kaleidoscope overhead, catching the myriad sequins and shimmers of white shirts and silvery shoes as the dancers swirled around to the big band sounds of Corrie Caldwell's Star-lighters.

One glimpse into the ballroom sent them rushing for the loo and the powder room.

The noise of giggling girls, all pushing and shoving for the mirrors, eyeing each other up, giving silent marks out of ten, was deafening as they handed in winter coats and bootees, chiffon headscarves that preserved stiff bouffants from the Grimbleton westerly wind.

That first sashay onto the dance floor was im-portant. The gang hunted in a pack until they got split up when it came to twisting time and the lads came edging ever closer to join in the danc-ing, among them Paul Jerviss, who scrubbed up smart in a dinner jacket. He eyed them all with interest. He looked so full of himself; Connie just turned her back on him and let Rosa fend off his charm offensive.

Rosa was the star on the dance floor. She wore a tight-fitting scarlet slub satin dress with layers of black cancan petticoats underneath that flashed as she swirled around. It was very theatrical but it suited her Latino looks. Cynthia Howarden played safe in turquoise brocade with buttons at the waist covered in material and inverted pleats, a style straight from the Butterick pattern book. Connie settled on an unusual shade of green grosgrain, a shift. Her sandy-red hair was already escaping from the armoury of pins into coils of curls, and one of the false eyelashes was coming loose at the edge, making her blink.

There were women in long dresses, some ancient sequined ballroom gowns, others in short cocktail dresses, and Rosa said that Sylvio's team had been hard at work all day setting hair for the occasion into cottage-loaf buns, flicked-up ends like the Silvikrin advert and lacquered stiff into meringues.

Up on the balcony couples looked down from their tables on the dancers and Connie felt like a performing seal in a circus. It was an old-fashioned sort of dance, with waltz and quickstep, and then a bit of rock and roll.

There was a drum roll and the compere asked all the contestants to head for the stage to receive a number to pin on their dress before the competition began. They were allotted a partner to dance the waltz with so as to introduce them to the audience and judges. Connie's legs felt like spaghetti as Joy made for the stage.

She hoped all those misspent wet playtimes in

the gym and Mr Milburn's sweaty tuition would bear fruit. Joy would not be daunted, she was sure. She could lead a two-left-footed blind elephant round a dance floor, if required.

Rosa was also in the competition. She was ace at the twist and jive but they never had ballroom dancing practice at the convent so she was looking awkward. Then the music changed to rock and roll and she was out there showing off, as usual. Their partners were stiff and useless, so Joy edged herself away and added a few hand movements to liven up her pretty meagre performance. There were thirty girls on the floor, all putting their best foot forward, trying to get noticed as the panel of dignitaries walked around the edge of the dancers with their notepads. The girls felt like prize specimens in some cattle auction. Tonia was right, but Connie was not going to give her the satisfaction of knowing so.

Cynthia waved to her cousin, Vinnie, who was one of the star judges. She was not allowed to enter. 'Look there's Denny Gregson, the centre forward. He's so dishy,' she shouted, waving again.

Joy was bearing up at all the attention. Her dress was shimmering in the light. Connie felt so proud of her. She really was the belle of the ball in that purple silk. The young football stars were handsome enough in their dinner jackets and sleek crew cuts, and they eyed her with interest too.

'Denny Gregson's father's an alderman, one of the judges too,' Cynthia whispered from the sidelines.

'Give him a big smile, Joy. Keep going, you look

gorgeous tonight,' her friends shouted, but she didn't hear.

Then it was cha-cha-cha time, and more showing off in the red corner as Rosa wiggled her bum in all directions.

You're not going to have it all your own way tonight, Connie thought. Joy's years of being Little Miss Dumpy were long gone. She made Spanish movements with her hands and stamped in time to the rhythm. They all hoped it was good enough to get her into round two. Everyone was clapping, cheering her on, so she must be doing something right.

Then the dancing was over and there was another rush to the loo to repair faces, hair and laddered stockings, spraying on Coty L'Aimant before the supper break and cabaret.

'Weren't Rosa and Joy great?' Connie said but her friends ignored her.

'Have you seen Denny Gregson? Isn't he the most?' said Rosa, with a whistle.

No, Connie thought. Not this time, Rosa. You get everything: the lead role in the town play, dancing solos, sex when you want it, being God's gift to manhood. You don't need any more accolades.

Connie thought of all the effort Lee and Susan had put into her and Joy's outfits. Would the Winstanley true grit see Joy through to victory? She hoped so. For all they still weren't speaking, Joy was family after all. They were all she had now.

The finger buffet was a spread of sandwiches, puffy vol-au-vents, cheese straws and chocolate gateaux, but Joy was too nervous now to eat a thing. The fizzy Babycham made her hiccup.

They sat down to watch in awe as Joan Regan performed her numbers. She was so sophisticated in tight-fitting black satin gown with chiffony sleeves dotted with sequins sparkling in the lights. Then there was a sequence dance for the oldies, and some more twisting.

Rosa was bringing over Paul Jerviss and his student friends but when Connie looked at him all she could think about was Geraldine Keane's tramlines of lovebites, and it made her smirk. She was determined not to dance with anyone. Then there was another drum roll as the judges announced the final eight girls in alphabetical order.

'...Number 21, Rosaria Santini ... Number 29, Shirley Unsworth ... and finally Number 30, Miss Joy Winstanley!'

Cynthia and Connie were on their feet shouting, 'There! What did I tell you?' but Joy could hardly believe it. Down to the last eight out of thirty! She was pushed forward for the final line-up on the stage.

'Our Miss *Mercury* represents the face of Grimbleton to the district for twelve months,' said Alderman Gregson in a gruff voice. He was tough-looking, with a walrus moustache going grey at the temples, but there was a twinkle in his eye. He towered over the little mayor, who was weighed down with a large gold chain and looked nervous. 'We will ask each of the girls to come up to the mike and say a few words about themselves and why they want to represent the paper. We are looking for poise and presentation at this stage.'

Oh heck, Joy thought. What would she say? The

sweat was pouring down her cleavage, and thank goodness for the underarm pads. 'Men perspire and ladies glow,' Granny Esme said. The girls on stage were glowing like candles.

If only Mummy was here to see her triumph. Being a Winstanley had its advantages and she could listen to what the others said to get some ideas.

When it was Rosa's turn she calmly sauntered to the mike as if she were born to the limelight. She paused and smiled at the audience. 'Hi, I'm Rosa Santini. You might have seen me in the Little Theatre production of *Romeo and Juliet*. I love acting and dancing, and it's my ambition to go on the stage. You may also recognise my surname too but I won't make a plug for the Casablanca coffee bar just yet. If I am chosen to be Miss *Mercury*, I will look forward to putting the name of Grimbleton on the map.' She paused, knowing she would get a good clap. It was a slick performance.

'I'm Beryl Saddleworth. I'm a nurse probationer at the General Hospital, working on the maternity ward. I support the Grasshoppers each week.' The audience cheered loudly. 'My hobbies are knitting sweaters and going dancing. Thank you.' She smiled weakly and almost ran off the stage.

'My name is Shirley Unsworth and I'm sixteen. I hope to go to university. I play tennis for the school and teach in Sunday school at Longley Methodist Church. My hobbies are macramé and bird-watching.'

Now Joy was last for the spotlight. No one would want to know she worked for her aunt's travel agency, or that she lived in a boarding

157

house, or that she had made her own dress for the ball. What on earth was she going to say?

'Thank you for your votes tonight,' Joy smiled at the judges in the darkness, taking a stab at where they might be. 'My name is Joy Liat Winstanley. I have come a long way to be here tonight, all the way from Burma where I was born. I wish my father, Freddie Winstanley, was here tonight to enjoy this wonderful evening but he was one of the forgotten army and like so many Grimbleton heroes did not come home to tell his tales. This town has welcomed so many strangers like me and given us refuge and a good education. As your representative I would look forward to being an ambassador for all that is good about our friendly town. If not, I look forward to many more years of enjoying the lively news each week in the *Mercury*. Thank you.' She paused, smiled and left the platform shaking.

All she wanted was to rush down into the darkness, to be swallowed into the clapping crowds, patting her on the back until she was sore. Why had she said all that? It was rubbish, the lot of it, off the top of her head, and yet she'd enjoyed saying it. It had just poured out in a gush. It was too serious for a Press Ball. She was too serious for a Miss *Mercury*. She must hide from her gang, pink and flustered.

A hand grabbed her arm and spun her round. 'Not so fast,' said a deep voice, and she found herself staring into the flashing eyes of Denny Gregson. 'Can I have the next dance?' he asked, looking her straight in the eyes. 'You have such lovely eyes,' he winked.

158

'I need to freshen up,' she stammered.

'The next dance is mine then? I'll be waiting,' he said, leaning on the marble pillar. Her heart thumped with excitement.

The girls were squashed in the powder room, holding a conference, fixing shiny faces and suspenders, looking up at Joy with admiration.

'You were great,' said Rosa.

'Nice little speech, playing on the patriotic heartstrings,' Connie whispered. 'What would they think if they knew what our Freddie really got up to in the Middle East?' She giggled but one look at the hurt in Joy's eyes shut her up. 'Good luck.'

Joy ignored her again. 'I was only trying to be honest. It was better than saying I liked crochet and *Come Dancing* on the TV,' she snapped turning her back on Connie.

You're such a jealous cow, Joy thought, rushing out to see if Denny was waiting but there was no one outside. She didn't know whether to be pleased or insulted. He had found better game on the dance floor.

It was goodbye to any friendship with Joy now, Connie sighed. Why had she opened her big mouth again?

The band was rolling out the drums for the final announcement. The mayor and Joan Regan were with the judges on the platform, holding a statue of the winged Mercury to present to the winner. The ballroom floor was full of couples and the press men with cameras.

'On behalf of the Board of *Grimbleton Mercury*,

it gives me great pleasure to announce the winner of the contest. All you girls were grand, charming and a glory to the eye. It was a difficult decision but we were looking for someone who would represent the standards of our journal, decent, fresh and a credit to the community. We feel that Miss Joy Winstanley will fit the bill nicely as Miss *Mercury* 1962. Come and receive your prize from Miss Joan Regan... Thank you... Give her a cheer! Miss Winstanley? Where is she?' he called. 'The prize will be a gala night out with our own hero, Mr Denholme Gregson... I reckon the missus would have something to say if I take her out myself.' Everyone laughed, 'Don't be shy!'

Connie could hardly breathe for excitement as Joy was pushed forward to face the cameras flashing, receiving the statue from the showbiz star, trying to smile, though her eyes were wide with amazement. Joy's big moment. They chose well, Connie thought without a tinge of envy.

There he was again with his arms open. Denny Gregson was waiting to escort her for the victory waltz and she felt like a princess as the people clapped her on.

'I thought you'd be the winner,' he laughed. 'You played a blinder with your speech. Alderman Roberts lost his son in a POW camp. So, Miss Winstanley, what do you think of your prize?' He was gripping her tightly. She could smell the smoke on his breath.

'The statue is very unusual,' she replied, flummoxed by his attention.

'Not that, silly, a night out with me in a posh

160

hotel, a dinner dance and an outfit from Costas boutique.'

'It sounds good,' she replied, flashbulbs making her blink.

'Don't be so gushing!' he laughed. 'You are beautiful. I knew you'd win. Vinnie's wishing he was the prize and not the judge. I wasn't expecting such an array of talent.'

'I think Rosa should have won,' she whispered.

'There's enough Eyeties in this town on the up. Our Rosie's been around a bit. She's a little too hot for Miss *Mercury*,' said Denny.

'What do you mean? Rosa's my friend,' Joy snapped.

'Keep your hair on. The *Mercury* wants a fresh face on its front page. A local hero's daughter makes good copy. You said the right things and pushed the button for yourself.' He added, 'Clever girl to play the sympathy vote.'

'I didn't mean it to come out like that,' she said. 'Working for my aunt is not exactly exciting, is it?'

'So did you really come from Burma?' he asked.

'Mama is Anglo-Burmese,' she replied, 'half and half.'

'A touch of the tar brush then,' he winked. 'I'd keep that under your hat, if I were you. You look more like Olivia De Havilland than Suzie Wong.'

'Suzie Wong is Chinese,' she corrected.

'Anyway... Who's the copper nob?' He turned to examine Connie, hovering on the edge of the floor.

Joy turned and smiled. 'Just someone I know.'

'Can I drive you home?' he smiled, showing perfect teeth and a dimple on his right cheek.

'I'm not sure. I was supposed to share a taxi with my friends,' she answered.

'You won't mind, will you, ginger?' he shouted across the floor to Connie. 'This princess is going home in style,' he said. 'I want her all to myself so we can get to know each other before our big date. Do you like football?'

'Yes, of course. I've been watching the team for years, good times and bad,' Joy laughed.

'Pity,' he replied. 'The boss likes girlfriends who hate the game and don't bother with matches unless it's the Cup.'

'Am I your girlfriend, then?' Joy was gazing up at his dark eyes, wondering what to make of his cocksure manner.

'Of course,' he winked. 'Miss *Mercury* was handpicked just for me.'

Connie was rooted to the spot, sick to her stomach by Joy's words and an uneasy feeling. All she wanted was for them to be friends again and now they were even further apart.

'Like a dance?'

Connie turned to see the grinning face of Paul Jerviss holding out his hand.

'Who's askin'?' She looked him up and down.

'I'm askin'.'

'No, thanks.' She shook her head and turned away leaving him standing puzzled and wondering what he'd done wrong this time.

'Cocky so-and-so,' she muttered, knowing she'd have loved to have a bop with Mr Swivel

Hips. What was up with her? Joy's dismissal of her had stunned her, that was what.

No sooner had she fled under the balcony when Neville sidled up. 'You know who you just turned down? Rosa would kill to get in his trousers.'

'Shut it, Nev, don't be crude!' she snapped. Neville was that sharp he'd cut himself one day.

'Ooh ... do I detect a touch of the green-eyed monster? Our Joy getting too much attention, is she?'

'Don't talk such rot. I reckon it was a put-up job. That Romeo had his eye on her all night and his father did the rest. Rosa thought it was in the bag and she's got a face on her like thunder. There'll be no living with either of them now.'

'Rosa's too big for this town. Her turn will come. Our Joy is a regular little Miss Stay-at-Home. She'll suit Gregsy well enough. He's a bit too beefy for my liking, but Jerviss is something else,' Neville sighed.

'What about me then?' She felt like a wilting flower out of its vase.

'The jury's out still, I'm afraid. You need to broaden your horizons so I'm taking you out on the town.'

'This is the town, silly.'

'This is Hicksville. We're off to Manchester, your taxi awaits. It's time I showed you how the other half live, young lady, but first you'd better get out of those glad rags. Where we're going you'll be mistaken for a drag queen,' he ordered.

'A what?'

'Patience, patience, cousin of mine. All will be revealed in good time... Just another Winstanley secret coming out of the bag...'

'Now I'm intrigued,' Connie laughed. 'Lead on Macduff!'

11

Neville

Neville drove towards the city lights in Ivy's Triumph Herald, not quite sure he'd done the right thing, but he'd seen Connie's distress, the sadness in those tired eyes. She and Joy were bickering like whores on a street corner. Poor cow needed cheering up and he needed to share his own secrets with someone he could trust. He sensed of all his cousins, she'd be the one to understand. He'd got it so wrong with Joy and the dieting fiasco. Connie was an orphan and too clever by half, but she'd got it wrong with Joy too and was paying the price.

It was fun managing them all as the Silkies but the future Beverley Sisters they were not. Rosa had the talent, Joy had the looks, but Connie was wooden on stage and lacklustre. She had no allure, too tall and angular, and her hair was neither red nor blonde. He smiled. She must have something, though, for Paul Jerviss was eyeing her up. Poor cow!

But at least they were family and the Waverley was still his safe house. Here he was stuck with parents who couldn't stand the sight of each other, who coxed and boxed in and out of their house like figures in their cuckoo clock on the landing. He wished they'd just get on with separating but neither was in a hurry to set things in motion.

No wonder he'd always preferred the noise of the Waverley to the silence of his dull home. His dad wore a look of resignation on his face. He'd wanted a football crazy, rootin' tootin' pinball wizard for a son, not the apology for manhood that he must appear on the surface. Ivy fussed over him as if he was still in short trousers.

'Wait till you get in the army, son,' Levi snapped, not realising he'd been deferred from conscription until call-up was abandoned. Shame! He'd have loved to have been all lads together for a while. Now he was stuck in Grimbleton, nine until six learning the business, such as it was. Things were changing in health foods. There was talk of fitness powders to bulk up muscle, chemists were getting in on the act with herbal shampoos and remedies. They were going to have to fight their corner with some new products to stay in profit.

He'd loved doing *Romeo and Juliet*. Alex Macauley had shown him and Basil more of the Manchester scene. What an eye-opener that was: all those secret dives and clubs, cafés and bars where boys like him could find their own kind. Basil had a ball and found a fella, but Neville was more of a look-and-learn type. There was a secret code that got you into the right places, an old language, Polari, the queer man's language which got you admitted to where you felt at home. The

165

famous Tommy Ducks, the Snake Pit, the basement café of Lewis's, the one in Peter Street, but it was a whispered world.

Danger of discovery meant gaol, a stretch in Strangeways prison, public disgrace. Cottaging in toilets was the worst place to find friends. The police set honeytraps. They'd got John Gielgud, the famous actor, that way, Alex warned.

For Neville it was a relief to know he wasn't the only poof in the world. Why could his cousins harp on about their boyfriends and love triangles, and he say nothing about the gorgeous GIs from Burtonwood Camp or the chorus boys at the theatre whom he danced with? Why couldn't he live his life in peace without the threat of arrest over his head?

There was a whole crowd like him who wanted to lead normal lives, have boyfriends, set up home discreetly. How many others led double lives, getting married, going into the Church to hide their true nature but giving him the old one-two bold stare just the same?

There were some queers who you soon learned to avoid. All they were after was young flesh, teenage boys to corrupt, pass around among themselves for group orgies, films and other rubbishy stuff. He was careful when offered a drink by a stranger. He'd heard tales of boys losing a whole weekend in a cloud of drink and drugs, waking tied up, beaten, raped and filmed.

Then there were the sad old biddies who were past their prime, dressed to the nines, full make-up and dyed hair, slack jowls trying to buy some taut flesh to pleasure. He was young and hand-

166

some enough to be noticed, but he found the outrageous queens, camp as a row of tents, not his type at all. They were loud and bitchy, like pantomime dames.

He just wanted to find love, like Rosa and the girls: a gorgeous guy in leathers with a guitar and a great voice, who was not afraid to be himself.

There were very few straight lookers open on the scene. If they were in the music business it would be the death of their rock-and-roll career if they were compromised by bad publicity.

Tony Amos knew the managers who took advantage of straight guys wanting record deals, taking first pickings of eager boys. Most lads would try anything once if it would get them a good deal. They had a bit of fun, saw a new side of life and then went back to their careers and girlfriends. He didn't want one of them either.

Tonight he was going to shock Miss Connie Prim out of her doldrums. It was time she grew up. She was half-Greek, for goodness' sake! Home of the gods who certainly swung both ways when it suited them.

He was glad it was all out about Uncle Freddie's adventures. Mother was furious that Esme was going to give them a share in the business as well as the Waverley.

He wished he'd been in the war. Billy 'The Handlebars' told such whopping stories about his life in the RAF, and little 'Pixie' said he had had such fun in the desert. Even straight lads take their comforts where they can when under fire. There was a hidden tolerance then that quickly disappeared when the boys returned

167

home. Now everyone was supposed to marry, raise kids, live in boxes and conform, however unhappy they were inside.

Look at his dad, miserable, down the Legion most nights or sneaking off with Shirley from the stocking bar. His mother spent his money like there was no tomorrow. He loved it at Gran's up Sutter's Fold. She never asked those awkward questions: Where've you been all night? Why do you go into Manchester with that Basil? When are you going to bring a nice girl home for tea?

Never, if he had anything to do with it. He had all the girl friends he needed in his cousins and Rosa. Funny how they'd fought as kids but now he enjoyed their company. Winstanleys stick together and he'd been their manager even if their gigs were little more than church hall dos, youth club venues and talent contests. He was trying to get them on TV but it was another league and that was where Sid Moss might come in handy. They'd met up in a club, had a dance, fooled around a bit, nothing serious. He might introduce him to Connie ... perhaps not. He ought to see the Silkies all together and get a pro's view of their act. They did have something but lacked a good song. Joy needed to be up front with Rosa. He still liked their 'Chantilly Lace', but competition for groups now was hotter than ever. Everyone was on the lookout for the next big thing. Their act was old hat.

He turned to Connie but she was flat out asleep. Wait till I take you down the cellar, you won't know what's hit you, he smiled to himself.

Connie woke with a start. It was dark and they were parked alongside tall buildings. Where was she?

'Wakey wakey!' Neville shook her arm. 'Time for a party.'

'Where're we going?' She staggered out of the low seat, her hair tangled. She was cold in her black trews and thin top.

'There's a club round the corner ... not far.' They slipped down a side street to a dimly lit entrance passing a black-faced doorman, clattering down the steps into a vaulted cellar. Neville waved to one or two men dancing together. 'Hi, Dudley.'

'Who's the palone?' Dudley replied, pointing at Connie.

'My cousin Connie,' Neville yelled over the music. 'I'm showing her the sights.' They all grinned and waved.

Connie stuck to Neville like a limpet, her eyes on stalks. The boys were dancing, kissing, fondling in a slow waltz. 'Where are we?'

'Never you mind. Enjoy! It's not everybody who gets to see the haunts of Manchester. The sights you see when you haven't a gun,' Nev joked.

'Is this where you come with Basil?' She'd heard about such places, where boys met boys. She'd discussed Shelagh Delaney's play *A Taste of Honey* in school. This was like the old Coal Hole in Grimbleton, only noisier and more lively, and hardly a female in sight – just one, standing at the bar in a very flashy frock with a fur stole, real mink, and blonde hair like Marilyn Monroe. When she ordered her drink the voice was deep

169

and smoky.

'She's a man!' Connie whispered.

'What took you so long to figure that out? Diamond Lil ... not bad legs. She does Danny La Rue impressions.'

Connie was trying not to stare but everything looked the same as the Coal Hole yet was so different. No one bothered her or tried to chat her up once they'd eyed her up and down.

'Where's your friend Basil? I presume he's one too?' She nudged him. 'Neville, you sly fox. All this time...'

'Didn't you ever guess?'

'Come on, I sensed you were always different and more a girl than a fella ... no offence but I never gave it that much thought. It's very cool, though. Wait until I tell the others.'

'No, you don't. This's our little secret. Rosa's got a gob on her and Joy would be shocked, but I can see you're not... Funny, I was waiting to see your jaw drop.'

'Sorry to disappoint you but I've read a lot of stuff. In London there's Soho – very hip but not so funny if you got found out. Promise me you won't do lavs.'

'What do you take me for, a fool?'

'Can we have a jive then?' she asked.

'I'll take you to a better place, a bit more your scene, if you like. This was just for starters.' Neville edged her back up the stairs.

How different he was here, Connie thought, relaxed, confident... But it would be a hard life if he was found out. Ivy would never accept a homosexual for a son and Levi would have a blue fit if he knew. It wasn't something any family bragged about. It would have to be their little secret.

What a weird family they were with all these secrets and lies. Their mothers were not war widows but refugees, and now this! She was touched Nev had shared his secret with her. It wasn't the shock he was expecting. He'd always loved dressing up, gossiping and had never been into sporty stuff. His only friend was Basil Philpot, who had never given them the eye like other boys did.

Out in the smoky night air she clung to his elbow. 'It must've been lonely for you growing up in Grimbleton.'

'Not really. I always had you lot to go around with. Boys think I'm straight as a plank. Now I've found somewhere...'

'Have you done it?' she whispered.

'Don't be nosy,' Nev laughed.

'Just asking 'cos I'm interested. How do you go about it?'

'Like anyone else, you look, you look again, you dance, you talk and find a quiet corner ... do you want all the sordid details?'

'No thank you,' she said.

'That was a tame place. You're not ready yet for the really big scene. Let's find the other club, more a jazz and blues place. There's a gig tonight you might like.'

They paid to get into the next club. On stage were four lads in leathers with long hair. Everyone was singing and swaying to their beat.

'This lot are from Liverpool; brave souls to venture into Manchester but they're all still alive

171

so they must be good.'

Connie watched transfixed. None of them was much to look at: one had a baby face, the tall one had a big nose. There was a hollow-cheeked guitarist but they gave their instruments some wellie. What a sound! 'Roll Over Beethoven' and then a version of 'My Bonnie Lies Over the Ocean.'

'They're good.' She clapped and bopped. 'What are they called?'

'The Beatles ... I think. They've done a stint in Hamburg. Everyone says they're the next big thing but I've heard better.'

On and on they played until the interval and then they disappeared. The place went wild for them but there was no encore.

'Probably gone to another gig. They've got a record out. I fancy the tall one,' Nev offered.

'The dark one with the guitar is for me,' Connie confided. Suddenly the night was alive. The Press Ball was forgotten, and all those petty jealousies, in that raucous music.

'Thanks, Nev!'

'What for?'

'You know ... for taking me out of myself. Mum's the word, though.'

'Please don't tell the others. People like me have to be so careful. Much as I hate my loving parents at times, I'd not want to shame them in public.'

'You've nothing to be ashamed of. It's just the way you are,' she replied.

'I'm afraid that's not what the law thinks. Being queer's a crime,' Nev sighed.

'Then the law's an ass. It'll change in time,' Connie answered.

'It has to ... for there's a lot of us about.'

That never-to-be-forgotten night when I saw the Beatles before they were really famous, Connie reminisces, waking from her dozing. What time is it? Neville was the first of us to shock the family to its core with his doings, but not the last. That honour went to me in due course, she sighs.

She stretches her legs and strolls to the Arrivals screen.

'It's late again.'

'Repairs in Manchester and they've lost all their slots over Europe,' says Sally, one of the holiday reps. 'I'd go for a drive, they'll be ages yet. Got family coming in? Do you live here?'

Everyone asks that of her. You are either ex-pats, tourists, or flitters like me. Half and half she usually replies. There is a little stone house in the hills in a village nobody has heard of. It belongs to the Papadakis family and they rent it to her. It's basic, cool and has a warm fire, for even in spring it can get cold at night.

As for family... It's all a bit awkward. They're still in shock at her sudden departure. What she's doing now must be done first in private. Time enough to spill the beans later.

Oh, come on! Why do you have to be late, today of all days?

She finds another coffee and sits trying to relax, but her mind is in turmoil. She has rehearsed this moment over and over again. Now her mind keeps flitting back into the past, to the bad old days before she did a Neville on the family.

'Only connect,' said E.M. Forster. How many times

173

has she used that quote to students?

Yet the seeds of all her troubles were surely all connected to those tumultuous years after Mama died. What else do you expect from a rudderless dinghy lost on a turbulent sea, drifting through the uncharted waters of first love towards a rocky shore?

PART II

GYMSLIPS AND BLUE JEANS

12

A Right Royal Wedding

Connie lost herself in sixth-form life in the following months and became an ardent Beatles fan. There were lots of new girls like herself who were keen on politics and jazz in school. They all wore black duffel coats and striped school scarves like proper students. No one else except Dr Friedmann seemed bothered about the Cuban Missile Crisis, the campaign for Nuclear Disarmament or interested in her black and white CND badge. No one laughed at the jokes in Private Eye.

Joy was full of preparations for her spring wedding to Denny Gregson. This engagement came as no surprise to the family apart from Connie. She was so wrapped up in her own life, Joy's excitement had passed her by. Rosa was in the chorus of a touring musical in Southampton. It was nearly Christmas and memories of Mama's death were painful, but she buried her head in work.

Somewhere between school and Division Street she tried to switch off student politics and tune back into Waverley gossip. The best bit of news was she'd been signed on to deliver the Christmas post and was meeting up at the sorting office with old school friends who were back from college to earn some dosh for the holidays.

Tramping the streets delivering cards was a slog

in this terrible winter. Connie was too fussy to wear wellies and soaked her best winkle-picker boots, which rubbed her toes and caused excruciating chilblains.

Who should be following the round in the postal van but Paul Jerviss, who, seeing her discomfort, gave her a lift. This time she didn't refuse. He introduced her to his gang of postmen and they all went for tea in the canteen to thaw out.

He was two years ahead of her and about to start his first medical wards. He was full of life at Leeds University Medical School. Connie was struggling to keep her end up but, being a mere schoolgirl, was not going to tell anyone how hard she was finding her studies, so she played the silent game. He asked her out with his crowd but with all her baby-sitting jobs and presents to buy there wasn't money left for nights out and she made one lame excuse after another until he got the message that he was not her type. Pity, really, because the more she saw of him alone, the more she sensed he was quite a right-on guy.

Joy and Connie were still being cool to each other but exchanged gifts. Connie bought Joy a fantastic baker-boy cap in red corduroy, but it was obvious that Joy'd expected something for her bottom drawer.

'Do you like my ring?' Joy shoved it in her face for the umpteenth time. It was a flashy solitaire diamond. There was no point in telling her about the exploitation of African workers in diamond mines.

'Very nice,' Connie muttered. 'Aren't you going to wait a bit longer before getting hitched?'

'Why? We love each other. Denny's got a big match coming and I want to go down to London as his wife, not his girlfriend.'

'But you hardly know him. It's only six months since you met.'

'So? Remember *West Side Story?* One day it'll happen to you and you'll know what I'm talking about.'

'I'm not sure about that. Look what happened to Tony and Maria.'

'Trust you to pour cold water over everything. I was going to ask you and Rosa to be my bridesmaids but if you feel like that...' Joy snapped.

'Hang about! I was just making a comment, not a criticism. Has Rosa agreed?'

'Of course. And you?'

'Of course, I'd be honoured,' Connie said, sensing Joy was doing it out of duty, not desire. How would it look if Rosa was a bridesmaid and not her?

Later that winter Rosa promised to come back for a dress fitting but none of them was prepared for the snow and blizzards that swept the north and the Pennines. The roads were blocked, schools were closed, pipes froze, the streets were piled high with snow, and everyone was struggling to keep warm. It was the worst winter on record.

Suddenly it was April and still the snow hung around on hills and side paths. Rosa'd not managed to get home to try on the dress. Auntie Su rang to remind her, and even Neville who was an usher, had called to make sure she got home early. Everyone was panicking about the snow piled up on the pavements and the freezing smog. There was nothing for it but to pray she caught the Trans-Pennine.

'Hurry up, Connie! Your taxi will be here soon,' shouted Auntie Su from the stairwell of Waverley House on the big day, shivering in her gold brocade dress and jacket two-piece. Her pillbox hat, decorated with golden feathers was perched on a chignon at the nape of her neck.

'I'm putting my duffel over my dress. I don't care how I look. We'll catch our death of cold in this chill,' Connie replied, looking out over the white rooftops of Division Street. A few stalwarts were gathered in the road waiting for the procession of black Daimlers decked with white ribbons to make their way through the rutted tracks in the snow to the parish church for Joy's wedding.

Auntie Lee's outfit was a sensible saxe-blue two-piece with matching hat; something that was serviceable, not gaudy like Auntie Su's concoction, which would gather moths in the wardrobe until there was another wedding in the family.

The water pipes had blocked up in Sutter's Fold so Gran Esme had to decamp to the Waverley. Everyone was slipping and sliding on the ice, and poor Joy's wedding dress was so flimsy that Auntie Lee had run up a white velvet cape edged with swansdown to stop her from freezing to death in the draughty church.

It was a good job Rosa took the hint and managed to get home earlier in the week as the Pennine railway was later closed. Connie had to admit that even Division Street looked beautiful in the snow. Auntie Su emptied the guesthouse to make room for any family to stay, decorating the hall and stairs in bright orange and brown wall-paper especially for this occasion. Connie was just glad to have Rosa as an ally in this lavish extravaganza. They could feed the starving of Africa for a month on what was being spent on this show.

No expense was being spared for 'the royal wedding' as Neville called it. 'Miss *Mercury* to marry Mr Football' read the headlines in the paper when the engagement was announced. It was all part of the run-up to the Cup Final and the Grasshoppers going all the way to Wembley, which had set the town afire with pride.

You're too young to be wed, Connie wanted to scream to Joy, but no one would take a blind bit of notice. If she put a damper on the whirlwind romance of the year, it would be seen as sour grapes. It had already been noticed that she hadn't got a young man in tow as a guest.

Joy now inhabited another planet; the world of *Brides* magazines and *Ideal Home*. Denny had the cash to put down on a new chalet bungalow on the Moorlands Estate. Was this the height of Joy's ambition? Connie mused.

Auntie Su was busy refitting the bridesmaids' dresses. Rosa and Connie only managed one dress fitting apiece. Connie made excuses it was too freezing to strip.

Connie's outfit was a fitted dress with sticky-out skirt the wrong size, with matching satin slippers. The colour was peacock blue but she'd never wear it again.

'I can't wear this,' she groaned, but Auntie Lee took some pins to the waist. 'This is not your wedding; just smile and look like a bridesmaid,'

181

she said.

'Marriage is an outmoded bourgeois habit,' Connie replied, quoting one of the leaders of their student debating society. Gran, who was helping, had a mouth full of pins and shook her head.

'We didn't make sacrifices so you come home spouting rubbish. If you've nothing positive to say, just be quiet. It's Joy's big day.'

'Don't worry. I'll make you proud one day,' she replied, but getting married in Grimbleton was not high on her list of ambitions.

'I hope so,' Gran nodded.

Connie thought that bridesmaids were about as much use in all the nuptial preparations as chocolate fireguards. They were there just to frame up the bride in all her glory.

Gathered in the hallway for a few brief minutes it was like the old days, chattering and bragging, trying not to shiver by the paraffin heater and wondering how to protect bare arms from the cold.

They were putting the finishing touches to their faces. A dab of powder to take the shine off the nose was all Connie normally did, but Rosa was making up as if for a big stage spotlights. 'Come here,' she said, and painted her face like a clown.

All the preparations for the wedding had everyone on edge. Gran was trying to keep Auntie Su calm, who was trying to keep Joy eating and resting, who was rushing round like a demented chicken so that everything would be perfect for her big day, while the Gregson family sat back and did bugger all but swank about their guest list.

There was something about Denny Gregson

Connie didn't like. They'd got off to a bad start and perhaps he thought she was a bad influence on his fiancée. Connie worried that Joy was being taken over by an alien. She never came out when Connie made the effort to include her in plans. She sometimes got the impression that he wanted to isolate her from her former friends.

He was charming when he wanted to be. Since he picked up Joy at the Press Ball they'd been inseparable. But there was a snobbish edge to the whole lot of them that annoyed Connie. Gran said that his mother, Irene Gregson on meeting Auntie Su had made it plain they were doing her a favour in taking Joy off her hands.

She wanted to take over the whole wedding palaver herself until Joy had insisted that Auntie Su must be involved. In the end poor Su was given the sewing jobs and little else. It did not augur well. Auntie Su had come home one evening in tears, feeling so left out. 'They say I can invite a hundred guests to fill the pews. I haven't the money to invite a hundred guests. I not know a hundred guests. What shall I do?' she cried.

Gran Esme was furious. 'Who does Arnold Gregson think he is? Nothing but a jumped-up coal merchant with a son who happens to have a killer right foot. The Winstanleys and the Cromptons were quality long before he made his mint, and Irene Gregson seems to forget that she came from the backstreets of Burnley to be his bride.

'Don't you worry,' she continued, 'we'll all chip in. If the Gregsons want to upstage us they have another think coming. The Winstanleys will pay their share and fill their pews Gran reassured her.

183

Auntie Lee's wedding had been a very modest affair, but such fun. This was going to be a bore.

In the end they filled the pews with Dr Friedmann and the Bertorellis, the Unsworths, Winstanley cousins and the Olive Oils.

The Gregsons insisted on putting their stamp on the whole caboodle: catering, hired dress suits, the Civic Hall, the lot, but nobody could control the weather. It was going to have the last laugh.

Half the football team turned up for the rehearsal, well oiled by the look of them and they carried Denny off to some club for a stag do. Joy looked tired and anxious, and the weight was dropping of her face and her bust again.

'I hope you haven't been starving yourself,' said Gran, knowing only a grandma could say such things and get away with it.

'No, Granny, I just can't remember to eat. I've so much to do,' Joy smiled.

'That lad of yours will need feeding up if he's to win the Cup for us,' Connie offered. 'The hopes of the town were resting on his shoulders.'

'I hope he'll make you a good husband, never mind the Cup. A wedding is easily arranged but a marriage takes much longer, Joy. You have to work at it – it's not all satin dresses and confetti,' said Gran as she hemmed Connie's frock.

Trust her to preach at Joy, but she did look so frail and vulnerable, so starry-eyed and not listening to a word Gran was saying that Connie felt a pang of fear for her.

Joy had never seen a marriage at work in her own family except Ivy and Levi, who were not much of an example. There was no man of the house to guide her in the usual ways of men. You certainly couldn't count Horace Milburn.

At least Denny had sorted him out one night. When Joy complained that he was bothering her, he stormed into the Waverley, up the stairs, and bashed open the salesman's door, gathered all his stuff and put it on the doorstep. The poor man was shivering in his stripy underpants. One look at Denny's red face and he went without a whimper. Everyone just stood there watching the drama. You didn't mess with Denny when his dander was up!

Dr Friedmann was kindly but distant and not your usual northern man. Once Gran had arrived in Division Street and was shocked to find Jacob doing the ironing while Su was out at the pictures. That was not normal behaviour in Grimbleton, but if Connie ever did get round to a serious relationship that would be what she'd expect from her lover.

Denny was too 'me Tarzan, you Jane' for her liking.

'My door is always open, Joy. I want you to be as happy as I was with my Redvers,' Esme patted her on the shoulder.

'I know, Gran, but Denny and I were meant for each other from the very first time we met. He's so generous and buys me anything I want. I am so lucky,' she replied.

Yuck, Connie thought. Joy had read too many Mills & Boons for her liking.

'Rosa! Connie! Is your door frozen up?' yelled Ivy's dulcet tones from the landing, breaking this reverie.

They opened the bedroom door, ready to face the world.

Ivy had broken the bank with her coffee and cream lace concoction and a bucket of silk flowers stuck on the back of her head, Jackie Kennedy-style. Division Street was in for quite a fashion show as they made for their taxis without breaking legs on the ice.

Connie now stood by the door wrapped in a borrowed mohair stole, trying not to look bored. She was not enjoying this charade one bit, and was sad that Joy had never forgiven her for forcing Auntie Su to reveal their secret kinship. There'd been awkward moments when they went to register the wedding and Auntie Su coughed up Joy's birth certificate and right-to-stay-in-Britain forms. The Gregsons were not impressed with a bastard daughter-in-law.

Connie's red-golden curls shimmered under the lamp, those telltale Winstanley genes coming to the fore. The hairdresser had piled and pinned the curls on top of her head. The style was neatly finished off with a bow, and the peacock satin looked good on both girls. Now she must smile and pretend to be enjoying Joy's big day. Left to her own devices she would have turned up in a duffel coat with her long hair hanging down and blue jeans covering her thin legs.

Rosa was smoking a cigarette in the kitchen, trying not to smudge her lipstick.

Then the bedroom door opened and Joy came down the stairs enveloped in a mist of veiling, looking achingly beautiful.

Connie shivered, wanting to hug her but that

186

would only crush her dress. A voice in her heart whispered, tell her you will always be there for her. Ask her not to shut you out of her life. You'll be there when she needs you... Don't be so morbid, she thought, shaking off this silly feeling with a flurry of train-straightening, making for the door as the snowflakes began to flutter like confetti on the pavement. It was time to leave the bride and Uncle Levi, who to everyone's surprise was doing the giving-away, and head for the church.

Things were never going to be the same.

Connie had to hand it to the Gregsons, they knew how to give a good party. Most weddings were finished at three with the triumphant exit of the bride and groom, dressed to the nines, and their taxi splattered with lard and confetti, tin cans trailing to the station. Not this wedding. The couple were off to Paris for a short break between training, and the flight wasn't until the morrow so they were spending their first night in the Midland Hotel, Manchester, a red brick palace famed for its celebrity guests.

Tonight they'd hired the Civic Hall for the bash to end all bashes: fairy lights twinkling, a buffet of rolls, vol-au-vents, pastries, Black Forest gateaux and a free bar.

On stage were the usual Starlighters combo, but a new rock singer was hired for later, who'd appeared on *Thank Your Lucky Stars*, it was rumoured.

Connie hoped it might be the Beatles but they were far too famous now, even for Gregson's pocket.

The ballroom was crowded with the corset-and-brocade friends of Irene Gregson. The great and the good of Grimbleton gathered was an awesome sight: the Chamber of Trade, the Masonic Brotherhood, the footballers and wives under the strict eye of Uncle Pete, and the Olive Oil Club, dressed like Jackie Kennedys. Maria was wearing her usual purple, Queenie in a floral number and Diana in a smart suit. It was good to see them laughing together but there was one missing – her beautiful mama – and the ache Connie felt for her not being there was unbearable.

Rosa linked arms with her, groaning at the band's attempts at pop music. She was heavily into John Leyton and his record 'Wild Wind'. Joy wanted Frankie Vaughan and Adam Faith numbers, but Connie loved Johnny Kidd and the Pirates, and the Beatles, especially George.

Suddenly pop music was on the news, television, and everyone was talking about the Liverpool groups, the Mersey Beat. But now in Grimbleton it was still just waltzes, cha-cha-chas and quick-steps for the oldies.

The bride and groom did a twirl round the floor. Joy did look happy in her long silk dress, her hair coiled into an enormous chignon dotted with stephanotis. Eighteen did seem so young to make such a commitment, but Joy was sure of herself. She had made her mother's dreams come true in marrying well. Su looked so proud. Connie knew when her turn came there'd be no parents to fuss over her. Better not to marry then, it was only a formality, after all. Who needed all this fuss?

Rosa sensed her retreating away from the dance

floor and pulled her back in. 'Come on, we'll do the skip jive and get something going, liven them up.'

Connie held back. 'Wait for the group. We can do it then.'

Neville was prowling round the edge of the floor. 'There you are...' He was dressed in the latest Mod suit style, though try as he might he couldn't get his hair to fall forward into a mop top. 'Come on, let's polish the floor. No wall-flowers, please. Silkie routines to the fore.'

'Not in this tight dress. My legs haven't seen daylight for what feels like years,' shouted Connie, 'and my winkle-pickers hurt.'

'And a nice pair they are too so stop moaning! Wait till you hear the group. They're something else! I saw them on *Oh Boy.*'

'Right then, let's get this hair pulled down and kick off our shoes,' Rosa smiled. 'Time to shake a leg.'

There was a roll of drums and the toastmaster announced the arrival of Mr Rick Romero and the Rollercoasters. Onto the stage jumped a bunch of boys with quiffs, setting out their drums and kit, all in tight jeans and T-shirts, not the usual dinner jacket and dicky bow crooners. Most of the oldies retreated to the bar and buffet, leaving the room half empty, but all the young Olive Oils hovered and lingered, hoping they'd be as good as everyone said.

The lights flickered, the spots came on, and onto the stage jumped a wild young man with long hair, a shirt slashed to the waist and the tightest leather pants.

Neville smirked and pursed his lips. 'Dig the tube down his pants ... is that for real or what?'

Connie nudged him to shut up.

Rosa sniggered. 'I know him... That's Martin Gorman or my name's Lita Roza... I'm sure he is. He got chucked out of the Salesian college for thumping one of the fathers... It's him... Rick Romero.'

There was an explosion of electric guitars and drum beat that got everyone's toes tapping, hips swaying and they were off at the double: 'Shake your body to the rhythm of my quaking heart'. Everyone was soon twisting and jiving and jumping about.

'He does his own songs,' shouted Neville, at the twist.

The dancers were going wild and all the young ones drifted back from the bars to listen. Denny and Vinnie Gratton were acting the fool and some of the girls bopped in a big circle. Connie felt the music from her toes to her fingertips; something deep inside was released by the beat. She joined the circle, swaying, gyrating like a savage in a jungle, Gran would say, but she didn't care. Her hair shook itself out of its bun, falling over her face, cascading in a curly mass down her back. The tight shoes were kicked off and she raised her skirt to undo her suspenders to a load of cheers. They were all lost in the beat.

Then Rick changed the tempo to one big ballad on everyone's lips, 'Tell Laura, I Love Her', the Ricky Valance hit.

Neville made a request and they sang 'Whole Lotta Woman'. The Silkies edged to the front, bride as well, and did their routine as before, miming the song and dancing so everyone could see and cheer them on.

When Connie looked up, Rick was staring down at her with interest. No one had ever looked at her like that except Paul Jerviss once, when she refused to go out with him. She was feeling hot and cold and scared all at the same time, not wanting the dancing to end. Soon the band's turn would wind up and she couldn't bear not to hear them again. She kept clapping and whistling with her fingers. 'Encore!' the dancers all yelled.

'Isn't he gorgeous?' chuckled Nev in her ear. 'He can beat my drum anytime ... long legs in leathers ... tasty!'

'You'll have to beat me off first!' Connie laughed. She stood there transfixed.

'Connie? Wake up, love. Everyone's staring at you.' She was standing in the middle of the ball-room, unable to move. 'Fetch her a Babycham or something,' Rosa shouted. 'The girl's been "sent".'

'I have to see him, speak to him, Rosa. I have to hear that music again.' There'd been a flashbulb going off in her head... This was what it was all about, love at first sight, the Romeo and Juliet moment, the Maria and Tony moment, the Lieutenant Cable and Liat moment in *South Pacific*. 'I have to see him again.'

Rosa was pulling her back to their table. 'It's all right, he's not going anywhere. His mam lives in Roper Avenue. He's a good Catholic boy, though I doubt she'd be happy with you on his arm...'

Once they'd done their gig, the band rushed their gear to the side of the stage.

191

'They'll be doing the second half somewhere else,' Nev pronounced, knowing how all these groups worked. 'The van'll be outside waiting for them.'

'We can follow them,' Connie replied. She wasn't going to let Rick Romero out of her sights.

'Steady on, love. How?'

'In your mother's car...'

'Do you think she'd let me take the Triumph Herald open top out of the garage at this time of night?'

'We'll get a taxi...'

'But it's Joy's big day. We can't just rush out. We've got to see the bride and groom off and catch the bouquet,' Rosa argued.

'Look, I've dressed up like a kewpie doll all day. I've flown the Winstanley flag, now it's my turn to have some fun. You do the honours for both of us. I'm off.'

'Constance, come right back here!' Rosa yelled. 'Oh, Nev, follow her. She's off her head!'

Connie was shooting off down the marble steps of the entrance hall to where a line of hopeful cabbies was parked, waiting to collect guests. She was just in time to see the old Bedford van, its funny exhaust smoking, coming out the side lane.

'Follow that van!' she yelled, and she and Neville jumped in.

She turned to Neville. 'Have you got any cash? I've got ten bob somewhere in this stupid Dorothy bag. I hope they're not going far.'

'If it's Manchester, you owe me big time,' her cousin snapped. 'The things I do for my cousins...'

'I'll remember you in my will,' she smiled.

'You will hell! You'll pay me back next Saturday and do my stint in the Market Hall.'

'Yer on!'

They were driving towards the Preston bypass where bikers could do a ton without being stopped. The Bedford was belching out smoke and coughing; sparks were flying.

'It's going to blow up, is that,' warned the taxi driver. 'Have they robbed you or summat?'

'No, it's Rick Romero and the Rollercoasters ... off to their next gig.'

'I don't think so, love. Their back end's just dropped off.'

The band was standing by the roadside, looking at the rear in disgust. Someone was kicking the wheels.

'Stop! Stop!' Connie ordered. 'We've got to help them.' She wound down the window. 'What's up?'

'Back end, exhaust ... it's died on us,' said her hero, his big Celtic-brown eyes flashing in her direction. 'It's you, Miss Ginger-Nut in the Civic, and your–'

'My cousin Neville. We were coming to hear you again.' She kicked Neville's shin.

''Fraid not. This is as far as we go. Shame, we'd got a great gig in Preston.'

'You can still make it. Take our taxi,' Connie offered. Nev was opening and closing his mouth like a fish out of water.

'But we've got all our gear.'

'Nev will ring the AA. They can tow the van back.' Neville's face was a picture of pained fury. For a second she thought he'd turned into his mother in one of her strops.

'If you're sure... Thanks. I owe you. What's your name?'

'Constandina Winstanley,' Neville shouted, 'so no funny business.'

'Blimey, that's a mouthful,' Rick smiled. 'We'll pay your taxi fare. Van belongs to Jack Southern, Plover Street.'

'Call me Connie,' she shouted as they piled everything into the taxi, in the boot, on their knees. Then they shot off while Nev stood holding the keys.

'Never again... Another fine mess you've got me into. Where's the nearest phone box?'

'Don't ask me,' Connie muttered, shivering in her brocade and mohair stole. It was going to be a long wait. 'Let's walk this way and hope for the best.'

Nothing mattered but that Rick Romero had smiled at her, knew her name and owed her one.

And that's how it began, with a clapped-out old van. Connie's life turned upside down, turned round into a whirl of gigs, parties and living for each precious weekend. So what if her prep was late or her revision for A levels put on hold? Life was for living now, in the shadow of Rick's growing success.

He'd called at the market stall to repay their kindness in helping them out. He looked quite ordinary in civvies – jeans and a cord jacket – his curly black hair falling onto his collar. Connie could hardly breathe when she saw him standing in the aisle while she closed over the curtains with

Uncle Levi breathing down her neck with curiosity. She'd paid her due to Neville as promised.

'Did the gig go well?' she asked, feeling awkward at first.

'It did, thanks to you. Here...' He shoved a record sleeve into her hands, signed on the cover. 'Thanks to you we might have a record deal with Tony Amos, the impresario. He'd come especially to look us over that night. If we'd not turned up ... who knows, we might have blown it? Thank God for you, my St Concertina, turning up like that... Fancy a coffee?'

'I'm Marty Gorman,' he said.

'Yes, I know, Rosa told me.'

'She's a cool chick, and on the stage.'

'She's doing a summer season at Butlins, a Red Coat. She's waiting to be discovered too.'

'I'm a student, art college, sort of... This is our chance to make the big time so I'm letting things slide. How about you?'

'A levels, a year early ... not sure what next. If I pass I'll do scholarship papers, I suppose.'

'You must be clever.'

'Not at all,' she blushed, brushing the compliment aside. Rock stars didn't go for blue stockings.

'Did your cousin forgive you for dumping him with our old jalopy? It has finally gone to the knacker's yard, but Jack's dad's lent us his fish van for weekends. You have to have wheels in this job.'

Connie wanted this moment to go on for ever. Here she was, striding through the town to the Casablanca with its dim lights, stuccoed white walls, posters and candles in bottles. She felt six

195

feet tall, tossing her flame hair, wrapping her
trusty duffel coat around her, for it was still cold.

'So you like our sound? You and your friends
were certainly adding to the floor show.'

Connie blushed again. 'We had a little group –
Rosa, the bride and me – called the Silkies.
Skiffle, folk and a bit of pop, just local stuff.'

'So I've some competition then. Do you still...?'
He paused, leaning forward, and her heart nearly
flipped.

'Joy's married now, of course; Rosa's left and I
have exams,' Connie explained. 'The parting of
the ways.'

'I bet your parents are relieved. Mam worries
that I'll never make a living. My dad's a builder.'

Gormans, of course, Connie mused. They built
Sutter's Fold. 'Doesn't he want you in the business?'

'Not sure. I have three brothers. They'll be
more likely to go in than me. And you? Family
businesses are a bit of a tightrope. Do your
parents want you to follow on?'

'They're dead. That was Uncle Levi you saw
earlier. My dad died after the war.'

'I'm sorry.'

'I'm half-Greek too, not a Catholic.'

'So that's the big name then. Constandina does
sound like a squeeze-box.'

'Exactly so. It's Connie.'

'And Marty, not Rick. One of Jack's poncy
ideas. Funny how we've lived in the same town
and never met before.'

'We'd go to different schools. I'm at Grimbleton Girls' Division.'

'So you are clever.'

'Oh, shut, it! And you?'

'St Francis de la Salle and St Joseph's ... until I walked.'

'So Rosa told me.'

'Nothing's secret in this town, is it?' he laughed.

'Suppose not, but you must have had your reasons,' she added.

'The Brothers were strict, too strict. One of them like beating little boys so I beat him with his own stick and that was me out, but not before I got him sorted and thrown out. Bullies and pervs, some of them, alongside real saintly priests. I don't understand religion.'

'Neither do I,' she nodded. 'I was brought up Greek Orthodox until Mama died last year.'

'It must be hard.' He paused and those treacle eyes looked concerned. 'Who do you live with?'

How could she explain the complicated living arrangements of the Waverley, these days? Auntie Su was a sort of half-mother; Gran Esme, and Joy, her half-sister and all being related to the same man?

'I live with aunties who are not quite aunties, if you know what I mean,' she tried to explain, and giggled. He laughed and they relaxed. Who wanted to talk about families when this dreamboat was in front of her?

'Fancy a night out with us? You could help in the back. It'll be a squash but I reckon I owe you one.'

'Can I go home and change? I stink of liniment cream.'

'Wait until you ride in the van, you'll honk of cod and kippers. It's only Wigan tonight. Tomorrow, Southport and Ormskirk. We'll have all the cats of Lancashire on our tail.'

'Almost Beatles territory,' she quipped.

'I wish. They're great guys and deserve their success but I only hope they leave us some space at the top. It's hard in the second division.'

'Tell that to the Grasshoppers if they don't improve in the league. You're first division and no mistake.'

'So you're coming then?'

'Try and stop me,' she grinned.

Wait until she told Joy she was going out with a rock star! Then she recalled she was on her honeymoon and Rosa was at an audition. Connie sighed. Stop the clock, she thought. I want this moment to go on for ever.

13

The Summer of Rock'n'Roll, 1963

In the bleak weeks after the wedding when winter refused to yield up to a proper spring, Esme was feeling flat; the wedding was over. All the family solidarity, the show of strength against the Gregsons, the speech-making and patting on backs had gone as well as expected. She'd sat on the bride's table with Neville, making fun of all their pretentious showing-off, feeling superior. Winstanleys were old money, or at least her side, the Cromptons, were. Now there was just the photographs, the splendour of the church service against a backdrop of snow flurries just a distant memory, and all that was left were bills and the chilblains.

But then came the run-up to Wembley and the excitement of coach trips to London, waving a Grasshopper's scarf. Lily and half the town went by train, while Joy was staying with the footballers' wives, segregated from their husbands until the match was over and hopefully won.

Esme sat glued to the TV in Sutter's Fold with her neighbour, Mr Ramsden, trying to spot Lily and Pete in the crowds. The match was a howler, with little action until the last five minutes when the Grasshoppers were pipped at the post by a late goal, an own goal, attributed to a mis-kick from Denny to his defence that slid through the goalie's feet by mistake. The whole town went into mourning and the Gregsons went very quiet.

Later she made a formal visit with Su and Lily to Moorlands Drive to have tea with Denny and Joy in their new home. Denny skedaddled after ten minutes, leaving Joy to entertain them alone. There was the usual show of wedding presents to admire: china and a hostess trolley, a G Plan sideboard and table with matching chairs. There was an array of expensive stainless-steel teapots and condiments, vases and prints on the walls. The sitting-room curtains were red linen with swirling patterns of black and gold, which made her eyes water, they were that busy.

She thought Joy looked tired and tense, and wondered if there was a honeymoon baby on the way. The new bride filled a three-tiered silver cake stand with scones and buns and walnut cake for them to work their way through. She was proving to be an excellent little baker but Esme felt hurt that she was treating them more like visitors than family.

'Has anyone seen our Connie lately?' she asked.

Joy shook her head. 'She's got exams soon. I expect she's busy studying.'

'Huh!' snapped Su. 'I wish she was. Never in for more than five minutes, I was saying to Jacob only the other day. You must speak with her. I think there is some boy behind all this but when I ask she clams shut. Perhaps, Daw Esme, you will give her pieces of your mind?'

'Best let her be. Happen losing her mother like that makes her tired. She's a bright girl. She knows what's expected of her.'

'But she is out till all hours of the night and all she does is sing to those records. She has only visited Joy once. That's not like her either, and I still haven't forgiven her for worrying Joy before her wedding.'

Joy sat picking at her scone. 'Oh, Mummy, don't go on about it.'

'They had to know some time, Susan,' Esme tried to defend Connie. 'Perhaps we did them a disservice keeping it from them, but it was done for the best. Connie will wake up to her studying. She's still young to be doing them exams.'

Later, alone in her bungalow, in the dark of the night, all these worries wrapped themselves around her chest. So much tension in the world nowadays. Hadn't they fought two World Wars for some peace? She hated listening to the news at times.

Her only comfort was memories of happier days when her own children were young: excursions to Llandudno, trips to Morecambe Bay, Redvers by her side and the whole future ahead of them. How quickly those days pass and how long is widowhood.

This new world, with its glamorous presidents, pop stars and two channels of rubbishy television was not one she felt comfortable with any more: all that talk of sex and money and power. No one seemed satisfied with their lot. Macmillan was right, they'd never had it so good, but look what a mess the Continent was in.

It was dreadful to hanker after the past, not the future. It troubled her. How could she advise this new generation as head of the household if she didn't keep up with affairs?

Her children didn't need her any more, or their children. She was good for baby-sitting, presents at Christmas and not much else. Old age was not for cowards. She'd felt so tired lately and all she was fit for was a good read and a cup of cocoa.

Then came the knock at the front door, shaking her awake. Who was that? She was glad she'd had a chain fitted to the door.

'Who is it?' she shouted, holding her silver-topped walking cane for good measure.

'Only me, Gran... Connie!'

Esme opened the door, all fingers and thumbs. Something must be up but there she was, all legs and hair, with Freddie's cheeky grin on her face.

'Sorry I'm a bit late but I've a favour to ask.'

'Don't stand there, come in. Put the kettle on. It's never too late to see a smiling face. I'm glad

201

you've called. I was wanting a word.'

'About what?' The girl's face changed at once. 'What's up? You're not ill?'

'Just make us some cocoa and put a bit of rum in it. The doc recommends it for a good night's sleep.'

'Gran, you devil! You're supposed to be TT,' Connie laughed.

'And you're supposed to be at home with your textbooks.'

'We did a great gig in Bolton tonight. Marty's got an audition for *Search for Stars* with Carroll Leavis. Isn't that great?'

'Marty who?'

'Martin Gorman... Rick Romero ... the wedding band. Honest, Gran, you were there, didn't you hear them?'

'I saw you dancing like a savage.'

'I knew you'd say that.'

'So Billy Gorman's son is flavour of the month. They're Catholics, and we don't mix, as a rule.'

'That's old hat! This is the sixties; no one bothers about that now.'

'Oh, but they do, young lady. Scratch under the surface and Marty Gorman will be looking for a nice girl from Our Lady of Sorrows – a Rosa, for instance. She's a left footer, not someone of our persuasion.'

'That's just bigotry. You'll love him when you meet him. He's so good on stage and he's got his big chance, thanks to Neville.'

'What's our Neville got to do with the price of fish?'

'He knows someone in Manchester who fixed

them an audition.'

'And where might you fit into all this? You've got exams in a month.'

'I can always take them next year. That's what I came to ask you. Can I borrow some money for a trip? We're going to do a student gig in Switzerland. I can go with them. I want to see what it's like, help behind the scenes. I've been writing a few songs ... strumming a bit. I've got loads of ideas. Oh, please, Gran.' Freddie's blue eyes were suddenly pleading in her direction. 'I never got to go on the school trip.'

'How will you get there?'

'We've got a new Transit – well, almost newish. We'll take camping stoves and sleeping bags, roughing it like in Guide camp. It's just I need the ferry crossing and spends until we earn out at the gig. I'll get a little wage.'

'I wouldn't begrudge you a holiday after all you've been through. You can pay me back by being a help to Su with the boarding house now that Ana–' Esme saw the girl's eyes filling up. 'I know it's been hard for you, and with Joy getting wed ... a break after the exams'll do you good.'

'No, Gran. That's the point. I can't do the exams this year. I'll do them next when I'm eighteen. We're going in two weeks.'

Esme felt weak at the knees at this news. 'You've studied for two years in the fast stream. It's what your mother would've wanted for you, Connie.'

'I know, but it can wait and this can't. I just *have* to go with Marty.'

'Are you going to be living with those boys in a van?'

'And their girlfriends too. It's all very respect-able.' Connie never could lie and her cheeks were flushing up.

'You be careful. I hope young Gorman is a gentleman.' Now it was Esme's turn to blush. 'You know what I mean.'

'Oh, it's not like that.'

'It's always like that when lads and lassies mix. If he's a good Catholic boy, there'll be ... no precautions taken.'

'Gra-an! We're not like that.'

'Given a week in a van and you will be. You're too young and I don't want any more trouble in the family. It's been bad enough...'

'Just because Freddie couldn't keep his flies buttoned up, I shouldn't be punished.'

'This is not punishment. It's an order. You have exams and our reputation. Be reasonable. Plenty of time for trips after your exams are over. That's all I'm asking.'

'But I want to go now.'

'I know you do, but not with my money you don't. Want doesn't get every time. So think on. Just be patient. There's a whole world ahead of you.'

'Not if they drop a nuclear bomb on us, there isn't,' Connie replied.

'Don't cheek your elders. We know best, and going off, living over the brush with some chap in a van is not the Winstanley way, and there's an end to it!'

'It's not fair. I bet if I were a boy you wouldn't mind. Nev can stay out all night and no one bothers.'

'I wouldn't be too sure about that. He's over eighteen and knows his own mind and earns a wage. He doesn't have studies to consider.'

'Oh, bugger the studies. I'm off. If you won't help me I'll find someone who will.' Connie jumped up and grabbed her scruffy duffel coat, her badges rattling, and fled out the front door, banging it so hard it nearly broke the window glass. Then there was silence.

Esme made for the cupboard and swigged down some neat rum. What did I say? How can the girl be so stupid as to ditch everything on a whim for a Gorman?

She sat back and sighed. There could be only one explanation. Connie was in the full flush of first love, a dangerous time. There'd be no reasoning with the child. Suddenly Esme was afraid.

Su was up early on the morning of Connie's first History A level paper. It was a lovely June morning, wall-to-wall paraffin-blue sky. She wanted to make sure the girl got a decent breakfast down her for the long slog ahead.

At least the girl had stayed in, for once, and gone to bed early, washed and tidied up without the usual moan. She'd gone to see Jacob in his room and then said she had to swot and not to wake her too early.

Since Joy's marriage, Su felt the draught of only one girl in the house and quiet Dr Friedmann kept himself to himself during term time. The two of them had gone out to the new Chinese restaurant in town. It wasn't like Burmese food but she'd smelled the spices frying and it had brought back memories of home. The pictures of her life before Freddie were fading fast. She was an English lady now. Jacob was a good friend and it was nice to have an honourable man in the house. In Horace Milburn they'd harboured a Peeping Tom, so next time references would be examined more closely. She must be more careful. She felt so alone. When Ana was alive she longed for the house to herself: all those comings and goings at all hours of the day. Now she would love to see Ana poring over the newspaper, chattering away to herself as she concocted her spicy stews. The house was too silent. How she wished she could hear Ana and Connie spitting out one of their blazing rows.

She sighed. She was sure that Joy was expecting her first grandchild. What a happy event to come, if only the girl wasn't so sick and thin-looking.

Su knocked on Connie's door. 'Eight o'clock, rise and shine. Come to the cookhouse door, boys,' she sang. There was no response. 'Connie, wake up, don't be late. It's a big day!' She opened the door gingerly. The room was tidy, too tidy. It smelled of smoky clothes and perfume. The bed was made but not slept in. It felt cold.

'Connie?' Perhaps she was in the new little bathroom, but that door was open.

'Jacob!' she cried, running down the attic stairs. He was busy gathering his papers into his briefcase. 'Have you seen Connie go out?'

'No.' He looked up, puzzled. 'But she did borrow ten pounds from me last night and a map. She's planning a holiday abroad after the exams, I think. She asked for her papers and the

206

passport we applied for for her when she was adopted. What's up? Did I do wrong?'

'No ... but her school case is in her room and her uniform. Her bed is empty. I must see if the old rucksack is under the stairs... Oh, no, not on the day of her first exam... She wouldn't just leave without a word. I'll ring Joy. She will know.'

Su was shaking with the realisation that Connie had hoodwinked them.

Joy knew nothing, however, and was sleepy and perplexed. 'Try Gran. She might know.'

Esme groaned at her news. 'Why, that little minx! I told her she couldn't go.'

'Go where?'

'To Switzerland, to some rock-and-roll do with her boyfriend and his band.'

'The pop singer at the wedding ... she's eloped with him?' Su was shaking even more now. 'Not Connie ... on the day of her exam. Ana would turn in her grave. How dare she do such a dishonourable thing? Why didn't you warn me?'

There was a pause. 'I thought my refusal was word enough. Evidently this young generation don't respect their elders' advice. It'll end in tears and we'll have to pick up the pieces. The disobedient puppy, to shame us like this. Wait until Ivy hears; she'll make a meal out of this for years. I could slap her, I really could, and not a word?'

'Now don't get your blood pressure up, Daw Esme. You know what the doctor said,' Su advised. 'Take a tablet and lie down and we'll sort it out this end.'

Jacob produced a cup of proper tea with no milk. Su sat down, suddenly weak and frustrated.

She'd tried to do her best by Connie, but one minute she was all smiles and helpfulness, the next the door banged and there were sullen silences, hours spent in her room listening to those terrible records. She didn't visit Joy or write to Rosa like she used to do. All she did was make a racket in the attic. She said she was composing music but Mozart never sounded like that.

'Oh, Jacob,' she sighed. 'Where did I go wrong?'

He smiled from the doorway in his shabby tweed jacket and faded corduroys, which were shiny at the knees. 'Drink your tea. The girl is over sixteen, old enough to take her life in her own hands, and who can blame the poor mixed-up child? She'll learn that running away is easy enough, it's staying away that's harder.'

'The selfish, thoughtless girl. She is shaming us all!' Su sighed into her cup.

'Susan, she's young and impatient to spread her wings. Let her be. She'll be back soon enough.'

'Do we want her back, I am thinking.'

'She is family and you are the only one she has. Think of Daedalus and his son, Icarus, who flew too high with his waxed wings. Youth has its own way of doing things. She has to learn maybe the hard way.'

Su smiled. Jacob was a good man. He had a way of seeing things. 'You see the good in everyone.'

'That is because I have no close ties to pick fault with.'

'I'm sorry, I forget...' She knew how much he missed his homeland. 'But you wouldn't want the Winstanleys. We're a handful at the best of times. Look at the mess we make of things,' Su added.

'That's better, you smile again,' Jacob replied. 'I think you Winstanleys are a force to be reckoned with. They brought you halfway across the world; you'll bring Connie back in line one way or another. Now I must go. Let me know if I can do anything.'

'I'll pay you the money back,' Su shouted after him.

'Connie will do that. She has a good heart.'

Susan sat back smiling. If only all the other guests were as wise and kind as Jacob Friedmann.

14

Summer Holiday

Connie sat in the back of the Ford Transit, her heart thumping, leaning on the rucksack, trying to take in what she had just done: sneaking out of the house in the dark, meeting up at Jack's place and driving south through the night. Now Jack, in his pork-pie hat, was blowing on his harmonica as if they were extras in the *Summer Holiday* film. His girlfriend, Sandy, was asleep over his lap, her eye make-up blotched round her eyes. Lorne Dobson was blotto already, smoking that stupid joint.

Marty and Des O'Malley were up front sharing the driving, while she was tucked up in a corner over the back wheels trying not to feel sick.

'You've done it! Bye, school ... bye bye, Grimbleton ... *au revoir*, Winstanleys. No one can stop me now,' she thought. Connie's big adventure had begun and she'd no regrets. She was trying to stay cool but Lorne's joint was getting to her. It always made her feel sick. They were on the A6 in Derbyshire somewhere. Looking for an all-night transport café.

Tony Amos was joining them in London. He'd arranged a special recording session in a top studio and she was part of the roadie team. This beat History A level Part I.

She felt mean, leaning on Dr Friedmann for some cash and getting him to find her passport. It had been part of the deal after Mama died that she became a Winstanley proper and she'd insisted on having a proper ten-year passport, not a visitor's card.

All her market stall savings were drawn out of the Post Office. There was just about enough to pay her share until the band got paid. Everyone was used to sharing food, cigs, sleeping bags. She'd roughed it enough in the Guides at Auntie Lee's camps to know how to keep clean. There was a letter in the post to Division Street, asking them not to worry and explaining why she must have this chance now.

She shared her sleeping bag with Marty but they hadn't done much but the usual petting in the back of the van. He was very careful round her and she wondered if Gran's warning was true that he'd prefer her to be a Catholic.

When he was on stage she watched other girls screaming at him and begging him to come to them. It made her feel so proud that he'd chosen her. When the screams died down she was the one to keep his bed warm. Now she was living her dream, even if her bones shook. This was the freedom of the open road, their own Route 66 across America, and Jack Kerouac, her beat hero, would be proud, even if this was only the A6 to London. They were living the dream: Rick Romero and the Rollercoasters, beat merchants in leathers, were on the road to fame. She looked around at the motley bunch, not sure what to make of them.

Jacko and Sandra were now a steady item. Lorne and Des took on the girls after the gigs and played the field. They liked a pint or five before a gig and came on smelling like a brewery.

Marty got short with them. 'You'd better not mess up at the session. This is the big one, guys. You can get as high as you like afterwards.'

'Yes, boss,' they mocked.

Connie saw red. Didn't they realise how rubbish they were after a skinful – slurring voices, silly antics on stage and losing the key? Why did they have to get so tanked up to perform? She'd tried the spliffs and the pills but couldn't see the point. None of them was the better for them.

Des and Marty had to stay awake all night so Des produced a tin of Benzies to keep them alert. Then Marty wouldn't sleep and needed some of Jack's mum's Valium for the jitters. Connie was too excited to need anything, just so grateful to be part of the gang. Wrapping her faithful old duffel round herself like a blanket, she tried to sleep. It was going to be a long night's ride ... what a good title for a song. She let the words float inside her head, found a pencil stub and her little jotting pad.

A long night's ride from nowhere land...
Leaving it all behind
A long night's ride to somewhere land...
With you by my side...

Marty drove through the garden suburbs at dawn and onto the golden stone of the city buildings. This was where it was all happening: the Beatles, Cliff and the Shadows, Johnny Kidd and the Pirates. Move over, boys, he grinned to himself. Rick and the Rollercoasters will be the next big thing.

Even at this hour, he'd never seen so much traffic – taxis, red buses – and tall grey office blocks loomed above them. Where did all these people come from? He felt small, scared and excited all at the same time, but he wanted to savour every minute of their experience. The recording session, the chance to meet an agent who was interested in them, and then on to the Continent for the gig in Switzerland at some international student gathering. One of Jacko's mates, Billy Froggatt, had fixed it up for them. Marty had a sinking feeling there'd not be much dosh in it, just travelling expenses. The cellars of Hamburg it was not, but he could put Continental tour on his billing.

'Let's find the Two Is coffee bar,' yelled Sandy. 'Has anyone got a map?'

'Park up first. I need another slash!' yelled Lorne, who smelled like a Moroccan hookah wallah.

The Two Is on the Kings Road was where Marty's heroes had been discovered. The rock-

and-roll manager, Larry Parnes – 'Mr Parnes Shillings and Pence' – was the top dude on everyone's lips. He could make or break you with one sneer or one telephone call: Parlaphone, EMI, Decca, Columbia ... all the big record companies were here. To get a chart hit, their record must get to the ear of the right manager. It was hard graft, luck and good connections. They had to pull together and make some luck happen.

The whiff in the van was getting worse. There were just too many of them and all their equipment as well. Sandy was the latest of Jacko's conquests, pretty in the dollybird sort of way, but she was a useless hanger on. She was here for the ride, not like young Connie, who was already a star. She shoved the map from her rucksack. 'Be prepared,' she laughed. She had a good voice too. He'd heard her rehearsing lyrics in the back; a special kid, but he wished she hadn't skipped her exams to jump on board. Sometimes she looked at him as if he were some god, and called him Rick instead of Marty.

He was just another Lancashire lad hoping to make his name and fortune in the big bad city where hundreds of others were after the same crock of gold.

The Beatles had raised the bar with their hit songs and own special brand of music and lyrics. If only you could bottle that sort of success, he sighed. Bands had relied so long on covering American hits and climbing the charts. Now it was time to write your own or buy the best of British song-writing talent. They would need a top-brass manager and a good agent.

How could he match some of the instrumental stuff, Karl Denver's version of 'Wimoweh' or the Shadows' hits? There were no easy routes to success, but coming to London might just give them the edge and some professional criticism. The guys in the trade would assess his chances of success or send them back home to plaster walls for his dad.

Tony said he had talent and could go far, given the right songs and image. They'd all chucked in jobs and studies to come this far. He just hoped when the time came they wouldn't let each other down and make a Horlicks of their bid for stardom.

Des was sound, Jacko was iffy and Lorne a piss artist at times, always humping some tart while they were setting up stage.

The only kid he could trust was Connie. She'd been the first serious girl he'd ever gone round with. She'd lost her mam and had no dad, and was so bright it scared him. She hung on his every word and that scared him too. Those intense blue eyes, like a bottle of Quink, and that magnificent mane of coppery gold hair. She was striking in an odd sort of way. Yet she brought out the brother in him more than the lover, and that worried him. They'd made out a few times now but something stopped him when it came to full sex. Was it his mother's voice warning, 'What do you want with a half-Greek heathen? Be wary of those Winstanleys. I've heard some funny tales about them. She's the sort to eat you alive, suck you dry and then spit you out.'

'Mam, she's a great kid and she's clever.'

'Then she'll run rings round you. Clever girls

are the worst. They're not natural. They jump before you know you've shouted.'

'Con's not like that.'

'All girls are like that when they've got their eye fixed in your direction. She's not the one for you, Martin.'

'I'm not looking for a wife. We just want to have some fun.'

'That was not what you were brought up to believe. We mate for life, not here and there like some dog and bitch on heat. The Church is wiser than you.'

'You're so old-fashioned. This is the sixties, not the Victorian age,' he argued, but his mother just shook her head.

'You'll learn, son ... you'll learn, and so'll she. There's a price to pay for everything. Promise me one thing, pet.'

Marty had paused from his packing. 'Now what?'

'Take your chance. Yer only young once. If a chance's offered to you, go for it but don't tie yourself down yet. You young ones have chances we never got. Plenty of time for girls. Don't get side-tracked from your goal by a pretty face.'

Marty smiled, knowing his mam was behind him in this quest. What chances had she forfeited to bring up the Gorman brood?

They found some waste ground to park up and wandered down the Kings Road, star struck, trying to look cool, yet feeling like country bump-kins. Marty sensed the creative energy of the place and the wealth; the clothes shops, the designer windows, girls sashaying down the street. Sandy and Connie stared in admiration at the fashions in the boutiques. If he made it, this is what he could expect too, Marty smiled to himself. This was where he belonged.

They dined on bacon butties and Coca-Cola. Everyone had to stay sober for the interview. He'd kill Lorne if he skived off and blew it.

The studio was in an old workshop in a back-street, up some wooden steps. It was like a barn, divided up into sound booths and little units. There was a room for them to rehearse and set up their gear.

No one bothered with them or fussed over them, just took their particulars and checked their appointment. There was a group of folk singers doing their recording, and lights were flashing, warning everyone to keep out of the way. There was so much more than strumming a tune in front of a mike to make a good tape: sound engin-eers, studio producers, assistants, session artists and background vocalists, managers, agents, a whole bevy of background boys were involved, and the Rollercoasters had none of them to hand. Marty felt small beer in this set-up.

They assembled their stall in silence, no one looking at the others much, tired from the journey, and hung over, and not a little overawed by the professionals around them.

'I thought this was going to be some smart outfit. We could do this in Manchester for half the price,' Lorne sneered staring round at the décor.

'Tony said this was kosher ... some fancy studios rip you off with promises. Their demo tapes are rubbish. We'll get a decent tape out of this lot.' Marty tried to sound confident.

'What does that poofter know? We've been had!' Lorne snapped.

'Tony's not like that,' Marty argued.

'What planet did you drop off? Tony Amos is out for all he can get – a bit of leg over, bit of a blow job, I saw the way he looks at you.' Lorne laughed and then coughed on his cigarette. 'You can be a right altar boy at times. He didn't get anything from us so he's just sent us on this wild-goose chase. He's having you on.'

Marty felt sick. Why was Lorne winding him up? Getting him rattled so he'd belt out numbers with a bit more aggression, letting the fury out on the guitar, or what? Now he was confused.

'You're a bowl of shit, Dobsy!'

'Belt up, you two.' Des jumped forward. 'Lorne, give us a hand.'

'Take no notice of him.' Connie moved in. 'He's no room to talk. He'd have it off with half the audience, given a chance.'

'I didn't know Tony Amos was a powder puff.'

'So what if he is?' she replied. 'It doesn't stop him spotting talent.'

'But to use boys for–'

'Oh, come on. Half the film stars in Hollywood would never have made it to the screen ... even I know about casting couches,' Connie laughed.

'I hate queers,' Marty said.

'No you don't. They're just the same as we are but love differently, that's all.'

'What do you know about queers in your grammar school?'

'Enough to know they're human beings. They

eat, wash, pee. Work for a living...We all share the same planet.'

'If he'd come on to me, I'd have battered him.'

'And he sensed it so he leaves you alone.'

'For a kid you know a bit more than you let on,' he smiled, hugging her.

'Let's just say there'd be a few masterpieces, ballets, operas, sonatas, plays and ballads and hits that wouldn't be here but for "queers" as you call them. I hate that word.'

'So who do you know in that sort of world, then?'

'My lips are sealed but they're no better or worse than we are, so shut up!'

Mam was right, Connie was a bright button and generous with it. He was intrigued at her spirited defence of pervs. His own experience at the Salesian had put him off men like that for life.

Then it was time to warm up, rehearse and do their takes. One bit took five shots when Lorne kept fluffing his entry. They listened to the roughs. That was agony enough. In his heart Marty knew that although they were on beat, it was an ordinary song and a so-so sound. What they were missing was a killer song with a good riff. They were better than most, but not unique. Four men banging drums and guitars might be the fashion right now but they would never be the Beatles. But there were other groups doing well in the charts: the Springfields, the Seekers. Connie's voice was ringing in the back of Marty's head. What they needed was a girl on stage to brighten up the act.

'No, I can't ... I can't sing up front.' Connie

218

leaned away from him, against the wall of the van. The others had gone window-shopping.

'But you've been a Silkie. You can do it,' Marty insisted.

'That was different. It was just me and my best friends...'

'Give it a try. We can rehearse some numbers and do something at the gig. What do you play?'

'The piano, a bit, a few guitar chords and the recorder,' she said, hoping that might squash this stupid notion. Much as she adored him, she was no Rosa.

'With your hair down and a long skirt, you'll look folksy. We can do a few Springfield numbers.' Marty wasn't going to take no for an answer.

'But it's all other people's songs. Have you written anything yourself?' she asked, hoping to knock him off course.

'Bits and pieces ... nothing that would stand up. I'm more a tunes man than lyrics,' he offered.

'I have some words. We could see if they matched up,' she said. 'But what will the lads say to me coming on board?'

'They'll do as they're told. I'm the gaffer,' he winked. 'Lorne will be too stoned to care.'

'He scares me. Why is he never sober?'

'Dunno. It's his life. I guess underneath he's not so laid-back as he'd like to think.'

'You mean he's scared?'

'Aren't we all before we go on stage? I could piss for England before a show. It takes guts to put yourself out there. But you've got a good voice. It's got a rich timbre.'

'What's timbre?' she asked, losing herself in

those dark eyes.

'Depth and richness, a throatiness, like Judith Durham. It must be the Greek in you. Have you seen Nana Mouskouri, the one with the glasses? We could pass you off for Greek if it wasn't for that red hair.'

'That's where you're wrong. This mop is part Cretan. They're famous for their special red hair. It's the Minoan goddess in me,' she laughed, tossing it into his face.

'I stand corrected. Mam said you were a clever one.'

'What else did she say?'

'Nothing much, but told me to look after you.'

'That was kind but I'm not your little sister, am I?'

She stared him out with all the love she felt for him. 'Come here, my black-eyed gypsy rover!' She opened her arms to him and he fell into them. For once the van was empty and they fell back kissing, deeper and deeper. This time there was no holding back on either side and Connie felt the wonder of making love among the rumpled sleeping bags with the sounds of traffic hooting past. This was what she'd wanted the first time she'd ever met him. If it meant singing in front of some student gig, she'd give it a go. What was there to lose.'

'That was your first time,' Marty sighed as they dozed and lay content, sharing a cigarette like they did in films.

Connie nodded. 'And I hope it won't be the last. Come here, I like it.'

'You know that folk song, "The Gypsy Rover"

– why don't we try that out?' She set him thinking ... try a new angle. They'd got a few weeks' travelling to get the harmonies right and try it out on students too.

'Oh, do shut up! The others will be back soon,' Connie laughed, and he did as he was told.

15

Colours of Love

Joy had never felt so sick, ill or drained of energy. It was a struggle to get out of bed to go to work, get Denny's breakfast of bacon and eggs, without heaving and retching in the bathroom. No matter what she was feeling he demanded the same routine each morning, one that made her nauseous with just the smell.

All those months she'd starved herself and now she'd give anything to enjoy a square meal, especially one she hadn't cooked herself.

'Can't we go out for tea?' she'd asked one evening.

'Not with you looking like a dog's dinner, all fat and frumpy,' Denny snorted in her direction. Why did he sneer because she had a little tummy bulge? The pregnancy news had not gone down well at all.

'Are you sure this sprog is mine?' he asked when she told him.

It had taken all her strength to stay calm and

reply, 'You took me on our wedding night. I bled … isn't that enough?'

'Well, with you orientals you can never be sure.' He turned over and started to snore, leaving her gasping at his insults.

What had happened to the charming Denny Gregson who wooed her like a princess and married her in such style? Even on their honeymoon in Paris he'd taken her so roughly with no thought for her soreness. She got terrible cramps when she peed and he'd laughed, left her alone in the bedroom, coming back hours later smelling of Gauloise and brandy and someone else's perfume.

Then came the disastrous mistake on the pitch at the Cup Final. One minute he was King of the Grasshoppers and then… Her heart bled for him as he stared down at his feet, forlorn and lost in the agony of his blunder. She'd wanted to run down onto the pitch and console him, but of course she had to stay put and try to shrug it off when the other wives looked at him with scorn. No wonder he was down in the dumps. She thought her good news would cheer him up but all he could think of was that match.

'Look, love, it's only a game. Think of all the times you came good for them and scored in the last five minutes,' she offered, to no avail.

'You're only as good as your last match. Coach was furious, the lads didn't speak to me and Dad was shamed in the director's box. I'll never live it down.'

She'd tried to comfort him but he preferred his mother's arms to hers, staying out and drinking late, then coming home foul-mouthed and tetchy. Now he said she must stop work and stay at home. She wasn't allowed to mix with the other footballers' wives either.

'I want you in the house, keeping it spick and span where I can see you. I don't want them seeing you blowing up like a balloon. It's bad enough the baby having wog blood in its veins. If it comes out black ... it'll have to go. I'm not having no darkie in my house.'

'Denny! Why are you saying such things?' Joy cried, but he just shoved her away roughly. 'You cheated me. You should've told me you were foreign. I knew your mother was a bit iffy but she is a Winstanley.'

'And so am I! I have a British passport and only a quarter of me is Burmese. My father fought for his country, and my grandfather... You should be proud. Don't worry, the baby will be white.'

'I'd better be or else...'

It was like living with a stranger. If she gave up her part-time work, she would be a prisoner in this neat and tidy house with nothing to do but knit matinée coats and bootees.

How she ached for the old days with the Silkies and the bustle of the Waverley. She missed Rosa, who was appearing in Butlins in Yorkshire for the season. She missed naughty Connie, running off with a rock band. There was one postcard from her in London, saying she was fine and going on to Dover and the Continent. Her departure had left a gap too. There was no one to share her worries with but Mummy, and she didn't want to get her upset. Mummy thought things were hunky-dory. Even Neville wasn't around much now. She'd like to learn to drive but Denny said no wife of his was going to bump his Ford Consul.

Here she was, stuck in a cul-de-sac with older couples who kept themselves to themselves. All she had to look forward to was trips to the shops, the doctor's and the library.

She did listen to the wireless a lot, to *Woman's Hour* in the afternoon with her feet up, knitting, and to the afternoon plays. In the off season, Denny was driving for his dad and training part time. She had to be sure his dinner was on the table or there was trouble. He once threw a fish pie across the room because it was lukewarm.

Now she lay in the darkness, feeling the bump growing, the baby snug and warm inside, and she felt such love and pride. She was the first of her gang to be a mother and this baby would have a mummy and daddy, properly married, safe and comfortable. This was what she'd always dreamed of and yet... Was this it? Is this what marriage was all about? At eighteen it was feeling more like being in prison, a life sentence. Where had her nice Denny gone? When would he return? She sighed. Why was nothing ever how you dreamed it'd be?

Neville read Connie's postcard with envy. There she was, sampling the bright lights of London with her gorgeous hunk, making records, hitting the town, and here was he, stuck on the market stall while his dad was at a cricket match for the afternoon. He was bearing the brunt of Grandma's fury and Mother gloating that she knew that girl would come to a sticky end one day.

'Mum, she's lost her mother, she's all mixed up,

have a heart.'

Ivy sniffed and ignored him. 'That'll teach Esme to take sides. Now who's got egg on her face?'

He didn't understand his mother's hatred of Su and Ana. It all went back to that B.F.O. with Maria when they were little. His dad was much more reasonable, but then he had secrets of his own. Nev couldn't wait to find a place of his own away from their bickering and fussing.

He'd marked out some possible venues to rent in the *Mercury*, and was reading them when he became aware of a customer hovering. Neville looked up to see an Adonis in blue jeans, smallish, with a mop of brown hair quiffed up, just like the American film star Fabian. It was lust at first sight!

Neville felt himself blushing, trying not to stare as the lad pointed to some embrocation ointment, smiling, raising one eyebrow. 'It's not for me, it's for my nana. She's got a bad back.'

'She ought to try the osteopath in Silvergate. I can give you his name.' Neville was trying to sound professional, but feeling a wally in his white coat.

'She won't go. Doesn't leave the house, not since Grandpa passed away, but thanks.' He paused. 'Don't I know you from somewhere?' The boy eyed him again.

Was that a stare or not? Neville was confused.

'Not like my gran then. Never in. Gallivanting all over town, given half a chance, and me her chauffeur.'

'You've got a car?'

'I share it with my Mum: a Triumph Herald.'

'Nice... Skiffle, that's where I saw you. You were

in a skiffle band that came to our youth club once. It was you, wasn't it? You were good.'

Neville flushed. 'That was ages ago and then I managed a girl group – the Silkies, my cousins. It was hard work. They can bitch each other hairless.'

'Don't I know it. I've got three sisters, yap, yap, yap... So what're you doing here?'

'Minding the family fortune until teatime. Dad's at the cricket club or down at the football. My uncle is the coach there. Not my cup of tea, is sport.'

'Mine neither. I'm into dramatics.' The boy paused. 'We've got a big show coming soon: *Annie Get Your Gun.*'

'Funny, I did a bit myself. I was in *Romeo and Juliet* over at the town hall. Did you see it? We did a bit at the Lawns School too.' He dropped that in to impress.

'Lucky you. I was at St Vincent's Secondary and they did nothing like that. I'm junior lead in Annie. You should come and see us. They need young ones in the chorus.'

'I might well do that but who'll I be getting an autograph from then?' He flashed an octane smile in the boy's direction. 'I'm Neville Winstanley.'

'Trevor ... Trevor Gilligan.' Their hands touched briefly as Neville gave him the change.

'See you around then?' Was that a promise or an invitation? How could Nev be sure? As Trevor turned to leave, he shouted after him, 'Get us some tickets then – two, for me and my gran, for the Saturday night. If I'm not here my dad will settle up with you. He owes me big time.'

'Not your girlfriend then?'

'You're a cheeky one.' Neville couldn't resist winking.

'It takes one to know one,' came the quick riposte from Trevor, whose back view was as good as the front.

Cheeky tart, Neville smiled. Things in Grimbleton had suddenly taken a turn for the better.

After the musical finished, Neville went backstage to see Trevor in his war paint. In his eyes, the boy lit up the stage every time he came on. He was a natural comic with a fine voice, coquettish and confident, and sang in tune, which was more than some of the old souls in the chorus could, creaking cowboys with phoney accents. But it was fun and Gran had enjoyed it too.

'Fancy a drink somewhere?' he offered. 'I can take Gran back while you change.'

'Sorry, there's an after-show party so I'll have to stay on.'

'That's OK then,' Neville replied, disappointed.

'Wait ... look. I'd love to meet up. Tuesday night?' Trevor offered.

'You're on. I'll borrow the car. We can nip into Manchester. I know a few clubs...'

'I bet you do.' Trevor winked. 'Nothing pervy, though. I'm a good boy.'

'I'm sure you are but I'm not.' Neville looked him straight in the eye.

'That's what I like to hear. Be seeing you Tuesday then. Can't wait.'

Neither can I, thought Neville. Wasn't lust a wonderful thing?

Rosa sat on the hard chair of the agent's office in Manchester, staring up at the pictures of theatrical stars, now fading from the light of the window: cheeky chappies in funny suits, busty blondes, and matinée idols with slicked-back hair and David Niven smiles. She had to get herself fixed up for when her stint at Butlins finished: panto, variety acts. The season was short and she didn't intend going home.

Holiday camps were not like boarding schools, more like POW camps, especially one on the north-east coast of England. It was hard work entertaining babies and grannies, but it got her an equity card and some good experience. There were so many hopefuls wanting work – dancers, singers, comedians, resting actors and a bunch of handsome Red Coats, who took her to see the bright lights of Scarborough and tried to get her into their chalets after lights out. It was hilarious, the tricks they got up to, but rules were rules and she was Miss Free and Fancy. It was a contract she was after, and the name of a good agent.

Now she was waiting for an appointment in Manchester to see Dilly Sherman of Strauss, Black and Sherman Associates, to whom she'd written years ago. Miss Sherman dealt with stage. Rosa hoped she'd make a good impression.

She pulled out the postcard from Connie with the picture of the Tower of London. She was up for the chop with the Winstanleys since her runaway act. Mamma and Susan were full of her midnight elopement as if it was something terrible.

Good luck to her for taking her chance. Exams weren't everything, following your dream was, and at least Maria was keen for her to get into show-business. Going off with Marty Gorman and his band was a bit risky, though. She hoped it worked out.

'Miss Santini?' A little woman with a fizz of orange hair stared at her sharply. 'Come inside.' There was hardly room to squeeze through the pile of files and typewriters to a tiny chair. The room was thick with smoke.

'I read your letter ... bits of this and that ... Butlins is a good training ground for working an audience... So what are you after? I can't promise much up north. Variety is dying on its feet and panto with it. Television is king now. Musicals pull in girls from the stage schools in London. Hmm...' She puffed on her cigarette. 'You have classical ... jazz and tap, I see ... amateur acting. Your voice ... can you give me something, a tape?'

Rosa shook her head.

'What are you, eighteen...? Is this your real name? That explains the Italian looks. Just give me a few lines of a song.'

What on earth could she sing? Rosa felt her throat close over. Deep breaths. She sang the first few lines from an aria from *West Side Story*, giving it as much soul and volume as she could.

'Fine, in tune, good control ... you'll do.' Dilly paused and rustled through some papers. 'Look, to be honest, I've nothing for you except Sadie Lane is looking for a new backing group.'

'Shady who?' Rosa misheard, and Dilly roared with laughter.

'Sadie Lane, the band singer.'

'I thought she was dead,' Rosa replied.

'Hardly, dearie. Large as life and twice as big. She did well in the late forties with Anne Shelton, Tessie O'Shea and Dorothy Squires. She's trying to revive her career in the current climate so it means younger voices and a decent song.'

'Where would I fit in?'

'An audition first. She's very particular – a bit too particular – that's why the last lot walked out mid-tour. You have to understand she was once near the top of the bill on the variety circuit. Others might retire but not our Sadie. I have her requirements here. You'll see what I mean.'

She shoved a letter across for Rosa to look at.

Dear Dilly,

I got rid of the last load of shit last week. Get me some fresh girls with good voices who can sing in tune this time. I want no lookers, no niggers, no dykes, no blondes, dark, small and dumpy, no upstaging little shysters. If they move an eyelash they're out. This is my show, not the stairway to the stars.

Try harder this time, darling,
Sadie

'It'll be no rose garden but you'll get some good shows and make contacts. Would you be willing to pad up for the audition? You're on the petite side. Scrape the curls back and put on fake glasses. She's as blind as a bat but too vain to wear specs. Sadie is well past her prime but she's clinging on with the claws of a tiger.

'Don't believe a word she says either about her devoted husband, the Battle of Britain pilot. He was a fitter in RAF maintenance. The nearest he got to a Spitfire was scraping the crashed ones off the tarmac. There is one poor adopted son who was packed off to some boarding institution at the age of four and calls her "the mater". Poor Sadie, she's a monster and as fake as a glass eye but I keep her on as a warning. She did her morale bit in the war and kept the theatres busy in the fifties, but everyone's home watching TV now. She needs a hit song – a novelty song would do it. Are you interested?'

'I'll try anything once,' Rosa gulped.

'That's the spirit. Be professional, stay in her shadow and you'll be fine. Step into her limelight and you'll be out faster than Stirling Moss. But remember, go plain or she'll have you for breakfast. Wear black to show off her glitz.'

'No one wears glitz but Alma Cogan,' Rosa quipped, thinking of the glamorous young singer.

'I know, dearie. Sadie still thinks she's in the fifties... Having second thoughts? It's all I have on the books.'

'I'll take it. I might not get through the audition.'

'Turn up like you are now and you'll not get past the door, but think of it as a performance. She's got a casting in the Midland Hotel. Sing whatever she asks you and fawn over her past glories and you'll be fine.'

Rosa sat amongst the hopefuls in the ballroom of the hotel, waiting for the arrival of the Queen of Sheba. Looking around at the competition she could spot Dilly's girls at once. They were dressed in black, flat shoes, padded jumpers, no make up

231

except round the eyes and mouth. The others were kitted out in tight pants, Brigitte Bardot hairstyles and the highest of winkle-picker heels.

It wasn't going to be the best of jobs but she'd gone home to Grimbleton trying to pretend it was her big break. Mamma was rushing round the salon telling everyone her daughter was going to sing with Sadie Lane. What if she didn't pass muster?

There was a fanfare of yapping dogs and two full-sized poodles rushed into the room. One cocked its leg on a gilt chair and sprayed the floor. Then came Mr Battle of Britain with his cavalry twill trousers, tweeds and moustache. Rosa thought of the famous cookery artist and her husband, Fanny Cradock and Johnny.

Sadie made her regal entrance wrapped in a mink stole over a silvery brocade dress, with beautiful shoes that showed off a pair of still shapely calves and ankles, but the rest... definitely outsize, corseted with steel to make some indentations where a waist should be and emphasise the sort of cleavage you could lose a biscuit down and never find the crumbs. Her white-blonde hair was fluffed up like a meringue nest, and her make-up was an inch thick. She was the star, the Queen Mother, the shark in this fish pond of minnows.

Rosa sank back into her chair. Who would Sadie be swallowing?

'Sadie's got a head so big, I bet no one could get past her on the stairs,' whispered the girl in black next to her. 'You must be with Miss Sherman too.' She grinned, eyeing Rosa up and down.

'How'd you guess?' Rosa winked. 'Rosa Santini.'

'Melanie Diamond ... break a leg.'

'You too,' Rosa smiled.

Miss Lane sat on her throne, lining them all up on stage and shuffling them around without anyone singing a word.

'What do you think, Reggie?'

He shrugged his shoulders and left her to it. Half the girls were dismissed there and then.

'I only want three of you,' Sadie barked, parading up and down the remaining ten, eyeing them all carefully. 'You.' Rosa stepped forward. 'You next.' Melanie joined her. 'And you over there ... what's your name?'

The plump girl blushed. 'Gabriella Blenkinsop.'

'You can be Gabby. Now sing the music you were given. I want action and timing.' 'How Much is that Doggie in the Window?' was the novelty song, and they all sang dutifully, trying to look together. Gabby had a good alto voice and she harmonised well with the other two.

'Stop! That's enough, Reggie,' she ordered the husband who was playing on the piano. 'You'll have to do. All dark, same height and blend OK. We shall think of a name for you. Who's your agent?'

'Miss Sherman,' Rosa offered, and the others nodded. 'She knows what I like. I'll sort it out with her then.'

That was it: no hand-shaking or formal welcome, more like class dismissed, and an order to return to a studio in Manchester on the next Monday morning. Rosa was going to have to rush back north, pack her bags and head home.

Mamma would want to come and see her perform, and them all looking like a dog's dinner. Perhaps better to say nothing.

'I'm supposed to be at school,' said little Gabby, who needed no padding at all.

'It's a job. We're on the circuit – who knows what might turn up? It'll be fun,' Melanie encouraged them.

'With that monster?' Rosa giggled, and they huddled together.

'Welcome to the madhouse. Let me get this kit off. I'm sweating.' Melanie pulled some foam out of her waistband.

'Me too. How will we stand it under the spotlights?'

'Mine's real,' Gabby sighed.

'Don't worry, she'll soon sweat it off you, but let's get a contract before we reveal all. We have to make her look glam and thirty,' Melanie said, looking at her watch.

'Thirty. She's nearly fifty. Fair, fat and fifty, I reckon! What does that make us, then?' Rosa said.

'Employed!' Melanie laughed. 'We can eat at the end of the week, pay rent and buy nylons. Who cares if we look like Baa baa black sheep, three bags full behind her?'

'I do. I was hoping to be a Vernons Girl or a new Beverley Sister. My mamma thinks I'm sharing the bill,' Rosa sighed. It was so important for Mamma to think she was a star.

'Don't say anything. Just do the job, let her think what she likes and no one will recognise us in this rigout. I dread to think what she'll drape us in. Sackcloth and ashes ... to show off all her sequins.

We'll be part of the backdrop curtains,' Melanie added, her black eyes flashing with mischief.

'She's the one who ought to be in black,' Gabby offered.

'Shall I tell her or shall you?' Rosa asked, and they burst out laughing again. 'How am I going to keep a straight face watching that derrière swaying in the breeze?'

'We're professionals, doing whatever is required for as long as we can. If she gets too bad we'll have our revenge,' Melanie whispered.

'How?' Gabby was all ears.

'Don't know yet, but we'll think of something.'

'You're on!' Rosa said. 'See you on Monday. I've got to dash.'

There was just time to get a train back to York and on to Scarborough after seeing Miss Sherman and signing up, time to ring up the salon to tell Maria the good news, or at least to tell her a version that might have her mother putting a notice in the *Mercury*.

16

The War Baby Blues

The band stayed in London all through June, much longer than they expected, hoping for a contract, living out of the van, cadging from friends where they could, but when the money ran out they took to busking with guitars and tambourines, under subways and stations, in parks until they were moved on.

Connie went to visit Auntie Diana, Mama's old friend who was nursing at St Thomas's Hospital and sharing a flat nearby with her friend Hazel. They were kindness itself, inviting her friends for a meal and a chance to bath and freshen up.

Connie was ashamed of all their scruffy clothes and ragged hair, but Diana took all in her stride. It was good to feel clean and tidy, and eat proper food from a table, not some hurried mush from a transport café.

'You young people do things differently, I must say,' Diana lectured them in her pukka voice. 'All I ask is you keep in touch with your families. Susan is worried. She asked me to look out for you. I know you'd not pass my door but you must be fair to your families too.' Connie sensed there was a lot more she could say but was holding back out of politeness and reserve.

Diana was one of the original Olive Oils who came up for Mama's funeral and promised to keep an open door if ever she needed to talk over things. Diana was so correct, and the band all rose to the occasion, behaving themselves like squaddies before an officer.

To Connie she was a reminder of home and all she'd sacrificed to live this exciting adventure. If only it wasn't so scary having to sing with Marty in doorways in a strange city, but she was so besotted with him and anxious to please.

One night she sat outside their van under the July stars and revised that very first ballad written ages ago, in her school exercise book.

'The colours of my love are like a rainbow in the sky, the colours of my love I give to you, midnight blue and silver, reflections in your eyes... the colours of my love I give to you.' The words just fell into a tune in her head but she didn't tell anyone that these little songs often burst out of nowhere, waking her up at night, begging to be written down before they were forgotten.

Usually she turned over, not wanting to disturb anyone, and by morning they were almost gone, just a haunting line that would nag away all morning.

The band had trawled the demo tape around the record companies to no avail. The Carroll Leavis audition didn't materialise but Tony Amos came down, as promised, to find them a gig in a coffee bar in Camden Town.

'I wanted you to be in the Two Is,' Sandra sighed, looking out of the café window and down at the dusty curtains. 'All the students are on their vacs ... it'll be dead.'

'We have to look on this as a start; it's better than the pavement,' Connie defended.

'O-ooh! Who's talking "we" all of a sudden? You're not in the group yet,' Sandy snapped. 'I could do what you've done so far.'

'Not with that foghorn you call a voice,' Marty jumped into Connie's corner. 'Connie sings real good and she's on the beat.'

'Pardon me for breathing, I'm sure.' Sandy backed off. 'Jack says you don't pull birds to listen if there's a girl on the stage.'

'Then Jack should tell me himself, not hide behind your skirt.'

Sandra stomped off in a huff.

'If only she knew he's been trying to ditch her for weeks, but she clings like a limpet,' Marty confided. 'We suggested she got herself a job as a waitress but Sandy's here for the ride and miffed that you get to sing.'

Connie felt a million dollars after this back-handed compliment.

It was Lorne Dobson who voiced everyone's frustration later in the evening. 'I thought we were going abroad, not camping up in some back alley with rats sniffing round our rubbish.'

'Patience, mate. We've plenty of time, yet. The gig's not for ages. We've got to make our mark down here,' Marty argued. They were all feeling hot and dusty, hungry and disappointed, and the cracks were showing. No one was eager to snatch them up to make records. This coffee bar was not exactly big time, but it was all there was.

Connie plucked up courage to ask if she could sing 'Colours of My Love' when they were busking. 'It's just a little thing that came to me.' Strumming a few chords, she was shaking as she started to sing the melody. Marty listened, and the other boys, then joined in when she repeated it.

'You have something there, the words ... very romantic. Nice one, Con!'

'I wrote it for you,' she whispered, gazing at him.

'Great, we can use it as a breather between the fast numbers. Play it again.'

'It's not exactly our style,' said Des, breaking the spell.

'Sure thing, but it's a gentle ballad... Connie will sing it well.'

This is how she got to rehearsing and it made its debut the following evening to a smoky half-empty café in a heat wave.

'You should write them down, music score, everything,' Marty suggested afterwards, when they were alone. 'Have you any others?'

'Not really, just ideas, lines... They appear first thing in the morning or in the middle of the night.'

'Keep a jotter by your sleeping bag and wake me up if you have a good tune. We could do with some fresh stuff to take to Switzerland.'

'When are we going?'

'I got the dates wrong – not until the end of August, so we'll just have to busk our way through the summer for food and petrol. This getting discovered is taking longer than I thought,' Marty sighed.

'But it's great being together ... living over the brush,' she laughed, thinking about the nights they shared in the sleeping bag.

Marty flushed. 'I'd better do something about that. We don't want any accidents, do we?'

'Sandra says there's a pill you can take to stop the chance of conceiving. You have to take it every night... I know you're not allowed to take precautions,' Connie said, trying not to burn up, 'but I'm not a Catholic so it's OK what I do. Shall I find out more?'

'You're a doll! What would we do without you to organise us?'

What she didn't tell him was that Diana had taken her aside in the kitchen and told her if she was old enough to be living with her boyfriend then she was old enough to prevent pregnancy and to get herself to a special clinic where they would kit her out with a device she must put inside her, covered with cream, and she'd be safe. 'Just tell them you'll be getting married soon, no names, no pack drill. They'll fit you up properly. Better safe than sorry. You owe that to your family.'

She'd gone with Sandra, but the whole business was messy and it needed a toilet or washroom to set herself up. Every time she squeezed the cap ready to insert it, it shot across the dirty floor and she had to start all over again. A pill would be so much better, but they were expensive and beyond her budget. How unromantic it was to have to guess if they were going to have sex, but better than the alternative. Then she sang a little ditty to the tune of 'The Big Ship Sails on the Alley Alley Oh' to relax herself: 'My dutch cap sails on the bathroom floor, the toilet floor, the washroom floor. My dutch cap sails all over the floor till the first day of September!'

But she'd taken herself in hand and got control. Now she really felt a responsible woman, not a lovestruck teenager. Marty could love her more frequently if he knew they were protected. She thought of Mama and Su, who'd not any control over their bodies. If they had, she and Joy wouldn't exist. What would Mama have thought of all this? It was so painful to know she'd never see her again, that she wasn't at home waiting for news. If Mama was still alive, would she have dared to do this?

Perhaps it was time to write home and make her peace with Granny. She didn't want them to think her ungrateful for all they'd done for her, but now she was free of constraints, she was going to make the most of it.

Marty was feeling more and more anxious as the summer rolled on. Their dreams were just not happening. No one was interested in the group. At least there were three coffee bars that gave them food and drinks in return for some numbers, but their reception was lukewarm. Everyone was raving about the R and B sessions at the Marquee Club in Oxford Street. There were new West London boys on the block called the Rolling Stones, London's answer to the Beatles. He'd gone to see them and they were wild. Beside them, the Rollercoasters were tame, yesterday's men. No wonder they weren't getting signed up.

He'd asked Tony Amos to watch their act to give him some encouragement, but his words had only made things worse.

'To be brutal, Marty, on last night's performance, it's never going to work. You've gone too samey ... no distinctive sound or beat and no sex appeal. Sorry, but I don't see it happening. You've seen the Stones. The girls love wild and raunchy, not *Ready, Steady, Go!* safe stuff. That girl's got to go for a start.'

'Who, Connie?'

'The girls out there want to know you're available, you see what I'm getting at?'

Marty wasn't going to let Tony dismiss her like that. 'She's singing her own stuff. Her voice is another Judith Durham.'

'But she's no looker. Leggy and wild-haired, fine for a folk singer but not if you want to hit the big time. I want you more wild gypsy rover, sex on

241

legs. Whatever happened to the tight leathers? Snake-hipped and scruffy is the next big thing, and what's with all this ballad stuff? No one wants ballads. Smoochy fifties crooners are dead in the water for this generation. Give them sex, lots of bump and grind. "Colours of My Love" is fine for the likes of Dickie Valentine and folk songs are two a penny.'

'Connie wrote that for us,' Marty replied, sick to the stomach at Tony's attack.

'Ditch it, let her go sell her itsy-bitsy tunes. They won't cut in this market. To be honest, it's time you went solo. I can do far more with Ricky Romero than with the whole shebang. Go with the times, leave the no-hopers behind, get off your lazy butt and go solo.'

Marty stepped back in shock. Was Tony giving him the come-on, getting his hands on his real investment? 'But they're my mates,' he argued.

'So? Friends will want the best for you.'

'We have a gig on the Continent.'

'Do it and then walk away. Go solo and build up another sound. Everyone's doing it, shedding the slack, ditching the birds in favour of a better image. If you want to make it in this business, ditch the steady chick, ditch the group and stay close to the London scene. You've got the looks. You're carrying the rest of them but you don't need personal trappings at this stage in your career. You'll get plenty of that when you're famous. Make a sacrifice now. I'm telling you for your own good... Well, you did ask me for my opinion. It wasn't what you wanted to hear but what you needed to hear. That's what I'm paid for.'

242

They had a beer and a smoke in a backstreet pub, then Tony left. Marty was stunned. What was being asked of him was unthinkable: to ditch his friends, walk away, tell Con to go home. He wouldn't do it. He couldn't do it. And yet he wanted to be a big star, make his name and prove homespun Grimbleton lads could break into the big time. What was worse was that in his heart he knew Tony's cruel words had the ring of truth in them. That was why the doors of the recording studios were shutting in their faces.

He thought about the gossip. Loads of bands split, reshaped. Even the Beatles hadn't been without their ruthless shake-ups. Guys reinvented themselves with new names and new acts and new musicians, but loyalty was something he couldn't ditch lightly. The tour must go on and he would have to distance himself somehow, make the separation as painless as possible. Fat chance! The others would hate him for what he was contemplating now, and then there was Connie. Oh hell! What was he going to do about her?

They were halfway to Dover in the van when Connie sensed something wasn't right. Was it back home? She wanted to stop right there to find a call box, but they were late. There had been this niggling feeling in the pit of her stomach all week, some sixth sense, a butterfly flutter that wouldn't go away. Marty had taken to walking off by himself, and when she offered to come, he'd waved her away. 'Need to think.'

His lovemaking was rushed and most nights he turned his back on her. Was it something in

243

Grimbleton, bad news from home?

Des drove, cursing. They were late for the evening ferry. Connie felt a surge of excitement when she saw the Channel port in the distance. At last she was going abroad. At last she was going to leave England for another adventure.

There was a deafening silence from home. She'd given them all Diana's address but none of them was writing. What did she expect after running away? She thought about Joy and how she was settling for so little: a Grimbleton suburb, hubby and baby in pram with a dribbling nose. Joy was fast becoming a stranger. Connie still had that vision of her enveloped in a white veil on her wedding day like some virgin sacrifice, and she experienced again that flutter of unease. Had Joy had an accident? Was their friendship really at an end now she was married? At least Rosa wrote back to say she was touring with a backup group and it was hard work, and not to tell Maria it was a rubbish job.

Now the band was on its way to some international student convention on the Swiss border. It was going to be so exciting except that Sandra talked non-stop until Connie's ears were aching. Then the exhaust began to roar and the van spluttered, drawing attention from passing cars.

'I thought you said they'd changed the exhaust for us?' Marty yelled at Jack, watching his black eyebrows knitting together into a frown.

'There wasn't the cash. It'll do later. What's a puff of smoke between friends?' he shouted, but Marty was not amused.

There wasn't time to phone home before they

embarked, and soon Connie watched the waves crashing against the ship in the darkness while some of the others rushed to the loos to be sick. Only then she felt again the instinct to call home. She watched Marty on the top deck, pacing the boards, lost in his own world. His face was stern and he kept shaking his head as he talked to himself.

'Can I help?' she offered. 'You look worried.'

'Just lay off, give me some peace, Con. Don't follow me around like a lap dog.'

His words slapped her across the cheeks more than any blow.

At Calais she went in search of a telephone. It took an age to get through and there were only a few minutes to speak to Auntie Su.

'Thank God, Connie, where are you? I rang Diana and she said you'd disappeared again. What is going on? I can hear ship horns.' Su sounded anxious and far away. 'Come home, we need you. Grandma Esme has broken her hip in her garden.'

'I can't. I'm in France. When did this happen?' Connie asked. How could that instinct be so accurate? 'Is she OK?'

'She's not taking it very well. I need you to help me.' Su was shouting, but the line was weak. There was a pause. 'Why are you in France? Time to come home.'

'I can't. I have a commitment here with the band. Can't Joy help?'

'Joy is on bed rest, doctor's orders.'

'I'll send a card... I'll come back at the end of the month,' Connie shouted. 'Look, I'm on my way to Switzerland for a student gathering. I can't come home now.' She was crying down the phone.

'Grandma Esme is more important than some student party. This is family. There is still time. Do not shame us,' Su was pleading.

'I can't. I will write to her.'

'Don't bother!' The line went dead. Connie felt terrible. Perhaps she ought to go back on the return ferry.

'What's up? Trouble't Mill?' Marty came up behind her.

'My gran's had a fall,' she said flatly. 'Auntie Su says I ought to go home now.'

'Then you'd better go,' Marty jumped in.

'No, I have a song to sing.'

'We can manage without you. Catch the return ferry back.'

Why was he trying to get shut of her?

'We're here now and my French is better than yours, I expect. I've never been abroad before. I'm not turning back now. Gran's tough; she'll recover. I can help out when we go back.' No Winstanley was going to ruin her big holiday.

'Suit yourself, but I still think you'd be better off going home.'

Connie wished she hadn't rung. Now she felt mean and the uneasy feeling was just getting worse.

They drove through the night down moonlit roads lined with poplars, sleeping in a ditch by a cabbage patch in sleeping bags lined up for warmth. There was no time for any romantic trysts as they woke, stiff as boards and ravenous. They breakfasted by the roadside, sharing batons of white crusty bread and fruit. It was enough to be on foreign soil listening to the bustle of French villages coming to life, the toot of horns and the smell of smoky cafés where they stopped for bowls of hot chocolate.

They whizzed through the battlefields of the Great War without stopping, past those sad gardens full of white crosses. Connie's head was reeling with Auntie Su hanging up on her. She had shamed the family in not respecting tradition, after all they had done for her, but Gran had sent her away empty-handed and she felt she owed the old lady nothing. They rattled on through the countryside, miles and miles of lonely straight roads, and she fell asleep with exhaustion to escape everyone's moaning and barking at each other. They arrived late at the camp, hidden on the slopes near Interlaken on the second night, tired, hungry and dishevelled. Connie fell into her allotted bunk without a murmur.

It was like being at Guide camp, segregated into bunkhouses, taking turns to do washing-up and setting tables, preparing meals by rote. The campsite was damp and cold at night, with thin blankets. Connie and Sandy were sharing with two other students, who stared at their dirty clothes with disapproval. It was then that they realised this was no jolly students' shindig but a political convention of international student action groups, a hotbed of left-wing socialist groups, who had come to be lectured and talked at, preparing for political action.

Eva was one of the leading German students,

with ripples of white-gold hair rolling down her back. She wore jeans and a leather waistcoat. Her English was perfect, her ice-blue eyes discerning. Marty and Des seemed to be consulting her at every turn.

'Trust us to land in some hotbed of socialist action. Wait until we get hold of Billy Froggatt! Does this look like one long party to you? The aim of this lot is to stir up student unrest, prepare them for battle,' Marty said, sifting through all the leaflets on display in the meeting hall.

The lectures were in German and English in a barrack-like dining hall, which also served as a bar. There were small discussion groups and splinter groups for the leaders to muster enthusiasm and swap ideas. There were German documentaries with subtitles, which lulled Connie to sleep with boredom.

Why were they here? Was this what they'd busked for, given up normal lives? Connie tried not to think of Gran, struggling in plaster on her own. Neville would do his bit, she knew, but she couldn't help feeling guilty. The best part of her day was drinking beer and attending gatherings in the evening after supper.

None of them had ever tasted this sort of Continental food: bowls of yoghurt and chopped fruit bitter to the tongue, plates of cold meats, sausages and deep cauldrons of vegetables served up like a stew with sauerkraut and pickles, vast cheese boards. Breakfast was just bread and hot milky coffee substitute, and for packed lunch on walking days there was a lump of holey cheese, a hunk of bread and an apple.

Eva's group were friendly and walked alongside Marty and the boys on the hike. She drew them like a magnet. Connie struggled in tight black leather boots that rubbed her heels after a mile and pinched her toes, giving blisters the size of eggs.

On the evening after their first walk, Marty gathered them together. 'We've got a problem. They don't want rock'n'roll, they want folk and protest. We're supposed to be some subversive cell from Leeds Uni, not singing Western capitalist music. Eva says we must fit in or not sing at all. I don't believe it. All this way for nothing! He's lead us up a gumtree. Wait till I get my hands on your friend Billy!' He was pointing at Jack and Sandy. Then he disappeared to continue his talk with Eva.

Connie felt dumped like heavy baggage. She was left to her own devices, sitting under a tree with a guitar trying not to feel sick. Marty hadn't been near her for days. What had she done wrong? It was as if she was just one of the group and no one special, and that hurt. Perhaps if she could write them a song they might be able to perform and everything would be all right again? She'd taken his advice and written down the bits and pieces that popped into her head. What they needed now was a folksy number, something like Joan Baez sang, but tunes didn't come so easily to her.

Connie shut her eyes, wondering if this was her punishment for not going home, then drifted off into a daydream and woke up with a line: 'I've got the war baby blues.' All of them were war babies, born when their countries were enemies. Now they were children of peace, a peace proving so fragile, threatened by nuclear war: Berlin, Russia, Hungary, America, Cuba, the Bay of Pigs invasion fiasco. Had nothing been learned after two World Wars?

She thought about Freddie, the dad she never knew. Was she like him in any way? Had his death in Palestine been worthwhile or just another pointless accident of war?

Soldier, soldier gone for slaughter,
Left his daughter baby blue,
Soldier soldier, what you fought for
Left the kid you never knew.

She repeated it in her head over and over until she found the tune of an old folk song, the one they used in *Z Cars* on the TV.

'Sandy, wake up. How does this sound?' she asked, wondering if the lyrics made any sense to anyone else.

Soldier, soldier gone for slaughter
Left the kid, you never knew
Soldier soldier, what you fought for.
Only flags, red, white and blue.

'That's brilliant!' said Marty, giving her a hug.

Once they got hold of the idea everyone stayed behind in the barracks to practise the harmonies and get the song off pat. Even Lorne Dobson gave Connie a hug and laughed.

'You've saved our bacon. We can add a few more verses and the usual protest CND songs but you bet, when they're all drunk and we bash

250

out a few numbers, they'll be up and dancing on the floor. This is a weird place and no mistake, a cross between a nunnery and a prisoner-of-war camp, and it gives me the willies. All that political stuff – they are so deadly serious about it. Marty seems very taken with Eva,' he added in a whisper, making mischief.

'So?' Connie smiled through her teeth. 'We're not joined at the hip.'

'Just as well then.' He winked at her.

On the last night of their gig, Connie stood up and introduced their new number with a new-found pride.

'I'd like to dedicate this to my dad, Freddie, who I never knew, who died in Palestine at the hands of Israeli separatists, and my late mother, Ana, who was a partisan in Crete, a prisoner of war and refugee.'

She sang first, the others joined in. They sang it straight off, adding a few more verses. The catchy tune soon caught on with first the English students and then the others. Everyone seemed pleased, and the beer flowed, and then some of the Brits asked for a few beat numbers and no one objected, and soon everybody was dancing just as Lorne predicted.

Connie was high with the success, looking round for Marty. He was dancing with Eva and her friend and not looking in her direction at all.

'What did I tell you?' Lorne whispered. 'That Lorelei German *Mädchen* has stolen his eyes.'

'So I see,' Connie said, knocking back the spice beers as if they were fizzy pop. 'Come on then. Let's beat them at their own game,' she said to

251

him, trying to look cool, but fuming inside. They danced and did the shake, fooled around, but she didn't care. Lorne could move like the devil, his hair flopping over his forehead, his eyes rolling as he sent himself up. He might not be the world's greatest looker but he did have a strange hypnotic allure when he was dancing, his limbs loose and suggestive, his hips thrusting.

'Have another,' he said, shoving a glass in her hand, and she just let the drink flow over her. What was the point? When she looked across the room neither Marty nor Eva was there dancing. If he was out there in the moonlight with Eva what was the point of crying into her beer? Two could play at that silly game, she smiled, and took hold of Lorne's hand and put it round her waist. Time to see if the famous Lorne's loins were as good as their reputation.

It was a brief, careless, headstrong act of drunken sex, but revenge was sweet. They tripped in the darkness, stumbling over each other, giggling and kissing. Lorne was expert at removing hooks, buttons, bras and other impediments. They were both so sozzled she couldn't recall whether it was good or not when she woke up at dawn on the damp grass with such a hangover and a tongue like a cork doormat. She attempted to totter back to her bunk.

Marty was already up, packing the van with a face like thunder.

'Where the hell did you get to last night?' he demanded.

'Not a million yards from where you were with Eva, I expect,' she snapped back.

'How could you be so stupid? We were here to sing, not fool around,' he replied, ignoring her jibe.

'Speak for yourself,' she sneered. 'I had a great time.'

'Yes, I saw you making doe eyes at Lorne. For God's sake, you must have been out of your head. You disappoint me, Connie. That was cheap and it'll make problems. How could you stoop so low?'

'Is he bothering you, honey?' Lorne staggered forth with his rucksack, putting his arms around Connie.

She wriggled free. 'I'm fine. I'll go and pack. Show's over, I suspect.' She was feeling sick and stupid and very small.

'You can say that again,' said Marty. 'We've made no money. The van's on its last legs.'

'This's been a complete waste of time,' Des added, slinging his rucksack back into the van. 'All that stupid propaganda, what's it all in aid of?'

'Ask Marty. He was the one having private lectures with the lovely Eva. I bet she was a trap to hook you into their schemes to change the world.'

'And you can belt up or smoke a joint, Dobson. You haven't exactly helped things along,' Marty exploded.

'Don't go blaming me for Connie's little night on the tiles. You started it.'

'Oh, shut it!'

'No, you shut it. You don't order us around like Mr Hitler. We're a group, a democratic, not autocratic, collective – decision makers. At least I've learned that in the last past few days.'

'Bullshit, Dobson. This band is rubbish without

a leader. You're always half cut and now you screw my girl.'

'I'm not your girl, or anybody's, for that matter,' piped Connie. 'So shut up, the both of you.' It was awful to see everything disintegrating like this. She was sobering up fast and now she was feeling cheap and silly.

'Well, I might as well tell you ... I'm out of it,' said Marty, as Jack, Des, Lorne circled round him with Connie and Sandra clinging on to each other. 'I'm leaving, going solo. I've had an offer. It just hasn't worked out, has it? We've had three months and this fiasco is the last straw.'

Everyone stood shocked, heads down, but Marty continued, 'It's better we split up now. You can all regroup. I want to do other stuff ... experiment. Tony has some ideas.'

'Has that poofter been feeling you up then?' Lorne sneered.

Marty leaped at him and punched him. 'Just shut it, big mouth. You think with your dick!'

Connie couldn't stand it and turned away in tears. 'What about me then?' she whispered.

Marty pulled her to the side, out of earshot, of the others. 'Look, Connie, you're still a kid. Go back and finish your studies, make up with your family. I'm not ready to be tied down. Write some more songs and send them out. But I'm travelling solo from now on.'

The journey back was long, dreary and full of tension. Everyone was shocked by Marty's defection. The van's exhaust finally gave up and they had a struggle to find enough cash to have it wired together. They scrumped apples off trees and had to share a loaf of bread and drink water, hunger making them all tetchy. Lorne kept trying to snuggle up to Connie but she was having none of it.

What a stupid thing to have done in a drunken haze, and with Lorne, of all people. She couldn't stand him. He was just a port in a storm and she'd been so angry and hurt she'd lashed out and hurt herself even more. All she had to look forward to was going back north and trying to make amends.

Everything was changed. She felt soiled and full of remorse. Marty had been planning this defection all along. That was why he'd gone cold, distanced himself and made up to Eva. No wonder she had felt something was going wrong. The summer of love was well and truly over.

As she hung over the rails of the ferry trying to breathe in the sea air, sensing everything was over, words drifted into her head.

You packed the suitcase full of my dreams and
  threw it down the stairs
When you cheated on me.
You put a stop to all my loving schemes and
  chucked them from the window
When you cheated on me.
What did I do to deserve all this pain? How can
  I ever trust you again?
I'm standing at the bus stop now, with nowhere
  to go, and the fog's coming down
A suitcase full of broken dreams, nowhere to go
  and the fog's coming down.

Through her tears, Connie ferreted in her

rucksack and pulled out the jotting pad. At least she'd learned one thing from Marty Gorman. Never miss some good lyrics.

Connie paces the airport lounge, looking at her watch. Why doesn't the plane land? She explained so much in her letters, trying to set her story in the context of those distant times.

The colours of the swinging sixties might have been oranges and limes and purples, black and white, geometric stripes and swirls, but when Connie thinks of that time she sees only grey and denim and mourning shades. They say if you can remember your student days in the sixties – all that measuring time through coffee spoons – then you weren't really there, she sighs. Sex, drugs and rock and roll were supposed to begin in 1963. That's not true, of course.

She'd done it all: sex, purple hearts, smoked grass, listened to the Beatles' first big albums through tears and pain and grief. Recalling every month of that time as if it was yesterday.

It's hard growing up without a mother's love to guide you.

All that was left was to hitchhike back to Grimbleton to eat humble pie, tail between legs.

There was a frosty chill in the air when she dumped her bags in the hall at Waverley. Her room was let and she was sent to live with Gran as her nursemaid. Every rebellion has its price.

'Do you think you can just swan back here and take up where you left off? Go back to school? You blotted your copybook there by not sitting your exams and we had to pay the fees. It's the technical college and work for you.' Gran had had the last word as usual.

There was always this hole in my heart, a gaping void in the middle waiting to be filled. First when Mama died and then later... Whatever I did to try to fill the gap, it never closed up, she sighs. How could it when that first summer of love was over and the winter of pain began?

17

23 November 1963

'I hear the runaway came back to Division Street and got short shrift from that Susan ... quite right too. Now the girl's up at Esme's, making herself useful, for once,' said Ivy, watching her son preening himself in the mirror. 'I see you've bought another new shirt. We'll have to get a bigger wardrobe, you've got that much stuff, Neville,' she added, eyeing him up. 'Black and white stripes is a bit loud... You look like a spiv. Dancing ... or out with that Trevor again?'

'Might be.' Neville was cagey. His mother was always sniffing around, waiting for him to bring Trevor home, but he never would.

'I hear he's off the Willows council estate and rough with it. What about Basil? You used to be right pally with him. I liked him. His dad is a dentist.'

'Basil's moved to Manchester.'

'Got a girlfriend, has he?'

'Something like that,' he replied. How could he

257

tell his mother that Basil was living in Didsbury with a guy twice his age, a right silver fox who played in the Hallé Orchestra.

'I wish you'd bring your friends back so I can meet them,' she continued.

So you can vet them, more like, he thought. She'd take one look at Trevor and think him common, rough-spoken and not good enough to be a friend for her precious son. God only knew what she'd think if she knew the truth about their relationship.

'Trevor and me thought we'd try further afield,' he lied. 'Go for a Chinese and then on to Manchester.'

'Well, put some petrol in the car then. I'm not forking out for your trips. Trevor should pay his whack. He gets enough free rides these days.'

'Oh, don't be mean. He's got his widowed mother to support.'

'Aye, and on a plasterer's wage, I gather. I can't see what you two have in common at all except the Operatic.'

She'd have a fit if she knew what they got up to after the rehearsals were over. Trevor was as keen as he was with their lovemaking – fast and furious and the best he'd ever had. Sometimes it was as much as they could do to keep their hands off each other in public. How could his fussy mother understand any of that? Now, his father was living with Shirley most of the time while Mum was growing fat in front of the television every night. He'd feel sorry for her if she wasn't so nosy.

'I'll be late so don't wait up,' he shouted as he straightened his tie. How could he tell her he was in love, courting and full of plans?

They met up as usual at the Golden Dragon for chow mein, chips and banana fritters, chatting over their day like an old couple. Trevor had taken his mother shopping and round the Saturday market. He was rehearsing his new part for the next show, *Oklahoma!*, with their voice coach, Audrey Ramsden, and he was plastering up a bedroom wall for one of his neighbours in his spare time.

'I looked like a snowman when I finished,' he smiled.

'You don't now; you smell divine,' Neville said.

'I like the new shirt, it's very trendy,' Trevor replied.

'Only the best for the best. Where shall we go from here?' Neville asked.

Trevor winked. 'What about Leaper's View. It's quiet up there and we haven't seen each other for days.' There was promise in those flashing eyes.

Neville grinned. 'Leaper's View it is then. I'll just go and settle up.'

'No, it's my treat,' Trevor replied. 'You always pay. It makes me feel like a kept man.'

'I wish we could live together, you and me, sharing a bed like any normal couple,' said Neville, knowing such a dream was never going to happen for them.

'We're not normal, though, are we?' Trevor said softly. 'We're not free to do as we please. We have to be careful. I don't want anyone to get hurt.'

'That's what I like about you, Trevor, you're so thoughtful. I get so frustrated and mad. It's not fair. We aren't bothering anyone else, are we?'

They drove up through the town, the foggy lights

and the streets fading as they turned from the suburbs into country lanes and up to the moor and the layby that looked down over the whole of the Lancashire plain. There was only one saloon car at the corner, its windows already steamed up.

'I love it here,' Trevor said. 'It's like the whole world's at our feet.' He nestled his head on Nev's shoulder. 'I wish we could stay here for ever, just you and me.'

'You'd soon get cramp,' Neville quipped, pulling him down onto his lap.

They tussled and kissed, unbuttoning themselves, aroused by the taste and scent of each other.

'I'll never get enough of you,' Neville sighed, his fingers wandering over Trevor's bulge.

Then a torch blinded them for a second. Christ! He couldn't see. A voice was shouting and a fist banging on the window.

'Get out, you perverts, out of the car. What have we here?'

'Just a couple of queers on the job, Constable.'

'Do you see what I see? Is that a trunk I see, popping out of those trousers? Blimey, it's more like a stovepipe. Out! Names...?'

Trevor covered his eyes. 'Please, we were doing no harm,' he pleaded.

'That's what they all say, sonny. What you are doing is against the law and we are here to uphold the law of the land. Save your defence for the bench. We've been told puffs like you are using Leaper's View as a rendezvous.'

The other constable got out his notebook. 'Names, addresses, and no lies.'

Neville felt sick, shaking. 'Look, we've taken your warning, just leave it at that, for pity's sake,' he argued. Trevor was sobbing. 'Let him go, just take me.'

'Out, the both of yous, or we'll call for reinforcements and they will not hesitate to use force. Come on chaps, the game's up. Time to pay your due. It's the police station for both of you.'

Esme watched her granddaughter vacuuming round the room like one of the Furies. Since her return, Connie was making a real effort to make up for letting her down. But there was silence between them that was worrying. The girl was peaky, with rings under her eyes, and the bounce had gone out of her. That Gorman lad had dumped her as she'd always sensed he might. It didn't do to mix faiths in Grimbleton.

Now he was back in London making records, and the rest of the band, it appeared, were back in town trying to find work.

Connie was now at the technical college to do her A-level resits. At least she could resit them in November, and it was a relief to see her with her head down in her books, silly madam, but the light had gone out of her eyes as if the dream had died. She looked just as she had when Ana died.

This dratted hip was slow to mend and stiffening her up, and it was so painful. If this was old age, you could keep it. She was like a creaking gate on rusty hinges; every move across the room must be calculated and aided with two sticks. Dr Gilchrist said she must keep moving or else, but cleaning was out of the question, walking, shopping, all the pleasures she had taken for granted, were off limits. It was a slow shuffle, a game of cards, the TV, gramophone, and visiting friends the highlight of her day. Connie circled round her, quiet, polite, almost too dutiful. Esme could see her heart was aching but now that she was home, all's well that ended well. Though Connie hadn't apologised for letting them down and running away. It was as if these young ones thought it was their right to do what they pleased with themselves. What had happened to their sense of duty and responsibility within the family? She'd hardly seen Joy since the summer – on bed rest still, or so they said. Su wouldn't let her leave the house much. Denny didn't want her being bothered by visitors either.

It was now she missed Ana, whose nursing would have given Esme good care. Levi was still in disgrace, having ditched his home to live with Shirley, the blonde bombshell on the stocking bar. Ivy was going round like a demented widow until Esme told her to pull herself together and get a proper job. Now she was working in the dress department of Whiteleys store, pretending all was well when it wasn't. What was happening to her family?

Only Neville had bothered to come and take her out but she couldn't get into the Triumph. They had to use the work's van. At least he'd taken her across the town to visit old friends. It was sad thinking of all those outings in the old days when the kiddies were little: the Olive Oil Club, Ana, Su, Maria, Diana, Queenie, gone or busy with their own lives now. Lily was kind but

Arthur was at that grabbing stage, and into her cupboards like a whirling dervish, wanting to play football all the time. A chip off the old block there. She was glad when they had gone home.

'Want a cuppa?' Connie asked. 'Cocoa or Nescafé?'

'A pot of tea will do nicely. You've bottomed this room properly. Come and sit down.'

'If it's all right, I'll go to bed. I'm whacked. I can't keep my eyes open, but I'll bring you a drink. Shall I switch on the TV?'

'You might as well, if you're going to bed.'

Connie switched on the box in the corner cabinet. The news was on.

'It's not that time already, is it? No ... hang on. It's something to do with America,' Connie said, standing by the door. The sound always took a long time to come through.

'Oh, no!' There was a scene of a motorcade in Dallas, the president and his wife, in her pink pillbox hat, and the chaos and the car speeding off. 'What's going on?'

'John Kennedy's been shot, and he's dead, Gran. The president of America's dead ... he was doing such a good job,' Connie gasped, almost in tears. 'Why do the good die young?'

Esme thought of little Travis and Freddie and Ana. 'His poor wife and kiddies,' she said. 'What is this world coming to? Fetch the brandy ... dear, oh dear. Is it the Russians? Turn the sound up.'

They sat there, sipping brandy and tea as bulletin after bulletin unfolded on that November evening, unaware that the doorbell was ringing until someone was banging with their fist.

'Who on earth is that?' Esme said. 'I bet it's Edna from next door, wanting to talk it all over. Go and see who it is, love.'

Connie brought Neville into the room. 'You've heard then about Kennedy?' she said.

Neville nodded, pale-faced, grim. 'Everybody's talking about it in the street, Gran.' He stood hesitating.

'Isn't it terrible news? Not another war. I thought he'd sorted out the Russians and all those Cuban missiles,' she continued, but Neville said nothing, standing before them, shaking. 'What's up, son? You look as if you've seen a ghost.'

'I've been arrested, Gran,' he cried, falling into her arms like a little boy, sobbing. 'I'm in trouble and I don't know what to do.'

'Connie, get us another cup. It can't be that bad, surely.' But she felt her heart skipping beats and her legs wobbling beneath her. He didn't look drunk. He wasn't the type, not like his father. Perhaps he wasn't the sharpest knife in the drawer but Neville had a steady job and was enjoying being in the amateur dramatics.

'I can't tell Mum and Dad. They'll kill me,' he wept breaking down. 'We weren't doing any harm to anybody,' he said, looking up, and she noticed, not for the first time, how attractive, how appealing his eyes were, fringed with dark lashes, almost girlish. A terrible thought stabbed Esme but she pushed it back... 'Go on then, spill the beans. Your gran is all ears,' she said. 'Turn the telly down, Connie.'

'Trevor and I weren't doing any harm,' he whispered.

'Trevor?' she asked.

'Trevor is my friend, my chum. We'd been out for a few drinks, and to the Chinese and then for a ride in the car,' he replied, not looking her in the face.

'So? What's the harm in that or did you crash the car?'

'No, Gran, there wasn't an accident. We went up to Leaper's View for some air. You can see the lights of Manchester down the plain. We often go there to ... talk,' he said.

Esme went cold, knowing it was a notorious spot for lovers to canoodle.

'You weren't being Peeping Toms, were you?'

'They were spying on *us*,' he croaked.

'Who?' This was all too confusing so late at night.

'The coppers. Two policemen came and put their torches on us when we were...' Neville halted, unable to go on.

'When you were doing what?' She didn't understand. 'Watching the view?'

'Not exactly. You see, we were being friendly and they put their torch on us and arrested us.'

'When you were chatting?' she said coldly. The silence was deafening.

'No, we were kissing and such...' he whispered. 'There were other cars, but they didn't go spying on them did they? If it were Connie and her boy-friend out in the car no one would bother them, but because it's two men ... we're finished, exposed in the papers. Dad'll kill me,' he wept. 'It's not fair.'

She looked at his crumpled face, his eyes filled

265

with tears. 'Eeh, son, I didn't think you were that type of a lad but I suppose you allus were a bit different. I put it down to Ivy's spoiling. You tell your parents the truth... Don't let them read it in the papers first. I expect Ivy will want to marry you off to prove your innocence, but they'll want what's best for you, I'm sure,' she offered, more in hope than certainty. It would rock them to their foundations and they'd each blame the other.

'However did you get mixed up with them nancy boys?' she sighed. No point shillyshallying.

'It's not like that, Gran. I can't help it. I love Trevor. You'll like him,' he said.

'How old is he?' she asked.

'Old enough to know his own mind,' Neville replied.

'That's a relief. You can get sent to prison for interfering with young boys,' she answered, thinking about the Lord Montagu case a few years back. 'By heck, you know how to make life complicated.'

'I didn't choose to be this way. We're harming no one, but now the whole town will laugh at us and I'll have to go away.'

'Perhaps you will after the fuss dies down, but now you have to face the music, show your mettle, be a man not a mouse,' she ordered.

'Dad'll call me queer and Mother will never speak to me again... I feel like jumping off a cliff.'

'Oh, no you don't! That's the easy way, son. Show them you're strong, that you choose to own up to who you are. That's all I can say. I'll be proud of you if you answer your charge bravely. We won't desert you, will we, Connie?'

Connie put her arm around her cousin and gave him a hug.

'Will you tell them for me?' he pleaded.

'Have you not heard one word I've said? Just do it!' Esme ordered. 'Besides, there are far worse things in life than being queer,' she offered, surprised at her own broad-mindedness. There'd been some funny love affairs when she was a suffragette, and she often wondered about Diana Unsworth.

'Like what?' he sighed, looking for crumbs of comfort.

'Like being mean-spirited and a hypocrite, for a start, or being violent to kiddies and animals, being a bully and a liar. What you do with your private life is up to you?'

'Come on, it's late. I expect you want a bed on the sofa. No point in going home now. It'll look better in the light of day.'

'I feel such a fool.'

'What does Trevor think?'

'I don't know. They wouldn't let me see him. What a bloody mess!'

'None of that language in this house. It's a messy business being different, right enough. People like us all to be the same, think the same thoughts, and them in the right order. It makes us feel safe, I suppose. Look at the mess our Freddie got into,' she sighed.

'That was different. He wasn't a queer and everyone hates queers,' said Neville.

'I don't know about that son, but I'm tired. We'll talk about it tomorrow. Good night and God bless... Pray for that widow and kiddies in

America,' she said, touching his lips with her finger.

'Gran, you're a good egg.'

'A scrambled egg, perhaps,' she replied, managing a weak laugh. 'All I need now is sleep and plenty of it. And keep the television down low if you're watching the news. We'll find a way through, won't we?'

When Esme was safe in her bedroom, Connie and Neville huddled under a blanket in the lounge, sipping Horlicks and dunking biscuits, watching the news reports.

'What am I going to do, Con? They'll kill me... Those coppers were waiting up there on the off chance, hidden in the bushes. They thought it was a joke. It's our lives they're messing with. How can I face Strangeways? I've heard such tales about what they do to guys like me in there.'

'It won't come to that. The family will find a good lawyer. You've never been in any trouble before. You're nineteen. It'll be OK.' The truth was she'd heard the same things, but why put the fear of God into him now?

'Trevor's only seventeen... Oh, it's such a mess.'

'It's not as bad as the mess I'm in, Nev. I think I'm pregnant.' Her worst fears were finally given voice.

Neville looked up. 'You are joking?'

'I wish I was. I've missed two periods. I've never done that before. My bra is tight and I feel sick each morning.'

'Have you told Marty Gorman?'

'He's gone to Hamburg.'

'You must contact him. He'll do the honourable thing.'

'I can't.' How could she tell anyone she wasn't sure whose baby it was?

'If you won't then I will. No one knocks up my cousin and gets away with it!' he added.

'Thanks, but it's more complicated than that. I did something stupid. Please leave it to me. I'll sort something out. You have enough on your plate. Don't tell a soul, I beg you. I'm trusting you with this. Promise?'

'What do you take me for? Have you seen a doctor?'

'No, not yet. I wanted to be sure. I wish my mama was here. She'd know what to do.'

'You must tell someone soon... Joy or Rosa. They'll help you.'

'I can't, Nev. I'm so scared!'

'Me too. How am I going to break the news?'

'Maybe like Gran says ... just come out with it and see what happens. I'll come with you, if you like, for support.'

'I suppose we could do it together. They wouldn't know who to beat up first.' Neville gave a false giggle.

'That's better,' Con whispered. 'There's got to be a funny side somewhere in all this, but the future's bleak for both of us right now.'

'We could cook them a meal, invite them to lunch, soften them up on roast beef and Yorkshires...'

Connie couldn't believe he was being serious. 'I can't cook in my condition. I'd throw up all over them,' she replied.

'But I can,' said Neville. 'I wasn't joking. Kill two birds with one stone.'

'Better make it a chicken then,' Connie said.

'Think about it. Only those who need to know: Gran, Su and my parents. We stand together on this one, kiddo. Remember the family motto: Family First and Foremost.'

'It'll have to be soon. Gran'll be so furious. I'll get chucked out,' Connie groaned.

'It'll be hatchets at dawn for me. My lot will just bury me in the back garden. Oh, Connie, why do we do these things?'

'Because we are who we are. I didn't think, and you forgot to be careful,' Connie sighed.

'We both forgot to be careful,' Neville replied.

Connie sat in the college, not taking a word in. Everyone was talking about the assassination of President Kennedy and his poor family, saying where they were when they heard the terrible news. All she could think about was her own predicament and Neville's court case, all the shame coming on the family and her future.

How could she look after a child and do her studies, make a home? Would Su let her back to the Waverley or could she stay with Gran in Sutter's Fold. What if Neville, her only ally, was sent to prison?

What no one must know was that she wasn't sure who the father of this baby could be. Was it Marty, or Lorne Dobson after that one drunken spree? She'd no idea, and that fact alone would make her a slut in anyone's eyes. Better to say nothing, better to hold her doubts to herself.

They would be too stunned to take much in at first so she had time to make plans now her A levels were resat. Studying had been her one consolation and she felt sure her results would get her a university place, but first there would be a summer baby to see to.

The thought of trying to get rid of it never entered her head. The poor thing hadn't asked to be born, but it deserved a chance in life. She'd heard tales of knitting needles and hooks, gin baths and other extreme measures. There were clinics where rich girls could get sorted by discreet doctors, but she was not one of them. Mama had given her a chance of life by coming here. She had been so strong and brave, and Connie must be the same now.

On the way home, she took a detour by the allotment where Mama used to grow vegetables, and sat on the old stool where they used to pod broad beans for their special bean stew.

'Mama, what shall I do? You once knew what I am feeling now. How do I soften the blow? Auntie Su must have felt the same, but Gran, Ivy, Levi – how will they react?' Auntie Lee would be a good listener, she knew, but she felt so ashamed of herself. *Why did you have to die before I realised just how strong and special you were? No one worries about you like your own mother.* Now she was gone, and everything was unsafe.

Now she was dangling over a precipice, with Neville holding the very slack rope. Joy was too ill to help and Rosa was far away. Neville was right: they just had to help each other out on Sunday when the Winstanleys were going to get

271

the shock of their lives, and no mistake. One thing was certain: most of them would have indigestion by the time the meal was over.

'What's all this in aid of?' said Esme when she got back from chapel to find the table was laid for six with the best embroidered cloth, the one with hollyhocks in the corner. She had prayed to the Almighty to send a miracle of understanding and compassion for poor Neville. It wasn't his fault he was born that way. Her husband, Redvers, used to say it was written right through the rock if a man was inclined to his own... There was no changing them, but she wasn't sure.

Now there was a distinct tincture of burning fat, gravy and roasting meat. Connie's best attempt at apple pie crust looked a bit like rubber rings, and the best crystal still had the dust on it. It was like setting the table for the prodigal son.

So, that was Neville's scheme? He was going to tell his mother and father in the safety of a strange house? But who was the sixth place for? Not Trevor Gilligan, surely?

Then the mystery deepened when Susan drove up in her smart Mini. She'd been to the parish church. Connie was busy in the kitchen with her head down. She'd gone so thin since coming back from her trip and hardly ate a morsel. But she and Neville were apparently doing this as a thank you.

Ivy came up on the bus, having refused a lift from Levi. He was put out at missing his own dinner. But Gran had insisted he came when he rang to see what the fuss was about.

'You'd better come along. I know Ivy's coming.

They're doing a meal especially for the family. You can have your tea at Shirley's later, but I want you to promise to drive our Ivy back home.'

'I'm getting a divorce, Mother.'

'Not while I'm alive, you won't. There's been no divorces in this family. You made your vows quick enough, so stick with them a while longer.'

'Oh, Mother, there's no shame in it nowadays.'

'There is in my book. I shall cut you out of my will.'

'Mam, this life is not a rehearsal,' he offered.

'It is ... for the world to come. You're on trial in this life.'

'Do you really believe that?'

'The Lord sends little tests to prove our mettle.' Wait till you hear what he is sending you today, she thought. 'Just turn up. Believe me, it's important.'

Connie's heart was thumping in her chest. She just wanted to blurt it all out and get it over with, but this was Neville's big moment; hers would come later. She tested the roast potatoes as Neville was hovering over the gravy. He was such a fusspot when it came to food, always bossing her around. She'd put fresh flowers on the table, linen napkins and water glasses, and Neville had bought a bottle of expensive wine. The thought of alcohol turned Connie's stomach.

'What are we celebrating?' said Ivy, puffing as she removed her fur hat and coat. 'It's a steep walk up that hill.'

'Levi could have fetched you,' said Esme.

'I'd rather walk, thank you. I'm not putting my behind on any seat Shirley Fletcher has been

273

sitting on. You never know what I might catch,' she sniffed. 'He's late, as usual. And is this all your work, Constance?' she sniffed, 'My, you're looking peaky. That French air didn't do much good for you then, did it.'

'Come into the sitting room and admire the view. Susan's already here,' Connie said, biting her tongue.

'Is this some family powwow? I'm honoured to be invited, I'm sure,' said Ivy, sitting down on the most comfortable chair and nodding in Su's direction. 'How's the mother-to-be be? What's all this in aid of?'

Su smiled. 'I don't know. I got a summons like you. Joy is on bed rest. They can't get her blood pressure down. I am so worried.'

'Connie and I thought it was about time we had a family gathering to thank Gran for her hospitality and to...' Neville paused.

'Anyone for sherry?' Connie passed the flutes around on a silver tray, trying not to shake it too much.

Then the front door flew open and Levi filled the hall. 'Sorry I'm late folks. How's the legs, Mother?'

'It's my hip, and it is on the mend, or it was.'

'Good ... good.'

Connie blurted out, 'Is that the gravy?'

'There's a good smell coming from the kitchen. Has Connie been busy?'

'Neville's done it, actually,' said Connie.

Levi looked at his son. 'You don't take after your pa, then. I wouldn't know one oven knob from the other,' he laughed, face pink with exertion. 'So what's new?'

'Would you like to sit down, Dad? There's something I've got to tell you and I'm going to say it only once.'

Connie jumped in. 'What Neville wants to say is that dinner is ready. Let's put everyone at the table. It's a shame to waste all this good cooking.'

Now everyone was nervous, polite, unsure, passing the vegetables around, making small talk. Connie sat at one end with Su to her left and Gran on the other side. Neville put Levi on his right next to Su, and his mother next to Gran so his parents were opposite and not touching.

When the first course was over, to great acclaim, Connie rushed in with her apple pie, with apologies for the rubbery pastry.

'These apples are a bit tart,' commented Ivy.

'I'll get the sugar bowl.' Neville jumped up.

'Sorry, I forgot to sweeten them,' said Connie.

'Look, what's going on?' Levi was flustered. 'I may be thick but I guess we're not here to discuss the price of fish. Out with it. What's up? Do you want a loan? Who's got the sack? Who's crashed the car?'

'Nothing like that, Dad,' Neville faltered, looking to Connie for courage. She nodded and crossed her fingers under the table.

'Then what?' Levi snapped.

'I'm queer.'

'You're what!'

'I'm queer, and me and my friend have been arrested. That's what's up.'

No one spoke. Su busied herself with eating the pudding. Gran briefly covered her face with her napkin.

'He's in a spot of bother, that's all, but we can get a good lawyer. They were targeted,' she said.

'Where?' Levi stuttered.

'Leaper's View.'

'Ivy, did you know?' Levi continued. Everyone was turning to Ivy, who was quietly choking on her apple pie, purple in the face. 'Say something, Ivy ... Ivy? She's going to pass out. Someone do something quickly!'

Auntie Su rushed behind Ivy's chair and thumped her between the shoulder blades. An apple skin shot out of her mouth onto the table cloth.

Connie apologised, 'Oh, sorry, I forgot to peel them.'

Ivy still didn't speak but sat there, rigid.

'I think she's gone into shock,' said Gran, patting her on the hand. 'Ivy, come on, now, it's not that bad. He could have been done for murder or fraud.'

'But what about my grandchildren?' was all she said. 'I want my grandchildren. Every mother wants grandchildren. And if he doesn't get himself wed... He has to get married.'

'I don't think she's taking it in,' said Gran. 'Look, Ivy, your son isn't the marrying kind, as they say. He's a bachelor boy.'

'This is private stuff – why do we have to share it out here?' Levi said, looking at Su and Connie, red in the face. 'Did you know, Mother?'

'Only a few days ago, the night when President Kennedy died. I told him not to hide away and to be a man, and he has. He's done the right thing and now we must do the right thing by him. He is your son.'

'He's no son of mine! A poofter! I'll never live it down at the Legion. A soldier's son, and all.'

'Lots of famous soldiers have loved men,' Connie interrupted. 'Alexander the Great, Achilles ... even Monty was supposed–'

'Don't you dare call the hero of Alamein a poof! He'll have to have treatment. They can give them electric shocks or pills to take away the urges.'

'But what about my grandchildren?' said Ivy.

'Oh, pipe down about your grandchildren, Ivy.'

'Don't you tell me to pipe down, you adulterer! It's all your fault for not being a proper father to him.'

'It's all your fault for pandering to his every whim and making a sissy out of him.'

'Don't you blame me!'

'Shut up moaning. The sooner I'm divorced from you the better.'

'I'll never divorce you!' said Ivy.

'Stop it, both of you! I've told you now, so you can go and I'll not bother you again. I can sort out my own mess without your help. Now you know, so you can all go home. The show's over. I'll be better off living here with Gran.'

'Mother, have you been interfering again?' Levi accused.

Susan stood to leave. 'This is private. I will leave you to your family discussions.'

'You are family,' Gran said. 'Connie wanted you here. Why, I don't know.'

'Because,' Connie gulped. The dreaded moment had come. 'Because Neville is not the only one in trouble. I am pregnant ... three months pregnant!'

Neville stood beside her with his hands on her shoulders. 'She came to support me so I am supporting her.'

'I don't believe it! Not all this palaver all over again. Like mother, like daughter. Connie, how could you do this to us? I thowt you'd have more sense!' Gran spluttered.

'I wasn't thinking of the family when I was doing it,' she quipped.

'Don't you get funny with me, girl. I had to put up with you as babies, all that fakery. Don't you ever learn? How dare you bring shame on the family? I warned you when you ran off, making a fool of yourself...' Gran was puce in the face, struggling for breath. 'You'll be the death of me!'

Susan went to hold Connie's hand. 'I can't take you – the rooms are all let.'

'Well, she's not staying here. I can't cope with a baby at my time of life and my bad hip.'

'I'm not asking for charity. I just need somewhere to stay for a while until my exam results come through. I'll get a job and pay my way for as long as I can.'

'You can stay with us,' said Ivy, smiling. 'Stay with Neville and me. We will look after you.'

Neville's hand stiffened on Connie's shoulder. 'What's brought this change of heart, Mother? You never have a good word to say about Connie.'

'But it's different now.'

'Why?' Everyone was looking puzzled.

'There's one condition, though,' Ivy added.

Levi smiled. 'I knew there would be. She never does anything for free.'

'It's a simple solution to all our problems.

278

Connie will marry Neville ... first cousins can. The baby will be brought up a Winstanley. I have my grandchild. Connie can go to college. The police will not charge a young married man with a baby on the way.'

'She's talking out of her backside as usual. Take no notice, she's off her head,' laughed Levi.

'Wait on,' said Gran. 'Ivy's got a point. If they marry, we keep it in the family, all the scandal. Once Neville's married he can put all this nonsense behind him for good. No one need ever know. It's worth thinking over.'

'But we're more like brother and sister,' Neville said, shocked, and Connie sat stunned.

'So what? There doesn't need to be any of that side of married life. You'll have a kiddy and no one will be any the wiser.'

'But I'm not its father!' he protested.

'I suppose it's one of Gorman's, is it?' Gran added.

Connie said nothing.

'We close ranks, keep this in the family, and the pregnancy will be another nine-day wonder,' Gran continued.

'But I don't want to marry Neville. I don't want to marry anyone.' Connie stood up.

'You'll do as you're told,' Gran shouted. 'You brought this on yourself. If you want a roof over your head, you'll do what I suggest or you're no granddaughter of mine!'

Connie had never seen Gran so angry and hard. Her eyes were flashing like sparks. Connie turned to Neville. 'Say something, Nev. Tell them it's a crazy idea. It won't work.'

'Does it have to? You'll get protection and I get some respect,' he replied.

'And I get my grandchild,' Ivy chuckled.

'It's the only offer on the table, Con. We have to think about it.'

'It's a stupid idea,' said Levi, standing to leave. 'If you don't mind, I'm out of here. You've all gone mad. Su, do you want a lift?'

'Thank you, but I have the car. Jacob is walking up to join me. We want to visit Joy and go for a run. Now Joy is safely married I am thinking for myself for a change.'

'You do right,' said Gran. 'These young ones have got the answer to their troubles in their own hands now. Let them stew on all this for a few days. I'm sure we can rustle up a shotgun wedding in a week or two... I'm off to bed for a rest.'

Neville faced the mountain of washing-up with a sigh. It had not gone how he had expected, and Mother's little outburst had taken the breath out of him. Marry Connie, father another man's baby, live with her as man and wife? How on earth could he do it and see Trevor on the side?

He loved Trevor. He didn't want to dump him but that was the price of getting out of this mess – saying it was just a moment's aberration, done under duress. He could explain that he was engaged and his fiancée was standing by him. There was a baby on the way, a baby he needed to support. It would look good before the judge.

Connie would have a permanent baby-sitter in Ivy. In fact, she'd be able to leave the baby there and do her studying if she wanted to. And yet he'd seen the look on Connie's face when Ivy made the suggestion, made her ultimatum. He was shocked to see how quick Gran was to jump to Ivy's defence.

The idea was all too slick and tempting, but he felt uneasy. Could he possibly go through with such a wild scheme?

18

A Truce

For three weeks Connie went along with their plans. She was taken in secret to see Dr Gilchrist, prodded and poked, pronounced healthy and given iron tablets and free milk tokens. Ivy even bought her a sack dress. Connie looked like a humbug in its black and silver stripes. There were plans to have the reception at their house, seeing as it would be a small wedding, soon after Christmas and before Connie got too big.

Neville saw his lawyers to make his defence but was still fretting about Trevor.

'His mother won't let me through the door,' he said to Connie. 'She says he's got flu, but I don't believe her. They hope to get us off with a caution, especially under the circumstances of your pregnancy. It's like Mam said, they are putting it down to an act against nature and it won't happen again.'

Ivy was all over them like a rash. She'd set aside

281

the boxroom for the nursery. They would have her bedroom and she'd have the back bedroom, three generations in one tiny semi-detached, but not for long. She'd already called on Esme to suggest if Susan was serious with Dr Friedmann, then wasn't it time that she moved out to live nearer to Joy and the baby so they could all go back to the Waverley, the big family house, where Connie could do the housekeeping and go to night school and it would be like old times? Neville would be running the Health and Herbs market stall and she would be able to give up her job and look after the baby for all time. Ivy was all for giving the tenants their notice there and then.

Connie felt sick every time she thought of living with Ivy again. Yet Neville's defence lay in her compliance, and she would not let him down. But as the tiny life fluttered inside her, she knew that she must do the best for this baby, no matter what. But something didn't feel right in her heart and in her gut.

One afternoon she took herself off after college to Longsight Square and the travel agency where Auntie Lee ran the business alongside Avril Crumblehume. They welcomed her in and Connie suggested she might take her aunt to Santini's for a tea break.

They sat in the espresso bar, where once Connie had felt so cool and with it, and now felt sick at the smell of the Gaggia machine.

'I expect Granny has told you my troubles,' she whispered.

Lee held out her hand and nodded. 'I'm sorry, yes, Esme couldn't contain herself. I gather they've made plans for you and Neville. Is that what you want?'

Connie bowed her head. 'I've no choice. It helps Neville out, and Ivy seems to be supporting us.'

'Ivy is out for herself. She will take over your baby. I'd offer to help myself, but Arthur is so active and demanding. He's in nursery part time and there's the business. I just can't help out.'

'I realise that but I have to continue studying. I've messed everything up.'

'You have told the father?'

'No, I can't. He's in showbusiness. It would never work, and it wasn't his fault.'

'Come on, it takes two to tango,' her aunt offered. 'I was wondering if Diana might be able to help. She's always a good listening post. She's got a job near Leeds now, and I know you visited her in London.'

Connie smiled, recalling those busking days. 'She saved us from rotting in our own clothes, gave us a meal, let us wash off the grime. I don't want to impose. We never met Hazel, her friend. She was on duty.'

'Well, they've moved in together to run some nursing home for children with handicaps. Let me give you her address, just in case...'

'Just in case?'

'I ought not to be saying this, Connie, but for Ana's sake I will. Don't always take the first option on offer. There are other ways forward.'

'Like what? If I let them down I'm out on my own,' Connie replied. This was not what she was expecting to hear from her aunt.

'You know the story of how Peter and I met just

283

before I was getting married, how I nearly made it to the altar with the wrong man, but I'd ducked out, to everyone's relief at the last minute? Listen to your heart and your bowels; they never lie: if there is relief and peace in this decision being made for you, go for it, but if not, please be careful,' Lee said, leaning forward so no one could catch their conversation.

'Why are you saying this to me now?' Connie asked.

'Because I care about you, Connie. I was the first person to hold you when I brought your mama from the airport and I promised her I would see you right. I do miss her. She, of all people, would have understood. Oh ... look at the time! I'd better go back.'

They both sniffed back their tears into their cups.

'Think on, trust your gut to tell you what is right.' Lee then wrote down Diana Unsworth's address outside Leeds and left it on the table.

Neville was closing up after a hectic Friday afternoon in the market. New orders had arrived in boxes to be sorted, labelled and shelved, and invoices checked over, while his dad fussed over the counter, sorting out misplaced packets of pulses and dried nuts. Pre-Christmas was always a busy time. Their vegetarian section was going well because of all the articles in the women's magazines about meatless cookery and healthy living.

Neville was sweeping up. His dad had been so silent with him of late, opening his mouth as if to give him an earful and then shutting it with a sigh. Why didn't he just come out with it and say that he was disgusted with him, sick at the thought of having a homo for a son, a Jessie and a soft quilt. But he had gone to the police station with him and stood by him, attended the first hearing and all the solicitor's meetings.

His mother was too busy trying to fix up the wedding on the quiet and buying baby knitting patterns.

'Do you fancy a pint?' Levi said. 'I reckon we've earned it this afternoon. You've nothing to rush back for?'

'I guess not.' Neville hesitated, not sure if he was in for another lecture. 'You'll have to pay, though. I'm skint.'

'You'll be a lot more skint once you're wed,' was his dad's comment as they drew the tarpaulin curtain across the stall. They walked across town side by side. Funny how his dad had shrunk, and it was Neville who was looking down on his father now. They slipped into the King's Arms next to the Variety Theatre, which was being turned into a bingo hall, sat in a corner by the fire and supped in silence.

'Neville, are you sure about this do?' Levi fumbled for words.

'You mean me and Connie? What choice do I have? It's all been decided. I suppose it makes sense for both of us.'

'Does it? In my eyes it's a damn silly idea.'

'Really?'

'You aren't suited. She's a clever girl in trouble, and you are a businessman, one who's not inclined to marriage. It'll be a disaster, in my book.

285

Heed a father's warning!'

'But they've built a case round this marriage and fatherhood. It makes me normal.' Neville looked up, shocked, by his father's stance.

'Son, you're not normal. I mean, you never were... I've been looking back. You were different right from the start. You always preferred Ana and Su's girls to rough and tumble with the street boys. You liked the stage and dressing up, not rugby and football. Was there any funny business at that school? Did anyone interfere with you?' Levi was blushing.

'No, Dad, just the usual boys mucking about and taking the mick. The Lawns was never my cup of tea, but there was Baz. We got by ... just. Why are you saying this, all of a sudden? I don't understand.' He had never had a heart-to-heart with his father before. It felt strange.

'All you need to know is I'm your dad. Whatever else you are ... you're my lad and I'll stand by you. I don't want you getting tied down like this just to please your mum and Gran. I may be a Winstanley, but I've seen enough hanky-panky in this family to know Ivy is not a good influence.

'I never really loved her. She sort of dazzled me and I sleepwalked into marriage after I'd been a prisoner of war. And that's another thing – I saw things there. Men took comfort from each other. There were romances of a sort, some lasting right the way through, some flirting. It's natural in a camp, but then I got to thinking we don't choose how we are.

'Your mum was a pretty typist with big ideas but she has a mean streak. She did something nasty once that had terrible consequences for others, but that's another story. I've never forgiven her that and she knows it, and I wanted to leave years ago but I thought I was doing the right thing by staying. Now you're grown up, old enough to stand on your own. You'll get by without all this family interference. I'll see to that.'

Neville didn't know what to say, he was so touched at his father's honesty. 'I thought you hated me.'

'You're my only son, even though you've chosen a lonely path to live. How can I hate you? I got my life back after the war and a kiddie for my troubles. Our Freddie never got that, but we have to do right by his kiddie too.'

'I don't want to let Connie down. She's in a pickle.'

'She'll get by. If you hitch up together you'll hate each other, and the poor baby will suffer too. Imagine Ivy as its only granny...'

'But the family—'

'Bugger the family, for once. It's every man for himself. Sup up and think on.'

'Rosa's home! Maria phoned Su. She's back from her tour for two days over Christmas. The Monster has given them time off,' yelled Connie, who was busy washing up for Joy, who sat like a beached whale in her maternity smock. This high blood pressure business was a pain. What if it happened to her?

She'd come to admire their nursery bedroom in lemon and green candy stripes with matching curtains from Sanderson's which were the latest must-have accessory. There was a white cot and a Moses basket lined with yellow gingham and lace. The room was piled up with new equipment, a baby bath, nappy bucket and potty set, lovely cot bedding, a wardrobe full of rompers and nighties, hand-knitted shawls and a mound of Terry towelling nappies, muslins, baby towels and a beautiful basket full of powders and creams and nappy pins.

'Have you still got Precious Teddy?' she asked, looking for the battered old toy that came from Burma, all those years ago.

Joy nodded. 'Mummy has it, but Mrs Gregson says everything must be new and hygienic. They have ordered a pram for us: a Silver Cross, but of course it's bad luck to have such a thing in the house. So it's staying in the shop.'

Setting up a junior must cost hundreds of pounds, Connie sighed, looking over the equipment. How could a small baby need so much stuff? There was a sterilising unit, bottles, and she'd seen Joy's list, which was daunting.

'How are you feeling?' she asked, staring round the nursery bedroom with awe. How on earth was she going to afford all this?

'It feels as if it's happening to someone else,' Joy said, patting her tummy. 'How will I ever deliver this football? Denny says I look like an elephant and the sooner I'm back to normal the better. He wants a boy, of course.'

He'll get what he's given, thought Connie. Fatherhood hadn't softened him much then, but she just smiled. *How I wish I could tell you my news. How I wish I could confide in you, but I promised your mother not to burden you with any of*

288

this until the baby was safely in its pram.

'Perhaps then you can come out and see Rosa tonight, just the three of us together like old times. We'll treat you to a Chinese meal or something.'

'I'm not sure. Denny doesn't like me going out in public.'

'But, Joy, we're your family, for goodness' sake. Once you have the baby, we'll hardly see you.'

'I'll ask him later,' she promised.

Oh, no you won't, sensed Connie, so she hung around until he came through the door. 'I'm collecting Joy at seven,' she announced to him. 'Rosa is home on a flying visit. This is our last chance before Joy's confined to barracks so ... seven o'clock tonight, right?'

Denny stared at her, 'She'll need a taxi.'

'No, I've passed my driving test, didn't I tell you? Thanks to Neville I passed it first time, so I've got Gran's wheels, for a change. Seven o'clock sharp.' There was no reply, but Connie knew she'd caught him on the hop.

Later she dressed with care in the new black and silver sack dress that hid her bump, and put on masses of eye make-up, a Dusty Springfield attempt, piling her hair into an enormous beehive. She must keep her tail up and it was Christmas even if she didn't feel at all in the mood.

The town streets were strung with fairy lights, and Christmas trees were lit in the bay windows along Division Street. The shops were full of toys and gifts but all she felt was panic inside. Lee's words kept echoing in her head. Could she really make a life without Winstanley support? Should she marry Neville and be damned? Could she bear to live with Ivy? How she wished she could believe it would work out, but to let Neville down...

Joy was waiting on the doorstep with an enormous cloak wrapped round her bump. 'I have to be back by ten,' she said, 'so don't let's be late.'

'Will you turn into a pumpkin then?' Connie laughed. 'He certainly keeps you on a tight leash, young Gregson.'

'It's his way of showing he cares,' Joy answered. 'He doesn't want anything to happen to the baby, that's all.'

'It's not due for another three weeks, is it?'

'I know, but he doesn't like me out on my own.'

'You're not on your own, Joy. One night out in months ... honestly. How do you put up with it?'

Joy looked ahead as she spoke. 'Marriage is another world, Connie. You do things for each other. You make sacrifices, you look to each other. Denny says I don't need any other friends than him. Denny says I should be content to stay at home.'

'Denny says ... Denny says. What do you say, or have you lost your tongue?'

'Connie, he is my husband. I must obey him.'

'What twaddle! This is the 1960s not the 1860s. We're free to think what we like. He doesn't own you.'

'You don't understand how it is,' Joy protested. 'You single girls are all free to please yourselves. When the baby comes we will be complete.'

'So it's goodbye Connie and goodbye Rosa, is it?'

'No, of course not, but it can't ever be the

290

same, can it?'

'Why not? You're not joined at the hip to him.' Connie stalled the gears in frustration at such nonsense.

'When the baby comes,' Joy added, 'it changes your life. You become the most important thing in its life. It will need me night and day and it's a helpless being that needs its mother's devotion. It will take up all my time, I just won't be the Joy you knew. I shall be a different Joy ... a real mother. So my baby and husband will come first in all things.'

'So this is your farewell outing then, with the Silkies?' Connie drove grim-faced. She didn't want to hear all this stuff about a baby taking over your life. How could it do that and there still be room for her life? Ivy was waiting in the wings to do all the mother care. Neville would ignore it and go to work. Where would she fit into all these plans?

Am I too young and selfish to be tied down by such a burden? she sighed, but said nothing.

'I hope I've not offended you,' Joy added, taking the silence for hurt.

'Of course not. It's just a lot to take in, isn't it, this childbirth stuff?' Connie replied.

'When your turn comes, you will understand better.'

Will I? Connie thought. From where she was sitting nothing was making any sense at all.

Rosa was waiting at the restaurant dressed in a mohair lilac coat, purple shift dress underneath, her hair swept up in an enormous black beehive.

291

She had dangling earrings and pair of panda eyes lined with kohl, with mascara on her false eyelashes. She took one look at Joy and burst out laughing.

'Nellie the elephant!' she sang.

Joy was not amused. 'Don't sing that. Denny sings it all the time.'

Rosa stared at Connie too. 'So what are you doing in Neville's old school blazer?' she said, examining her dress. 'You look like a mint humbug!' They were hugging and laughing at the same time. 'And you've filled out a bit. It suits you. And the hair, wow! How many sparrows are nesting in that hairdo?'

They found a corner bench, sat down and never stopped talking. Catching up was so much fun. Rosa was full of life with the New Silkies, Sadie Lane's backing group. 'She's a monster... always trying to forget to pay us. When she's living it up in the Queens Hotel, we get shoved in the serf's boarding house in a backstreet by the railway line. She drives around in a Rolls-Royce and we have to catch the bus. Sadie doesn't miss a trick. "Darlinks, you were divine but which bitch missed that first entry? I vant no wiggling of the hips,"' Rosa mimicked. 'So I said, "But that's what all the other backing artistes do in a live concert ... the Vernons Girls do it. They have their moves choreographed to fit in with the lyrics," says I, and she is down my throat like one of the Furies. "Don't you be clever with me, duckie. I know your little game ... and when did you lose all that weight?" That was the night I forgot to pad up my dress. Mamma says women of her age either widen or wither. Poor old

Sadie is expanding so fast and we have to look like three Billy Bunters, and it gets so hot on stage. Mel said, "It's the change. It does that to women." "What change?" Sadie jumps in. "There's no change in this routine." She's got ears like a microphone and eyes like a hawk looking for its dinner... By the way, she liked your song, "Colours of My Love".'

'What song is this?' Joy was all ears. 'I didn't know you were writing songs, Connie.'

'She's good. I like "The Last Bus Home". I think Sadie might buy some. It's awfully sad, though,' said Rosa.

Connie smiled. She'd sent Rosa some of her summer songs in a letter, not explaining why she'd written them, of course.

'We'll make sure she does buy them.'

'Thanks, I could do with the cash,' Connie said. She'd not written anything for ages.

'Sadie is desperate for a chart hit but she is past it, honestly. It's so sad. If she wasn't such a bitch, I'd feel sorry for her. Gabby, Mel and me are thinking of striking out on our own. We've had enough of the old trout.'

Joy burst out laughing. It was good to see her so relaxed. 'Ooh!' she yelled. 'You've given me a stitch in my side.'

The waiters brought the chow mein with crispy noodles. The restaurant was packed for Christmas parties, with a noisy bustle of students, home for the vacation, half tight on beer, making the usual racket in the background.

'They ought to get an Indian restaurant here. The food is delicious: curries, papadums, chapattis. Gabby cooks us stuff with spices. Her family were in India after the war. But enough about me, me, me... I was sorry about the romance with Marty ending.' Rosa hesitated. 'I hear he's gone solo. He got to number forty with "Pocket Full of Stars".'

'Did he? I helped him with that one too,' Connie said, trying to sound casual, her heart leaping at the sound of his name. She'd been secretly watching his progress up the charts in *New Musical Express*. Part of her was glad he was doing well, but she was angry that he'd not included her in the credits.

'Then you ought to copyright your songs with an agent, and soon. Why not go and see Dilly Sherman in Manchester? I've got her number. I'm sure she'll help you. What went wrong with the two of you?'

'I suppose the usual stuff. He didn't want to be tied down.'

'He's right in a way. Here today, gone to-morrow, and all those girls flinging themselves in his face ... perhaps he felt it was only fair.'

Connie didn't want to hear any more. 'How about you?' she asked.

'No one special – most of the handsome guys I meet would prefer Neville. How is our fourth girl, OK?'

Connie was cagey with her reply.

'Mamma said he's in trouble but she didn't say what for. Confess all, Connie.'

'Sorry, I really can't say much. It's all a storm in a teacup.'

Joy was smiling and then twitched. 'Do you

294

mind if I stand up? This stitch is getting worse, I think I'd better go to the loo. I've got such wind.'

'I think it's more than wind inside that dress, darlinks!' Rosa giggled. 'Sadie would love you singing behind her.'

'I'll come with you,' said Connie. 'Just in case.'

'In case of what?' Rosa asked.

'I don't know. I just promised to look after her.' The toilet was a cramped little cubbyhole and Connie stood outside. It was so good with them altogether as if it were old times, but it wasn't. She'd had to lie about Neville, hide her own secrets, and pretend everything was all right. If only she could tell them, but it was better left as it was...

Then she heard Joy shouting through the door.

'Connie. I can't breathe!'

Connie pushed open the door gingerly. Joy was bent double in agony. 'It must be something I've eaten. I can't move ... the pain is all round my belly.'

'It's not the noodles,' said Connie, 'I think you've started. I'd better get some help.'

'Don't leave me, I'm scared.'

'Just give me a sec.'

There was a queue forming behind her. Connie passed the word down the line. 'Is there a nurse or doctor anywhere in the restaurant?' Then Joy let out a yell that everybody could hear. There was silence and real concern now. Suddenly a face appeared at the ladies door. 'Can I help? I'm a medic in training.'

Connie looked up to see the familiar face of Paul Jerviss standing in the door.

'I can't move her. She's not due for three weeks. We were laughing and then she got a stitch,' Connie offered, feeling her cheeks flushing at the sight of him.

Everybody cleared a space as the drama unfolded. Paul edged his way through the door, sat Joy down on the toilet seat and began to feel her tummy as the contractions ripped through.

'That's hard. How many have you had like this?'

'They're all like this,' Joy whimpered. 'What's happening?'

'Baby is what's happening, Joy. I don't like the size of those swollen ankles. We've got to get you to the hospital now. They'll phone us an ambulance. When I saw you come in I thought you wouldn't have long to go. You're very low-slung. Try to breathe through like they taught you in class.'

'But I didn't go to the relaxation class. Denny said they were not for the likes of us. They'd be no use...'

'Pity about that. I'm told ladies find them very useful, but no matter, try to let go when the pain comes, try not to fight the contraction,' he ordered. 'Connie, can you collect her things? Long time no see,' he smiled.

Connie was too shocked to say anything. She sped back to their bench seat and told Rosa.

'Hell's bells, a Christmas baby! Someone had better warn Denny and Susan. I'm sure the restaurant will let us use their phone. How exciting.'

'I must go with Joy to the hospital. You go home and warn everyone who needs to know, Rosa.'

'Was that who I thought it was? Dr Kildare

Jerviss ministering to the sick?'

'She's not sick, just pregnant,' Connie snapped.

'I know that, stupid. Don't be so touchy. Anyone would think you were in labour, by the looks of you!' Rosa laughed at her own joke.

If only you knew, Connie's heart cried, but now was not the time to tell her troubles.

She sat opposite Paul in the ambulance, unable to utter a sensible word. Of all the people to be sitting in the back of the Golden Dragon, with his crowd of students, he had to be the first volunteer. He was still handsome, rugged, floppy-haired. She recalled their conversation all those years ago, and the death of his little brother. Now he could be Joy's midwife.

'It's a good job I've just started on the obs and gynae ward,' Paul smiled. 'I've been reading up on swollen ankles but I'd be useless when it comes to delivery. How's things with you? Are you back for the vacation?'

'No,' Connie sighed. 'Just finished my resits ... bit of a hiccup. Maybe next year,' she said. Maybe not – who was she kidding? Connie had lost her chance of a university education for good now. She was as tied as Joy was – tied by family loyalty, tied by pregnancy, tied by her own stupid mistakes. Suddenly she felt so fed up and stupid. She wanted to cry and to her horror tears started to run down her cheeks.'

'Hey, don't worry, she'll be fine, and she'll be in the right place,' Paul assured. 'The contractions might stop and then she'll go home, but it's a pity she hasn't been to relaxation classes. They are supposed to make a difference in labour.'

'How would you know?' Joy muttered between gasps.

'I suppose I wouldn't,' he said, giving Connie one of those Jerviss eye-ups that made her go all shaky. 'Family all well?' he asked politely.

'Tickety-boo,' she replied, not looking at him.

Then they arrived at the entrance hall of the maternity hospital and found a wheelchair. Joy was swallowed up into the bowels of the building, a midwife pushing her along the corridor.

'I'd better wait here until Denny comes. I promised I'd look after her,' Connie said.

'I'll wait too, if you like,' Paul offered.

'No, I'm fine ... go back to your friends. I think it'll be ages yet.'

'Yes, Doctor,' he teased. 'You might well be right, but let us know how she goes on. A few hours later and it might have been my first delivery. I'd better go home and read up a bit more,' he said, smiling and waving as he left.

And I'd better sit here and contemplate just where I will be in five months' time, thought Connie. And why was it I turned him down for Marty Gorman? For a pair of tight leathers, as I recall. Why do I make a mess of everything, and how can I ever think of marrying Neville? What on earth am I going to do now?

It was Christmas Eve and they were shutting shop early once the last stragglers had picked up their jars of mincemeat and spices. It had been Neville's idea to make a display of all the stuff needed for cakes and fancy goods and cookery. A one-stop shop for busy housewives. They'd brought extra treats, like diabetic sweets, jellies and gluten-free items, and sold almost all of their stock, but his heart wasn't in their success. It was at the hospital, where Joy was still in labour and Trevor Gilligan was having his stomach pumped.

He'd known something wasn't right the way Trev's mother slammed the door in his face. He'd been frantic to know what was happening. One of his regulars, Mrs Davidson, lived next door to the Gilligans, and Neville pumped her for information as nonchalantly as he could.

'Everything all right with Trevor and his mother? I've not seen anything of them for weeks. Is she bad again?' he asked.

'Oh, I'm not surprised,' said Mrs Davidson. 'We heard – and I shouldn't be telling you this – young Trevor tried to do away himself ... trouble with the police,' she whispered. 'An ambulance came in the night, and her a widow. What a terrible thing to do to his mum. He's been sent away.'

'Sent away where?' Neville tried to hang on to the counter and looked normal.

'To that place up by Moor Bank School with the bars on the window, silly blighter... What does a young man want to do that for? He's all she's got after Alf got killed on the railway line in the fog. But I shouldn't be telling tales, should I? Must dash, got the whole family coming tomorrow.' Off she shuffled with her Beecham's Pills and arrowroot powder, leaving Neville staring into space.

'Oh, Trevor, I'm sorry. What did you do that for? Please God, he'll be OK.' He felt sick with worry and he couldn't make things better by visiting, either. All he could do was to write a letter, send him some money.

What was the matter with this world when a nice boy has to try killing himself because he is different? Why should guys like him be married off just to please his family, father a child he didn't want? It wasn't fair and it wasn't right. But Connie needed his protection. How could he think of letting her down?

Merry bleeding Christmas! He wanted to sleep until it was all over. At least they'd pushed the court case back for another month and by then he'd be a married man. But the thought gave him no comfort at all.

19

A Cracker of a Christmas

Christmas dinner was going to be a minor affair this year as Su and Jacob were visiting Joy, who gave birth after much stopping and starting to a tiny little girl, who they called Kimberley Dawn. She weighed in at just four pounds, so they were keeping mother and baby in hospital until she gained more weight. Denny was eating at his mother's, as usual.

Esme thought they should name the baby something Christmassy, like Carol or Noelle or even Nichola. She was relieved the baby was safe, and Joy seemed none the worse for her ordeal.

'Holly would be a good name,' Connie said. 'Or Ivy...'

She was smirking as she was preparing the last of the mince pie pastry under strict supervision. Someone had to teach the minx to cook.

'I suppose she'll be called Kim for short,' Esme replied without enthusiasm, filling the cake tins, inspecting the pastry crust. 'You should always have a tin spare in case of visitors. You never know who'll be popping in to give the season's greetings.'

The house was trimmed up and she'd counted the Christmas cards to see if there were as many as last year. It didn't look good to have only a few on display. Connie had hardly sent any of her own.

True to form, Levi came first with some parcels for under the tree. On his own, of course; Shirley was not welcome at Sutter's Fold.

'Your first great-grandchild,' he said, swigging the Christmas sherry down with relish. 'Has our Neville been in yet?'

'He's at the Royal, I think, to see Joy, but he'll be here for his Christmas dinner with Ivy and Connie, of course. Lily and Peter are going to the Walshes with Arthur this year. It's only fair to turn and turn about, but we'll give them a belt loosener, don't worry, while you've got off with the fancy piece. I don't know what I've done to deserve this shame, I really don't!' Esme sighed. 'You've all put years on me!'

'But you are old, Mother,' Levi teased. 'You've had your three score years and ten. Merry Christmas and I'll see you on Boxing Day then, for my tea. I hope Ivy will not be here then?'

301

'Oh, Levi, you should never have married her in the first place. Divorce is a terrible thing. She'll want her share. She brought up your child and now you shame us.'

'She can have the house. I'll have the business. Shirley's place is cosy and there's always a bed for Neville.'

'Neville and Connie will stay with her. That's been agreed.'

'Then I won't interfere, seeing as you've sorted it all out as usual to your satisfaction, not theirs.'

'What's that supposed to mean? Not every family would take in a fallen woman and a nancy boy. We're doing our Christian best for the baby, like we did for Freddie's little mistakes. Winstanleys stick by their own, as you well know. I've bailed you out enough times.'

'Yes, yes, sermon over. I must be off. If Neville wants me he knows where I'm at. Cheerio, one and all, and have a nice day tomorrow.'

He's getting more like his brother Freddie by the minute, Esme thought. Since he dumped his wife he'd lost weight and got some sparkle back in his eyes. Levi was never her favourite child but he'd cut out the boozing and come on. He'd had a rough war as a prisoner, and there was still things he'd never talk about with her; things he'd seen twenty years ago. Funny how soldiers were still paying a price for defending their country, and their families suffered too.

She was glad Neville hadn't been conscripted, even if it might have made a man of him. She just didn't understand him. This David and Jonathan thing between him and his friend was all there in

302

the Bible too. Love between men was as old as history, and soldiers seemed to do it a lot. But she put that down to them being on their own without any women.

The family must stick together in this and see off any threats to its unity. Esme felt like she was the glue sticking everyone together, but it was wearing thin in parts and she was tired.

Connie was gearing herself up to visiting Joy, knowing it would be her own turn next, and she still hadn't managed to master a simple pearl plain stitch. Her knitting was only up to dish-cloths standard, but there were a few months yet to lick her into shape.

How she'd manage living with Ivy was another matter. Two women in the kitchen was always bad news. She looked back to when Su, Ana and Ivy had fought over their food cupboards in the Waverley. Those were times of rationing and foreign girls wanting fancy food, but they'd been happy days. Together they'd stopped Lily from making a big mistake and marrying Walter Platt.

Poor soul, he was still not wed and living with his mother, wondering why life had passed him by.

Connie was trying her best to please but her eyes were dull and her shoulders stooped like Lily's had before the Olive Oil Club took her in hand. Esme hoped Connie had got some good pals in Joy and Rosa to back her up. She and Joy would be young mums together, just like Ana and Su. Funny how history repeated itself.

Now Ana was gone and Su had turned to Jacob Friedmann for company. Two lonely people finding love late in life. She'd had Redvers for such a short time, and lost two of her children. She hoped Neville and Connie would make a go of things for the baby's sake. No one else need know their predicament. It wasn't an ideal start, a false marriage, but it was all that was on offer for the moment. So why was she feeling so guilty? Why did she feel uneasy in forcing them together? Why did Walter and Lily's long engagement come to mind, and how desperate she had been to change that? All this was too confusing for Christmas Eve. Time to sit down and listen to the carols on the wireless from King's College, Cambridge. That would soothe her jumping heartbeat. Then Christmas would really begin.

Connie sat in her room wrapping parcels with a heavy heart. She hated the festive season, since Ana's death. Even Joy's safe delivery couldn't dispel her gloom. And then there was a tune on Radio Luxembourg, 'Anyone Who Had a Heart'. It made her want to weep. Who was there left who really cared about her in that special way? The little teddy she'd bought for Kim sat staring at her with its beady eyes. If only she was a child again.

Joy's baby was in a bassinet, tiny, red-faced, ugly, swaddled like the baby in the manger, and all she'd felt looking at it was panic to have to go through what Joy had suffered: tearing, stitches and soreness. She'd added soaps and pretty talcum powder for the new mother, and lavender cologne, hoping it would remind her that she was still Joy and not just a mother smelling of baby sick.

For Rosa she'd bought a bone clip for her hair and offered her the last of her songs to show to

Shady Sadie. Since her pregnancy she'd not written a thing. For Neville she'd bought one of those hand-crocheted ties that were all the rage on the fashion pages. For Granny Esme a pretty photograph album to put all the family pictures in that were still in a shoebox in her wardrobe. Then there was a toy for little Arthur and some chocolates for Auntie Lee and Maria, and a tin of cigarettes for Uncle Levi.

Another Christmas and how would she make it through? What would Mama make of all this? Connie wrapped a scarf up for Auntie Su, and a ballpoint pen for Jacob, who was always losing his glasses and his pens.

In January she'd be a married woman, but with the same surname. It was going to be a farce from start to finish, and dishonest, but that was all there was on offer.

She'd received a card from Diana Unsworth and a note saying: 'I shall be home in Grimbleton on Boxing Day. Come and see me.' How strange. Auntie Lee must have told her the score, but there was nothing she could do now.

She thought of Ricky Romero going solo, touring abroad. First love seemed so silly now. Then she thought of that night with Lorne Dobson. How could she forgive herself for that? To be just another of his cheap conquests and maybe to have created a new life.

Then Paul Jerviss's face flashed into her inner eye; such a decent guy but his sort wouldn't look twice at a girl like her now. Pity is all he would feel so she might as well face it. Her life was over before it'd begun. Buck up and make the best of things; don't fight what can't be altered.

Then her baby kicked. 'I know, I know...' Connie patted her belly. 'It's not your fault. You didn't ask to be born. Don't worry, I'm doing the best I can for you even if it's going to be hell on earth for me.'

It must have been nearly midnight when Neville knocked them up. Gran was snoring over her medicinal brandy wine and didn't hear him. Connie was sitting cross-legged on the floor, trying to coax the fire into life and find some Christmas spirit.

'I just had to come. You heard about Trevor, have you?'

'Shush! No,' Connie replied. 'You'd better come in but don't wake Gran. What's up?'

'He tried to kill himself with pills, his mother's barbies, but he took too many and made himself sick, and now they've put him on the psychiatric ward at Moor Bank. I've been trying to visit but I'm not family and they won't let me in to see him. I've been so worried. I knew something was up, daft happorth!' Neville was crying.

'I expect he felt trapped, ashamed, scared and confused. He ought to join our club,' Connie said without emotion.

'Is that how you are feeling too?'

'You as well?' she said.

Neville nodded. 'I don't know how to say this, Connie, but I can't do it. I can't marry you.'

'I know,' she sighed, but he kept on trying to explain. 'I know, Neville, neither can I.' He wasn't hearing so she shook him to make him listen.

'You can't?' Nev looked up with relief in his eyes.

'No, it's not fair to you or me to tie ourselves down like this, and it's not fair to my baby either.'

'I don't know what to say.'

'There's nothing to say. It was a daft idea: a desperate idea and not ours. Here, I'll pour you some Glühwein; the only good thing I picked up in Switzerland. You warm wine, with these bundles of spices in a package. It'll give you Dutch courage. I'm so glad you've said your piece.'

'I'm sorry.'

'What for? One of us had to put a stop to this sham before we got to the altar. It's just dishonest, and for what? To give my baby a name? It's already got that name, so nothing changes, does it? I can't live with Ivy. We would kill each other, and she's always loathed us girls. All she wants is the baby for herself.'

'I'm sorry Con. Everyone said it would help my case if I got wed. I don't know what to say now.'

'Stop apologising for a start. We can still go along with it in public ... but there is one question left. Are you going to tell the family or shall I?'

Neville sipped the hot mug with a sigh. 'I think you know the answer to that one.'

Connie smiled. 'Merry Christmas – while it lasts.'

Christmas Day followed the usual pattern: church, presents, sherry, soup and then a fat capon with all the trimmings. Neville kept looking at Connie for courage as his mother kept wittering away about the wedding arrangements. They waited until the pudding was lit and the sixpences found, just in case there was another choking episode, and then both of them stood up and told Gran and Ivy about their joint decision.

'We're not getting married. It's not a good idea.'

'Is this some silly joke?' Esme spluttered, her paper hat slipping over her ears. 'Tell them, Ivy. They can't do this, after bringing our family name into the public shame after all we've done for you, and it's almost arranged.'

'No it's not, not by us. You'll thank us in the end for being honest,' said Connie, sitting down. 'I'm surprised at you, Granny, going along with this mad scheme, pretending we're suited, letting us make a mockery of marriage for everyone's respectability. Ivy I can understand – she'll do anything to get her own way – but you can't order us about like little kids. We've both made our minds up alone.'

'It's not right and I'm not doing it,' Neville added.

'Well, be it on your own heads,' said Esme, wagging her finger. 'Don't expect me to bail you out. Not a penny, not a penny will I give you. You can fend for yourselves! There'll be nothing from me ever again!'

Connie felt awful. She'd never cheeked her gran like this before.

Neville stood his ground. 'I'm a working man, I don't need you to bribe me.'

'Are you indeed?' Esme sniffed, pointing at Connie. 'She's not bringing any baby to this house if she's unwed. You'll leave this house right now, and I never want to see your face again. I won't be putting a roof over a bastard's head. I have enough to cope with with my jippy hip and rheumatics.'

'You did last time,' Connie argued. 'You gave my mother a home, but I won't stay where I'm not welcome... I'll manage somehow,' she said, rising to leave.

'Not in this town you won't, you wicked girl!' Esme continued, feeling the heat of too much sherry and punch.

'Don't worry, I'll find somewhere else to stay so my shame won't come to your door.' Even as Connie spoke her heart was racing at what they had just done, but the gloves were off and she was giving as good as she got.

'Ivy?' Esme turned to Neville's mother for support. 'Say something.'

Everyone was looking at Ivy, whose cheeks were glowing, eyes glinting in fury. She suddenly got up, her chest swelling, and she whisked the tablecloth off the table like a magician, spilling pudding plates, glasses, candlesticks, sending them spinning onto the floor. With one great wail of fury she went for Connie, beating her on her chest, pounding her with her fists. 'Whore of Babylon, wicked girl, spawn of the devil!'

Neville jumped to restrain her. 'Gran, do something. Give her some water!'

'I'll give her water,' Esme said, grabbing the crystal jug from the sideboard and throwing the contents over Ivy's head, soaking her, shocking her into silence. 'Stop it, you silly woman, calm yourself... Neville, get that girl out of the house. Now see what you've both done. You've sent your poor mother over the edge. Go and tell Edna next door to ring the doctor, and send for Levi. This is what comes from your wickedness. Never darken my door again, either of you. I'm finished with you. You young ones are nothing but trouble!'

Connie stood frozen with shock in the driveway, shaking and sobbing. The wind from across the moors chilled her even more. Gran had never been like this, ever, and Ivy had gone berserk. There was madness in her eyes, a gleam of a murderous hate, all because she was depriving her of a baby, a baby she would have ruined and possessed for herself. But for Gran to banish her like that...

Neville was quick to make up some story to Edna about his mother being upset. Everyone knew about Levi's defection so they would put this down to reaction to stress.

They both sat in the Triumph Herald, sharing their last cigarette, looking at each other with dismay, waiting for the doctor to arrive.

'We've done it now, so where next?' said Connie.

'I've got a bed at my dad's, at Shirley's. He was the one who put the doubt in my mind. He'll understand.'

'Take me to the Walshes' then. I'm sure Auntie Lee will give me a sofa for the night. When things cool down, Gran'll see sense. It was Lee who made me change my mind.'

'So the Winstanley family hasn't deserted us altogether. At least there's some comfort in that. I'm sorry about Mum. Are you OK? Did she hurt you? We ought to get you checked over,' Neville said with concern.

'No, leave it. I'm just shocked. I thought she was going to kill me.'

'She's crazy, nuts... Must be her time of life ...

you know menny wotsit.'

'I expect she'll calm down. It's all this about your dad too. But Gran... She's made a right fool of herself. Too much ginger wine. She'll come round. It's not her life to live, is it? They can't make us do what we don't want to do. I was banking on living here a bit longer but it's better if I leave Grimbleton and see this through on my own.'

Connie was scared just saying those words out loud. How on earth would she survive now?

'I'll be behind you. I'll see you right, you've only got to ask,' Neville said.

'I know, but I think there's somewhere I can go where no one will bother me,' Connie sighed, feeling drained of all emotion.

'Where?' Neville was curious.

'I'll tell you later. Just drop me off with Auntie Lee, but not a word to anyone else – except your dad, of course. We have to keep it in the family.'

'And Joy?'

'Not yet. She's got her hands full. I'll tell her when I tell Rosa but not yet. Oh, Neville, we made a mess of it, didn't we?' Connie cried.

'But it had to be done. There was never going to be a good time to thwart their dream and burst the bubble. I just wish Gran hadn't been so angry, though. Still, it's done now.'

Connie nodded, feeling sick and weary. Now she must throw herself on the mercy of another Winstanley and trust to luck that there was a solution.' What a mess, what a terrible mess, and on Christmas Day too.

Rosa was puzzled her letter to Connie was

returned with 'NOT KNOWN AT THIS AD-DRESS' on the envelope. What was going on? She'd heard from her mother that Ivy Winstanley was a patient in Moor Bank, that Neville's name was in the paper on a gross indecency charge and Connie had left town suddenly.

How come? She'd not even got her resit results yet. Why was she being so secretive?

Rosa had duly visited Joy and the baby with her present, but Joy was confined to barracks, little Kim looking beautiful as tiny babies do, so even Joy didn't know where Connie had gone and she was too spaced out to care. Susan was fussing round her and trying to get her to eat properly. It was all very odd, Rosa thought, looking back over the holiday while standing in the wings waiting for Shady Sadie to make her big entrance.

The diva was singing one of Connie's ballads belting it out old style. This was a solo number and the backing group had to fade into the wings while Madam made her grand finale. Rosa didn't know if Connie had got round to getting a contract and having her lyrics registered. She was such a dozy brush these days. Papadaki, they decided, was a good name for her as a lyrics writer. Everyone liked Greek films and Melina Mercouri. Sadie wanted to do a recording of the song and Rosa thought Connie ought to know.

Life with the Monster was not getting any easier now that even Gabby was slim and need-ing padding up. How else on the wages they re-ceived could they not starve in order to afford nylons and make-up?

Mean? Rosa laughed, thinking about Maria's

joke. 'She's so mean she'd have the fleas off your back and sell them on!'

Sylvio's hairdressing salon was going well. They'd bought out Mr Lavaroni when he retired. Sylvio was training up staff to do the new sharp cuts made famous by Vidal Sassoon, cutting hair into sharp geometric shapes to go with Mary Quant dresses. They all wanted straight curtains of hair and a fringe. Mel Diamond had long black straight hair and looked fantastic off stage, but Sadie made them wear horrible wigs.

It was Mel who had found the sheet music score of 'Colours of My Love'. It had a picture of Sadie when she was about twenty-five on the cover, all bust and teeth. Rosa searched the credits. Only the music of Morris Lavatzza was mentioned.

'But it's Connie's song,' Rosa said. 'They can't do this!'

'She already has – stolen the lyrics. They do that if they're not tied down,' Mel sighed.

Rosa was furious. How dare she? It was the last straw. How on earth could she tell Connie when she didn't even know where she was? Connie might hear it and think she'd sold her short. 'What a monster. I've had it up to here with her,' sighed Rosa.

'Haven't we all?' Gabby said. 'I want to go home soon. I'm sick of travelling. She treats us like muck.'

'We have to do something ... show her up. I'm not going to wiggle my bum in a fat suit any more.'

It was Mel who suggested the perfect revenge. It took a bit of rehearsing and bribing the orchestra, who never got any praise from the prima donna

313

either. They were performing at another big press ball near Manchester, a bit like the old *Mercury* Press Ball all those years ago. Sadie was the star act, and they were about to do the unthinkable. The girls had worked out a way to whip off their costumes to music like a striptease during one of her big numbers. Rosa knew it might be professional suicide but thinking about Sadie's skulduggery made it even stevens somehow.

Sadie started with her usual slow tempo stuff, flirting with the audience while the girls stood behind her, swaying and oohing and ahhing in harmony. Then Danny on the drums did a flourish and off came the wigs, the fat skirts and tops, to reveal the girls in skimpy, glitzy outfits, fishnet tights and high heels as they stepped into the limelight to cheers and applause from the men. They were young, fit, slim and in tune. They gave the audience a wonderful finale.

Sadie, old pro that she was, managed to fix a grimace that passed as delight, smiling and clapping them on as she announced, 'My girls, the New Silkies. Give them a big hand!'

Everyone stomped and shouted encore, but Sadie bundled them off the podium, incandescent with fury, her green tasselled dress shimmering and shaking. 'How dare you? How dare you do that to me?' she screamed. 'I'll see that you will never work in this country again.'

'Neither will you,' said Rosa, standing firm. 'I can prove you stole that song and claimed it as your own. My friend wrote that song. She should get the credit, not you.'

'You ungrateful girl!'

'You mean old has-been, isn't it time you retired? You're too old for the beat scene. Try the working men's clubs, the graveyard of yesterday's stars!'

'I've never been talked to like this in my life. You are finished in this business, all of you.'

'We'll see.'

'I shall tell Dilly Sherman.'

'You do that and we'll go to the papers with our pitiful story: how famous star left us starving in a bedsit.'

'I did not!'

'You owe us a month's pay,' Mel yelled.

'Kiss my arse!' came the reply, and a shoe flew into her face.

Connie took Mel and Gabby back to Dilly, who ushered them into the office.

'Yes, I've heard about your tantrum. I did warn you. But what's all this about "Colours of My Love"?'

'It is true, honest. Every bit of it was written by Connie Winstanley, my friend. She sent it me to look over, and all the other songs,' Rosa said. 'Look, I have the originals.'

'Silly girl must register them. Bring her work here. I know someone who can deal with it.'

'But she's disappeared. I don't think she's in the business any more. She ought to get royalties to her song if it's a hit. Sadie is a thief!'

'Oh, she's not the only one to claim a song as her own, but I hear you got your own back.' Dilly sat back to hear their version of the events.

'You should've seen us,' Mel finished, swinging her curtains of hair with excitement.

'I don't want to know, young lady. The best

315

thing I can do is get all of you out of the country and quick. I hear there's a cruise ship going to South Africa, wanting singers and dancers. I hope you've all kept up your classes at the barre.'

'Can ducks swim?' Rosa laughed. 'Yes, we can still do the Tiller Girl high kicks and the splits.'

'Then get yourself down to Southampton *tout de suite* and put some distance between you and Sadie's wrath. Who needs enemies with clients like you? I don't know what I am going to do with you,' Dilly continued, sighing. 'Go on, all of you, you're giving me a heart attack.'

'I'm going to go back home to West Hartlepool. I've had enough,' said Gabby.

'Sensible girl,' said Dilly. 'It's rough in the second and third division. Only the big stars get the perks, and it's a short life as a dancer. Look at Sadie Lane and be warned. Nothing lasts in show business. Everyone wants the next big act. She was young once, and had her moment in the limelight, then puff ... it is gone. Take it from me, girls, find yourselves a good man and stick to him like glue.'

'Thank you, Miss Sherman,' Rosa said, but she wasn't listening for a reply. She'd had far too much to think about. Auditioning for a cruise? Sunshine, ships, glamour and new horizons. Wait till Mamma heard this news. She could go into Grimbleton with her tail up this time, say her farewells. If only Connie was here to share the good news. Why had she disappeared?

Joy sat looking out of the window. Kim was crying again. She was never satisfied, gulping down the bottled milk, then doubling up with wind and

316

sick, screaming. Breast-feeding had just not worked out. Joy's nipples were so sore, her head thumping with all the advice Mummy kept throwing her way: do this, do that, let her scream, put her down in the garden, keep her by your side... And then Denny's mother hovering over her: 'Take no notice of Susan, she's out of date.'

Denny was slow to fall in love with his daughter. She wasn't the boy he was wanting, but she was fair-skinned with eyes already like chocolate buttons and a mop of curly brown hair. Joy had never seen anything so beautiful, such a tiny body. But she was afraid to wake her, change her, touch her. It was Mummy who swaddled her tight and organised her layette. Mummy was doing everything, all because Joy had no energy to move or think or eat. Her limbs were like lead weights. This was not how she was expecting to feel. How could she be so afraid of such a tiny thing?

Sometimes she would lie on the sofa all day and not move if no one was coming. Everyone was still feeding them and fussing over the baby, but all she wanted to do was sleep, sleep, sleep.

Rosa called in, bringing gossip and tales, but Joy wasn't interested. Connie had been gone since Boxing Day and no one would say where or why. She'd left a little teddy bear and a card, just like some polite acquaintance. Joy had been upstairs when Connie called round and Denny had thanked her and let her go, not telling Joy for days afterwards that Connie had come

Denny didn't like her friends, her mother or Mummy's boyfriend, Dr Friedmann, calling him a Yid. It was Dr Friedmann who asked how she was, looked concerned and suggested she talked to her doctor, but she didn't have the energy to get dressed some days, let alone catch a bus. If only she could drive, and why was she so tired all the time? Why did nothing feel right inside her head? Everything was jumbled up, night was day and day was night, and still Kimberley cried and cried and Joy felt such a miserable failure at being a mother. This time last year she was a bride, belle of the ball. Then there was Paris and Wembley and then sickness and now nothing. What was wrong with her? If only Rosa and Connie were here to cheer her up. But they had deserted her too. Rosa was on the high seas, dancing on some cruise ship with her friend Mel. So be it ... she wasn't bothered. And as for Connie? What had she done wrong to be so abandoned and deserted and left to soothe this crying, feeding machine in front of her?

Joy curled up in a ball and cried. I don't want to be here. I don't want to be Kim's mummy. I don't know how... I want to die.

Lee Walsh banged on Esme's door as she was dozing. 'Mother! I know you are in,' she shouted through the letter box. 'I want a word with you. What do you mean sending Connie's letter back. Maria told me. Let me in or shall we have this conversation so the whole of Sutter's Fold can hear?'

Esme shuffled to the door and opened it reluctantly.

She'd had a cruel visit from Levi on Boxing Day. She expected this would be much the same. 'What's all the fuss? She doesn't live here and I don't care to know where she is now. I gather I've you to thank for changing her mind.'

'I didn't need to persuade her. It was the most ridiculous idea in the first place. I just can't believe my own mother could behave in such a harsh fashion with her own kith and kin. What's got into you?'

'Don't you go telling me what to do. I've had an earful from Levi on the subject but I won't be budged. It's bad enough Neville being in the papers and poor Ivy having treatment in hospital for her nerves.'

'Don't poor Ivy, me. You know what she did to Marco Santini all those years ago, and she would sacrifice her own son for her own ends. Don't go making an example of her, Mother. You are so very wrong about this. Poor Connie needs our help, not our condemnation. She's not the first or last who makes a wrong decision and has to pay for it. I am ashamed of you! You're not the woman I once knew ... who took in strangers and their babies out of the good of her heart.'

'I'm too old. Wait until you're my age. It'll be a different story then when Arthur starts playing you up. I have given my life to bringing up this family. It's time I had a rest from nappies and noise. It's my due.' Why were her children taking sides against her in this matter?

'All Connie needs is a place to support her child. She'll do the rest...'

'Like her mother, having to go off to work and leave me to baby-sit. I did it once but not again. I'm too old.'

'Old? Old is a number in your head. You don't

want to do it, and I can understand why, but to throw her on the mercy of strangers... I hope you know what you've done?'

'Why, what's she up to now? Where is she?'

'Safe, no thanks to you. You threw her out on Christmas Day! I never thought you mean-spirited but now I see a crabby old woman who thinks only of her comforts.'

'Don't you dare talk to your mother like that!'

'I'll speak as I find. I don't like who you've become.'

'Suit yourself. This is who I am now, but I won't change my mind.'

'Then there's nothing more to be said. If Connie's not welcome here then neither am I! Put that in your pipe and smoke it!' Lee shouted. 'I hope you enjoy your peace and quiet. There'll be plenty of it from now on, Mother!'

The door banged as Lee left in a huff and a puff.

Esme sat down, stunned by this cruel outburst. Only a daughter knew how to wound, where to put the dagger to her heart. Why were they all ganging up on her? Arrest, divorce, pregnancy – she couldn't hack it any more. Someone had to do the right thing, make a stand for Christian morality and respectability in this godless age. To condone Connie's situation was wrong, wasn't it?

He who is without sin, cast the first stone... And yet, why did Jesus's words toll like a bell in her ears?

20

Exile

Diana Unsworth's staff flat was spacious, with two bedrooms. It was attached to the children's hostel, once a great Victorian house on the outskirts of Leeds. Most of the week, Diana lived alone and then her friend Hazel would come to visit from London by train.

Hazel was a fellow nurse Guider, a part-time lover, Connie suspected. They shared a bed even before she'd taken over the second bedroom, which Diana used as an office. The two of them were kind, friendly but correct.

'You can stay here as long as it is possible – until the confinement, that is. Perhaps you can give me a hand with the patients as an orderly; nothing too strenuous in your condition,' Diana offered.

Auntie Lee had taken her along to the Unsworths on Boxing Day, to their little party. Diana had whisked Connie into the kitchen to talk in private.

'Oh dear, you are in trouble, aren't you? But what's broke can be fixed,' she smiled. 'You can stay with me for a while. No one will know you and there are places you can go when it gets close to your time. I fear you're going to have to make some big decisions, Connie. The biggest decisions of your life is whether to keep this child or find it a home. It's not easy to put kids into a nursery these days. Since the war most of them have closed, and you'll have to work. Adoption would give the baby a chance with parents in a better position than you to bring up a child.' Diana could be so direct, looking at her with those slate-grey eyes. 'If only your mother were alive,' she sighed. 'Such a pity.'

'I don't want adoption. I'll manage on my own.'

'I think you'd better wait until it's born. The welfare officers will discuss these things better than I can, but babies cost money, Connie, a lot of money, so think carefully.' The seeds of doubt were already being sown, gently but firmly planted. Diana was making everything real.

Connie crossed over the Pennine Hills with a heavy heart. Gran's anger and Ivy's assault flashed into her mind. Better to go where nobody would judge her, but on bad mornings all she wanted to do was lie in bed. Then the little one inside had its own ideas and started to kick her into touch. 'What do you want me to do?' she whispered to it.

Diana kept her busy bathing children with weak limbs and hunched backs, boys who nodded and banged their heads against the cots. The hostel was full of handicapped children and another doubt was planted in Connie's mind. How would she cope if her baby was not healthy? What if it had been already harmed in some way?

She fought off the doubts but the picture of Joy's nursery, with all its equipment, worried her.

One day, window shopping in Schofield's baby department on The Headrow, she picked up a soft woollen blanket: blue, yellow and green plaid with a thick fringe, just right for a pram or cot, and not too expensive. On impulse she bought it and brushed it across her face. It smelled new and soft.

Then for the first time she wondered what it would be like; a boy or a girl, ginger-haired, or dark like Marty or Lorne? She couldn't recall exactly what colour his hair was, it was so plastered in gel. She knew so little about them. Her baby would be its own person with its own genes. It was nothing to do with them, and yet, of course, it was.

One pram blanket wasn't much of a layette but it was a start. The day was edging ever closer when her bulge would get difficult to conceal, but no one around here would care what happened then. She was tall and slim, and when she stood up straight there was nothing much to see.

It was agony to pass a nursery store window and see the racks of rompers and pram suits reminding her of what was to come.

Joy was wrapped up in her new life and Rosa was halfway across the world, on her way from Southampton. Connie had never felt so alone and yet so coldly focused on what to do, but a creeping inertia filled her limbs too, a heaviness that kept her lying under the covers, reading, as if to escape making a single decision.

She presented herself, at Diana's insistence, to the local doctor. Dr Shearling was of the old school, an ex-missionary. She sensed he was of the brigade that said you don't touch the opposite sex anywhere but on the unclothed arm unless you are engaged, and then it was better to marry than to burn.

He examined her coldly. He tried not to show his exasperation that she was so far on and that she'd not taken any precautions whilst 'indulging in careless behaviour'.

'If you must be reckless then take precautions. You look like an intelligent girl. What a sorry end for your life,' he said.

He dismissed her as if she was a silly girl but Connie was no longer in awe of the medical profession. Dr Friedmann had told them too many funny stories about his colleagues for her to take them seriously.

'I want to continue with my education,' she said. 'I'll find a nursery or a part-time job.'

'You're mighty sure of yourself,' he sneered. 'I've met many sorry lassies like you, and none of them yet has managed to bring up a baby without the support of their family or a young man willing to take them on. You can't just walk into a day nursery these days.' He was pouring his bucket of cold water on her fantasies like Diana.

Connie stood up to leave.

'Wait,' he said. 'Have you thought of adoption, giving the bairn to parents who are in a better position to bring up a child properly?'

The very word made her hackles rise. 'No,' she said. 'I don't want that. It won't come to that.'

'Then get on the phone to your mother right now and go home,' he ordered.

'My mother is dead and no one in the family can take me in. I want to stay here and find work. I'm not due until May. I'll find something,' she insisted. No one was going to tell her what to do, especially not some po-faced doctor who didn't know the first thing about her.

'In that case we'll find you a place in a hostel for unmarried mothers and babies. You have your confinement and then you think again about adoption. The welfare officers will discuss options for you, both before and after the bairn is born,' he replied, looking at his watch and writing out a form and prescription for the usual iron tablets and free orange juice.

Connie stood out on the concrete steps, clutching her forms, blinking in the sunshine. What were hostels for mothers and babies? Perhaps if she went into a home it would give her time to plan the future. Only Diana need know she was there. She'd find some excuses to cover her tracks with everyone else.

She could earn enough to buy a pram and layette, find a room; a cot didn't take up much space. There had to be a day nursery somewhere for factory workers, but how could she fund all that on a care assistant's wage?

Perhaps it was better to give up now. Every time she came up with a solution there was an obstacle right behind it. She was eighteen and unqualified for any job. She'd not got her results yet.

She put her hand on her bulge and knew she must look after this unborn child. The two of them were locked together. 'I'll think of something for us, don't worry,' she whispered.

Then came an unexpected letter from Neville. Joy was asking Connie to write to her to be a godmother to Kim in April. Enclosed was a little picture of Kimberley in her pram, looking like a miniature Auntie Su.

After all this, Joy wanted her to receive such an honour?

The letter thrilled and terrified her. Joy was reaching out to her in asking her to do this honour, but there was no way that she could stand up in a church and make vows in this state. Stricken with terror, ashamed and paralysed with not knowing what to do, she had to find an excuse. If she refused, Joy would think she didn't care and be hurt.

In desperation she rang Neville at the Market Hall office. 'What shall I do?' she cried.

'She's asked Rosa but she's out at sea... Auntie Su would tell her the truth about your condition but Joy's not well. I don't think she'd understand.'

'No, she mustn't suspect. I'll think of something. There has to be a way.'

Next morning she woke up with the perfect solution. She was going to take her cue from Joy's old tricks. She walked into town, made a purchase, then wrote back enthusiastically, saying she was working with Diana for a while but accepted the role of godmother with pleasure. She enclosed a little stainless-steel christening mug with a bunny rabbit engraved on the front, telling her she was sending the gift in advance.

On the Saturday before the christening she rang Auntie Lee complaining of diarrhoea and stomach cramps. 'You know I can't come in my condition. Tell them I thought it unwise to bring infection to a new baby and hope they'll all understand.'

'How are you?' said Lee with concern in her voice.

'Coping. Diana and Hazel are kind. They are

326

finding me somewhere to stay. How's Gran?'

'We've had words. She won't bend, Connie. I wish I could help...'

'Don't worry, I'm managing.' She had already composed a letter to Joy and Denny, promising to visit as soon as she could. 'I've sent Kim's present. Are they well?'

Lee was hesitant. 'Su is worried. Joy has gone very thin again. Denny had a hamstring injury. He's been dropped from the first team and is out of training. He's drinking a lot. She hasn't seen much of Joy lately, or the baby, but Joy will make an excellent mother when she settles down,' she added.

'I'm sure she will,' Connie croaked, but she sensed Lee was worried. If only she could bury her head in Mama's warm lap as she had as a child, to tell her what a mess she was making of her own life. If only she could hear the forgiveness in her voice, she wouldn't be now out in this wilderness on this scary journey into the unknown.

'Are you sure *you're* all right?' Lee was sensing her hesitation.

'I'm fine,' Connie lied, wishing she was with her aunt right now to ask her what to do. It was hard being exiled from friends and family, not knowing if she'd ever be allowed to return.

Diana, true to her word, found the name of a hostel, somewhere in the Yorkshire Dales near Sowerthwaite, where they took girls on an extended stay, but then their hopes were dashed when news came that it was full. So now she was down for the local hostel. Interviews followed with a midwife and welfare officer, and a list of requirements she must bring for her confinement.

The orderly job was her only means of income to buy all these extras. It was time to save every penny, walking instead of taking a bus. Sometimes she lived in a pretend world where people smiled and asked when she was due. She was careful always to wear gloves so no one could see the ringless finger. Hubby's away at sea, she told the other staff.

One afternoon she took a trip out to Rawnsworth by bus to find the hostel that would soon be her home. It was hidden behind a high wall with a copper beech hedge and green wrought-iron gates. The house was like a huge preparatory school made from some mill owner's mansion, discreetly unnamed, with no signs of life.

Dr Shearling had confirmed arrangements for entry into the hostel two weeks before Connie's due date. In a funny way it was exciting. This would be a refuge from further deception, a refuge from having to conceal her condition, a relief to be among others in the same boat. No more pretending or wearing that awful corset that clinched her belly and cut into her skin. Here she could hide away and make plans.

The only good news on the horizon was that she had passed her A levels with flying colours. Neville was sending on her mail. There was nothing from Gran, though.

No one knew where she was except Diana and Neville. It was better that way.

Connie packed her suitcase with care, the little blanket she'd bought on the top. Once she was behind those green gates all would be safe. And after that? She could think no further ahead than the birth. How her back ached, her ankles swollen with the heat. Now she was looking forward to a good rest.

Diana kissed her and waved her off from the car. 'I'll come and visit you. Remember, you're not alone.'

'How can I thank you?' Connie cried, feeling tearful. 'You've kept me sane.'

'It's what your mother would expect from me. Don't be too proud to ask for help, but do remember what the doctor said. Please don't think me cruel but there are so many childless couples longing for a baby to love... You've got your whole life ahead of you, a chance for a fresh start. You're only eighteen, don't burden yourself with a child. There's not going to be much family support. Without that you'll sink. Don't condemn your child to poverty and a poor start in life just because you think you should do the right thing. Give it a chance of a better life.'

Connie didn't want to hear all this, not now, not yet... 'Bye, Diana. Come and see me, please.' It was enough to be hidden out of sight, exiled, confined to barracks for the duration. She daren't think more than one day ahead. That prospect was too daunting.

It felt a long slog up the driveway of Green End House with two canvas holdalls. She rang the bell in the portico entrance, breathless with exertion and nerves, and a very pregnant young girl opened the door.

'Another lamb to the slaughter, Miss Willow!' she shouted in a broad Yorkshire accent, and a middle-aged woman came down the corridor, wiping her hands on her apron.

'That's enough, Doreen. Come in, come in. You must be Miss Winstanley?' she said with an emphasis on the word 'Miss'. 'You're one of Dr Shearling's girls. We were expecting you last week. It's a full house, I'm afraid,' she said, looking Connie up and down.

She had on her best smock pinafore dress and flat ballet pumps. 'Sorry I'm late. I was helping my aunt in Leeds,' she offered, but the woman wasn't listening. She was busy pulling Connie's bags from the doorstep.

'What on earth have you got in here, the kitchen sink? Let's be having you. Doreen will show you round. I have an emergency on. One of the girls has gone into labour. So we'll do the formalities later,' she said.

'Home sweet home,' Doreen, who looked about fourteen, giggled. Connie had never seen a bump so large on such a small girl.

'Don't mind her. That's Miss Willow – we call her Pussy – purring one minute and snapping the next. She's in charge when Matron is busy. I'm Doreen Hewett.' She held out her hand shyly.

'Connie Winstanley,' she replied, trying to be brave and friendly when she was completely terrified. The hall was gracious, with a mosaic-tiled floor, a winding oak stairway with a stained-glass window on the landing, shot through with sunlight. There was an unmistakable smell of Jeyes fluid and burned toast.

The day room was full of battered armchairs and a minute television. Under the stairs sat a line of very old bucket prams. There was a print of Jesus holding the lamp, the Holman Hunt portrait, placed halfway up the stairs, and Connie could hear the noise of a baby wailing somewhere in competition with a radio.

Suddenly she felt desperate, so alone and full of shame, bewildered by the incongruity of such elegant rooms and such battered furnishings, as if the house had been emptied of anything that would give it colour and warmth and taste. Anything was good enough for girls who were no better than they should be, seemed to be the order of the day.

The windows were open and the draughts rattled the sashes. Doreen wobbled up the stairs to show Connie the dorms. 'Antenatals to the left, and mothers and babies to the right,' she smiled. 'Bathroom down the corridor, but don't lock the door in case you need help, and watch your purse…'

Connie's heart sank. What sort of place was this?

'It's rest time on the bed for an hour now, feet up and no titivating.' Doreen pointed to a girl lying with two slices of cucumber on her eyelids. 'Matron doesn't like make-up or nail polish on the bedspreads.'

'What's it like here?' Connie asked, sitting on the iron bed, feeling the mattress with dismay.

'Well, it's not Butlins,' Doreen smiled, 'but it'll do.'

'You look fit to burst. When's it due?'

'They think it's twins, worse luck,' she sighed.

'Any time now, and you?'

How on earth was this child going to look after twins? 'About ten days, I hope. I can't fit into anything,' Connie moaned. 'I just hope there's not another heatwave coming our way.'

Her corner of the five-bedded room consisted of a bed and a locker, a small wardrobe, a chair and a hook behind the door. There was a large marble fireplace blocked up and an elaborate plasterwork ceiling that had seen better days. The room could do with a lick of fresh paint. The floor was lino-leum in a pattern full of dizzy stripes. The curtains were unlined and skimpy. The view out from the bedroom was over the front lawn. There were no flowerbeds, no terraces, nothing but a monkey puzzle tree and the high hedge that screened the inmates shame from the world outside.

The other girls were lying down, bumps in the air, eyeing Connie with interest. Doreen was taking her duty seriously and introduced her. 'This is Sheila and June and Evelyn Sixsmith. This is Connie.'

Connie smiled at each one in turn.

'Welcome to heartbreak hotel,' said June, who looked about her own age.

It didn't take long to unpack, with her back turned for privacy, pulling out a pile of books: Brontës, Gaskell, George Eliot, ready for next term's tuition if she ever got the chance to go to university. When she'd finished she could see everyone staring in amazement as if she was a creature from another planet.

'You'll never read all them here,' laughed Evelyn, who was brown-skinned with a scar across her cheek. 'They keep you far too busy for reading.'

'I have to read. I'm going to be a student,' Connie explained.

'Poor you,' said Doreen, patting her stomach. 'I was glad when they chucked me out of school.'

In no time Miss Willow appeared and summoned Connie to meet Matron Holroyd, who looked just like a deflated Hattie Jacques. Together these two guardians, tall and short, looked like a clothes peg and prop. Connie surrendered her supplementary benefit book and her antenatal card, which listed all the personal details asked for except the name of the baby's father.

'Your parents' occupations?'

'Soldier and nurse, but they're both dead,' she said. There was a stubborn part that was determined to hold back bits of herself from them. It was as if it wasn't her sitting in front of them like some naughty schoolgirl, but her own double: Konstandina Papadaki.

'I gather you have not decided about the baby yet,' said Miss Holroyd, looking at her notes from Dr Shearling. 'So what are your plans?'

It was a reasonable request, but Connie was on guard.

'I want to start a degree course, if possible,' she replied.

'And the baby, who will be looking after the baby?' Matron continued.

'I don't know yet,' Connie said, feeling weary of questions.

'This is a Christian foundation supported by the council. It is our duty to guide you to a wise decision. We have to account for all expenditure and comply with statutory regulations that require us to give you six weeks to decide. We believe in giving every new infant the best possible chance in life. It is hard to burden any baby with the stigma of being illegitimate when there are hundreds of good people desperate to give it a proper family life. You owe it to the innocent party in all this to do what is best for it, not you. Babies need mothers and fathers if they are to grow up healthy and successful.'

Most girls she'd grown up with had had no real fathers but how could she argue with Matron? Besides, she was too tired now to comment. None of this was making any sense.

'There are homes waiting for a child with your special credentials,' Matron continued.

Connie was puzzled, looking up questioningly.

'You are obviously a clever girl, and I presume the father is a student too.'

'My mother was Greek and the father is a pop singer,' Connie replied, hoping it would put her off.

'No one will hold that against the child,' Matron answered. 'Is there a possibility of a reconciliation?'

Connie shook her head. 'This is all my responsibility now.'

'All the more reason to be a sensible girl and give Baby up for adoption,' Matron said. 'We can take it away at birth or you can keep Baby for two weeks and then see where we stand. If you sign the adoption papers there's no point in spinning out the agony. It doesn't do to get too attached.'

Connie was not having any of it. 'Do I give

birth here?'

'Goodness, no! You go to the local maternity wing of the hospital, like everybody else, to be monitored and delivered. You can stay the statutory ten days on the ward, then back here to discuss things with welfare department.' Then she leaned over to give Connie a sheet of rules to sign.

'We expect good behaviour at all times, no alcohol on the premises and no men visitors. All other visits by permission, and no phone calls without permission. Church on Sunday. I see you've put yourself down as Greek Orthodox. We don't cater for foreign, any other religion must be arranged in advance. There is cooking and light cleaning duties for antenatals. If you do bring Baby back here, then you must be prepared to look after your baby at all times. I hope you brought a suitable layette and two of everything. A baby is not a doll. They make unreasonable demands. We find reality is a hard taskmaster. It sorts the sheep from the goats, the faint-hearted from the natural mother. You don't look the type to me.'

Connie sat back, defeated by the brusque no-nonsense arguments. The home was a model of efficiency but where was the compassion? They must come and go by the due date, deposit and deliver their burden, and be dismissed to make way for others to follow.

She must either take on the child or walk away. This was the terrible choice facing her. There would be no time to brood over options with meals to prepare, cleaning, laundry, check-ups, prayers over meals and enforced rests.

For one brief minute Connie thought about

packing her bags and catching the first train back to Grimbleton, and to hell with the lot of them. But she hadn't the energy to budge.

A cluster of young mums with babies talked about their birthings and their stitches and their imminent departure dates. Each of the rest was waiting to join their club, knowing full well their turn for the agony would come. They sat sipping afternoon tea in little huddles. It was like some bizarre boarding school full of bloated schoolgirls. Doreen gave her the lowdown on those in their dorm.

'Evelyn went with a black man from Jamaica. She was in a school for delinquent girls but her mam might have her back. June's a nurse, brainy like you. She's going to keep her baby, if she can face her dad. Sheila's engaged but her mam won't let them marry until the baby is out of the way and adopted. No wedding, and no going back home if she keeps it. What can she do? She doesn't want to fall out with her mum. So they don't want anyone to know she's in here.'

'What about you?' Connie said. Doreen was so young.

'I got copped at the fairground. He works the dodgems for Pat Collins; here today and gone tomorrow. My brothers went after him but he vamoosed, didn't he, leaving me up the duff.'

It was easy talking to these girls, different though they all were. They were all in the same sorry mess. 'I'm hoping to keep my baby,' Connie explained.

'Better you than me,' Doreen replied, eyeing her pile of books. 'Doesn't all that book learning put wrinkles on your face?'

Connie sat at the dinner table with June later that day. They were about the same age but plain-looking as June was, there was a silent strength and passion to her that reminded Connie of her heroine, Emily Brontë. Her parents were strict Plymouth Brethren. Hers was another sad tale of getting carried away by first love.

'I thought he was the love of my life but he wasn't ready to settle down. He was a medic and suggested I had an abortion. He was going to take me back in the middle of the night into theatre. He wanted one of his mates to give me a D and C. How could I get rid of a life? Now he's seeing someone else.'

Connie agreed it was a drastic option and she wouldn't have had a clue how to go about it, not to mention that it was illegal. She'd just felt she had to see things through to the end like June, but then what?

What a sorry bunch of sisters they were. But as the days went on they drew strength from each other, packing and unpacking their maternity cases: sanitary towels, maternity size; nappy pins; muslins; thin nighties; vests and bootees; hats and bonnets; talc and cod liver oil; pram suits and towels. Only the best for Connie's baby would do and she'd been extravagant just to prove a point, using every pound Neville sent.

But she realised how silly she'd been to bounce into a shop pretending she was married and buying the most expensive things just to make her feel better for a few minutes. Now she had nothing in her purse but change for phone calls.

On Saturday night Connie was deep into

Middlemarch, while June was reading Dr Spock's childcare manual, quoting them bits from time to time. Evelyn was trying to knit a rainbow-coloured bonnet. Sheila was writing daily letters to her fiancé, begging him to run away to Gretna Green with their baby. Doreen had nothing prepared. Her mother called in from time to time, a worried little woman in a headscarf, holding a cigarette out in front of her as if to ward off the evil eye.

Doreen liked going to the newsagent's for sweets and magazines, but her legs were swelling and she found it difficult to move. Sometimes June and Connie took the chance to escape into the sunshine. June was full of plans for her baby. Connie couldn't think so far ahead as if part of her brain was frozen with fear.

There was a television allowed, but not on Sunday when they had to attend Calvary Church, morning and evening. It was torture, sitting on those hard pews with aching backs and heartburn, listening to some old man who loved the sound of his own voice. They sat upstairs in the old servants' gallery like delinquents, ushered out before the last hymn so the Sunday School wouldn't see their bulging shame. The weather was so warm they had few suitable clothes to wear but cotton print smocks over straining skirts.

Once a week they were escorted to the maternity wing of the teaching hospital for the usual pre-birth check-ups. They sat with the other mums-to-be, who stared at their ringless fingers with silent pity in their eyes.

'Mrs Winstanley?' Connie looked up, thinking there was someone else with the name.

338

'Mrs Constance Winstanley!' Why were they calling her Mrs?

'It's only Miss Winstanley,' she whispered to the nurse.

'Not in here it isn't,' she snapped, palpating the bump. 'Head not engaged. Otherwise full term and a good size.'

'Can I go now?' Connie asked, feeling naked on the couch.

'Down the corridor for blood pressure and urine and scales,' the nurse ordered, not bothering to look at her.

It was at this point, Evelyn, whose blood pressure was going through the roof and whose ankles were swollen, was admitted for an induction.

'What's an induction?' asked Doreen, worriedly.

'They put your feet in stirrups, snip your water bag and give you an enema and a pessary to get you going. Evelyn's got signs of toxaemia and that can be dangerous,' said June who was their fount of medical knowledge.

'I wish I hadn't asked,' moaned Doreen.

Next morning they heard that Evelyn had had a boy, six pounds twelve ounces.

I hope by the time she comes back I'll be well on the way myself, Connie thought.

Sheila went next in the middle of the night, a week early, followed by Doreen, who had an emergency Caesarean.

'Three down, two to go,' Connie smiled to June. They'd had time to get to know each other and often escaped through a back garden gate into a snicket and walked in the summer evening to get some fresh air. June was terrified of telling her parents. They were very strict and had hopes of her becoming a medical missionary in Borneo.

It was hard to explain to June why Connie refused to tell her friends what was happening to her. Perhaps she was too proud to admit she'd messed up and too proud to ask for help. She'd always been the good girl. She wanted them to think of her still as the clever Connie who'd flounced off to find fame and fortune with her boyfriend. None of those lies mattered now. She was going to face giving birth on her own in a strange place.

Days later, even June deserted her. She'd had the runs and, being too shy to warn anyone, had locked herself in the bathroom. Then there were screams and a panic, and Miss Willow had climbed up the stepladder to get through the open window while an ambulance was called. Baby Matthew Brownley was born in the ambulance in a layby on the A65.

Suddenly there was just Connie left waiting impatiently, absorbed in her George Eliot but missing the gang who'd become her confidantes. Evelyn returned with Errol, Sheila with Lorraine. Doreen's twins, Donna and Darren, were kept in the hospital, being underweight and sick. Doreen never saw them again. Darren died and Donna went straight into a foster home. Still Connie's bulge didn't budge.

Seeing the state of her new-found mates was worrying. There was too much time to brood and watch them struggling to nurse their babies and heal their stitches. She'd now been in Green End for nearly three weeks and it was becoming her world. When would it all end?

21

Lullabye

'Get yourself on a number thirty-six bus, Connie. If that driver doesn't get you going, nothing will. He's a right bone-shaker,' Evelyn yelled, while little Errol was nuzzling her breast with relish. The poor girl winced every time she changed position on her rubber cushion.

'Who would have told me that bliss is a salt bath? Fifty stitches and I can feel every one of them. I'm not letting no willy up there ever again,' she winked. Despite her grumblings, Evelyn had taken to motherhood. A tribe of sisters called who took it in turns to juggle the tiny creature. She was going to go back to the detention centre for a few months while her family would look after her son.

At Connie's next examination the doctor gave her a rough internal that rattled her down to her toes, all to no avail. This lazy blighter was content to sit curled up. Doreen was sent home early and they clubbed together to send flowers for the tiny baby that didn't survive. She was going to get a job in a woollen mill as soon as she was fifteen. They all hugged her tight and wished her well.

'She's one tough cookie,' Sheila whispered. Doreen had never mentioned Donna once. But the stitches across her stomach told another story. Connie had heard her crying in the lavatory when she thought she was alone. She'd crept away, not wanting to disturb her private grief.

When June came back with Matthew, she was amazed to find Connie still with the antenatals. She put her little boy in her arms and he smelled of warm sweet condensed milk. All their babies were different: Errol was chubby and squat; Lorraine was long, with no hair. Matthew looked sharp and alert like his mother. Connie wondered just what her baby would be like if and when it bothered to turn up.

'I am not giving him up,' June whispered. 'I prayed with the chaplain and wrote to my parents in Halifax and told them the truth. I asked them to pray for guidance and to come and see their grandson. There's a nursery at the hospital and I will try to get him in there, if I can. The Lord will find a way through,' she smiled, her eyes shining with hope. June was radiant. Connie felt sick. If only she had her courage and faith...

'It's not fair,' she cried. They were all through their ordeal and hers was still to come. She wanted to be back with them in the mother and baby room; she needed their support. It was funny how the world outside no longer existed. They were all cut off, cocooned behind the hedges of Green End.

'Come and watch Benny Hill!' shouted Sheila, and Connie shuffled down to join her on the sofa. They were all laughing. Benny Hill was silly and rude, so even Connie started to giggle and couldn't stop. She was wetting herself with laughter, but the trickle soon became a warm flood that soaked her skirt and the seat, and she jumped up.

'I've started! I've started!' She was dancing around with relief.

'Shut up.' They were all glued to the screen. Connie crept up the stairs, leaving a trail of water, checking her bag, changing herself ready for the big showdown to begin.

What was there to say about birthing a first baby? Every detail of that evening was imprinted on her mind. The Beatles music on the radio. The journey in the ambulance and back again, when she couldn't produce a contraction worth measuring.

She returned, deflated, lying awake, looking through the curtains into the night sky humming an annoying tune that stuck in her brain. Something must happen soon, so she had a bath, with Matron hovering behind the door but still nothing. They had shaved her pubic hair with a scratchy razor, and she felt naked and silly without that familiar tuft. 'Hands, knees and bumpsey daisy.' She was singing it to her bump.

Matron suggested she took castor oil, and that she would give her an enema to hurry things along. Drinking the stuff was worse than everything else put together. She went through all that rigmarole and still not a contraction to show for it.

'I'm afraid you will have to go back. You're vulnerable to infection now your waters have broken. They'll start you off if you don't oblige.'

So it was back in the ambulance once more, wheeled in a chair like an invalid, desperate for the loo. Then she was put in a sort of dentist's chair and into the stirrups, feet in a sling, bottom to the air and the indignity of a line of gynaecology students examining her procedure.

It was then, to her horror, she saw a familiar face in gown and mask, trying not to catch her eye. She was so embarrassed. Paul Jerviss stared and then looked away. Connie was mortified. It was then that she cried out, 'Why won't this bloody thing come out?'

A dapper little man with a carnation in his buttonhole, obviously the consultant, felt around her. 'Put Mother on a drip,' he ordered.

It was Paul who had to insert the needle into her hand. At least he had the grace to blush as he fumbled for the vein. 'Sorry ... I'll try again.'

'It's OK. You have to practise on someone,' she offered. What else were they to do but pretend neither knew the other?

Within half an hour she wished she had not been in such a hurry to deliver, still trying to avoid the eye of Paul. This was the stuff of nightmares. Of all the hospitals in the North of England he'd ended up here!

She had read the leaflets and listened to the girls' tales of woe but nothing prepared her for the agony as the contractions ripped through her in waves. She cried out for Mama in long-forgotten Greek, screamed the place down until someone took pity on her cursing and swearing, sticking something into her thigh and she drifted away.

Then it wore off and she struggled to gain some control of this vicelike grip of new pain burning its way out of her body. When the pushing began they heaved her onto her back.

'Why do I have to push against gravity?' she gasped.

'So we catch the little devil without straining our backs,' said a jolly midwife. 'It won't be long now.'

She was a liar and Connie was tiring. A doctor came with a lamp on his head and ferreted for scissors and still that stupid song rang in her head. She hummed, trying to forget that it was Paul bending over her, encouraging her on with the pushing, Paul about to deliver her baby.

'Just a snip,' said the midwife, and Connie thought about poor Evelyn and her stitches. Why was she laughing and pushing? Then suddenly with another push and a gush it was all over. Everyone fell silent, but Paul lifted the baby up to her and said, 'It's a girl!'

She saw the tiny creature turn from puce to pink with a helmet of red hair and then it was whisked away in a towel.

'What's wrong? Why are you taking it? Paul, please. I want my baby!' Connie screamed. 'Give me my baby!'

The midwife stood in the doorway for a moment, cradling the bundle. 'We're to take this one away...' she whispered to the doctor on duty.

'Are you sure?' she heard Paul intervene. 'Is it in her notes?' Someone brought her card and there was a discussion. Connie was exhausted. But she had to see the baby again. Nothing was decided. How could they do this to her? 'Oh, please, let me have my baby!' There was further discussion in the corridor and then suddenly Paul brought the baby back. He smiled. 'They got the wrong mother.'

Connie fingered the tiny hands, her plump cheeks and loved what she saw. I have created this out of my own body. How beautiful she is, she sighed.

The colours of my love I give to you.

Then a terrible thought nagged at her. What was she going to do? She was wheeled into the postnatal ward where the nurses were brusque. Everyone could see the U on her notes, which meant she was unmarried.

She was attempting to breast-feed when a nurse shoved a bottle in her hand. 'Don't start what you won't finish!' Connie wanted the ground to swallow her up. The other girls on the ward must think she was giving her baby away and she saw them looking at her with disgust.

Connie tried to feed her baby but she was so tense and inexperienced. No one wanted to help her master it but she was going to try all the same. The baby struggled with the nipple, not latching on properly. Why did Evelyn and June find it so easy, and not her? Was the baby rejecting her too? She cried so much that she gave in to the bottle and the baby wolfed it down.

Visiting time was the worst as husbands shuffled onto the squeaking ward, armed with flowers and presents. The other girls spent all afternoon making themselves ready to hold court with their families. Connie pretended not to care and carried on with her George Eliot, pulling the curtains around her so as not to see the families worshipping their new arrival. She wrote to tell Diana the news and got a big card back by return and a promise to visit soon.

She wanted to cuddle her baby all the time but they didn't like them being handled except for feeds. Desperate to groom her and sniff her, cuddle her, she disobeyed instructions and they took the cot away, saying she would spoil the baby.

They were on borrowed time, the two of them, days filled with feeds and nappies and rests. The other girls kept to themselves, sneaking off the ward for cigarettes and illicit wanders down the corridors. Connie wanted this time to go on for ever, but then the chaplain of Green End, the Revd Terry Anderton, came to talk things over with her about adoption.

'Shall we pray about it?' he offered when she said it was too soon for her to decide. He seemed a pleasant enough sort of priest, with big ears that stuck out like jug handles. She kept her eyes on his imperfection to distract from his words.

'I am Greek Orthodox,' Connie replied, hoping he'd leave.

'God hears in every language,' he smiled, but he didn't pursue his arguments. She had earned a reprieve.

When they got back to the hostel it was not the same. There was a new intake of mums-in-waiting, the place full to bursting. Miss Willow said it was all this pop music making girls loose and easy prey.

She took one look at Connie's baby and asked, 'What are you calling her for now?'

There was only one name in Connie's head for this precious infant. 'Anastasia ... after her grandmother. It is the custom,' she replied proudly.

'That's a handful for a tiny mite,' was Miss Willow's reply.

'I think it's a beautiful name,' June offered,

seeing the look on Connie's face.

'It was my mother's name and her grand-mother's name before that. She'll probably get called Anna for short,' Connie said, suddenly feeling sick that it might not be her who would shorten it.

June's parents were coming to collect her. They had written to offer forgiveness. June was jumping with relief but Connie felt jealous. She'd like to think that Mama would have been like them but she couldn't be sure of anyone else now, not even Diana, who had not visited. She was on her own.

Sheila went home without Lorraine. Her mother would not relent and insisted she came home alone or else be out on the street. It was a tearful farewell when her fiancé came to collect her. She made one last trip back to Leeds with her baby and came back distraught. How could a mother do that to her child? Sheila's plight was driving home to Connie now what a stigma being an unmarried mother was.

Connie clung to her baby, trying to work out plans. She owed it to everyone to do something with her A levels, but Anastasia must come first. She deserved the best in the world, this bright-eyed, perfect creature. She must have a lovely home, a good education, with two parents to dote on her, not one who would be tired, resentful and hard up.

All she could offer was second best. If she had married Neville things would be different, but that was not an option now. Not even 'a breast full of milk' as Rossetti's hymn said. She might find a grotty bedsit and they'd live on love with no trimmings. It wasn't enough. Love was about doing the best for your loved one, no matter what. The chaplain said if God could sacrifice his only son to die on the cross, he would give her the strength to give up her daughter into a loving home waiting to receive her even now.

How could she not believe he was right? She was so racked with guilt and fear and shame, knowing she was too irresponsible to look after this little thing in her arms. At night she whipped herself with every reason why she was not worthy to keep her baby. But still she held out from signing those forms.

Everyone was older, wiser, and slowly they were taking the decision out of her hands, gently, persistently wearing down her resolve to find a practical solution. In desperation she'd even written to Gran, begging her to reconsider. Now she was wavering, exhausted, and putty in their hands. Never had she felt so alone, so torn between what was right or wrong, selfish or noble, alone on a raft drowning in the crushing waves of arguments, pressed down from all sides. How could she not capsize?

One glorious morning in June, when roses wafted their heady scent down the path, Connie took her own via dolorosa to the welfare office in town. The baby was in a borrowed carrycot, green canvas with a hood, topped with the blue check blanket, for mornings could be chilly. She'd made a woolly pompom toy for Anna to look at, and round the baby's neck Connie put her own gold crucifix with the Greek cruciform shape, given to her on her confirmation years ago. Anna had to have something of her. The baby was dressed in a brand-new knitted pram suit, turquoise and white stripes, from a pattern borrowed from June. The colour suited her eyes, those aquamarine eyes. Everybody commented upon them, but no one was willing to take a picture of them. She still refused to sign the forms. She wouldn't, not yet, not until she was sure.

A woman in a tweed suit accompanied her, afraid that she might run off.

'Can she keep her name? She must keep her name,' Connie insisted to the assembled officials. 'It is part of her heritage.'

No one spoke.

'And the gold cross?' she pleaded, pointing, but they shook their heads.

'It will be in her file for safekeeping. Baby must have a fresh start. You can have no say in her future. Perhaps one day she may request information. Perhaps not,' said the social worker, ready to lift the carrycot.

But Connie leaped up. 'Let me hold my baby one more time,' she cried, desperate now for every second to be an hour. 'She will have loving parents?' she asked, trying to be brave in the face of all this cold officialdom.

'Of course. They've been waiting a long time,' came the reply, and Connie guessed they were waiting somewhere in the building, ready to collect this unexpected treasure.

'Can I walk her to them?' she pleaded.

'No,' said the woman, restraining her. 'There must be no contact for her sake. It only unsettles everyone... Say your goodbyes to baby here and I will take her to her new home.'

'I must give her something so she knows how much I love her,' Connie whispered, hardly able to breathe.

'You have given her the gift of life and opportunity. That is enough.' The woman lifted up the carrycot again. 'You can keep this. It's too warm for baby,' she said. 'You have all her other clothes for us,' handing back the blanket as if to compensate for the bundle in her arms, picking up the baby's bag. Then they edged through the door.

'But I love her,' Connie sobbed, blinded by terror and tears. 'I can't do this... I won't.'

She collapsed into the arms of the chaplain, who suddenly appeared out of nowhere. Her face was buried in the blanket, sniffing the sweetness of talcum and baby. She sobbed and sobbed until there were no more tears.

'Time to go home, Connie.'

She didn't remember the journey back to Green End. All her friends had left and that night she heard her song on the radio again. 'The colours of my love I give to you...' Connie got up, packed her bags and left in the middle of the night, walking towards Leeds with the tune racing through her head. There was still time. She hadn't signed those forms yet.

Connie wakes on the bench. Every detail of that afternoon is scratched into her heart. How can a wrong thing be done for all the right reasons? Oh, for the wisdom of hindsight. If only she'd been strong instead of weak, determined instead of uncertain. If only she'd waited a little while longer, hung out for her rights. But that was then, this is now. The young ones have no idea what her generation went through. The past is a different country indeed.

The minute her baby left her that was when she knew she'd done the wrong thing. All her life she's searched for her, in her dreams, in prams outside shops, in clinics just in case there was a little sandy-haired baby called Anna with turquoise eyes who was born on the 25 May 1964.

Every birthday for years afterwards, she lit a candle, sent a card for her file, telling her all her news and her address just in case ... but no matter, there was never any reply or confirmation that her daughter ever received any information.

For thirty years it was forbidden for her to make any approach once she signed those forms. All her rights were gone at a stroke of the pen. They wore her down. They wore her down until she signed away her hope, condemned to ache like this for the rest of her life. It never went away. It tore you apart, the void at the centre of her being, that hole in the heart where a little icon sits behind a burning candle.

If only she had waited, if only she'd been strong enough to hold out those six long weeks, things might have been different. In the small hours of the night she prayed to her icon that they would be reunited one day. The blanket was all that was left to remind her, hidden, waiting. The flame at the heart of her never went out, not even in the darkest hours. There has to be a kernel of hope at the heart of things.

PART III

WIVES AND OTHER LOVERS

22

Dr Valium

Esme walked through the door to a pile of mail on the floor and the stale smell of an empty house. She'd been away for nearly a month, renting a room in a farmhouse outside Grange-over-Sands for a change of air, but the trip was over and all she had to show for it was a pile of washing. Welcome home! She sighed to herself, staring at the kitchen, as clean as she'd left it. She was getting used to her own company these days.

Since the big falling out in the New Year, Lily and Levi had scarcely crossed her door; the occasional duty visit and polite chitchat about nothing. The business with Connie and Neville had split the family in two, and it hurt. Heaven preserve you from ungrateful children, she sighed again. After all she'd done for this family too.

She'd been the only one to visit Ivy in that awful place with bars at the window and seen to her comforts when she got back home. Neville's court case had knocked the stuffing out of his mother and she'd forbidden him to visit.

Not a word of gratitude from any of them. Levi and Neville were expanding their business into the High Street without consulting her. Neville was on probation. He wasn't speaking to her either.

Only Susan bothered to come round, wheeling

little Kim to give Joy a break. The christening had been a churchy affair and not a word from anyone about Connie, for whom Susan had stood proxy as godmother. Did you ever hear such a thing! Standing proxy for someone else who was supposed to be making vows on behalf of the baby. What was wrong with adult baptism when the kiddy was old enough to know its own mind? When she'd told them her view at the buffet lunch in Rene Gregson's fancy parlour, everyone went silent and turned away.

She was out of the loop, out of range for them to just pop in, and too proud to admit she was lonely and missing the hubbub of her errant children and their offspring. She'd not seen young Arthur for months. She was too proud to admit she might have made a big mistake in taking Ivy's side in the quarrel.

Last night she'd had such a strange dream. Freddie was standing at the top of the stairs at the Waverley. He was asking for his daughter. One minute it was him and he sort of merged into Connie, and then they stood side by side, identical. They kept opening and shutting doors, looking for something. She was frozen at the bottom of the stairs, unable to help, wanting to reach out to her dead son but her arms wouldn't move. Worst of all, he kept glaring down at her as if she'd done something wrong, shaking his head, and she woke up all of a to-do... That look on his face was still there at the back of her eyes when she shut them.

On the train coming home she kept thinking about Connie and if she'd had the baby. Lily would know, and Neville, but no one was saying anything important to her now.

A quiet empty house, a house where nothing was messed up, no chatter but the wireless for company, no one to walk round the garden with sharing the view, this was what she'd returned to. A house without love and life and noise and bustle was a house, not a home. Poor Ivy lived like this in her empty little palace, peering out of the net curtains, her eyes dulled with drugs to help her nerves. Was this death sentence going to be her fate too?

Oh, Redvers, what have I done? Could I have got it all wrong? What do I do now? she sighed, looking at his portrait for inspiration.

Making a cup of tea with the milk left on the doorstep, she ferreted through the post; the usual bills, appointments, a few postcards and then the unmistakable handwriting of her granddaughter. She tore it open and went in search of her reading specs.

Connie's scrawl was always difficult to read but the letter was short, neat, almost a child's writing.

Dear Granny,

This is to let you know I had a baby girl, called Anastasia, after Mama. I want to keep her but without a roof over our heads it will be impossible. They have suggested she is better off adopted and have given me six weeks to decide. I am begging you to reconsider what you said before. You are my last hope.

Connie and Anna xx

PS, send the reply to Green End, Rawnsworth, Nr Leeds.

Esme took off her glasses, her heart thumping. It was a sign: first the dream and then the letter. The Lord was giving her a clear indication of His will. Then she noted the postmark. It was a month old already.

Connie didn't know how she had landed up at the hostel. All she could recall of that terrible night was walking for miles until dawn. She could have gone to Diana's flat but there was no more energy left inside her to face anyone she knew. So she kept walking. Someone had found her lying in a doorway, her feet bleeding, bought her a cup of tea and a bacon sandwich and taken her to St George's Crypt in the middle of the town where the tramps and homeless found beds and food. Everything was a blur of tears and weariness, as if she was sleep-walking through the day searching, searching prams and baby shops, parks and streets, just in case she'd find Anna.

The mission found her a job selling ice cream in a park, handing dripping cones to sticky fingers – babies, children, parents, always searching their faces just in case. Days turned into weeks. Soon the summer holidays would be over and she could turn her mind to study, to filling in forms for a place somewhere, if only she could concentrate. Nothing mattered any more but putting one foot in front of the other.

They found her digs off Clarendon Road, a squalid bedroom in a back-to-back house, but it was all she could afford, and close to the university if she ever got there. People like her didn't deserve any better. When you break the rules you had to be punished and brought into line, she thought.

She plucked up courage to take a bus to Green End to collect the rest of her things but no one she knew was there any longer, and everything had been sent back to Diana's address. That's when she knew she must face reality and go back to Grove Park once more. She looked in the cracked mirror at her reflection. Her hair was cropped into a bubble of curls after she caught nits, her skin blotchy and pale, with dark circles under her eyes. She wore baggy trousers and a man's black T-shirt. No one bothered her in the street when she looked such a scruff. Her once-beautiful breasts had shrunk to nothing. She could pass for a boy.

It took all her courage to knock on that door. Diana stood back at the sight of her.

'Connie! Where have you been? We've been searching for you! I thought you'd gone home. Everyone's so worried. Come in... Look at the state of you!'

She wolfed down her first proper meal for weeks and Diana slid a letter onto the table. 'This was readdressed here ... from Grimbleton.'

'Does everyone know now?' she said, not looking up. 'Only those who knew before ... and those you've told yourself. Is that from who I think it is?'

Connie nodded and took it into the spare room to read.

Dear Connie,

Thank you for letting me know you are safe. I have reconsidered my position in the light of your

359

present circumstances. I feel it is my Christian duty to offer you and Baby a proper home. I did it for your mother and I will do it for you. Your father expects it from me. I cannot rest easy thinking that one of our next generation might not live among its own and we don't give Winstanleys away.

Come home.

Grandma Esme

Enclosed is your train fare.

Connie froze, chilled to the core by those words. Only last month, faced with the prospect of a homeless future and a tiny baby in tow, she'd gone of her own accord to the welfare office to sign the forms of consent in the sixth week. She had hung out to the bitter end for just such news as this. Now it was too late. She had walked away from her daughter for good, surrendering any hope of them being together. Too late, Gran... Too late...

That night she made her first attempt to end it all.

She woke up in hospital with Diana looking down at her.

'Oh, Connie ... how could you do that to us? It's not the answer ... taking my patients' pills and swallowing them. I'm ashamed of you. What were you thinking of?'

Connie turned her face to the wall. She wasn't thinking anything at all. She just wanted to go to sleep and not wake up. The pain was too much to bear.

'I've rung your aunt and they'll be coming for you. I can't take responsibility for you now ...

what a stupid thing to do! There will be other babies, happier times. You just have to put all this behind you. No use moping here. Better to go back to your family and make yourself useful.'

Connie didn't want to hear any of this. She just wanted to go to sleep. Her throat was raw from the stomach pump. The nurses didn't look at her with sympathy. What did they know of how she was feeling? Diana was being tough for a reason, but Connie was too tired to listen to a lecture and now the Winstanleys would gang up on her too. Why weren't they there when she really needed them?

It was Auntie Lee and Uncle Pete who brought her home and deposited her at Gran's house. Esme was fussing over her as if she was an invalid but no one asked anything about the baby or the adoption. The baby who never came home was a subject no one wanted to address. It was as if none of it had ever happened and now she must get on with her own life as a free agent. She slumped on the sofa and sunk herself into an old woman's routine.

She had no appetite, couldn't be bothered to wash or go out much. Who was there to visit? Joy and her baby were the last people she wanted to see. Granny had a line of photos of little Kim on her sideboard, and there was a postcard from Rosa, who was on a ship bound for Australia.

On trips to town she often saw grammar school girls in their gymslips and red blazers, full of confidence and the giggles. How she envied and resented them. She felt like tapping them on the shoulder to say: 'Don't bother with all those text-books. Go out and enjoy yourselves now. Don't bother with college, it just delays the journey from one life to another.'

'Isn't it about time you washed your hair? It looks a mess,' Gran nagged, handing her a towel.

Connie didn't need anyone to tell her she looked a mess, a stick insect.

'And put something on a little more cheerful. You look as if you're going to a funeral.'

'I'll wear what I want,' Connie snapped, knowing Esme was right. All she wore was grey or black because she felt dead inside, colourless, drab, a walking ghost, and sometimes the urge to end it all suggested itself again in her mind. *This time do it properly. Go where no one will find you. Buy a bottle of painkillers and some gin, anything to relieve the pain in your heart.* It was as if she was walking under a heavy grey, cloud that hovered over everything she did.

Walking through Sutter's Copse with the autumn leaves drifting down on her like confetti, she sobbed. Where was little Anna now? Why had she been so weak and let her go?

Gran shoved platefuls of pies and stews, soup and puddings before Connie, trying to make up for all that had happened but she was too choked to eat anything. Gran prattled on about Freddie, Connie's dad, as if he was still a little boy. I didn't know him, she thought, and he would never know me. I abandoned my baby as he abandoned us.

Perhaps if she went to see the doctor it might help, but then the look on Paul Jerviss's face when she was in labour froze her resolve. Lily had said he was back at Grimbleton Royal, finishing off his training. How would she cope if

362

she bumped into him in a corridor? She couldn't face anyone she knew. There must be other places to seek help.

It was Dr Friedmann who suggested she went to a new surgery across town where there were a team of doctors to choose from. He'd heard one of his colleagues there was good with patients with 'depression'.

'I'm not mental,' Connie snapped. 'I'm just tired. You could give me something to pep me up.'

'You've had enough uppers, young lady. You need help and you know I can't do it, not since Su and I got together. I'm family now. Dr Blackie is the man for you. He'll give you time and prescribe, if necessary. He's got a special interest in the mind and mental health.'

There was no choice but to make an appointment and register as a new patient. She was desperate for an instant cure, but one look at the strange little man sitting behind an enormous desk with half-moon glasses sliding down his nose and she was not so sure.

'How may I help, young lady?'

'I'm not sure... Everything's an effort. I ran away and came back home in disgrace. I was fed up and took an overdose ... an accidental one,' she lied.

'Tell me how you're feeling now,' he asked.

'Terrible. Can't be bothered with anyone or anything.'

'How do you intend to keep yourself – live off benefit, get a job ... or sponge off your family?' he challenged her. 'I hear you're related to Dr Friedmann.'

'What's that got to do with anything?'

'Don't be so tetchy,' he shot back. 'I'm trying to get the full picture.'

'I don't want the whole world knowing I'm here,' she argued.

'You are very defensive, Miss Winstanley. Why are you so angry?' He was not ruffled by her outburst.

'I'm not angry. I'm tired. I don't want to talk about it any more, thank you. I just need something to buck me up so I can make some decisions.'

'I can give you something but I do want to know why you are so angry with the world. Who has hurt you, or are you angry with yourself? In my experience, girls who overdose are crying out for help. Help with what?'

She didn't like his emphasis on girls and being a silly teenager. He was poking and prying into her life and she wasn't having any of it.

'I had a boyfriend and he let me down. I thought I was going to college but I'm not fit for anything,' she offered, hoping to put him off.

'So now you are sulking?' He smiled as if he had discovered the key to her sadness.

'I suppose so. Nothing has gone right this last year and now I'm home, it's not the same.'

'I don't suppose it is, young lady. So why stay around?'

'I've no job, no money and no energy. It's an effort to get dressed of a morning or eat. I don't want to face the day, any day.'

'That does sound like depression to me and we have tablets to lift that mood, but you're a little young to have given up on life.'

'I've not given up. I just don't see a way through the fog.' That bit was true enough.

'Then let's lift the fog and it'll be clearer.' He wrote out a prescription. 'Come back in two weeks and let's see if this helps your mood.' He smiled, satisfied.

Connie snatched the paper and fled out into the waiting room. She'd got a bottle full of pills and hadn't told him a thing. Round one to her. His writing was atrocious and she couldn't read what the pills were but Jacob would know. She'd give them a try and if they were useless, then she'd swallow the lot and finish things off properly this time.

Rosa read her mother's letter with concern. Maria had seen Connie in the street one afternoon and she'd almost ignored her, looking like a zombie, like an old woman, a shadow of her former self. The family were worried about her. She hadn't gone to university and was back working in Neville's shop but she was no advert for Health and Herbs, not the state she was in.

Perhaps she ought to write to her and tell her all her news ... perhaps not. She didn't want to upset her again. She sat in her dressing room smiling at her own image in the mirror. Her face was beaming, blushing, her eyes bright. She was in love and it was so unexpected and exciting.

They were entertaining on the ship bound for Australia. It was a good crew, lots of handsome officers, some nice passengers too. She and Mel danced and sang in the troupe. The weather was fabulous and she'd got her sea legs. It was a huge ship with a first-class deck and top entertainers, magicians, comedians, top-notch pianist and big band, and a guest rock artist with his band.

There were rumours that Gerry and the Pacemakers were on board but when she went to watch the sound check rehearsal who should she bump into but Marty Gorman, strumming up a storm on his guitar. God! He was gorgeous! She'd forgotten how good he was on stage and she stared up at him in disbelief.

'Up the Grasshoppers!' she yelled, and he looked down and smiled.

'Are they still in the First Division? Hey, don't I know you from somewhere?'

'Nice try, but yes, you do. Our Lady of Sorrows ... one of the bumblebees. I knew your brother, Vincent ... in my class. Rosa Santini – you knew my friend.'

'You're one of Connie's mates? How is she?' He ruffled his hair with his hand as if he was nervous.

'Fine, no thanks to you,' she snapped waltzing off.

'Wait!' he cried, jumping off the podium. 'I can explain. I had to strike out on my own. I didn't mean to upset anyone.'

'Well, you did, and her family were furious with her when she got back.'

'I'm sorry. Give her my best when you see her again. Did she do her exams in the end?'

Rosa nodded but she wasn't going to let him off the hook. 'I've not seen her for yonks, but you could sing a few of her songs and help get her name on some song sheets. She's already had one stolen from her.'

'How come?'

Connie told him all about Shady Sadie and 'Colours of My Love'.

'I have one or two of hers but they're not my style now. Fancy a drink?'

'No, thanks ... things to do.' Rosa tore herself away, trying to play it cool. How could she even think of chatting up Connie's old flame?

The flowers came every night before the show: roses, pretty bouquets from the florist's shop flown in from South Africa; wonderful exotic blooms, oranges, golds and crimson.

Mel was green with envy. 'Treat 'em mean, keep 'em keen, is it?'

'Shipboard romances don't last; you should know that by now,' Rosa argued, but she crept at the back of the theatre none the less to see his act most nights when she was free.

Would Connie mind if she had a secret fling? It was all over with them but it was only a year ago. She didn't want to upset Con, but what the eye didn't see... They were young, full of lust and miles from shore. Why shouldn't she have a good time? It wouldn't last. She'd seen enough of these stars to know they had a girl at every gig, hotel room and house, but she was curious. What a feather in her cap to make out with Ricky Romero, the Gypsy King, even if he was just Marty Gorman from Roper Avenue. There were still three more weeks before they docked. Perhaps it was time to let her guard down and give him the once-over. Nothing too heavy, just a bit of fun before he set off on his tour down under and she cruised back home. All work and no play was a mug's game, especially aboard an ocean-going liner. Connie would never know a thing...

Jacob made Connie give the pills to Gran when she got home. He'd left instructions that she was to be treated like a child and doled them out one at a time. He needn't have bothered, for they were useless. If she was tired before, now she was exhausted, ten times more lethargic, and dry-mouthed, sleeping night and day, dragging her limbs back and forth, her lips unable to articulate words. She felt like one of those victims in a horror movie, night of the living dead.

'I can't be doing with these,' she complained when she returned to see Dr Blackie, plonking the packet on his desk. 'I can't think straight. Dr Friedmann wonders if the dosage is too high.'

The doctor wasn't impressed with her diagnosis or Jacob's. 'I am the one who decides your dosage. Perhaps you're not as depressed as you thought. We'll try something else but first I want to hear all about your mood.' He shone a lamp in her eyes so she blinked and couldn't see his face at first.

She didn't want to tell him anything about her moods. She was sick of them. 'I just want to feel some brightness, to see colours again, to feel life is worth living. I have no moods, just one long continuous grey fug to push through.'

He handed out another prescription and told her to come back in two weeks again. The pills this time had the opposite effect, making her twitchy and restless. Her mind was racing ahead and it reminded her of the purple hearts they popped to keep awake when they were living in the van, her heart racing and thudding in her ears. She couldn't eat.

Back she went and she could see he was sick of the sight of her. 'I give you medication to slow you down, and to speed you up but none of it works. Have you thought that it isn't medication you need but a proper job with prospects, time fulfilled so you don't keep dwelling on your disappointments? I'm not sure you are telling me the whole truth about your stay in Leeds, but without honesty I can't help you.' He peered over his glasses and she stood up to leave. 'Perhaps if I send for your notes from your doctor there I might get a fuller picture.'

If he got those he'd know about her pregnancy, and the family would be shamed all over again.

'You're right. I've taken up too much of your time. I'll find work and stick with the medication... Thank you,' she said. What a waste of time.

'I still want to see you in two weeks,' he ordered.

Not on your life, Dr Valium, she thought, racing out of the surgery on winged feet. Fear of discovery had done more than any tranquilliser. The fog was lifted for an instant. She would effect her own cure somehow. No more talking to a stranger who didn't understand just what she'd been through or bother to put her at ease enough to trust him with her secret sorrow. It felt like a Gestapo interrogation with that man.

Keep busy, don't mope about what you can't change, just keep busy... As if to prove her resolve she took a hike up to the Moorlands Estate to see her new goddaughter, Kim. If she could face mother and baby now, she could face anything.

23

The Tupperware Queen

Joy heard the doorbell ringing but sat tight. If she waited they might go away. She didn't want anyone to see her in this state, but she couldn't resist seeing who it was this time and pulled the net curtain aside to catch Connie staring up at her. She hadn't seen her for months.

'Oh, it's you... We were just resting,' she lied when she opened the door. How else could she explain herself still in a dressing gown and slippers at this hour? She had to look twice to see if this pale skinny woman with a bubble cut was really her half-sister.

'What happened to you?' Connie said, barging through the door, pointing to the bruise on Joy's cheek and her puffy lip. 'You look how I feel,' she quipped.

'I had an accident in the car, trying to steer and banged myself on the wheel.'

'I didn't know you drove,' Connie quizzed.

'I'm learning. I heard you were back. We were sort of expecting you. Come and see Kim, but don't wake her. I've only just got her off.' Another lie. She was happiest when Kim slept, and never woke her up.

'So what've you been doing in Leeds? I heard you went to Auntie Diana's.'

370

'Helping out at Grove Park with the youngsters. I meant to come for the baptism but you got my message when I was sick? Sorry about missing the christening.'

'You didn't miss much. There's been a bust-up in the family but no one will tell me why. Do you know?'

Connie shook her head and gave Kim a brief glance, then turned away.

'When she wakes you can hold her,' Joy smiled. It was good to have company.

'Better not ... I'm not good with babies,' Connie replied.

'Neither am I, she terrifies me,' Joy confessed. 'Mummy takes her when she can, and Irene, of course. They dote on her.' Another lie. Denny's parents hardly visited these days. His father took one look at his granddaughter, at her olive skin and black hair, and called her a piccaninny.

Joy showed her round the house. It was spick and span, ready for tonight's event, with all the cushions plumped up and the dishes put away, as Denny insisted. You couldn't tell there was a baby in the house.

'It's all very neat.'

'Denny likes it that way. I've got a do tonight,' Joy replied. Cleaning was the only thing that interested her. It stopped her from moping.

'Is he still with the Grasshoppers?'

'No.' Joy paused. No point telling her he'd been dropped from the team. 'He works for his father now in the coal company.' She heard herself sigh, thinking how bad-tempered he was these days, and how he spent evenings in the pub, then came home full of piss and wind and spoiling for a fight. She took to bed early, but if Kim woke, he lashed out and blamed her.

'Would you like a cup of tea? I'd ask you to stay but Den's home early these days and likes his meal on the table sharp. I've got a party tonight and I'm going to leave Kim at Mummy's.'

'Lucky you,' Connie smiled.

'Oh, not that sort of party, just Tupperware. I'm hosting tonight. Denny's night out, just the neighbours, not your sort of thing. You host and get a present for what is sold. Look.' Joy pointed to the shelves in the fridge filled with pastel-coloured plastic containers. 'It's really good stuff.'

They were being polite like strangers but she couldn't tell Connie just how bad things were or she'd burst into tears and Kim might wake up.

Connie sat on the edge of the Dralon sofa, trying not to make crumbs.

'How's things?' she was asking, and Joy was glad she had on her long-sleeved dressing gown so she'd not see the bruises up her arm. 'So when do you take your test?'

'What test?' Joy was puzzled.

'The driving test,' Connie said and Joy realised she'd been nearly caught out.

'Oh, not yet. I'm not very confident.'

'Will Denny let you use the car?' Connie was looking at her strangely.

'Eventually... I was half wondering if I could do some evening work but that's a long way off. Mummy will baby-sit. She's marvellous. I don't know what I'd do without her. You need your mum when you've had a baby. I'm sorry, that was tactless, but I'm so glad you called.'

'Shall we go out one evening then, you and me, and catch up?' Connie said.

'I'm not sure. I'd have to ask Denny.'

'Doesn't he baby-sit?'

'No, never. It's not a man's job, is it?'

'Never mind, your mum could do it instead.'

'Oh, no, she's not allowed to sit here. I have to take Kim round there, and now that she and Jacob are an item, it's not so easy.' She saw the look on Connie's face. 'But I'll ask. Have you heard from Rosa?'

'Just postcards ... from the high seas.' Connie sighed. 'And you?'

'Just postcards.' She looked at her watch. She must get Connie away before Den came home. There was so much still to do before the party. Her hand went out to wipe a mark off the table. Connie was watching her every move and the blue-black mark round her wrist.

'I'd better be off. Hope it goes well tonight.' Connie rose to leave, eyeing Joy carefully. 'And mind the steering wheel. That looks nasty to me.'

'Thanks for coming. Give me a ring and I'll make sure I'm dressed next time,' Joy laughed at her feeble joke, ushering Connie out of the hall and onto the drive. She shut the door quickly just as Kim woke up for another feed. Now she was late, the meal wasn't ready and Denny would be in a slap-happy mood again.

She'd seen Connie's envy of her pristine house, her baby, all the comforts of being a married couple, but oh, how she envied Connie's freedom. She'd give anything to be living like her and not a prisoner in her own home.

Connie didn't see Joy again for many weeks. For someone who was home all day she was elusive, and no mention was made of the outing. When she phoned Joy was always busy or couldn't get a sitter, Kimberley was sick or some such excuse. She began to wonder if Joy was giving her a message until Auntie Su said she hardly saw her daughter either.

'Denny keeps them to himself, and she doesn't seem herself, but I've offered to host a party for her next week. It'll be the only chance I'll get to see her on her own. You must come and give her some support.'

'I've no money for Tupperware,' Connie was quick to reply. It was not her scene at all, a gaggle of screaming women crushed in the parlour at the Waverley.

'I know, but the numbers count, and as long as we can find someone else to host another party Joy will be happy. You can help me look after little Kim.'

Connie didn't want to look at little Kim, she was too close in age to Anna, too much a reminder of what she'd done. How her life would've been if only she hadn't signed those papers. How could she bear to think of where the baby was and who was giving her the hugs and kisses that were hers by right?

Connie didn't go back to Dr Valium again – she daren't risk exposure – but helping out at the new shop in the High Street, having to get up each morning and put a smile on her face, was slowly helping to dispel some of the fug in her mind. There was a wage, money to buy records and clothes if only she could drum up some interest. It was as if she was marking time until she started some career.

How strange to have regressed back to familiar routines, going to the theatre with Neville. He was subdued since his public shaming. Trevor had disappeared out of town and Neville daren't put a foot wrong in case he was being targeted. At least going out with his cousin made things look normal, but she sensed he was as unhappy as she. Their lives were on hold.

If only Rosa would come home and Joy would get back to being her old self, if only they could turn the clock back to how things were, but all of them were living lives on separate tram tracks, waving from a distance. Nothing could ever be the same because her heart ached for her baby, the secret pain in her chest that never went away. This secret kept her apart as if she were surrounded by a prickly wire fence that sectioned her off from the rest of the family. Some of them knew she was there, but thought it best never to open the subject of why she was so distant. Others hadn't a clue and it must stay that way.

One Saturday morning she took herself off in Gran's old car over the Pennines to Leeds. She couldn't help it. She parked up in Leeds and strolled slowly and deliberately around the bustling market, the shopping centre and busy backstreets. She drove through Headingley and West Park, round the ring road, searching. There were red-haired toddlers. No baby fitted the fantasy, and the whole venture was stupid and a waste of petrol. The baby could be miles away by now, in York or Harrogate, Ripon or Bradford.

There was a picture of herself as a baby in her wallet, the first one taken at the Waverley in the back garden with Neville and Joy. She was praying her baby might look something like her, with that unmistakable hair, but this photo was so creased and worn. It was all she had to remind her of Anna. She drove back exhausted and tearful, wondering why she was punishing herself like this.

On the night of Joy's party, Connie helped Su set out the drawing room with chairs and a table to display all the plastic containers and utensils. Denny had dropped boxes of the stuff with a huff and a puff. He ignored Connie. He'd grown flabby and jowled, with a moustache to hide his petulant mouth.

'Where's little Kim? In the car?' Su asked with a politeness that worried Connie. It was almost as if she was afraid of him.

'She's gone to Mother's. Why Joy needs to do this rubbish I don't know,' he muttered. 'It's not as if she needs to work,' he smirked, looking directly at Connie.

'It's always good to have an interest,' Connie said. 'She must be good at selling.'

'She's useless. People feel sorry for her, that's all. They buy out of pity and I'm not having any of that,' he said, banging down the boxes. 'You sort them.'

'How's her driving,' Connie asked, more for something to say.

'What driving? No woman will be let loose in my Consul.'

'No, of course not. I must've got it wrong,' Connie backtracked. Were Joy's driving lessons a secret?

'Women are hopeless with four wheels unless it's a pram,' he laughed.

The neighbours in Division Street and some from Green Lane began to gather at seven, familiar faces who wanted to know all Connie's doings, but there was no sign of Joy. Su was beginning to panic by the time she burst through the door, white-faced, with another pile of boxes.

'Sorry I'm late. Rene was late for Kim, and Denny had gone out. I had to get a taxi.' She laughed it off but they could see she was trembling.

'I could've come for you,' Connie whispered. 'Here, let me help you set things up.'

If she wanted to be a top Tupperware saleswoman, Joy needed transport, and quick.

Joy delivered her spiel about a hundred uses for Tupperware containers from humble cornflake boxes to mustard pots and 'Party Susan', a hostess hors-d'oeuvres carousel. There were sealed cheese boxes, sandwich holders, milk jugs in sugared almond colours – turquoise, apricot and pale blue.

Joy came alive as she delivered her special pointers, special offers, skimming along the lines, describing their qualities so convincingly that Connie could feel the purses twitching in the handbags. There were even storage boxes for toys and sewing and tools. Everything was so versatile, not cheap but enticing. Who didn't want to have a tidy kitchen?

Soon everyone was scrabbling on the floor, opening lids, looking at catalogues and making orders. Joy looked neat in her matching twinset and pinafore dress. But Connie sensed an agitation under the surface.

No one else volunteered to host a party so Connie suggested that she and Gran do one in Sutter's Fold. There was such a look of relief on Joy's face. Su and Connie dished out the refreshments: trays full of crackers decorated with cream cheese and pineapple, pâté, bite-size sausages on sticks and cake squares and flapjacks.

Joy began to pack up her boxes. She looked tired but her order book was full enough for it to have been worthwhile.

'You're a natural saleswoman,' Connie said. 'You enjoy it?'

'It gets me out of the house,' Joy replied, turning away.

'Denny must be proud of you,' Connie added, but Joy just shrugged. 'How'll you get home?'

'On the bus. I'll leave the boxes for Den to pick up later.'

'It'll be good when you can drive then.' Connie was fishing.

'There's no point in learning. I'd never get the car.'

'But you said last time...' Connie began, and then paused. 'All that stuff about you learning to drive was a lie? Why?' Joy ignored her. 'Look, I'm driving you home. We can put the boxes on the back seat and in the boot.'

'No, that's kind but I can't trouble you.' Joy

smiled her professional smile but Connie wasn't fooled.

'I insist. I didn't buy anything. You must learn to drive, then you could take Kim out each day while Denny's at work.'

They collected up the boxes. Auntie Su wanted to give them supper but Joy was anxious to be off. 'It's getting late,' she pleaded, and sat in silence as Connie drove her back through the town. Joy was shivering. The Morris Traveller was draughty.

'You OK?' Connie asked, but Joy was lost in her own world, not hearing her. She shot out of the car before it had even stopped, grabbing the boxes. There were no lights on in the house. 'Is Denny not back yet?'

'No,' she sighed and there was such a look of relief on her face. 'It'll be fine now.'

'What'll be fine?' Connie asked.

'Nothing. Let's get these inside before...' Joy was like a whirlwind, whipping her stock through the door and into the cupboard under the stairs. The bigger stuff had to go into the garage. Connie was struggling to keep up.

'Just leave the rest on the doorstep,' Joy ordered. 'Fine, thanks... Thanks for the lift.' Joy was blocking Connie's path across the door. 'It's late. You've got the shop in the morning,' she said, dismissing her.

'I don't have to rush.' Connie was inviting herself in but Joy was pushing her back.

'Denny'll be back soon. It's better we leave it here,' she whispered.

'Denny doesn't like me much,' Connie said. There was no point in hiding the obvious.

'It's not that. You know how it is – an Englishman's home is his castle. He's not good with visitors late at night... We have a routine.'

'No worries, Joy, you don't have to explain.' Connie waved to her and jumped back in the car, feeling hurt. She was learning fast that once her friends were in couples they shut themselves off into their little nests from which she was excluded. Two's company, three's a crowd. Now they were almost polite strangers. All those years growing up together counted for nothing once a husband came into the equation.

But in her heart she sensed there was more in this – Joy's nervous agitation, her preoccupation with the time. Why on earth was she afraid of being late?

To Connie's surprise Gran was pleased with the coming invasion. She'd invited all the neighbours in the cul-de-sac to Joy's Tupperware display, and Lee and Maria came, together with news that Rosa was on her way home and docking in Southampton next week. At last a chance for them all to be together like old times! Rosa would be full of all her adventures. Letters and postcards were all very well, but there was nothing like a gathering. Surely Joy would get a night off to see her old friend too?

This time Connie arranged to pick up Joy early. She was not having her struggling on a bus. She knocked but there was no reply. Surely she hadn't forgotten the arrangement? Perhaps she was out of earshot?

'Joy! Joy! It's me!' she yelled, thinking she must be upstairs. 'I came early, let me in!'

380

'You can't come in. I can't come tonight,' a faint voice came from inside.

'Are you sick? You should've rung us. I can still cancel it. Are you in bed?' It was ridiculous shouting in the avenue.

'No, I'm in the loo!'

'Let me in. I'll call the doctor if you're ill.' There was no reply. Connie was furious. Why couldn't she have picked up the phone? Was it something she'd done to upset her? 'Why can't you let me in? Is it something I said?' Connie peered through the letterbox.

'It's not you ... it's me. I've been stupid.' Joy was coming down the stairs slowly in her blessed dressing gown again. She unlatched the door and Connie shot in, all guns blazing.

'What's going on? You could've rung!'

Joy was standing there dishevelled with a burst lip and black eye, a bruise that leeched across her cheek.

Connie stared in disbelief.

'It looks worse than it is,' Joy apologised.

'Another accident driving?' Connie shook her head.

'I bumped into a cupboard,' Joy replied.

'And I'm Marilyn Monroe. Pull the other one. Who did this to you, as if I need ask!'

'It's not what you think. He doesn't mean to. I just get him all wound up. I dither... Look, he's bought me this beautiful bunch of red roses,' she whispered, pointing to a crystal vase full of blooms.

Connie felt sick to the stomach at the sight of such an injury. 'I don't understand. Why is it your

381

fault he hits you?'

'He has a lot of worries ... the business isn't going so well... Everyone has electric fires and gas now... Kim cries in the night... No! He doesn't touch her but he needs his sleep. He doesn't mean it,' she said with such conviction it made Connie want to scream.

'Joy, has the doctor seen these bruises?'

'No, and you mustn't say anything or I'll never speak to you again. I'll deal with this in my own way. He loves me!'

'If he loved you he wouldn't do this to you. You're worth more than this.' Connie wanted to hug her sister, but as she made to Joy recoiled.

'It's not that bad. Don't tell tales, Connie, please. It's none of your business.' Joy flashed such a look at her. 'I'm sorry to have brought you out but I can't go like this, can I?'

'Then tell me what to do and I'll do it for you, just this once.' Connie gulped at what she was offering.

'Are you sure?'

'On one condition: that you don't let him hit you again, right? It's not going to happen again. Promise me?'

'I'm not the only one. Rene's been putting up with it for ages from Den's father. She says you get used to it.'

'Then more fool her. I won't let him do this to you.' Connie was on fire. She wanted to find Den and kick him in the goolies.

'Leave it be. Don't say anything. Don't make it worse. He won't do it again. I'll be careful not to provoke him.'

'Why should *you* be careful? He's the bully boy.'

'He really does love me. He just likes things to be just so. He doesn't like all my stock cluttering the house. I'll give up the party planning.'

'Listen to yourself ... and lose the one night out you get to be independent? What happened to you, Joy? No man is worth getting beaten for.'

'It's all right for you, Goody Two-Shoes. You're single and fancy free. You don't understand. Denny and I were young sweethearts, he's the father of my baby. He wants us to have another one soon. We have this lovely home. It'll get better. This is just a bad patch.'

'Oh, Joy, if only you knew...' Connie almost blurted out her own secret but this was not the time. Joy needed her help not another tale of woe. 'Let's get the boxes packed.'

They piled the stock in the car and Joy pointed out how to start the evening, go round the boxes and make sure everyone saw the catalogue and had a good feel of the product.

'They sell themselves. The salad washer is the latest offer. Get the money up front before you take orders, and find another venue, please.'

'I don't like to leave you like this. Rosa's coming home. We must all meet up.'

'We'll see. I don't want anyone seeing me like this.' Joy waved her off.

Connie drove back in a dream trying to remember everything, her heart aching for Joy's misery. She made up a cock-and-bull story about Joy being struck down with sickness. What made it worse was not the lies but colluding in Denny's nasty violence by saying nothing.

The funny thing was she had a great night. Gran was on form and had baked up a storm of goodies. Connie muddled through somehow, took orders, and found another venue close by.

There was a group of women who organised evenings where they met in each other's houses and had a programme of events. Most off them seemed to be housebound young mothers: one of their gang offered to host a party and was anxious to meet Joy: 'She might like to join us. We have discussions and speakers... Do you think she'd be interested?'

Connie made a note to tell Joy about this Housewives' Register and the playgroup someone was planning for toddlers.

How she wanted to tell Maria and Lee the real truth so they could warn Susan, but a promise was a promise. They had never split on her. But it wasn't right, and she lay in bed tossing and turning, trying to find ways to get Joy to see sense. How could she even think of living with such a monster?

Perhaps when Rosa returned Joy would fess up to her too and somehow together they could sort out this mess. Funny how concern for Joy's pain had made her forget her own sadness, Connie thought. She was needed here and that was enough.

24

Rosa

Rosa couldn't believe they were all sitting together in Santini's sipping cappuccinos as if they'd never been apart. That was the joy of old friendship; you just picked up where you left off. Yet both Joy and Connie were looking tense and tired and so pale.

The café was now La Dolce Vita Espresso Bar. Rosa's Santini cousins had cashed in the old juke box for yet another bulbous monster playing Beatles and the charts. Maria's old theatrical posters were gone and in their place were scenes from the Italian Riviera. Sophia Loren hung from a film poster alongside Rossano Brazzi, the heartthrob from *South Pacific*, who stared out with those sensuous lips. She glanced across the street to where the King's Theatre was now a bingo hall and looking its age. The place was buzzing. Enzo, her cousin, was sporting a Beatle haircut and his new wife, Elaine, was running round just like Mamma used to do. It was good to be back and there was so much to tell them.

She'd just had a furious row with Mamma and was glad to get out of that madhouse.

'How dare you come back here and tell me you're married! What nonsense is this? You are married when you stand before a priest, not a captain on a ship! What will Serafina say when she learns you have robbed her of being your brides-maid?'

'You've not heard a word I said. It was just a civil ceremony. We can have a party later and a blessing in church. Marty's not home yet for ages.'

'What girl gets married on ship and then leaves husband...?' Mamma's English was breaking down in an effort to cross-examine her.

'We both had contracts to fulfil. I couldn't let Mel down. Don't be cross with me. He's a good Catholic boy, like you always wanted.'

'What good Catholic boy lets you marry on a boat?'

'On a ship... It's a ship.'

'Don't get clever with me! I wiped your bottom not that long ago, don't forget. Do I have to start knitting?' Maria glared at her daughter's stomach with interest.

'Of course not. I'm on the pill.'

'Holy Mary, Mother of God, do you hear such blasphemy! There'll be no pills in my house. What does Mrs Gorman have to say to all this?'

'I haven't met her yet. Marty has written to her.'

'Why the rush? How will I tell my friends you have shamed me?'

'There's no shame in marrying someone you love. We thought it would be fun.'

'Marriage isn't fun, it's bloody hard work. You hardly know him... Out of sight, out of mind. Are you sure he'll come home?'

'I'm not listening to all this,' Rosa had argued. 'I'm meeting the girls. They'll be happy for me. Anyone would think we were living over the brush. Look, here's my rings and a picture to prove it. It was so romantic!'

'Tush ... romance. What has romance got to do with anything? This is a life sentence we are talking about. Have I had a day's rest since I married Sylvio? Work, work, business and babies. I didn't want that for you. I wanted you to be my star.'

'You wanted me to live your dream and I have. I've travelled the world and now I'm back for a while. I've found the one for me, so be happy for us.'

Why was everything between them such a battle? Mamma was never happy unless she was worrying over them, fussing over Luca, spoiling the boys. She and Marty just wanted to have fun and be together. It was funny how they just clicked into place, slotted together, laughing at the same things, sharing the same background. She'd found her soul mate and she was giddy with happiness. No one was going to pour cold water on her good news.

Rosa was being very mysterious. She was bronzed and wearing the shortest mini-skirt, Connie had ever seen, little more than a pelmet, and tights too, real nylon tights with white boots. Her hair was piled up into a tousle of curls and her eyes were made up like soot.

Joy had come with Kim, who was sitting in a high chair, sipping juice from a plastic beaker. Connie wondered if Anna would be feeding herself yet.

'You look a million dollars,' Connie smiled.

Rosa suddenly held out her ring finger to show off a beautiful solitaire diamond over a gold wedding band, and Joy and Connie shrieked.

'You dark horse! When, where and who?' Connie gasped. Rosa was married and hadn't told them!

'It was all a bit of a rush on board ship, like in the film *The African Queen*. We didn't even have a ring so we borrowed one from a passenger. It was so ... romantic. He had to go on to Australia to do a gig, but he's flying back soon and we'll have the biggest bash ever. It was in the papers there. I would've told you. It was all so sudden and I'm so happy. We couldn't believe it ... we both knew. "Just One Look" like the song.' Rosa began to sing the song.

'But who is this Mr Wonderful?' Joy asked. She'd brushed her hair forward into a long curtain and deep fringe, which hid a yellowing bruise.

'Oh, didn't I say? Someone you both know, actually.' Rosa's cheeks flushed. 'I hardly dare tell you.'

'Who?' They were both so curious now, leaning forward, all ears.

'Guess?'

'Not Paul Jerviss?' Joy asked.

'Don't be daft, he's a medic in the hospital,' Connie snapped. 'One of his mates?'

'Warm ... from the Salesian college. Who do we know who went into showbusiness from there?'

'Not Des O'Malley?' Connie said, but her heart was thumping. There was only one name left on her lips and she couldn't say it.

'Getting hotter by the minute. Look!' Rosa produced a wedding snap of the two of them looking smug, standing by the captain. 'Mr Snake-Hips Gorman. Marty. I married Ricky Romero!'

Connie went through the motions like a pro. She forced her cheeks to widen into a grin and whispered, 'How lovely. You both look very happy.'

'We are. It was just a bit of fun, us being miles from anywhere on the high seas. We got talking about home and families and friends. He sends his love to you, by the way. I knew you wouldn't mind me going out with him. It was ages ago, wasn't it?'

Connie felt sick, the coffee gagged in her throat. She couldn't swallow it down. A whirlwind romance... So much for Marty not being tied down.

'How's his career going? I haven't heard him in the charts for ages!'

'You won't. He's doing more technical stuff in recording studios, helping record companies.'

She was being vague. It hadn't worked out for him as he'd planned, then. 'Some session work and the odd gig. Just wait till you see him. He's so gorgeous.'

With one name Rosa had ruined this rendez-vous; with one photo, taken Connie right back to London and Switzerland and that terrible time afterwards. How could she ever tell her friend that Marty might be the father of her lost baby?

It was as if a glass shutter fell down between her and the others. She heard their prattle through muffled ears. She wanted to run out of Santini's and flee from Rosa's happiness. Why couldn't it have been her? Then she would have a baby sitting alongside Kim.

'Can I kip down with you for a few nights?' Rosa said to Joy. 'Mamma and me have fallen out. She thinks I've let the Church down but we're going to have a blessing with Mass and everything. She'll come round eventually. Serafina's not speaking to me either.'

'I'm sorry.' Joy looked panicked by this request. 'I'm not sure...'

'Forget it. I'd better go back and make my peace,' Rosa smiled.

'So what's going to happen to your showbiz career?' Connie asked.

'The *Gazette* asked me that. There'll be a spread in the paper on Friday: "Local Stars Make Good". Mamma doesn't know about that. She'll forgive me then. Marty wants us to travel together but I have had a great year. I missed all you lot, though.'

'You can't have a career and babies when they come,' Joy interrupted. 'A child has to come first, and our husbands, of course.'

'Listen to yourself. You do party planning – that's a career, or the beginning of one,' Connie couldn't resist. She turned to Rosa. 'She's quite a sales girl. Surely you can do both?'

'Joy's right in a way. To get to the top you have to be ruthless, dedicated, nothing must get in the way of your auditions or your next show. There were girls dancing on the ship who had babies back home and were pining for their little ones. I wouldn't want someone else bringing up my kids.'

Connie flinched at her words. Rosa had changed. She was softer round the edge. Love had replaced that burning ambition. How envious Connie was of her happiness.

'What do you think, Joy?' Connie pushed. 'Who comes first in your family?'

'Connie! You promised... She's talking off her head, Rosa. She thinks Denny and I are heading for divorce.'

Connie brushed Joy's fringe to the side to

reveal the bruises. 'Look at that. It isn't make-up. It's Denny's fist. Rosa should know the score. Not all marriages are made in heaven.'

'Is this true? Oh, Joy, I'd kill him if he did that to me,' Rosa whispered.

'You've both got it all wrong. For better or for worse, that's what I promised. I know we'll get through this. It's the drinking that does it. He's like his father. They can't hold it and it changes them. Honestly, we've discussed it and it won't happen again. Just leave it, both of you.'

Why did she not trust Joy to stand up to him, Connie wondered. Joy'd invested her whole life in her precious house and its carpets and furnishings. Kim was the coolest baby in town with her little outfits, but there wasn't a book in the house. What had happened to all Joy's reading, to all those travel plans? Now she was as isolated from her friends on that housing estate as Connie was in the family.

Joy was silent on the way back, but when they got closer to her house she exploded.

'How dare you tell Rosa my business like that? But I expect you were put out about Marty. You can be a grade-one cow, sometimes! You're just jealous,' she said, and Connie shuddered.

'I don't think so. Not of the life you're living now. I want to do something with my life first. Did you join the Register I told you about? Did they send you a programme?'

Joy nodded. 'When have I time to gad about with a load of chattering women? Party work takes up all my time. I don't need that sort of thing. I told you it was just a bad patch. Denny

391

was worried when you called round. He says to tell you it was all a misunderstanding.'

My arse, Connie thought. He knows I know. Perhaps that will keep her safe for a while, or will he put the bruises where they don't show?

'I could sit for you one night.' She was trying to make amends for telling Rosa.

'Thank you but you've done enough damage. Denny isn't keen to have people in our house.'

'But he goes out. Why not you?'

'Oh, shut it, Connie. Don't meddle in things you don't understand. Leave us alone to sort it out. What goes on behind closed doors is private. Don't interfere. Sort your own life out. Stop moping around. Do something useful or find a man of your own and then tell me how it feels.'

'I was only trying to help.'

'Well, you're not helping.'

They drove the rest of the way in silence. Connie was smarting from Joy's outburst. Kimberley was quiet in the back. She was such an appealing child, with those dark eyes and curls. How could Denny not recognise how lucky he was? If only Connie could believe that Joy would stand up for herself when the next fight came...

Neville looked at the stiff card invitation to Rosa and Marty's wedding with a smile. It would be the biggest bash the town had seen for years. 'Rock Star Marries Cruise Line Starlet', the paper announced. The fact that Marty wasn't Cliff Richard, the fact they were already married aboard ship, and Rosa was little more than a chorus girl, didn't seem to matter. Connie and he were going to go together. He wondered, as Marty's ex, just how she was feeling on top of everything else. It was almost a year since her baby was born and he still wondered who the father was. Connie was a closed book on that subject.

It was going to be a black-tie job in the big country house hotel outside town after a Nuptial Mass at St Wilfred's. The great and the good of Roman Catholic Grimbleton would be there: all that incense and knee-bending was very theatrical. He quite fancied converting if it weren't for all the other stuff he'd have to believe and practise.

He was being extra careful these days. No trips to Manchester clubs to eye the talent. The magistrates had been lenient, taking into account his youth, his family background and intended marriage, and he'd pleaded guilty to the offence. There was a fine and warning, but the case got the full treatment in the *Mercury*, the worst shame of all. He'd slinked behind the market stall for months afterwards, convinced no one would want him to serve them, but nothing was said to his face. His father stood by his side and he learned to grow a tough shell round his feelings. 'Smile and wave at yer troubles, sonny. It'll pass,' said one of his old customers. He could have hugged her for her compassion. Others didn't look him in the eye any more but snatched their coins and fled as if he was some nasty pervert.

It was a customer who told him that Trevor and his mother had exchanged their council house for one in Burnley. They'd never met again except in court. It was all so sad and unfair. What with his mother's breakdown, Gran, and Connie's baby,

Neville just kept his head down. He'd put his energies into setting up their health shop in the High Street. It was more like a chemist's shop, selling smellies and herbal products, soaps and packaged pills and potions.

He did visit Ivy, but she was distant and dopey, drifting through her days in a haze of cigarette smoke and television. Her breath smelled of cheap sherry and peppermints. She was no longer the firebrand he'd known and he felt sorry for her loneliness.

They'd smartened up the rooms above the shop so he could live there. It was a compact flat, but he'd had such fun making it funky with white walls and black furniture, abstract print curtains and jazzy pictures on the wall. There was nothing like having the key to his own door. If only there was someone to share it with, but there'd been no one on his radar since Trevor. How could there be?

Things were changing though. The *Guardian* had letters from homosexual men asking for a change in the law. There were moves afoot to allow some private relationships to flourish behind closed doors. The film *Victim* had raised discussion at the highest level. There was hope perhaps for the future. All he could do now was to subscribe to magazines that gave him a fix of talent and beautiful bodies, reminding him that he wasn't the only queer in the world.

Joy insisted Rene Gregson sat for Kim so she and Denny could enjoy the wedding without having to watch the clock. Susan and Jacob were guests of Maria and Sylvio Bertorelli. There'd been such a fuss over what to wear. Mummy wanted her to go Burmese style in a silk *longyi* and boxed jacket, but she knew Denny would sulk at this display of national pride.

If she were to keep him sweet she'd need to make a traditional evening dress, and soon. He'd not touched her since Connie's unexpected visit but she felt uneasy.

For once she had money to splash on some lovely brocade in a deep cherry-red colour. Her party plan business just kept getting better. Everyone wanted Tupperware in their kitchens. She'd been invited into some of the smartest homes, and her delivery was now so polished and slick she could sail through an evening, confident of success. Now Head Office had asked her to train up other starters, and she was learning to drive on the quiet with her earnings. It was good to have her own bank account and cheque book, which bought Kim extra treats and toys.

For the first time in months she felt more like her old self again and she'd even gone to one of the Housewives' Register meetings on the estate where they were talking of starting up a play-group for little ones in the local church hall. It would be run by the mothers themselves and manned on a rota system; a chance for children to mix and share pre-school activities. The idea was catching hold all over the country.

Twenty young mothers sat squashed in the sitting room, most of them living close by, making her welcome, jabbering away about things they'd read in the paper, or in a book or on the radio. When had she last thought about the world outside her own kitchen? She took Kim to play at their fund-raising coffee morning, and for the first time since her birth Joy no longer felt so isolated.

If only Denny would lift himself out of his black mood. He thought all her activities a waste of time but he did nothing except work and drink, not playing any sport, growing fat and driving coal lorries, which he said was demeaning.

'One day it'll all be yours,' she offered in sympathy, but he just shrugged.

'I'm just a glorified coal man.' He couldn't get over being dropped by the Grasshoppers. He hated Pete Walsh, the coach, Lee's husband, and by extension all the Winstanleys.

She suggested he do something useful, like training up youngsters into a team, talent-spotting, but he dismissed each idea with a withering look.

They were drifting apart and it scared her, but now they had a fabulous night to look forward to, a chance to be a couple again.

Joy cut out her material into a shift with a low back with a bow at the base and a long kick vent to show off her legs. She'd found a silk wrap to tone in among her mother's collection, and the feel of the silk and the sensuous colours made her yearn for the country of her birth. She could style her hair, thick and lustrous, into the traditional Burmese bun at the nape of her neck, and pin a corsage into it for effect. She wanted Denny to see her at her best. They were young and had all their life together ahead of them. Joy shivered. Why did that thought no longer give her any comfort at all?

Connie was struggling to summon up any enthusiasm for Rosa's wedding, and it wasn't because of Marty. She'd met him twice since he flew back and there was nothing there between them. He'd been kind and brotherly to her, she could see that now, never besotted or in love. In fact he'd humoured her but when she saw him gaze down at Rosa, his eyes lit up with adoration and sparkle. They had found something in each other and it glowed off them. If only she could be sure that Anna was not his child. Should she tell him but say that Anna could be Lorne Dobson's girl? It was just too shameful to discuss.

Now it was May and this time last year ... it was all so raw and sore and secret. No wonder she couldn't be bothered to find a new dress. She'd no money, but Gran was determined she'd not let the side down.

'You're only young once, treat yourself,' she said, shoving a pile of notes into her hand. It was conscience money, Connie thought: too much and too late. If only she'd been so generous last year, then life would be different all round. It was hard not to be resentful. 'Get something nice from Whiteleys,' Gran ordered and Connie did. Neville would moan if she turned up like second-hand Rose.

She found a turquoise-blue lacy slip dress with a matching coat. It was short and showed off her long legs. She'd had her ears pierced and treated herself to some long dangling turquoise and silver earrings and some pretty silver T-shaped shoes to flash up the outfit. Mustn't let the side down. They'd all be there: Su and Maria, Queenie Quigley, all the old Olive Oil Club faithfuls, except one of them was missing.

If only Mama were here to enjoy this fashion parade. Her absence was so powerful in this rotten year, but at least Rosa's big wedding would cap it off with something more cheerful.

25

Oh, What a Night!

Rosa stood back from the long mirror, puzzled at her reflection. Who was this stranger looking back at her, this elegant woman with eyes flashing like jet? Serafina was lifting up her dress at the back, trying to be the perfect bridesmaid.

She was glad she'd held out about the puffed-out wedding dress. She was already a married woman but she'd given into Maria's chunterings that no daughter of hers was going down the aisle in a mini-dress, showing next week's washing. They'd fought and cursed, slammed doors and stormed out, made up and compromised on this beautiful oyster-white fitted evening dress with crystal beading over the fitted bodice and a tight skirt gathered in the back into a fishtail net concoction. It was theatrical, thanks to Dilly Sherman, who'd found just the right boutique in King Street, Manchester.

Melanie Diamond was her other bridesmaid, having a crafty fag downstairs. Rosa felt mean not asking Connie and Joy, but both of them seemed relieved to be out of the limelight. Mel and Fina were happy in shocking-pink satin with puffed-out skirts and matching satin shoes. Their hair was piled up into cottage loaf buns with matching fuchsia head-bands. The colour suited their dark dramatic looks.

Marty was banished to his parents, who'd welcomed Rosa into the family with open arms, his big brothers crushing her fingers with handshakes.

Sylvio's team had everyone's hair under control, working since dawn, making sure everyone had a style to suit their outfits. She'd never called Sylvio 'Daddy' and kept a picture of Marco Santini in her prayerbook; she could hardly recall him now, but the smell of Dettol always took her back to a sad time when Auntie Lee took her home and she'd wet herself the night her father died. Sylvio had done a good job, though, and she was proud that he had stood by her mother when Salvi was born so quickly after their wedding. It had caused a terrible rift with the Santinis, one that was never going to heal. That was why she'd chosen St Wilfred's for the service, not Our Lady of Sorrows. Only her cousins would attend today.

Why did weddings bring out all these sad bits of family history? Memories of lost loved ones, petty arguments about who sat where and with whom, those not invited and why. She didn't want to think about all that stuff now. The service would be long and chilly in that concrete barn of a church, but it had to be done, and after that they'd have a night to remember. They were going to have a ball!

The church was packed inside and out with

hordes of sightseers wanting to catch a glimpse of the golden couple. The photographers were snapping away as they made their entrance together with their families in a break with tradition. Maria was dressed from head to toe in her favourite lilac with a pillbox of flowers stuck on the back of her head. The men were in pinstripes, black tie or dark suits, with white heather in their buttonholes for luck. The church was candlelit and sparkling, still smelling of varnish, the seats were hard and Neville noted the organ was electric. Everything was too modern for his taste. There was a sprinkling of his regular customers in stiff collars, looking scrubbed up for the solemn occasion.

The flowers were gorgeous, a riot of expensive blooms with rich foliage and tasteful arrangements. He'd never seen such extravagance and flair.

'Who did the flowers, not the church ladies?' he asked Joy to his left.

'The new florists in town, Consider the Lily … won a gold at Chelsea Flower Show, so Rosa said.'

'It brightens up the concrete, doesn't it?'

Joy nodded, looking gorgeous, and Denny sat stiff but sober. To his right Connie had made a Trojan effort but her eyes were sad and he guessed who she might be thinking about. They'd both survived the whirlwind of last year but he felt she was still drifting, not settling to anything much. She was wasted as a shop girl. Now Joy was busy making her empire and Rosa and Marty would leave town, what would become of her?

Thank God, Neville prayed, he and Connie hadn't married to please their folks. The sky hadn't fallen on them either but Rosa marrying Connie's old flame, and with such mystery around the baby's genes ... he wondered. But now was not the time to dwell on any of that.

Then the organ pipes struck up. Everyone stood. It wasn't the traditional Bridal march, but Purcell's Trumpet Tune and Air, very jaunty and original. The show was about to start.

The Country Club had done them proud, with great circular tables festooned with flowers and confetti roses, white linen and silver candelabras, a trio playing in the background as the guests wolfed their way through prawn cocktail, roast beef and Yorkshire pudding followed by Chantilly meringue and ice cream with crushed pineapple.

The speeches were mercifully short, funny enough, and poor Sylvio got carried away by his emotions, breaking into Italian. 'I never think when I am in this country against my will, one day I see my daughters in such a place. I am verra proud man. Rosa make me happy and Maria.' Tears into his hanky. 'I wish you all happy night.'

They toasted the couple, the family, the brides-maids. Connie just let it all wash over her. Go with the flow, the hipsters said. She was doing her best to look cheerful and involved. Rosa was happy. It was her turn for happiness, but what if she knew that Anna might be Marty's child? What then for their friendship? Why did these thoughts flash into her head? Night and day, listening to the radio, driving the car, standing in a bus queue, lying in the bath, she was struck by the force of her yearning. It was a stab wound into her heart

401

every time. Stop it! she chided herself. This is their day, not yours; their chance to start a new life together, not yours. Don't be so selfish!

Joy was watching Denny knocking back his wine during the toasts and asking for refills. She kept topping his glass up with water but he pushed it aside with a glare. Why did he spoil things by drinking too much? Was he nervous amongst her friends? Was it because they were in the public eye and he was known? Was it because he was bored and couldn't be bothered to make small talk with the woman sitting next to him, who was perfectly charming? She was trying not to draw attention to her ways of slowing down his drinking.

It took only a few too many glasses for him to switch from jolly and affable, confident and polite to edgy, aggressive and rude. At least he couldn't take his displeasure out in public. He'd save that until he went home. Tonight she'd sized up his mood and would make some excuse to go back with Mummy and Jacob. He could punch his pillow, not her.

Looking across at Rosa, she thought of her own wedding day, not that long ago, when she had been so trusting and overawed, thinking it was the pinnacle of a girl's life to go down the aisle with the first man who asked her.

Rosa had been round the world and Joy had hardly been out of town. Rosa had stories to tell but she had only horrendous memories of being flung across the bedroom floor, assaulted whether she wanted lovemaking or not, pinned against the wall in terror while Kim cried in the next room, tormented by Denny locking the doors, turning the lights out, pushing her onto the bed and forcing her legs apart. No woman should have to be at the mercy of such temper and fury. It was as if he hated her. She'd made so many excuses for him, lied and hid away, but something in her head had shifted. She was seeing him for what he was: weak, sullen and possessive. He wanted to control her every move and when she defied him he punished her. What sort of love was that?

Rosa had found her prince in Marty. They had so much in common. How she envied them their future together. How she wished she were fancy free like Connie. She looked at her husband for the first time with eyes rinsed clear of any sympathy. All she felt was revulsion as those terrible scenes of violence played themselves out like a film. *Am I stuck with you for the rest of my life? What have I done?*

She swallowed back her wine in a gulp and held out her glass for more.

The ballroom was on fire with dancing bodies twisting to the sound of some of Marty's old beat merchants. It was hot, smoky, sweaty, and jackets were off, the men glowed lime-lighted, fluorescent in the spinning glitterball as they jived. At nearly midnight they were still dancing, waltzing and chatting. Rosa was so excited that the wedding was going so well. Everyone was mixing and the drink was flowing. Her friends and family were all around her. Even Connie was letting her hair down with Neville.

Rosa was now Mrs Gorman in the eyes of

Mother Church and they were going off to Ireland from Holyhead the next morning to visit the Irish Gormans, who wanted to give them a proper Irish welcome with Guinness and jigs. This would be their first night alone together since Marty's return. Mamma had refused to let them kip down until Father Patrick had made them legal. Rosa was bursting with goodwill to all men but dying to have Marty to herself.

It was one of those moments when she wanted to catch every sensation, sound, the essence of a wonderful day, and bottle it up in a jar. What had she done to be so lucky? All the arrangements had worked, not a glitch to spoil the day. She wanted the night to go on for ever.

As she danced with her friends, all girls together, shaking their bodies and showing off, with Serafina doing a turn in the middle of them, she became aware of a kerfuffle at the side of the dance floor. They carried on, ignoring the horse-play, thinking it a bit of fun, and then she saw Joy looking anxious and leaving them to see what was happening. Rosa followed out of curiosity.

Joy could see Denny was in trouble.

'Shut yer fuckin' gob!' he gestured to Enzo Santini, who was raising his hands, ready to walk away. 'Say that again!'

'Look, mate, forget it ... you're drunk,' Enzo replied.

'Don't you walk away from me, you wop!' Denny was taunting the lad, who turned on him in anger.

'No wonder we lost the cup, old bandylegs here

lets the ball through his legs for an own goal! We lost because of you, Gregsy!'

Denny leaped to hit him but Enzo darted away.

Joy tried to restrain him. 'No, Den, not tonight ... not now!' she ordered.

He pushed her aside roughly. 'Shut up, you bitch!'

'No, I won't shut up. You are making an ass of yourself. Come on, let's go. You're not welcome here.'

'I'll bloody well go when I'm good and ready. No greasy spoon tells me where to get off!'

She tried again, but this time he knocked her sideways onto the table, sending the glasses flying.

'Don't you dare hit my friend, you drunken pig. I'll not have you hurting her. We all know your little game. Beat it!' Rosa stood looking up at him while Joy straightened her dress.

'Bugger off, you little show-off!' Denny picked Rosa up as if she was a piece of cloth and threw her down on the floor with contempt. Marty, Enzo and his brothers leaped on him and dragged him out of the room for a beating. Joy was screaming, 'they'll kill him!' And the band tried to play on. Connie and Neville were kneeling over the bride.

Maria came rushing forward with Jacob Friedmann. 'Rosa?' he said, and she eyed him with rolling eyes and fell asleep. Nobody spoke but Rosa didn't move.

'Fetch an ambulance,' Jacob ordered. 'Clear the floor and let her get some air.'

'Shall we carry her to the side?' Maria cried, patting her daughter's hand.

'Don't move her ... not yet. Just get everybody

out of here!'

Joy and Connie clung to each other as Neville drove them through the darkness to Grimbleton Royal. No one could believe what they'd just witnessed. Denny was flattened, kicked and beaten, arrested and in a police cell to sober up. Rosa was in the ambulance with Marty and Maria.

They stood in the grim hospital corridor in all their finery, bedraggled, smoking to soothe their nerves, watching nurses and doctors going in and out of the cubicle where Rosa lay. It was only a fall, so quick, but she wasn't waking up. Then they saw a white coat they recognised. Paul Jerviss was on duty and it was a relief to see his handsome face, grim as it was as he waved and rushed by.

They sat through the night, wondering what was going on behind those doors. A terrible drama was unfolding and Joy was shaking.

Neville was doing his best to calm their fears. 'It was just a bump on her head. Did you see the state of Denny when they'd finished with him? He'll be needing stitches when he comes out.'

'I don't want to talk about him,' Joy said. 'Not ever.'

'Shush,' Connie whispered. 'It's the shock.' She looked up to see Paul striding down to them, his tired eyes dull and serious. 'How is she?'

'Mrs Gorman is resting. She's conscious now...'

'Oh, thank God! Can we go and see her?'

'I'm afraid not. She'll have to be transferred from here to a specialist unit. We think she may have broken her back!'

Joy rushed out to be sick and Neville followed,

leaving Connie to face her old adversary. She stared uncomprehendingly into those blue pools. 'But it's her wedding night. It can't be serious. Rosa is a dancer.'

'I know. Marty told me. I'm sorry, we just don't know yet. It was a heavy fall onto a hard surface from height. I gather she was thrown backwards.'

'But you can't hurt yourself on a wooden floor.'

'It just depends if she caught the edging, the angle. She's a tiny thing.'

Connie sat stunned and he sat down next to her. 'How are you?' he said. 'I heard you were home.'

Connie didn't speak. 'Just a year ago ... when we last met ... I had to give her up ... the family made me give her up and then changed their minds but it was too late ... this very month.'

'I'm sorry. I wondered if that would be the outcome. You must be gutted.'

She didn't want to think about any of that now. Rosa was all that mattered now.

'Why, why ... why, Paul? Why Rosa and why now? It's not fair. It was Denny who did it to her. How do we live with that?'

'I don't know what to say. They'll do tests. It's a good place and if there's the slightest chance of recovery they'll suss it out and get her back on her feet again, I promise.' He drew close to comfort her and for once she sank into his shoulder, suddenly exhausted. Then she jumped back, embarrassed, feeling awkward.

'If there's anything I can do...' he offered, and she looked up at him with concern. He looked tired, bags under his eyes. He was a kind man doing a worthy job, way out of her league now, of course. He had purpose to his life, helping others live. How could she look him in the face after how they'd last met? If only things were different. He must think of her always as a victim, not an equal. What had she done to earn his respect? How she'd like to make him proud of her one day.

'You'd better go on your rounds. Don't let me hold you back,' she said. 'I must find Joy.'

'Take care, Connie. You look worn out.' He stood up and set off back towards the ward. She watched him walk away from her wistfully. If only... None of that. Rosa was going to need all her friends gunning for her, praying for her recovery. Nothing was going to be the same for her again.

Rosa woke up not knowing where she was and what was happening. It felt as if she'd been asleep for months. She could recall faces bending over her, white coats and nurses, Marty bending over to kiss her. Where was she? What had happened? Then the sickening reality washed over her in a wave of panic.

She was somewhere in hospital strapped to a bed, unable to move a muscle, lying helpless, trapped in a prison of restraints. She recalled the wedding day and the dance and the fight, and then everything went blank. No one would tell her what was wrong or why she was here but it was not looking good.

The priest on his rounds glided past her bed, not looking her in the face. Mamma cried when she visited and her brothers and sisters weren't allowed to come through the door in case they gave her a cold.

'When can I get up?' she begged the nurses.

'All in good time,' came the guarded reply. 'You need to rest your back.'

'Why can't I feel my legs?' she asked the doctor who read her notes and added his own.

He didn't look at her when he spoke. 'Don't be impatient, young lady. Healing takes time. We need to know what nature will do about this first.'

'What has nature got to do with this?' He was talking gibberish. Nature was leaves and acorns, blue skies and the seasons.

He sat down then. 'We think the fall on your back may have caused compression of the vertebrae that may have damaged axons – nerve endings, which carry the messages from your nerves to your brain. The extent of the damage is yet unknown. Only time will tell. We don't want you to move.'

'But I'm a dancer,' Rosa croaked, knowing all about muscle wastage and how it could weaken limbs. 'When will I walk again?'

'You won't unless you're very lucky. It depends on the extent of the damage. You were very unlucky to fall like that. Were you drunk?'

'It was my wedding night. Some drunk tried to knock his wife about and I stopped him so I got thrown.' That bit she suddenly recalled in a flash.

'I see.' The doctor stood up. 'What a pity...' He walked off, leaving her numb with the shock of his hard words. She stared up at the ceiling in disbelief. This must be a dream. This must be happening to someone else. How could she live trapped in a broken body for the rest of her life?

She turned her face to the wall and wanted to die.

Joy kept putting off the moment when she went to visit Rosa in hospital. She couldn't face what Denny had done to her friend. He'd been charged with grievous bodily harm. If she'd anything to do with it, he'd go to prison for a long time, but that was unlikely. The Gregson mafia would see to that.

Their marriage was over from the moment she went home to the Waverley with Kim. She stripped the house in Moorlands and insisted it be sold. She never wanted to see him or that place again, with all its bad memories.

No man was ever going to treat her like that again. She would bring up her daughter alone with the help of Su and Jacob. How grateful she was for a roof over her head and her family's protection, but now she would work full time and make her own way. She filed for separation and divorce on the grounds of cruelty, and if she had to she'd drag his family name through the mud in the papers.

How could she have ever been such a punch bag, such a wimp, such a trusting fool? How could she forgive herself for putting Rosa in such danger? She should've refused the invitation. She relived that terrible fight over and over again, trying to make it better, but nothing could change what had happened to her friend and it was all her fault. She was too ashamed to see Rosa, and the longer she left it the worse it got. How could she ever look her in the face again?

Connie spent the summer with her head in Winnicott's *The Child, the Family and the Outside World*,

410

tomes by Bowlby and Titmuss, and whatever books on the science of sociology she could get hold of. There was a place available for a degree course and she'd applied with Jacob's help and her good A levels. No more sitting around feeling sorry for herself, not with what Rosa was going through.

Rosa's suffering had galvanised Connie into making decisions for the future. There was so much to read and take on board and she wanted to be well prepared. It was ages since she'd done any studying and she felt so rusty. She would have to learn to share a room with a stranger, live off a grant, but Granny Esme had coughed up for her trunk and book list, no doubt relieved to have her back on track.

They tiptoed round each other at times. It was if Anna had never happened and that part of her life could all be shoved under the carpet. The love she'd felt for her as a child had shrivelled away. Esme had let her down, they'd all let her down, but most of all she'd let herself down in not holding out a little longer. They both sensed the anger inside her but Connie dare not speak out. It wasn't the time. One day perhaps, but now she was leaving for good to be a student and all because of Rosa's accident. How strange that someone else's tragedy should be a force for good.

Neville was determined to send Rosa the best bouquet he could afford and that meant searching out the florist who'd made such a display in St Wilfrid's. Consider the Lily was tucked behind the High Street down a cobbled alleyway, but once inside, the shop was an Aladdin's cave of blooms, foliage, vases: everything for the flower arranger. The smell of lilies was delicious, and Neville stood transfixed by this assault on his senses.

'Can I help you?' said a young man in jeans and smart shirt.

'I want something cheerful to send to hospital for a special patient. Something like your wife did for the Gorman–Santini wedding. It's for Rosa.'

'Yes, I heard about that in the paper ... terrible.' The man smiled. 'But it's me you have to thank. Nigel Norris, at your service!'

'You did those displays?' Then Neville saw the framed gold medal certificate from Chelsea. 'I heard about this but I assumed...'

'I know, everyone does, but it's been my obsession since I was a child. I just love colour.'

'So I see.' Neville appraised the guy before him. The signs were all there: the flamboyant designs, the scent of expensive aftershave and, yes, that giveaway stance but he was going to be careful. 'Neville Winstanley.' He held out his hand. 'Winstanley Health and Herbs, down the road. Business going well?'

'Early days but much better since the wedding, thank you. I've been open only a few months but Mrs Bertorelli has been so kind. I hope to do flower-arranging classes in the winter, a night school class at the technical school.'

Was he fishing for punters? Neville smiled and looked over his stock. 'Some of those ... and those, and those blowsy dahlias. I want something theatrical. Rosa was a dancer, but heaven knows now...' He sighed.

'I had a friend ... in National Service. He fell off the back of a lorry and broke his back. Paralysed from the neck down. You'll want some of this bronze foliage to set those off. I can do it now, or later, if you like?'

Was that an invitation? Neville felt the old familiar flutter in his groin. Here we go again. But hell, if Rosa's accident told him anything it was that life was for living now.

Rosa strained to listen to the radio to take her mind of her misery. It was one of her bad days when, try as she might, she felt a useless lump of broken meat. It was one of those days when she wished she'd never woken up from the accident. How could you be normal one day and a helpless cripple the next?

She wasn't the only poor sod here to be struggling. Tim across the end had dived into a swimming pool at the wrong end and broken his neck. Garry had been in a car accident. Barbara had complications with her spina bifida. They all had their off days too. Now it was her turn to feel sorry for herself.

Now Marty was talking about going back on the building site with his dad to put up a bungalow with everything on one level for a wheelchair. He had brought in plans, and she'd wanted to scream at him. She wanted to be normal, not confined to a wheelchair for the rest of her life. What about his career? How could she let him have to do all that intimate stuff?

Joy had come at last and cried in her arms. Poor Joy, exhausted by guilt and regret and blaming herself. It had been such an emotional visit and Rosa was left so drained.

Neville bounced in behind a bouquet the size of shrubbery, trying to be jokey and cheerful. There was a twinkle in his eyes that meant only one thing: he was on the prowl again. Good luck to him, she thought. Would she ever lie in Marty's arms again? Frustration was making her weep.

They'd wheeled in the television last night to watch some tame variety show and the dancers were awful – loose arms, bad timing and poor ideas – and it made her head buzz with frustration. I could do better with them than that. She might not be able to dance again but that didn't stop her from teaching it, choreographing routines. Lemody Liptrot, her old dancing teacher, had visited her and asked if there was anything she could do. Everyone wanted to help but it wasn't now she needed help, it would be later, when they were faced with the fact she was a permanent cripple. There had to be some hope. Day by endless day, in the stillness of her body she was learning to be patient, willing something to happen, but it was no use. The damage was done.

This battle with her moods and despair was making her head tingle. In fact, it was making her tingle all over. Suddenly she was becoming aware that the tingle had lodged itself down her left leg and into her ankle.

For a second she thought she was imagining the sensation. Something strange was happening down there ... a stirring, an itch? She didn't know what it was but she rang the bell and called for help, just in case...

414

PART IV

MOTHERS AND DAUGHTERS

26

December 1968

'Joy's on the phone!' shouted Gran. 'I told her you were sticking in your book again. You're taking my cupboards over with all them scrapbooks...'

Connie left her cuttings, bracing herself for Joy's usual litany of success and enthusiasms. She put her ear to the phone, mumbled a 'Hi' and let Joy spout forth.

'We're opening the new emporium on Tuesday ... a month's trading before Christmas, I hope. You must come to the launch; cheese and wine. Everyone will be there!'

'I'll try, but I'm on placement and I've loads of reports to do.'

It had been one of those days when she'd been rocked to her foundations, finding an old man dead, unvisited, frozen in his own living room, and she was in no mood for Christmas cheer.

'If Rosa can make the effort you can too. Anyone would think you'd gone into exile. It's going to be fantastic. You've just got to come. I won't take no for an answer. I've given you plenty of notice.'

'Yes, Joy, but no more matchmaking. I'm happy as I am.'

'Would I ever? I'm too busy trying to bag one for myself. Six thirty and dress up funky. No last-minute dropping out. I know you!'

Connie smiled. Joy meant well, trying to fix her up with dates, but this new job was draining her of every ounce of energy. Joy had taken on a new lease of life since her divorce and Connie must support her new venture. She would make an effort, and seeing Rosa was always a tonic.

She sat down to arrange her cuttings. It was a ritual at the end of every month to gather up all the news and local bits, snapshots and postcards for the year-books, as she called them now.

There was a picture of her on the steps of the Parkinson Building of Leeds University after her graduation, looking sombre in her cap and gown, and Gran standing proud as her guest. She'd had to go back to Leeds, of course. No other centre would do in case of a chance encounter with her little girl. It was stupid to yearn for her fantasy child like this but she couldn't help herself, the yearning never went away, or the guilt, but those three years had gone so quickly and now she was on a placement near Bolton for her social work qualification.

An upper second degree wasn't bad for all the work she put in between student demos and protests. It had been a terrible year: the assassination of Martin Luther King and then Bobby Kennedy but then the terrible betrayal of Czechoslovakia and the crushing of the 'Prague Spring' by Russian forces. She'd kept all the headlines out of respect, alongside more intimate family pieces from the local paper: the birth of Rosa's miracle baby, Amber Valentina, and Arthur Walsh making the youngest ever member of the Grimbleton Junior Football Team.

The reality of being a trainee social worker was hitting home; the realities of dealing with broken homes, violence and abuse, incest and unimaginable child neglect. It was another world away from her cosy billet with Gran at Sutter's Fold; the dark side of the 1960s, but this was what she'd chosen to do in reparation for her own betrayal.

How she wanted to be of public service to others, but it was a shock to see the deprivation and suffering in the backstreets of every town and large city on a scale that overwhelmed her at times. She had been so cosseted by the family as a child.

But the worst test of all came early on in her placement when she was sent to remove a baby from its adoptive parents. She was told to go and collect the baby, who'd been with his new family almost three months.

Now within the statutory period of grace, the birth mother had changed her mind and refused to sign the final consent forms. Good for her, Connie thought as she drove to a smart suburb outside Manchester. If only I'd been so strong, she sighed.

She knocked at the door, looking prim in her trouser suit. 'I've come for Simon,' she announced as if she was collecting some stray post. Mrs Sargent was standing in her dressing gown, smiling at first, but then her face crumpled.

'Ralph!' she shouted, and her husband tumbled down the stairs, half asleep. 'It's Miss Winstanley … you'd better come down.'

'Where's the baby?' Connie barged in as she had been taught.

'In his cot, asleep. What's wrong?'

'Then I'll get him, if you can put a few things together.' She was trying to be professional, cool and uninvolved. 'The sooner this is done...' She heard herself say.

'What's going on?' The man barred her way. 'You can't just walk in here and snatch our baby.'

'Mr Sargent, he's not your baby. The mother has had a change of heart and will not be signing her consent so he must go back into his birth family. Better just to do this now. We don't want to upset him.'

'What about his toys and his clothes? He needs a feed ... please. How can you be so cruel? Where is your authority?' The mother was fighting now. 'We thought you were on our side!'

Connie pulled the forms out of the bag and wafted them, looking round at the pretty rooms and the manicured lawns, the open aspect and obvious affluence of the couple.

'You can't do this, he's ours! We've waited so long for him,' Diane Sargent pleaded.

'He never was yours until the final consent forms were signed and they won't be now. He has to come with me. Don't make it hard on yourselves.'

The couple clung together in disbelief at her words. Then Mrs Sargent, as if in a dream, went upstairs and brought down the startled three-month-old, pink from sleep, and wrapped him in a shawl. He smelled of baby sweat and dried milk.

'How can you do this to us? You were glad enough for us to have Simon. We will report you!'

'I'm sorry, but it is the law. There will be other babies.' How could she say that to them when she

420

knew damn well that white babies were getting scarce since the pill and the abortion act? They'd be lucky to have another chance of adoption at their age.

She placed him in the waiting carrycot, but one look at her strange face and Simon howled. She put the new dummy in his mouth as she'd been told and he sucked on it in fury.

'He never needed one of those with us,' cried Mrs Sargent, bending over him, tucking him in. 'Please let us bring him in ourselves. He'll be frightened with strangers.'

Connie stood firm. She had right and might on her side. No one should separate a child from its rightful mother ever again. If she couldn't do this for herself, she would do it for some other poor mother.

She left the Sargents on the pavement sobbing as she drove back through Salford and Farnworth to a council estate in New Bury, but the baby cried so sore she had to stop the car and comfort him as best she could. The distraught faces of the couple kept flashing before her eyes. How could she do this to them? They had bonded with baby Simon and now he was torn away from the only parents he'd known, but the law was on the young mother's side. Why now did she want to take him back to the Sargents? This was not professional behaviour. Suddenly she was sweating and crying at what she had just done so coldly. For once bureaucracy seemed cruel, cold and clinical, and she was ashamed of her part in this act.

It didn't help when she turned up at the scruffy house with the battered-down fence and overgrown grass, where a girl of about fifteen snatched the infant from her.

'Darren's here,' she yelled, and everyone stood in the doorway, trying to pacify the screaming child.

'Thanks, love,' said a careworn mother who stood, fag in mouth, smiling. 'Give it here ... he looks well enough... Thanks. Best back with his own.' She pointed to the girl. 'She'll be his sister from now on. If anyone asks, he's my son. Her uncle did it to her. He's in gaol and he's going to have to pay for what he done to her.'

'I shall be visiting regularly,' Connie added, but they were all doting on the baby as if he was a new puppy.

'You do that, love, if you can find us in! Knock six times or we might think you're the rent man!' Darren's new mother laughed.

Why did she feel so confused, uncertain? He was back in this chaotic nest, his rightful place to grow up with a pack of lies about his parentage. She smiled. It was no different from what she and Joy had experienced, and it hadn't done them any harm – or had it? Nothing was certain any more but one thing was for sure, she didn't want to work with children. It was too close to the bone.

Now she was hoping to focus on work with the elderly. They might grumble and moan for hours, but dealing with their forms and assessments was safer than making judgements on families. She never wanted to be in that horrible dilemma again.

She loved it, though, and it was taking over her life, especially her social life. Gran was failing and needed someone around so here she was like a teenager, back living at home, on her way to becoming a right old maid.

Connie picked up the photo of Rosa and Amber at her christening. Rosa's recovery was slow but never complete, and although walking was difficult, she didn't complain about her lot. She travelled with Marty when she could. He was now in demand as a sound engineer for the stars, making records, setting up concerts in strange places.

Rosa took every therapy on offer, even acupuncture for the constant pain. She went with Maria on a pilgrimage to Lourdes and the result of her prayers, she was convinced, was Amber. No disability stopped her in her tracks. In public she put them all to shame, but Connie knew there were still private dark days when they sat smoking, talking about the old days.

She picked up a photo of them all on Gran's birthday: Neville and Nigel, Joy and Kim and Su, Levi, Shirley, and she thought of the absent ones ... her baby, her mother and some of the Olive Oils. Diana died suddenly of a brain haemorrhage. Her obituary cutting must go in. How had Connie thanked Diana for all her kindness and common sense? By hardly visiting her when she was a student in Leeds. It was too painful to return, too many memories to fight, and now she was dead. She had been such a link to Mama. Now she knew what was meant by 'thankless youth'.

Neville and Nigel lived over the premises of Consider the Lily. Since last year's act permitted some homosexual practices in private, they could live discreetly as a couple. Levi had made an honest woman of his Shirley now that Ivy had debunked to St Annes to run a boarding house with the proceeds of her settlement.

Connie kept these yearbooks faithfully, much to the teasing of the Winstanleys. Any quirky item that took her fancy went in there: theatre programmes, rude postcards, bills for expensive meals. Auntie Lee got to be District Commissioner for Brownies and got herself in the paper. Levi stood for the Town Council and lost, due to a fierce Gregson lobby.

Now the *Mercury* would be sending a reporter to Joy's launch of The Silk Route. With her exotic background and their mini tours as the Silkies, it seemed a good name for her fabric, furnishing and ethnic goods business. The Beatles were making all things eastern hip and cool. Never one to miss an opportunity, Joy was getting out of her home-selling empire and renting an old furniture shop in the centre of town to display fabrics, carved furniture from the Far East, jewellery, scarves and accessories for homes and gardens in psychedelic colours; cushions, stools and incense sticks. Grimbleton didn't know what was going to hit them.

Now she wore her hair hippy-style, long and straight, with clothes to match: swirling skirts and tie-dyed prints. Kim was her little shadow, now at private school. Connie's heart ached when she saw how much she'd grown.

On Tuesday night Connie made an effort to get herself there on time for once. The Winstanleys must support their own. 'All this work and no play makes a dull Jill!' Esme said, eyeing her preparations with dismay. 'Put some colour on your face and stop wearing black. Anyone would think you were going to a funeral. I don't know, Constance...Yer only young once!'

But she didn't feel young. She was nearly twenty-three, ancient. Fun was something she didn't do; drink and smoke, yes; the odd joint, yes; but fun ... what was that? Someone like her didn't deserve fun.

OK, tonight she would get out the mini-dress in green and turquoise swirls, put on those kooky sandals, even though it was freezing, and do a Twiggy on them. Thank God for coloured tights and long scarves. She'd not let the side down.

By the time she got her Mini parked up, she could hear the sitar music blaring out and the lights of The Silk Route blazing a welcome to a crush of young professionals, old school friends and family. Everyone was shuffling around examining stock while Auntie Su, in her traditional national dress, was keeping an eye they didn't spill their wine on the fabrics. She was bemused by the whole craze, whispering in Connie's ear, 'Who wants pictures of elephants on their curtains? All these clashing colours. It makes my head spin.'

'Take no notice of our chintzy lady,' laughed Jacob.

Rosa's sister, Serafina, was serving drinks on a tray, looking grown up, and Rosa was enthroned in her wheelchair, surrounded by a coterie of old school friends and cousins. There were some old school faces Connie recognised but she was in no hurry to join them.

Joy had such flair for colour and style. The shop would be a great success with the young couples wanting to set up home cheaply.

'Nigel helped her with the layout and décor,' Neville whispered proudly. 'It's very now, isn't it, all this junk ... very Biba.'

Would Joy's store be as famous as the celebrated shop in London?

'So you dragged yourself away from the television then?' Neville teased.

'I'm not that bad. I've reports I should be doing.'

'Pull the other one. I bet you're doing your scrapbooks. You'll be playing solo patience next.' He was not going to let her lack of social life drop.

'How did you guess?'

'Why do you bother? They're not exactly historical records, are they?'

'I'm recording our family life ... a snapshot of our times,' she said.

'Because?' he continued.

'One day we can look back and laugh, see ourselves and remember how it was.' That was the only explanation she was going to give anyone about her compulsion. They were there as a record so her children might look and learn ... if she ever had any.

'Hello, stranger. Long time, no see,' a voice whispered and she turned to find Paul Jerviss at her side. 'Where have you been hiding?'

'Have you an hour or two to spare and I'll tell you?' she laughed.

'Saw you got a degree in sociology. Well done.'

'Better late than never.' She gripped her glass, blushing. 'I'm doing my CSWQ. Would you believe me, a social worker?'

'You'll be excellent. So what do you think of the latest Winstanley enterprise?' he smiled, in no hurry to pass on into the mêlée.

'You have to hand it to my sister, she's ahead of the times. I hope Grimbleton is ready for innovation and all things ethnic.'

They laughed, picking up two more glasses as they wafted past them. 'Isn't Rosa doing well?' Paul nodded in her direction. 'After all she's been through, what a star. You know she's trying to get back into dance teaching? There's a lift in the building, so it's possible... She's amazing. In fact, I think you're all amazing!'

'Do you?' Connie felt hot at this compliment. Her tongue stuck to her teeth for a second. 'Do you work around here?'

'In general practice, buying into Doc Unsworth's practice. I'm a trainee.'

'In Green Lane?' Connie said, thinking about the big farmhouse where Diana's father had a surgery.

'No, they're building a new surgery and health centre on the allotment field.'

'Not on my mama's plot? She'll turn in her grave. We grew courgettes and garlic, green peppers when I was little. I still have an urge to get our plot back but if it's going to be dug over...'

'No, on the wasteland. The bit they used in the war but don't need now. It's been derelict for years.'

'I'm very pleased to hear it.' They laughed again and Connie felt strangely squiffy after two glasses of plonk. He was just being polite and friendly, and yet in no hurry to leave her side.

'I was hoping you'd be here. Joy said she'd invited you. I've been wanting to catch up with

427

you for ages but I know you're very busy.'

So that was Joy's little game, setting them up together. If only she knew how impossible that was.

'Fancy a drink when this show's over? I'd like to know how things are going.' He paused and gave her the right-on full-impact Jerviss stare.

Why not? Her heart leaped at this unexpected invitation. Thank God she'd made a decent effort for once. Why not? She wasn't his patient or a victim any more. They were equals, and hadn't she promised herself all those years ago that when the right time came she'd let him into her life a little.

'Thanks, I'd like that,' she smiled. 'Better circulate first, though. I must see Rosa and the others. See you later then?' she said, wobbling her way into the crowd. Why were her feet six inches off the ground?

Neville and Rosa winked across the room as Connie and Paul sidled out of the door together. Thumbs up to Joy, thought Neville. The doctor had fancied the pants off his cousin for years. God knows why, but he knew the score. Connie had told him Paul was there at the baby's birth. Connie had been living like a nun for years. She deserved a break.

Marty and Rosa lived for each other and Joy was too busy making money to have time for romance, while he, Neville, still couldn't believe his good luck in finding Nigel. There was no end to his creative talents: dressing windows, floral displays, cooking, homemaking. They fought like cats over

428

details, each being as fussy over décor as the other, but Nigel fitted into his life and business and he felt content for the first time in his life.

It still wasn't easy being pointed out as the odd couple. There'd been the odd brick thrown through their window and they were easy targets to be picked on until Nigel suggested they go to the judo club and train up to defend themselves. Now they were competing against each other for who would be first to a black belt. Not all queer couples looked like wilting pansies, and once word got round, no one bothered them.

Sometimes when they were sitting on the sofa with the lights low and the wine chilling, the smell of a perfect supper in the oven, Neville felt as if life couldn't get any better and wondered what he'd done to deserve such a gift.

Rosa waited for Marty's trunk call. She hated it when they were apart, but each separation made her more determined to manage as much as she could on her own. One of the blessings of a large family was the extra hands for pram walking when she was tired, picking up Amber when her back gave out on her and the pain made her wince. However bad she felt, one look at her beautiful daughter and she was filled with hope and energy. How could she have produced such a miracle?

The Gormans had adapted one of their show house chalet bungalows to take her wheelchair. There were rails to negotiate corners, a picture window straight out onto a patio with the best of views onto the hills.

Sometimes she wept at how cruel fate had been,

but then she wept for all the blessings of family and friends and how she was back in the studio training up hopefuls as best she could. On good days she could stand and demonstrate some *port de bras* and *attitudes*, some days nothing moved freely. This was the nature of the injury but the more she tried to keep active, the stronger those weak muscles might become.

Rest also helped, but how could you relax when Christmas was just round the corner and there were so many preparations to make? She was no invalid, and chewed off the ear of anyone who tried to help without her consent.

She smiled, thinking how Paul and Connie had slunk off on their first date and sensed it wouldn't be their last. How Rosa had chased him all those years ago as Connie had chased Marty and lived with him in a van!

It was about time Connie let her hair down. She lived life like a clenched fist, so tense, so serious, as if she carried the worries of the world on her shoulders. Something had happened while Rosa was cruising the high seas, no one knew what it was, but it had soured Connie's life. Now she prayed her friend might trust herself with Paul. He was the best catch going in Grimbleton, hers for the asking and always had been, no matter how many hearts he'd broken on the way.

She picked up her rosary to say a special prayer for her friend that whatever hurt she'd suffered in the past might be healed.

Esme, watched Connie putting the final touches to her toilette. This was more like the old Connie.

There was life in her face again. She was going to a New Year's Eve dinner dance at the Country Club with Paul Jerviss and his friends. It was a black tie affair and Connie had treated herself to a long lavender evening dress that Esme surveyed with surprise and approval. Time to dress it up a bit.

Her legs were tired and stiff as she made for her bedroom, but she brought out an old box containing a string of beautiful pearls to finish off the neckline. They belonged to her mother, worn on her own wedding day. 'That's better. Now you look a proper Winstanley at last!'

Connie smiled. 'Thanks.'

'Don't thank me. They're yours to wear on your wedding day.'

'Gran! I'm only going out to a dance.'

'I know, but you have to start somewhere, love, and he seems a nice young man. No one refuses a doctor in the family.'

'Gran! Don't embarrass me.' Then the doorbell rang and Connie brought her beau in for inspection.

Esme eyed him up with interest. 'You take care of this lass, young man or you'll have me to answer to,' she teased Paul, who had brought a corsage of orchids for Connie's dress.'

'I'm glad to see young men haven't forgotten how to treat a lady,' she smiled, nodding at his tall presence. 'You know you remind me of someone... Now off you go and shake a leg for me.'

'I'll call you at midnight and we'll come first footing, so leave the door unlocked,' Connie ordered.

'I'll see how I feel. I do like to watch Andy Stewart do his stuff on Hogmanay. Edna might call in with a dram and shortbread. Her hubby was in the Black Watch. We'll be fine. You go off and enjoy yourselves.'

She stoked up the fire and put the glasses on the table with some of her mince pies. It had been such a busy Christmas, comings and goings, family teas and chapel services, and now she was bone tired.

Seeing Connie looking flushed and excited lifted her spirit, but underneath was always the guilt of what had happened between them. It was never spoken about but there was an undercurrent of guilt on her own part and reticence on Connie's to stir up the past.

She'd tried to make it up to her as best she could. She'd given her a home and made good provision for her grandchildren when the time came. You can't turn the clock back and put things right, she sighed, but seeing Connie tonight had lifted a burden from her. That young man would be good for her. He had kind eyes and a flirtatious spark, just like Redvers all those years ago when he had come a-courting.

Esme watched the flames flickering in the fire and looked at the clock. A great wave of tiredness washed over her, seeping into her aching limbs. Time for forty winks before the Big Ben chimed in 1969.

It had been a magical night, dancing and singing, 'Auld Lang Syne'. The more Connie saw of Paul, the more she was beginning to relax in his company, but when they phoned Gran to wish her Happy New Year from the hotel there was no reply and Connie had that strange feeling, the one that came and went over the years. 'I have to go home,' she said, and Paul drove her back without a murmur.

The door was unlocked and Connie leaped into the sitting room. The fire had gone out, the glasses untouched. The television was blaring out. Edna hadn't been. Esme had simply sat down and fallen asleep. There would be no waking her now.

'Oh, Granny!' Connie cried, looking down at the grey face.

Paul checked her pulse and shook his head. Connie stood in shock.

'What a way to go, at peace with the world,' Paul whispered, wrapping the tartan blanket over the body. 'Come on, Con, let's go... There's nothing to be done at this hour. This is no place to spend the first day of year.'

'I can't just leave her like that. I've seen too many old people. Let's do it properly, put her on the bed. I wish I knew how to lay someone out.'

'I do,' Paul smiled. 'You're right. We'll put her into bed and leave her there till the morning. You're coming home with me.'

Connie had no energy to protest.

27

By the Wine-Dark Sea,

July 1969

Connie hung over the rails of the ferry boat watching the harbour lights at Piraeus drifting far into the darkness. She couldn't believe they'd made it so far, hitchhiking through Europe; through France, Italy, taking the train to Brindisi across to Patras, camping under the stars by the Olympic grove and now, after many detours around Athens, they were on their way to Crete.

Paul had wanted to do the straight route by plane but this was their honeymoon and she wanted it to be an adventure. They would never get a month off again, she was sure, and the un-expected legacy from Gran, combined with some royalties, meant they could go where they pleased and then fly home.

Who'd have thought 'War Baby Blues' would turn up a minor hit in the States as a Vietnam protest song? Who would have thought six months after meeting Paul at Joy's launch they would be married? She'd moved into Paul's flat the night Gran died and never left. No one batted an eyelid but Paul's new partners suggested that perhaps a local doctor living over the brush with his girlfriend was not exactly appropriate. They took the hint and booked themselves into the registry office with just Rosa, Neville and Joy as witnesses.

Their families were horrified but neither of them wanted any fuss. Connie wore a striped mini-dress and a huge floppy hat. Paul wore a South Sea Island shirt and flannels. Connie had seen enough formal weddings to want to break the mould.

Neville and Nigel put on a lavish surprise wedding breakfast in their new apartment and they were showered with gifts, no matter how they protested. For the first time in years Connie felt happy and content. She felt safe with Paul. They had no secrets from each other. He knew about Marty, and Lore, who had been killed in the terrible air crash at Perpignan in 1967. Paul had explained the science of reproduction to her and, much to her relief, assured her that the chances of Anna being Marty's baby now looked slim.

'You have to put it all behind you now, Con,' he ordered. 'Don't hanker after what's not going to happen. We'll have lots of children. Wherever she is, she'll be happy in the only life she's ever known. It doesn't do to brood.'

He was right but she resented him saying it out loud as if she was his patient. No point arguing that as long as she lived she'd never forget her lost child. None of that mattered now as she stood under the stars watching the mainland disappear. She was coming home. If only Mama were by her side, and yet in a funny way she felt her presence. Her excitement was growing and she didn't want to miss a second of the journey.

Getting into the country was not so easy now

the new regime was in power, but her command of basic Greek, her old papers and her British passport did the trick.

'I am taking my mother's bones back to her island,' she lied, pointing to her bag. The immigration officer shrugged, thinking them just another decadent hippy couple, but waved them through. Now on the night ferry to Chania, they'd kip on the floor in sleeping bags, lulled by the chug of the engines.

They woke to the ink-blue sky and shimmering heat, watching the ship dock in the harbour of Suda Bay, still shelled and cratered from the war.

I've come home, Connie thought, hanging over the side to drink in the grey hills, the burned ochre verges, the squat cube houses, nut-brown men on the harbour pulling the ropes. This was foreign soil. There had been unrest and civil war, and a military regime ruled with an iron fist. Strangers were considered suspicious but no one was going to stop Connie finding the village where Mama was born.

Grimbleton, with its cold, damp, smutty red brick seemed a million miles away from the brightness of this landscape.

They trundled down with their rucksacks. Paul's hair was bleached almost white already, and she wore a headscarf gathering up her hair from her neck, just like Mama used to do, swapping her shorts for a long skirt just in case she caused offence.

By now they knew the score: find transport into the main town but sit respectfully, man with man and girl with female if the bus was crowded, rent a room, take their bearings, buy basics for breakfast – bread, cheese, fruit and water – and then go exploring. They piled into a rickety bus, the object of much staring and comment with their brightly coloured clothes, driving through sandy avenues of eucalyptus trees, past elegant grey houses with balconies and bomb sites towards the town. Soon they reached the capital city of Chania and made for the sea. They found a room overlooking the Venetian harbour, just a bedroom with crisp clean sheets, a wooden bed, and jug and basin for washing. They fled from the heat into the backstreets where a taverna gave them fried octopus and a bowl of mountain green salads and lashings of rough Cretan wine that tasted of liquorice. Drunk with heat, wine and tiredness, they staggered back to their room for a siesta. There were not many foreign tourists and they were the object of much open hostility at first. Some of the children looked poor and unkempt. They crowded round, watching them eat their fruit with soulful eyes. Paul was careful always to drop a few coins as they left, watching the kids scrabble and fight to pick them up.

'Are you Germans?' the waiter asked, looking at Paul's blond hair.

Connie lashed them with her broken Greek. 'No! I am Konstandina Papadaki. My mother was Anastasia Papadaki, sister of Stelios Papadakis.'

But she couldn't recall the name of the village where they lived. 'To be so near and yet so far,' she cried, and Paul held her, making love to her, soothing away the tension from her body with massage and caresses.

'Be patient. We'll find it.'

'But how? Papadakis is such a common name. There are hundreds of men called Stelios. I have to find him... What if he is dead too?'

'If it's anything like Grimbleton, all you have to do is spread the word. If you kick one, all of them squeal. The jungle drums will do the rest. An English girl who speaks good Greek is here to find her mother's family. Wait and see.'

It was hard to contain her enthusiasm. Every shop they went into she surprised them with her Greek conversation; up the bombed backstreets, where people were suspicious of authority, careful with their opinions and neighbours, she met with silence.

On the Saturday they found the open fruit market where the farmers from all over the island arrived in donkey carts, and rusty vans brought in fresh produce: live chickens, rabbits in cages, barrels of cheese, olives in brine, oil, wine and raki. It was just as Mama had described all those years ago when the Olive Oils tried to reproduce her stews. Food was the true heart of everything here, Connie smiled.

Paul staggered down the aisle of shouting hawkers, mesmerised by the colours of tomatoes the size of tennis balls, melons, cherries, bunches of fresh herbs – mint and thyme – barrels of honey oozing golden drips. Connie followed behind in a long skirt and peasant headscarf, eyeing up the stall holders just in case.

'Do you know a Papadakis family?' she repeated. 'Anastasia - her sister, Eleni, was shot in the war.' Faces were guarded and inscrutable to read, pleasant but cautious. No one, it appeared, knew anything.

There was an older man sitting behind the family cheese stall, selling tubs of *mitizithra* and hard *graviera*, yoghurt curds. He was dressed old style in traditional dress, baggy trousers and black knee-length leather boots, a loose black shirt and a lacy bandana wrapped over his head. He listened as he flicked his amber worry beads over and over into his palm. 'Repeat,' he said, and Connie brought out her photo of Ana. 'She was with the *Andartes* in the hills ... a nurse, captured and sent to Germany... You knew her?' she cried, suddenly excited.

He tossed his head but said nothing.

She was almost crying. 'This is hopeless. Why won't anyone tell me anything?' Paul dragged her away. 'They had a terrible war and then a civil war, Communist against right wing, brother against brother. We don't know how it was for them. I think, for what it's worth, he recognised her. I watched his face... Just give them time.'

They walked along the harbour, looking out towards the lighthouse and harbour wall, watching the sun begin to dip down. They slipped into the shade of the backstreets to admire the ruined palaces and older buildings, through the souk of the leather shops, trying on sandals and bags and belts, sensing the history of this ancient city.

When they returned to their room there was a message asking them to go to a taverna close to the big indoor agora.

'See, what did I tell you? Bring your photos. It's a small place after all!' Paul laughed.

439

A man was waiting with a younger one of about twenty, dark with a moustache, both in traditional dress, flicking beads and smoking, eyeing Connie up. They stood.

'Are you Anastasia's girl?' the older man said in disbelief.

'Yes,' she replied with pride. 'My husband, Paul. We have photographs.'

'I don't need such things. You are like your mother ... but the hair. It is English hair?'

'My father's. Are you Stelios?'

'This is Dimitri, my son ... your cousin. We heard there is a girl in town asking questions but today you must be careful, but I can see you are Ana's girl. We never know if she is alive or die. She never wrote to her mama.'

What could Connie say? Her mother's sorry plight was not hers to tell, but she smiled. 'It is a long story and she never forgot this island. I promised her that one day I would come and find you to visit Eleni's grave, but I didn't know the name of her village when she died.'

'It is your village now. Come, collect your bags and stay with us. It is shameful that you live among strangers when family is close by. Come and meet your family. Be our honoured guest, and your husband.'

There was a pick-up lorry waiting, an ex-military vehicle that they sat in the back of, watching the town disappear into the dusk. The road ran along the coast and climbed high becoming just a sandy lane with olive trees on either side, and then little more than a donkey track into a hillside.

'The British fought their last battle here from those caves,' Stelios shouted. 'We hid in the fields, watching the soldiers retreat over the White Mountains and then we saw many of them creeping back as prisoners of war, ragged, barefoot. It was a terrible time but now ... times are difficult for us but one day...'

It felt like the whole village came out to greet them, lining the street, watching as the young couple jumped off their impromptu taxi into the cool darkness of the Papadakis house. They were engulfed in thick brown arms, hugged and welcomed, offered tiny glasses of fiery liquid. In the corner of the room sat a little woman in black who watched over the proceedings.

Connie was taken to meet her grandmother Eleftheria, and kneeled down at her feet to receive her welcome, overcome with emotion at this unexpected blessing.

'My Ana is come back from the dead.' She crossed herself three times. 'God is merciful indeed.' She smiled a toothless smile looking to the icon of the Virgin tucked in the right corner of the room, and to a sepia photo of three girls lined up against a wall, looking serious. Maria, Ana and Eleni. It was the first photo Connie had ever seen of her mother as a girl.

A great iron pot of stew appeared, and then another, bread, and a plate of beans in a rich tomato sauce. Paul and Connie tried to do justice to this honour, fearing that many had gone without a meal in order to give their guests the best. Neighbours called in with little gifts of lace and cheese, examining Connie's hair and her photographs, her

441

family snaps. Her Greek strained to grasp their dialect and speed of delivery. The barrage of questions never ended. What did Paul do? How much did he earn? Who were his father and grandfather? Paul sat back, accepting toasts until he was legless, but by then they had started up the music and the boys were out in the street dancing and he was expected to join in, copying their kicks and moves.

They were given the best family bed, hung with handwoven drapes, sheets edged with lace and striped wool blankets. Stelios and his wife, Christouli, slept in their children's room while Yaya slept on a ledge by the fire. Nothing was too much trouble. They told terrible tales of the cruelty of war and how the family had once harboured a British soldier in their cave in the hills.

They gave hints of how hard it was now under the colonels, but dangerous to protest. Only in the mantinades could they voice their sadness.

The rest of Connie and Paul's stay was spent exploring the hills, miles of limestone greenery, cooler, higher up and full of wildlife and the last of the summer flowers. They toured the olive groves, dipped into ancient Minoan remains, visited the cave grottos with their shrines, and swam in the tepid turquoise sea close to Kalives, a little fishing village nearby.

On the last night of their stay before another farewell feast, Connie slipped away with Yaya to the cemetery, to the Papadakis family tomb standing like a solid stone table sloping down. At its head was a shrine, photographs encased in glass with an oil lamp burning. Here was her grandfather in his dark suit; Eleni; Maria, who died in childbirth. Here they placed the precious photo of Ana, the one she loved best, looking young and relaxed on the allotment and, as was the custom, something personal to give a clue to who she was. By her grandfather there was a button from a military uniform. Connie placed her mother's nursing badge to show she was an SRN. Now she was back with her family where she belonged. Yaya smiled and took her hand.

When they'd asked about Ana's husband, she told the truth and said he'd died in the war. It didn't matter which one, did it? She had his name and his photo. They knew how she was placed in the Winstanley family and that was enough. She stood among the brown grass, overgrown clumps, wax flowers and other tombs. This is part of me, she sighed. Mama would've known this place well.

'I did what you asked, Mama. Rest in peace. You are home and I am home too now I've found your birthplace,' she smiled through her tears. This was not going to be her one and only visit. She would be back. One day I will bring my own family ... all of them, she vowed, wondering if she was already pregnant. A baby conceived on Crete ... so be it ... a new life and new start?

No matter what happened Anastasia would always be her first-born, wherever she was now. In returning to Crete she'd completed her mama's circle of life.

But when will I find the missing bit of myself?

28

Zoe, 1970

Everyone was puzzled when Connie booked herself into a private clinic for the coming birth. The partners' wives were sniffy. 'We like to fly the flag for our local maternity unit wherever possible,' advised Marianne, the senior partner's wife. 'I had all my three children there with no problems at all. So don't worry, babies deliver themselves. Given half a chance.'

'I had all mine at home,' said Celia, wife of the second in command and next one down the pecking order. 'It was lovely. We have to be seen to support our surgery and the midwives in the town.'

And you like to keep yourselves to yourselves behind the great iron gates of Albert Drive, playing bridge with your friends, sitting on charity committees and sending your children to public schools. They meant well, these middle-aged ladies, with their smart clothes and permed hair, but she found them so scary.

How could Connie begin to explain that she needed the privacy of a clinic where no one locally might see her medical records and deduce that this was not her first pregnancy? Paul wasn't bothered either way, but she was.

I really want to deliver out of town, she thought, but said nothing. She was learning fast that being a prospective junior partner's wife in an established practice meant bending to unwritten rules and traditions, supporting her husband, of course, at every turn, and no complaining.

Paul was expected to do all the unpopular on-call hours, cover for school holidays. They were expected to live within a mile of the new practice and to respond to emergencies, to be careful with patients socially, to conform to a standard of living, and above all to be seen to be paragons of virtue in public behaviour.

The honeymoon was over on their return and Connie's sickness made her condition soon evident. Everyone was congratulating them, but Connie felt panic. It was all too soon, she had hardly taken up her new social work post before she was having to hand in her resignation because no one expected a doctor's wife to work with a new baby in tow.

Rosa continued to make slow progress. She was busy crocheting a patchwork shawl of Afghan squares. Joy was already collecting up Kim's precious baby clothes from her cupboards in bags smelling of mothballs. They were thrilled to bits for her, and if ever there was a time to tell her friends about Anna it was now, but her courage failed. She just couldn't confess anything to them right now.

How different this pregnancy was, how public, how welcome. Everyone was giving her maternity clothes, baby equipment and loads of advice.

She did avail herself of a private relaxation class to learn the technique of psychoprophylaxis; learning to breathe in labour while tensing muscles. This time she'd not make a mess of things, this time she knew what to expect and all about the stages of labour and how to react physically to the pain. Everyone thought she was a first-time mum and guided her along as a novice. She took herself swimming and for long walks, and tried to feel excited, but it only made her remember that very first time and all the girls at Green End House. Where were they all now?

With Gran's generous legacy Connie and Paul were able to put a deposit against a mortgage to buy old Dr Unsworth's farmhouse on Green Lane. It wasn't far from the new Health Centre premises going up. Even this move was sniffed at by the partners' wives as extravagant for a newly married practitioner.

Lane House was a period stone house with a walled garden. Most of its land had long gone for building around it but there was still an acre and a half of trees and outbuildings, which gave it a rural air. Connie had loved it since a child, recalling those Boxing Day gatherings with Diana Unsworth. It smelled of soot and must. It had seen better days, but was a loving family home, shabby and spacious and airy again now that the Unsworths had taken away all the clutter of antique furniture to their retirement house in the Derbyshire Dales. Neville, Joy and the gang mucked in to help Connie and Paul move in, as every time Connie smelled fresh paint, she threw up.

A week later, Celia and Marianne paid a state visit, eyeing the interior with knowing nods, suggesting they could accompany her to art auctions so that she might collect suitable pieces to fill out the bare rooms. Connie smiled politely, knowing there were no funds left for that sort of luxury. Instead, with Nigel's help, they furnished the rooms with second-hand pine, an old Chesterfield and gaudy cushions, an Indian coffee table, painting the walls white, and bought a large scrubbed pine table and chairs through a newsagent's ad. For curtains Connie used old lace hand towels and tablecloths, embroidery and lace reminding her of Crete, and the gift of a hand-woven Cretan rug they hung on the wall like a painting.

Cynthia eyed this motley collection of junk with interest. 'You do have an eye, Connie, but I'm not sure what Dennis and Betty Unsworth would have made of it. The white makes all the rooms look lighter. But you must get in a gardener. It's looking very scruffy out there on the roadside and people will talk.'

Let them, Connie screamed inside, this is in my house and I'll do what I please, but she swallowed her fury and said nothing. 'More coffee, anyone? Pass the mugs across.'

'Don't you use your wedding china?' Celia looked with interest at Grandma Esme's Wedgwood in the cabinet.

'Not on your life! Granny Esme would turn in her grave if I risked those antique cups on these stone floors. They take no prisoners!'

'Then you ought to get fitted carpets. Much easier on the feet and for Baby when it crawls.' Marianne sipped from the pot mug.

'I rather liked the stone flags with rag rugs on them. It's traditional.'

Marianne sighed, 'But they do have some beautiful Chinese silk rugs in Mason's... I've been telling Charles that we need another one in the drawing room.'

'Rag rugs are fine. The baby will just have to learn to walk quickly,' Connie smiled, watching Celia wince at the thick pottery and the Nescafé.

'You do know you can get ground coffee in the Maypole? Did you get a percolator in your wedding presents?'

'Somewhere, but it's still in its box. Paul likes Nescafé and I can't touch the stuff, or tea, or I'm sick.'

'You might find it useful for your dinner parties,' Celia said, oblivious to Connie's reply.

'What dinner parties?'

'Dinner parties help to circulate you around the district, to meet other young professionals, advertise the practice. You'll meet such interesting people who might be helpful to us, and Paul might find some new friends.'

'I thought doctors can't advertise?' Connie said. 'I just like suppers by the fire with my friends.'

'That's all very well, but Paul has to make contacts. I hear you're very friendly with that flower man and his fancy boy. Is that wise?' Marianne said, her eyes roaming round the room.

'You mean Nigel and Neville. Nev's my cousin ... we're all family. Nigel helped me design this room. They've bought a derelict barn and outbuildings on the Preston Road. They're going to go in with Joy, my half-sister, and open a series of design shops and outlets with a café and car park. Just what Grimbleton needs, don't you think?' Connie smiled, watching their cheeks flush.

'I see,' said Marianne. 'It's just that we don't encourage those sort of liaisons.'

'Don't worry, the two of them go to the Blackie and Donovan surgery.'

'Oh, I didn't mean–'

'No, well, I'm sure you didn't mean to offend. Grimbleton's a small place. Kick one of us and we all squeal. I don't expect it was like that in Solihull, but you're right, we do have to be careful who we mix with,' Connie said, looking so innocent that Marianne and Celia weren't sure who had come out on top of the little spat.

I'm not one of you, am I? Connie thought. I'm too local, too Northern, too common, and I don't want to join your sort of snobby club. I've got all the friends I need in the world here. I'll do my share of wifely duties, but you won't take me over and turn me into a someone who thinks just because she's a doctor's wife she's somebody special.

'You are a lucky girl to live in such a period property. How on earth did you get hold of it?' Marianne eyed up the large hall and circular stairs with envy. 'It never came on the market.'

'Connections,' Connie grinned. 'Sometimes it pays to be local. Diana was my mother's friend. She was like an aunt to me, so her mother asked if we'd be interested when Paul joined the practice.'

'Oh, we never knew that, did we?' Celia looked at Marianne.

'I bet you didn't!' Connie smiled as Marianne put on her Jaeger coat to leave.

'Thank you so much for showing us round. We'd love to see it again in the summer when you've done the back garden. Are you getting in

449

a maternity nurse for your confinement?'

Connie smiled. 'I don't think so. We'll manage.' She didn't want anyone living in their house. What was wrong with how things were now? She loved all the friendship and collective effort that had gone into their homemaking. Those remarks about Nigel had really hurt but she must learn to swallow her fury. There was more to her new life with Paul than she had imagined.

Before they took him into partnership he'd been vetted, and his wife alongside him, wined and dined and given the once-over. She understood why they must fit into the ethos of their set-up but the rest sat uneasy on her.

The fact that Esme had been one of Crompton's Biscuits clan did hold some clout, distantly related to the famous spinning wheel inventor, Samuel Crompton of Hall'th Wood, near Bolton. The fact Connie was a university graduate and a grammar school scholar also went in her favour. Winstanley was still a name worthy of comment in the town.

If only you knew the half of my history you'd not have been so keen on Dr Paul's young wife, Connie mused, but that's for me to know and you never to find out. That's why I'm going to a private clinic. You play the ball where it lands, and she'd just scored a rounder.

Zoe's birth was natural, lengthy but straightforward. She slid into the world, took one look at her anxious parents and howled. Connie cried at the sight of her. She'd so wanted a boy, deep down, an ally, not a rival, and a reminder of the baby she'd already given away. Paul held the mite in his arms

450

and cried. They were soul mates from that second on, and Zoe was very much her own person.

'Why do all babies look like Winston Churchill?' Connie quipped, eyeing up this new arrival for any imperfections. So full of life, curious, already the baby's eyes flickered around, finding the light, searching her mother's face, squinting with fierce concentration. They had loads of names for a boy – Alexander, Philip, James – but only one girl's name came to mind, they could agree on: Zoe, Zoe Esme Jerviss.

It was Joy who held her and swooned, 'I want another baby. I want another. I thought you'd go for Anastasia,' she said, 'but Zoe is a lovely name.'

Connie felt she should have told Joy then how it was that the name was already used but the moment passed and she let it.

They chose something Greek with no strings and it suited this bundle of life. Connie and baby stayed in the clinic for a full two weeks, receiving visitors, cards, presents and revelling in the wonderful bouquets, cards, telegrams. She wrote to Yaya Papadaki enclosing a Polaroid snap of the two of them. Here was another girl, what a disappointment! Stelios would be raising his hands that Paul would have a dowry to find when the time came. Everyone thought how clever she was, how beautiful Baby looked in her wicker crib edged with net and lace in her little nursery decorated in white with great murals painted on the wall by Nigel as his gift to the baby. It was the funkiest nursery in the town, but it didn't meet with Marianne's approval.

'She'll never sleep a wink with those colours.'

And for once the matron was right.

This was no fantasy baby, who slept through the night at three weeks, who took to the breast when it was offered, like a native. This was Zoe, like her namesake, feisty, fighting the breast, screaming through the night, so they took to driving her round the block in the dark. Connie was desperate for peace to sleep, to think her own thoughts, but Zoe had other ideas. Nothing she did seemed to pacify her, and yet when Paul took over the baby, she relaxed and fell asleep on his shoulder.

'What am I doing wrong?' Connie cried to Rosa. 'I don't think she likes me very much.'

'Nonsense, just relax. She senses your tension and tenses up. It gives her wind,' came the calm reply. Why was Rosa, who had so much to complain about, the one whose door was always open for a fag and a scream?

Try as she might Connie felt afraid of her daughter. The power of those blue eyes eyeing her up, dismissing her futile efforts to be the perfect mum, was electric.

Just keep her busy, keep on the move, pushing her around in Joy's Silver Cross pram, visiting the shops, into the park, across town to see Rosa, anything to stave off the moment when they were alone together. Connie was exhausted, disappointed and lonely.

It didn't help that Paul was worked off his feet. He was never at home when she needed him. His half-day off seemed to get nibbled at the edges by unfinished visits and phone calls. There were practice meetings, drug reps taking them out for dinners, paperwork and filling in for the others in

452

emergencies. No one warned her just what hard work it was being on call, trying to calm down patients in distress when Paul was already on a night visit, and all against the background of a wailing child.

How she wished she had old Dr Valium's prescription in her bathroom cabinet. How would she ever have coped on her own, with little Anna? What a fantasy that was. This was the reality of motherhood. She was on her own, full stop, but they had to come to an accommodation, to some truce. What was wrong with Zoe? It felt so personal, as if her baby looked at her, screwed up her face and said, 'I don't rate you much as a mother. But my daddy is wonderful, so let's get on with it and you can tag along.'

It was as if that wailing bundle of energy just climbed into bed between them, separating them so they could only wave to each other from separate tracks.

One night when Paul was out on call and Zoe screamed and screamed, Connie shut the nursery door and ran into the night garden, far from the noise. I could kill you, she cried. Nothing I do is good enough for you and I can't cope any more. This can't go on.

She sat on the bench, sobbing. Why wasn't there anybody to put their arms around her and tell her she was doing a good job? She felt so alone and helpless. No one told her it would be like this. Now she knew why girls needed their mums at such a time of crisis, someone to take over, someone to console, but midnight was a lonely place to be with no comfort at hand.

'Don't leave Baby on her own, she needs you,' came a voice in her head. 'Go back in and tell her who is boss, try loving her and she will love you back.' Where did these words come from? What if she was choking or being sick in her distress? What if something terrible happened to this baby?

Connie raced through the garden up the stairs two at a time as she heard the rasps and little sobs of her crying child. Zoe was only a tiny baby in a strange world. I'm the grown-up here and she needs my comfort, she thought. Suddenly from nowhere a wave of such protective love and tenderness washed over her and she flung open the door, relieved to see Zoe was still breathing.

'Mummy's here... Come to Mummy.' She gathered up the hot bundle with such concern. 'There, there. Perhaps if I sing you a lullaby, it'll get better.'

The words and the tune to that famous 'Liverpool Lullaby' came into her head. She rocked the baby and sang some new words of her own.

How I love thee, baby mine
I'll climb the stars to make them thine
I'll fetch the moon right to your door
To shower your head with sleepy dust...

Zoe settled snuggled into her breast and sucked until she was drunk. You are mine, Connie smiled. No one will take my baby this time ... no one in the world. You are all I have and I'm the only mother you've got. We'll muddle along somehow.

When Paul found them later they were curled up together, dead to the world. The first of many battles had been won that night.

Connie smiles, thinking of Zoe, now a mother of two, herself a busy GP. Over the past few years she's been a source of strength and pride. Somewhere along the line they must have been good enough parents. Best of all she was there for her daughter when Sam and Susannah came along. It's always good when parents become friends in later life, but it's a gift not a right.

It was Zoe's suggestion that Connie came out here alone to sort out this business once and for all. Her children love Crete as much as she does.

After that first visit she and Paul had never stayed away long, and it got easier after the Colonels were deposed and even better when Greece was brought into the EU. That's when the tourist rush really began.

Connie and Paul have no need of a plot of land. There's always a family house at their disposal for a couple of weeks or more. First they came with baby Zoe, and then after Alex was born three years later. The children came out with Connie when they could to learn the language and meet Granny Ana's relations, who spoiled them rotten. Even Paul tried to muster some of the language, but gave up, promising that when he retires he'll try again.

Doctors in the seventies and eighties had it hard, on call night and day, extra clinics and constant change within the NHS. There never was time for Connie to have a full-time job. When she married Paul and his job she became married to the phone night and day, but she did try running the pre-school playgroup for a while, taking over Brownies when Auntie Lee retired, helping in The Silk Route when it expanded into the Country Style Homemaker outlet. This gave Joy and her new partner, Harry, time to go on trade visits to Thailand and the Far East. Kim was trained up to be the heir to the Empire.

Connie smiles, thinking how she struggled against her role as a doctor's wife but with middle age gradually she got sucked into its way of life. If she was bored and put upon, neglected and left to her own devices, she created her own social life. She grew used to finding a way through to be herself training first in listening skills, and then for a counselling certificate. Then she was asked to be a magistrate, though no one in that role was expected to harbour a secret like hers, a secret loss that never diminished. However long ago it happened, every time she looked at Zoe and Alex the pain of it stabbed her heart.

'The Manchester plane's landed, Connie.' One of the reps tapped her on the shoulder. 'Sorry about the delay but they'll be a little while yet. I'm afraid three British planes have landed at once and you know what that does for baggage!'

Connie began to feel the panic rising. Will there be anyone on that plane for me? *Even now she couldn't be sure.*

This is the final piece of the jigsaw... I've waited for the right time to open my heart; all those dutiful years of parent evenings, charitable committees, seeing Zoe and Alex through the difficult years to university and beyond, the prospect of retiring, all our plans for the future. There never seems a right time to go in search of the truth.

But fate had other ways of pulling her up short, she sighed.

Here I am waiting, and all because of a little lump...

29

The Cancer Eye, 2005

One night when they were christening the new mattress of the antique French bed Paul had bought for Connie's approaching sixtieth birthday, he paused, holding his fingers over her breast.

'How long have you had this lump?' he said.

'Oh, stop being a doctor!' Connie laughed. 'What lump?'

'The one I can feel here,' he replied, fingering into her breast. 'There's a thickness, and it's hard. Feel?'

'That's not a lump, it's just my breast, being my breast,' she whispered.

'Sit up,' he ordered as he palpated round her right breast, and in the soft candlelight she could see he wasn't joking. He led her own hand under the nipple to the round thick spot. 'And when was your last checkup?'

'I think I've got one soon,' she said, her heart sinking.

'I want you to see Alison tomorrow. She'll refer you to the Breast Clinic immediately.'

'You're joking, I'm fine. I've been off the HRT for three years now.' After the last episode of bad research results they'd agreed it wasn't worth the risk her taking it any more, what with her mother's history. They'd been so cautious, but Paul was

457

right. There was something as hard as a rock inside her. How could she not have noticed this?

They sat drinking tea until dawn and suddenly she kept fingering round the thickness.

'Have you not been examining yourself?' Paul sighed.

'I've been meaning to but I never get round to it,' she confessed.

'Oh, Connie! I thought you of all people would know what to look for?'

Then everything went into overdrive – appointments, mammograms, ultrasound scans, revealing a tumour that was certainly no benign cyst. In the days that followed Zoe and Alex rallied round. Joy, Rosa and Neville came to cheer her up.

'It'll be OK,' Joy smiled.

'But what if it's gone walkabout in my lymph glands? What if it's all too late?' Connie tried to put a brave face on her terror, drawing strength from the kindness of friends who had been through the ordeal themselves. She was being admitted to a special club of women who showed her their scars and talked of chemo and radiotherapy, prosthesis, reconstruction; a whole new vocabulary to learn.

Suddenly her busy world shrunk to a hospital bed, a kindly consultant and a wall plastered with pictures of Zoe's children, Sam and Susie, and Alex's new daughter, Esme-Kate. Why? How? Why now? Her mind was racing with the possibilities of a mortal wound. What if it was all too late? There were cards and a florist's shop full of encouragement and hope.

'If anyone can wrestle this thing to the ground,

you will, Connie!' Rosa and Marty wrote.

Zoe gave her reams of Internet information and books to read. Paul went quiet, and the night before the op sat on her bed, holding her hand. 'I know it'll be all right, but whatever it takes I'm not going to lose you or let you go. We'll battle this together.' She saw the tears in his eyes.

'What did I do to deserve you?' she replied, knowing, for all their scraps and the ups and downs in their marriage, it was a good one.

Why was this happening to them now? Why not? There were thousands of women like her each day battling with the same diagnosis. Was it the years on the pill or HRT? She was slim and fit enough, didn't smoke now. It wasn't fair, and yet she supposed there was always a randomness about life; it was just another of its little challenges to overcome.

But it was Neville's card that challenged her the most, with just a few words of Quaker wisdom he'd been given by a friend: 'Look thy sorrow mightily in the face and fathom it.'

What did that mean? Standing staring cancer in the face was not for cowards. How dependent she now felt on the good offices of Paul's colleagues, putting her trust in their skills to give her a second chance. And why should she be so lucky when others weren't?

I've done my job, passed on my genes to the next generation, who in turn have passed on theirs, she mused. Perhaps she was redundant in that respect, but not ready to pop her clogs and go quietly. I've only just got my bus pass, she laughed, but to lose a breast and the possibility of further, wearisome treatments was not on her agenda.

She lay alone after the operation, sore, tired, tearful and suddenly aware of Neville's words. The news was better than she had hoped. Her chances of remission were good. The lymph glands were clear. Perhaps there was a future after all, but the shock of it would take some time to settle down.

'You've got to live for now. The past is over. The future, who knows... The present is all we've got. That's how I got through,' said Rosa. 'I kept thinking of running my dancing classes again and having my own child. You have to be positive, Connie. Now you've got a cancer eye.'

'What's that?'

'It sees things differently. It's the eye of someone who's had a brush with their own mortality. It looks to see what really matters to you. It makes you do all the things you've dreamed of. Don't make too many plans and get bogged down. Just sort out any unfinished business and follow your heart. You've been given a gift of a second chance. Go for it, kiddo!'

Joy brought diet plans, vitamins and goodies to build up Connie's strength. 'When you're stronger we'll take days out, all of us. Your illness has brought me up sharp, made me take stock of my own life and slow down to rethink my priorities. There's so much of the world I want to see. I'd love to take Mummy back to Burma, if we can get permission. It's not the world she knew but I'm going to give it a try. Now is what matters!'

On the sixth night after her operation Connie couldn't sleep, her drain was slow to clear, her mind racing and she felt very alone. *Fathom it.* She knew from the practice how hidden grief could make people sick. Who was it that said that the mind can forget bad things but the body never forgets? This tissue rock of sadness and regret had grown quietly in her breast, close to her heart. This lump of sadness, never acknow- ledged, had turned rotten. *Fathom it.*

Yes, there was unfinished business in her life. Much as she loved her two children there was always the one she'd never held for long, the child she still held close to her heart, now grown to an adult, the child she could never forget.

No one can weigh such grief or the cost of it. All those lost years when she'd done nothing to find her – it was never the right time; the children were too young; the promises she made to those long dead; a myriad excuses. Who was there to hurt but herself?

If ever there was a right time to change things, it was now. The future was uncertain. *Fathom it.*

In the wee small hours of the night, she was doing just that. For years she'd skirted round this hole in her heart, patched it, darned it with silken excuses, filled the gap with busyness. But it was always there, this unfinished business.

So no more shillyshallying: it was time to open deeper wounds than the visible scar on her chest. That tissue would heal given time but the other wound must weep and heal as best it could. Why not start to search for information that was right- fully hers? There were new laws and guidelines for mothers such as she. Attitudes were chan- ging. She had rights too. Time to share her secret, to ask for help, to make some meaning out of this brush with death.

Fathom its depths and survive. When I'm stronger, I'll search for her, my firstborn, my daughter Anastasia, whatever it takes. I'm not going to give up until I know just where she is in this world.

'Meet me in Santini's Wine Bar, the drinks are on me,' was the message on Joy's mobile. What were they celebrating? Joy searched her diary to see if she'd forgotten a birthday.

Connie was amazing. She'd bounced back from her op in the past few months as if it had never happened. Paul had taken her off to Crete to convalesce and now she was back in town. It was going to be like old times.

Santini's was now on the up, she smiled, sinking back into soft leather armchairs, listening to a guitarist strumming in the corner, live music, good Italian wine and snacks, ciabatta sandwiches, salads and their gourmet ice creams. Grimbleton was riding high and The Silk Route was expanding into a whole complex of shops, cafés and tourist attractions. Kimberley was proving a good buyer with an eye for upmarket home accessories. She lived with her boyfriend, Mark, and their two children. The dynasty was secure.

Su had a granny flat in the barn conversion after Jacob died, and the Waverley was finally sold. They had bought the old farmhouse close to the business. Harry Tindale, Joy's partner, was out in Bali tracing some fabulous carved furniture for the shop. Life was good and all the better for Connie being back among them. When her sister fell sick,

462

it had been such a shock. The 'it happens to someone else, not one of yours' had struck home with a vengeance. Over the years, they'd fallen in and out with each other over stupid things but now they were closer than ever and she couldn't wait to see Connie bouncing back to life again.

Rosa struggled to get in her car with her sticks. Transferring from chair to seat took a bit of negotiating but she needed no excuse to hit the town tonight. Connie was home and it was a girl's night out, plus Neville. Time for the Silkies to hog the best sofa in Enzo's emporium and drink to Connie's permanent recovery.

Connie's life-changing experience was a second chance. Rosa knew what it was like to feel she'd got her life back, however restricted, and however painful it could be if she overdid things. Marty hovered over her like a clucking hen now that he'd retired.

They had built a studio from their garage where he still did some recording work and encouraged young hopefuls to make tracks. He'd picked up one or two stars in the making and passed them on to agents. Amber was in the States, flitting around LA. So far there'd been no breakthrough in her film career but Rosa was hopeful.

'I'm getting as bad as Mamma Mia with her press cuttings,' Rosa had confessed to Amber. 'Funny how the stage had struck into the next generation, Mamma would've been proud.'

She missed Maria now she was gone, those long nosy phone calls, her gossip, her sparkle, and Sylvio had shrunk at her passing. No one worries about you like your mother, and once she's gone, that link with past generations goes with her too: Valentina, Marco ... Sicily; just sepia photos in an old album and the Olive Oil Club of the 1940s. Only Lily and Su were left now, but Rosa determined she must remember to write down the names of all those relatives and friends for Amber.

Santini's was looking smart, with tubs of flowers at the door and hanging baskets. No one lived in the flat upstairs where she was born. The street was pedestrianised, but with good disabled parking, full of benches and signposts, and the King's Theatre was now an arts complex with a cinema, the Little Theatre and meeting rooms.

They still held a dancing display there at Christmas, a modest affair, given the size of the auditorium, but the parents packed it out to see their little darlings perform. The Rosa Santini School of Performing Arts had broadened out from a mere dancing class. It was more profitable to cash in on the celebrity culture and wannabe X *Factor* little stars with singing and drama classes. Rosa's role was mainly administrative now, but she had discovered a few budding acting careers and TV stars in her time.

Funny how it all came back to Santini's and the story of the lost pram, the two war widows, and the search for Mediterranean food in war-time Britain. They'd grown up with those stories. How times had changed. Now their own girls were dreaming dreams for the grandchildren in this very same place and after a few bevies the Silkies'd be comparing ailments by the end of the evening. There was nothing like a night out with friends!

Paul cleared away the plates from the outside table. It was one of those balmy summer evenings in late July when the sun was resting on the patio of Lane House, lingering over the wine and bowls of strawberries from the kitchen garden. Connie watched him sidle away, leaving her alone with Alex and Zoe, as they had planned. It wasn't often they got them on their own without their other halves but she needed to break her news to them gently.

'You look so well, Mum,' Alex offered. 'The rest in Chania did you good.'

'I know, and it gave me lots of time to think about things too. You know I believe this happened for a reason,' she said, taking in a deep breath, seeing Zoe squirm.

'No one knows why breast cancer develops, Mum. There are risk factors, of course. You were just unlucky.' Ever the Doctor, Zoe jumped in, as Connie knew she would.

'I'm not so sure. Have you heard the saying, if you don't weep, your body weeps for you?'

'That's just psychobabble!' Zoe again. 'What have you to weep about? You and dad have a lovely life, a good job and a beautiful house...'

Connie smiled. Trust a daughter to tell it how she sees it. Sons are gentler on their mothers. Zoe was straight to the point.

'It wasn't always like that, though. There was a time when I hadn't a friend in the world and not a bean, with everything collapsing round my head.'

'You never said,' Alex said. 'When was that? I don't remember.'

465

'There was a life before you were born, you know.' She smiled at her son. 'When I was fifteen I lost my mother and I went a little wild.'

'A sixties rock chick, yes, Auntie Joy told us,' Alex said.

'What Joy didn't tell you, because she didn't know, was that I got pregnant and had a baby in 1964. It was a brief fling with someone who's now dead but I had to give her away.' There, her secret was out of the bag and the sky hadn't fallen down.

No one spoke and she bowed her head. 'It was your dad who delivered her. One of those strange coincidences in life no one can explain.'

'I see,' said Zoe not able to look her mother in the face. 'Who else knows?'

'Only my grandma Esme, Auntie Lee and Su were told, and Neville and his father. It was a different world then, you have to understand. Respectability was everything and the Winstanley name wasn't to be sullied again so I had to do what the family thought best. When they changed their minds it was too late. I had to sign her away, my little girl. I only kept her for a few weeks but I had to do what was best for her too. Now I want to find her before it's too late. I feel I need your blessing before I begin.'

'Oh, Mum...' Zoe cried, rushing to her side. 'How awful, how sad... And all this time you've kept it to yourself?'

'I didn't want to hurt anyone. I don't know how I'll find her but I want to have a try. You are the first to know what I'm planning.'

Her children wrapped themselves round her, crying.

'Oh, Mum, you have to find her,' Alex said. 'Now I have little Esme-Kate ... the thought of losing her... How could they be so cruel to you?'

'They thought they were doing it for the best all round. Hushing up everything, sending me away – that was how it was done. You young ones have no idea how it was then.'

'Now it's so different. My surgery is full of girls wanting the morning-after pill or an abortion. It breaks my heart to see girls as young as twelve, pregnant because of some drunken dare or ignorance. No one cares a hoot, and that's just as bad. And yet, Mum, I know it sounds strange but I always sensed there was something.' Zoe sniffled, searching for a hanky. 'I've always felt a gap between us ... as if there was something unspoken, something hidden inside you I couldn't reach. I thought it was me you couldn't take to yet I knew that wasn't true. It's almost a relief to know this.' Zoe drew up her chair and put her arm round her mother with concern.

Connie felt her tears dripping but she needed to explain.

'I've learned that when something is unspoken, it doesn't disappear but it grows ever larger, like Banquo's ghost hovering, a silent presence; the absent face in the photograph more powerful than the ones you can see. You know Joy and my history, but it was hidden from us. I badgered my mother for facts when she was so ill. I have blamed myself ever since for forcing things into the open so I do the opposite to you. Can you forgive me?'

'For what? For goodness' sake, for something that happened long before we were born, in

467

another time and place,' Alex said.

'We'll help you find her, if you want to. I can go on the Net.' Dr Zoe was back in control. 'It just wouldn't happen today, would it? Marriage is an option, not an order. Look at Joy and Harry. They've never tied the knot but I suppose that was because of her first husband.'

'Thanks, both of you, but this is a journey I must make on my own for as long as it takes. There may be nothing at the end of it but tears, rejection and regrets. That's when I'll be needing your support. Besides, you must both give yourselves time to get used to the idea of having a half-sister. Pass me a glass, I need a stiff drink.'

'You'd better let me drive you to town, in that case,' said Alex. 'We don't want the local magistrate done for drink driving.'

'Neville's doing the honours. He's going to hold my hand while I tell the others tonight. They have a right to know. His mother tried to make us marry when she found out he was gay! The stories I could tell you – but I think I've shocked you enough.'

'Believe me, some of the things we got up to behind your back would shock you rigid,' Alex winked at Zoe. 'Secrets in the family: the soaps have nothing on us.'

Connie sank back, relieved to have come clean. It had gone better than she'd hoped but it was early days for all of them. The journey had hardly begun and now she must face her oldest friends, backed up by Dutch courage.

Joy sank back into the sofa speechless. What a

468

turn-up! How could they not have guessed? Connie's disappearing act for all those months, the family confabs behind closed doors and her absence from the christening, it all made sense in hindsight. Her own mother, sworn to secrecy for all these years, had never even hinted at Connie's plight.

'I wanted to tell you both,' Connie confessed. 'I nearly did, once or twice but...'

'I was a wreck after Kim was born. I would've been useless,' Joy offered.

'And I was off swanning round the world with your ex-boyfriend... It's not Marty's child, is it?' Rosa was like an arrow to the bull's-eye.

She could have hesitated and hedged her bets but Connie was not going down that route. 'I had a fling with Lorne Dobson!'

'Old swivel-hips. You know he died, poor Dobby?' Rosa added.

'Yes, I heard.' Connie wanted no complications. The baby must be his and his alone.

'So, now what? Where do you go to find her?' Joy said. 'The Internet?'

Connie nodded. 'Would it were that simple! There are tracing agencies, I can contact, lists to explore. I'll find my way somehow. I just don't want to withhold any more secrets from you. Neville's known from the beginning, and that's another thing. Tell them, Nev.'

He launched into a hilarious account of that terrible Christmas when Ivy went berserk. There was always a funny side to family dramas in hindsight. The line between tragedy and farce was very thin. Neville told the story with such drama, not missing a detail. How glad she was to have had his support for so many years.

'This is better than *EastEnders*,' Rosa laughed.

'Where do you think they get their plots from?' Neville quipped. 'Life is much more bizarre than fiction.'

'Let's drink to you finding her and soon, Connie. You deserve some luck.'

They raised their glasses yet again. It was going to be a long and boozy night. Connie sat back with relief. All who mattered to her knew. Whatever the next months would bring, she'd not be alone on this strangest of journeys into the unknown. Who else but friends and family would give her the courage to face whatever was ahead?

30

Anastasia

Connie began the journey at first with such enthusiasm, buoyed up by everyone's encouragement: searching the Web for the right agencies, contacting old colleagues from her brief social work career to ask for guidance. It was like a journey without a map reference, just a few signposts along the way.

Once she had a name it would be easy to find an address, but she knew that was the wrong approach. It was all right some mother turning up on the doorstep in a TV drama but it never worked in real life unless you were very lucky.

There were cul-de-sacs when her search bore no fruit. No baby was born on the day she gave birth. The West Riding was no more and the records scattered. In her mind's eye it'd all be straightforward, but doors shut and she began to despair.

'Keep going,' Paul said. 'We just haven't opened the right ones yet. It'll happen, you'll see.'

'Have you tried the National Children's Home archives, the Church of England Children's Society or the Catholic adoption agencies?' Everyone was being so helpful, so curious. She'd tried them all, to no avail. Furthermore, her own name was not on the list of children seeking to find their birth parents. That was a real downer. It was then Connie realised how late she'd left things. But it was only recently that birth parents had the right to go in search of their adopted children. At least she could put her own name down on that list, just in case.

It was time to dig deep into reserves of determination and obsession to make her dream come true. Anna was out there somewhere, not knowing how hard Connie was looking, but was it all too late?

It was Zoe who broke the deadlock. 'I'm not breaking confidentiality here but I have a patient, about your age, who was on the same mission. She found her child through Barnardos. It's worth a try.'

'They're one of the last on my list. Thanks. Can I ask how she got on?'

Zoe hesitated, looking at her mother with those piercing blue eyes. 'Not very well. She went through all the processes. They made contact with her son but then he decided he didn't want to meet her or have anything to do with her. His right, of course... Mum, you have to be prepared. She'd built herself up and now, well, you can guess. Sorry, that's not what you want to hear, is it?'

'I guess that's not unusual and I'm trying to brace myself for rejection, but at least I'll know she's alive and well. I'll have to be satisfied with the fact I made the effort.'

Connie smiled, putting a brave face on this news. Better to get on with her chores and duties and follow the lead, even if it led to the dark valley of despair.

Next morning she found the number to ring, made a tentative enquiry, listened to the implications of trying to trace her child, left all the relevant details with the agency, then went to visit Auntie Lee and Uncle Pete, who weren't well.

'I'm glad you've gone in search of your baby. I never agreed with Mother, as you know. We had a falling-out. I think the timing was bad for her and I know she regretted it to her dying day.'

This was news to Connie. 'What did she say?'

'"I was too hard on the girl... I let her down. We should never have let her give the baby away. I hope the Good Lord doesn't hold it against me." Then she smiled. "Our Connie's a Winstanley. She'll not give up on one of her own. Happen it'll be right one day."'

They sipped tea by a roaring fire and Connie felt enveloped in their concern and love. The shelves gleamed with all Pete's trophies, photos of him with footballing heroes of yesteryear: Bobby Charlton, Tom Finney and Nat Lofthouse. Arthur was now coaching the local juniors. He'd never gone as far as his dad but was a teacher at the independent grammar school.

Connie took herself round the shops just to cheer up her flagging spirits but her purse stayed closed. She was in no mood for such compensations.

At least her borders were getting a good weeding. All the tension of the past weeks drew her from the tyranny of the phone, out into the fresh air to flowers and shrubs, and the effort to keep on top of the veg plot. After forty, went the saying, women go for God or the garden, and she was putting all her energies into redesigning her flowerbeds. It took her mind off her disappointment, and when the phone rang she strolled to the one in the potting shed. Doctors have to have phones everywhere when they are on call.

'Is that Constance Jerviss, née Winstanley?' a voice said.

'It is. Who's speaking?' Not another sales plea from a charity?

'Is this a convenient time? I'm phoning on behalf of Barnados.'

'I'm in the garden...'

'I hope you're sitting down then. We've found a match!'

Connie collapsed on the sack of potting compost. 'Are you sure?'

The voice gave date and place of birth and date of the signing of the adoption papers. Everything tallied.

'What happens next?' Connie croaked, too shocked to take in the rest.

She's found, my daughter is found!

Oh, that life was so simple! She told only Paul the good news. She walked around the house hugging it around herself. The first stile was mounted into a green field where they would meet and be friends and live happily ever after, but this was 2006 and there are forms to fill and processes to go through, turnstiles and checks, and it was like trying to get through Manchester Airport after a bomb scare. She must be scanned, tested, counselled, and it all took time. She must wait for a counsellor-cum-mediator free to take on both parties, if needed, to act as a go-between, a liaison officer, a wise woman to guide them both through the path to a meeting place, and there was none free. It was all going to take months. Connie wanted to scream with frustration. *I can't wait that long. What if my cancer comes back?*

Those were dark months, holding on to just a hope until one day, six months later, she found herself sitting in a comfortable room with a box of tissues on the coffee table, facing a beautiful woman of mixed race called Marilyn, who gently explained the purpose of these counselling sessions and how they were necessary to prepare Connie for some future contact with her daughter, if she was agreeable.

She was now in the departure lounge waiting for boarding. The journey had really begun but there was no certainty that the plane would ever take off.

They talked through all her past, her hopes, nothing was left out, even the truth about Lorne and Marty. This was a room where the walls wept with all the sadnesses confessed, mistakes, uncertainties explored, all the tears shed.

Nothing was promised but listening and support, until one morning Marilyn came in with a beam on her face. 'We've made contact with your daughter and she is willing to proceed further. That's all I can say, but she wishes you to know her name is Joanna, Joanna May.'

Connie sped through the Manchester streets with wings on her feet. *I have a daughter called Joanna and she's willing to write to me.*

She found herself close to the cathedral and stepped inside. I have to thank someone for this, she prayed, lighting a candle, barely able to stop grinning. Joanna ... so close to the name she'd always called her, Anna.

Joanna ... what a beautiful name. Who are you? What do you look like? Will you write to me? Will we ever meet?

It has been a long and ardent courtship of letters, cards, emails, phone calls, photographs exchanges, tentative reachings out on both sides to understand why things had happened the way they did. There were tears and recriminations, misunderstandings and silences at times, but Marilyn was there, holding their hands each step of the way, guiding them ever closer to this first meeting.

'Fifty things you don't know about me!' Joanna sent a questionnaire for her birth mother to devour and Connie replied with a special scrapbook compiled by the Silkies. 'Fifty things you'll need to know about Connie.' It was full of old photos and quotes, her likes and dislikes, her outrageous clothes and gardening mania, even stuff Connie had long forgotten.

Life histories winged their way through the post and email. Joanna was married to Mike Kenyon with two boys, Harry and Freddie. She lived near Hebden Bridge, close to Sylvia Plath's grave. She taught modern languages at a further education college and supported Burnley football team. She had lived most of her life close to Bradford.

Then, when they felt ready, this plan was hatched, this holiday, this private honeymoon of sorts, away from prying eyes. Where better than Crete to share time?

Now is the moment of truth. Connie shakes as she stands at the barrier watching the first dribble of pale-faced passengers pushing trolleys out into the foyer. Where is she?

And then she sees Joanna, tall, sandy-haired, beautiful, just like her photo, just like the portrait of Freddie on the piano. They lock eyes in recognition and move towards each other in a gentle, tentative hug for all those missed years.

My daughter ... you're here, my firstborn at long last!

There are no words, only tears. One journey has ended and another wonderful journey is beginning. There's no certainties, only hope, but that is enough for now, Connie smiles as she guides her daughter into the sunlight.

Acknowledgements

Setting a story in a half-remembered era of your own life is always a challenge, especially when trying to drum up the pop music of the time, so I am indebted to *Beat Merchants* by Alan Clayson (Blandford Books, 1995) and *Hit Parade Heroes* by Dave McAteer (Hamlyn, 1993) for jogging my memory. The Beatles did perform at the Oasis Club in Manchester in 1962 but not exactly on the night I have chosen. Thanks to my school friend, Di Leigh, for the sartorial details I'd forgotten, to Peter and Christa Wiggin, for sharing some anecdotes about life as social workers in that era.

The fate of the young unmarried mother in the 60s has been well documented but I was very moved by Pauline Collins's own biography: *Letter to Louise* (Corgi, 1993).

It was only after I had written the first version of this book that a remarkable member of my own family shared her experience of having to give up her baby for adoption under family pressure and how she recently went about searching and finding this child through official channels. I am deeply indebted to you for giving me insights into how difficult and traumatic this was. I hope this story does justice to the trust you placed in me to convey how punishing those swinging sixties were if you stepped out of line.

However, all my characters are entirely fictitious, and any discrepancies or mistakes are entirely my own.

Once more I must praise my editor, Maxine Hitchcock, for some excellent suggestions, Yvonne Holland, my copy editor for her usual attention to detail and all the team at Avon.

A thank you also to my consultant, Mr A. Nejin for making sure I am still here to tell this tale.

Finally, a loving thank you to my husband David, for his practical support and encouragement during a difficult year.

This Large Print Book for the partially sighted, who cannot read normal print, is published under the auspices of

THE ULVERSCROFT FOUNDATION